HARLEM*MOON

BROADWAY

Also by Heather Neff

Blackgammon

Wisdom

ACCIDENT
of
BIRTH

A NOVEL

Heather Neff

Harlem Moon / Broadway Books
New York

Published by Harlem Moon, an imprint of Broadway Books,
a division of Random House, Inc.

PRINTED IN THE UNITED STATES OF AMERICA

HARLEM MOON, BROADWAY BOOKS, and the HARLEM
MOON logo, depicting a moon and a woman, are trademarks of
Random House, Inc. The figure in the Harlem Moon logo is inspired
by a graphic design by Aaron Douglas (1899–1979).

Visit our website at www.harlemmoon.com

Book design by Donna Sinisgalli

Library of Congress Cataloging-in-Publication Data
Neff, Heather.
Accident of birth : a novel / Heather Neff.
p. cm.
1. Triangles (Interpersonal relations)—Fiction. 2. African American
women—Fiction. 3. Political refugees—Fiction. 4. Trials
(Terrorism)—Fiction. 5. Alexandria (Va.)—Fiction. 6. Remarried
people—Fiction. 7. Massacres—Fiction. 8. Liberia—Fiction. I. Title.

PS3564.E2625A623 2004
813'.6—dc22   2004047411

ISBN 0-7679-1751-0

BVG 01

For Marcel and Aviva

The tree must have a stem
before it can grow.

Acknowledgments

Some sixty years ago my parents met and fell in love on the campus of a historically black college in Raleigh, North Carolina. My mother's stories about those days are an integral part of our family narrative, and in *Accident of Birth* I hoped to capture a sense of the vital role these colleges play in African American life. Absalom Jones College, as well as its students and staff, is nonetheless entirely fictitious. Only the name of the college, taken from the first Black priest in the Episcopal Church, is based on a real person.

I have long wanted to write a novel about the moral complexities of living in one of the world's most politically stable nations during a time of great international unrest. *Accident of Birth* is my humble attempt to do so. The Court of Human Rights, which I have situated in Berne, Switzerland, is also a product of my imagination, although it is loosely based on the very real International Criminal Court in the Netherlands.

I would like to thank all those who supported me in the writing of this book, including Janet Hill, executive editor of Harlem Moon and Doubleday vice president, associate editor Clarence Haynes, and my agent, Denise Stinson.

I'd also like to extend special thanks to the three people who continue to illuminate my life: my husband, Marcel; my daughter, Aviva; and my dear friend Tanisha M. Bailey.

ACCIDENT

of

BIRTH

Chapter 1

Alexandria, Virginia

2 0 0 4

Children with guns.

Barrels tilted downward, the weight of the steel forcing their knotty knees into mocking bows. Faces like plague masks, their leering grins hiding their indifference to the odors of rotting flesh and raw sewage in the equatorial sun. They speak quickly, and in a brief movement the cameras reveal their cavernous chests, hidden beneath uniforms with sleeves ripped off to accommodate the scarecrow arms. Their small feet vanish into laceless boots, the leather tongues torn sideways like the mutilated faces of the murdered. An elderly woman in rags flinches when one child raises his hand, and she slides off into the shadows, stooped in terror. The children laugh. One proudly hoists his rifle into the air and fires it.

It was late; long after midnight on a Tuesday. Although it could have been a Wednesday or a Thursday—nights without sleep all end up feeling the same to me.

I was sick of the television, even though I couldn't seem to turn it off. God knows I had more important things to think about: my big presentation for Senator Jacobs. The down payment on our next vacation. Even Marisa's orthodontist bills. I crossed the kitchen and took out the vanilla ice cream while the journalist droned on about the escalation of the civil war and new evidence proving that the Liberian military was recruiting orphans as young as nine years old as soldiers. *Of course*—I thought as I fished for a spoon in a rattling drawer and pried open the tight lid—*they know that children raised in death hate any evidence of life.*

Something bitter rose up in my throat, barely soothed by the melting sweetness of the ice cream. I pressed my hips against the counter, the spoon making a smooth orbit between the carton and my lips. I wouldn't think about those children. I couldn't think about them. It was pointless to think about them, because there was still so much to do right here, with my own life, and with the lives of my husband and daughter and the people I was trying to save here, in the comparative safety of America.

Comparative, I thought as the icy tip of the spoon again met my tongue. Rachid and his wife, Fatima, and their five children fled Afghanistan only to end up living in a two-room apartment in a neighborhood where I wouldn't let my dog run free for fear that someone would use it for target practice.

And what about the Ortiz family from Guatemala? The one our government wanted to put in a "safe, healthy" place? They ended up in a town in northern Michigan where the white supremacists take their shotguns to church.

The news broadcast moved on. My thoughts moved on. A rise in the price of gasoline, a heat wave in Texas. A fourteen-year-old caught in a hotel with a fifty-year-old man she'd met on the Internet—a man who intended to marry her the very next day. *Right.*

There I stood in my spotless porcelain kitchen, the sound turned down low so I wouldn't disturb Marisa or Carl, my eyes red from yet another night without sleep, my body hungry not for food but rather for something intangibly near and indescribably far away. I knew coffee would put an edge on my thoughts and drive that deep sense of the insatiable out into the night, but caffeine was not an option: I needed to get some sleep before that presentation on the resettlement of the Rwandan group. Senator Aaron Jacobs was coming down from the Hill to look at our operation, and I needed to at least *appear* to have everything under control.

I didn't get more than two hours of sleep that Tuesday night—but I finally turned off the TV and wrestled that news report into the darkest corner of my cave. On Wednesday morning I painted my face and put on a power suit and drove to my job as a specialist in the Office for the Placement of Permanent Refugees, on L'Enfant Plaza in downtown D.C. Welcoming Senator Jacobs with my trademark confidence and grace, I then laid out the facts with drop-jaw precision. The senator invited me to lunch, promising us more money from the Refugee Resettlement committee. I even got a compliment from my boss, who thought compliments were a foreign language.

And let's face it: I had good reason to be proud—our office had managed to find placements for over two thousand political asylum seekers in the past year. The upshot was that I had single-handedly convinced a bleached-white suburb to accept those forty Rwandans into its subsidized family housing: new homes for the Blacks, and much-needed color for the rest. I was helping America live up to its melting pot claims.

I made it through that entire week without making the mistake of letting the entrance to my cave slide open. Then came Saturday. I found myself standing in the living room, looking out at the early spring morning when that news report about those child soldiers in Liberia hit me again, like an anvil falling off a cliff in the cartoon of my life. I couldn't protect myself. Couldn't stop it from happening. Just like that stupid, pitiful coyote, I raised my eyes just in time to see it coming. Yet even then, it came in the most unexpected way.

It was the petals. Millions of them, littering the heady emerald grass like a widow's tears. Pure white—the color of mourning in many parts of the world. A blanket of them, like gossamer snow, settling around the roots of the blossoming crabapple trees.

Out of the corner of my eye I caught a glimpse of a silver and scarlet training suit as Marisa flounced down the stairs, exhaling demonstratively.

"Mom—I really don't feel like going to my lesson today."

I turned to look at her. "It's too late to cancel, honey."

"Don't you think I'm old enough to decide if I want to study piano?"

"No, Marisa, I don't."

"But Kelsey's not taking lessons anymore!"

"Kelsey's not the soloist with the District of Columbia's Youth Symphony."

"But I don't care if I'm their soloist!"

"That's right," I snapped, weary of this argument but secretly relieved that she had yanked me away from those petals. "You don't care if you have a gift. You don't care if that gift could get you into one of the best music schools in the world. You don't care if you could have a life surrounded by the beauty of music. No—you just want to spend your time shaking your rear and chasing boys, like everybody else."

"Oh, Mom!"

"'Oh Mom' nothing. Hurry up and get your shoes. You know I have a lot to do before the party tonight."

Ignoring the look of vengeance in her gray eyes, I kept my back to the window, focusing my thoughts on exactly what the morning would look like.

First I'd drive Marisa to the Conservatory, leaving her with her piano teacher, a papyrus-thin Austrian who was probably already performing back in the era of Kaiser Wilhelm.

Then I'd rush to the Gourmet Foods Market, gritting my teeth against the mind-numbing process of deciding which of two hundred green peppers would look most enticing when quartered and skewered for Carl's famous barbecued brochettes. During that hour I'd also buy the other items on the evening's menu: five bottles of Bordeaux, aged French Camembert, imported Gorgonzola and Brie, sour cream, strawberries, water crackers and cappuccino ice cream.

Then I'd jet back to the Conservatory, where I'd hope like hell that Marisa's lesson would be finished so that cappuccino ice cream wouldn't melt all over the leather upholstery of my new car.

When I got back to the house it would be my job to put together the perfect grill party for our closest friends, knowing all the while that Samantha would refuse everything but wine and salad (*"Reba, I've got to get into a swimsuit on our cruise in three weeks!"*). Desiree would find something wrong with the cheese (*"Reba, you really should shop at that little French grocery up near Chevy Chase!"*). And all of our husbands would be on a strict beer and bourbon diet.

"Mom?" Marisa's voice came from the kitchen. "I can't find my shoes!"

"In the garage, where you left them caked with mud last night."

"I didn't even want to go on that stupid hike!"

"It was good for you. And good for those little kids, too."

"I'm too old to do that campfire thing!"

"You wouldn't complain if you'd been making s'mores with some guys."

"You wouldn't let me go into the woods with any guys."

"You're still a little young to be starting fires with—"

"That's not fair, Mom! You were dating when you were sixteen."

"Eighteen," I laughed. "And you're only fifteen. Don't put any more years on me, okay?"

"Why is it that the only thing women ever worry about is getting older?"

"I worry about a whole lot more than that, baby."

"Sure," she said, coming to the kitchen door. "Like which outfit to wear to your *terribly* important meetings and which new car to buy and—"

"—how to finish the report that I have to present to the Resettlement Committee and which suburb would be least resistant to receiving one more family of non-English-speaking refugees from another genocide in central Europe—"

"*Boring!*"

"But *boring* pays for your basketball shoes, your braces, your trips to the Caribbean and, last but not least, that other car I'm planning to buy so that you won't wreck my car as soon as you get your driver's license!"

"Why do you always have to talk about money!"

"I talk about money because I spend my life helping people who don't have any."

"But that's not our fault."

"Maybe not," I said, picking up my keys and wallet. "But that doesn't mean we should take anything for granted."

There was a terse pause as Marisa calculated whether to push her grouchy mother into a real argument. I moved toward the door, ready to leave, but somehow my gaze was drawn once more to the window, where those tender white petals were still stirring in the breeze. As I watched, those white petals melted into children with guns. I heard the swishing of nylon as she came up behind me.

"Mom?" she whispered, her voice amazingly childlike.

"Yes?" I glanced at her and was surprised to look into the eyes of a young woman who shared my height. She had Carl's beauty—his cinnamon skin, gathering of freckles, and smoky gray eyes—but her mind was like mine.

"One day," she said innocently, her wide eyes steadily meeting mine, "I'm going to send you on a vacation to Maui."

"What?" Surprise lightened my voice.

"You've been everywhere else. And I don't know how else to pay you back for the day I'm going to wreck your beloved Volvo," she concluded, giving me the smile that had brought me to her father twenty years before.

"Pay me back by not complaining all the way to your lesson, okay?"

She rolled her eyes as if that were an ungodly thing to consider. But she didn't argue, so I decided to press my luck.

"And after we get home, you can pay me back by helping me get ready for the party."

"Are you feeling okay?" she joked, pressing her palm against my forehead as if checking my temperature.

"And one other thing," I added. "During the party, you can pay me back by not flirting too hard with Jimmy, no matter how fine he is!"

"Oh, no—that's asking *too* much!"

"Look: Your Auntie Desiree's my friend, but I don't want her for an in-law."

I was surprised when she hugged me, but when she pulled back I noticed that her gaze had fallen on the white petals, too. We stood side by side behind the picture window, a mother and daughter watching the death of beauty as it brought about the chance for new life.

———

He's *gone*, girl."

"He'll be back. That little bitch won't want him after he gets through paying Tamika a housing allowance and child support."

"She doesn't care as long as she can attach that M.D. to her name."

"Won't do her any good if she's stuck with a Hyundai and a Kmart closet."

"Honey, you don't know how long she's been working on him. Listen: Those types of bitches don't give a damn as long as they can wreck *somebody's* home—"

The voices of my two closest friends became the treble key against Grover Washington's "Mister Magic" and the laughter of our tanked-up husbands bursting from Carl's study. Marisa had vanished down the stairs to the family room with Jimmy as soon as she'd filled her plate with the food she liked, holding the thin wooden sticks of her father's barbecued shish kebab with her fine pianist's fingers. Now the adults had splintered off according to gender, the women settling into a good gossip on my slate-stoned patio and the men working on their third or fourth beers and becoming increasingly lewd, judging by the broken-glass tone of their laughter.

I glanced across the garden table through the tendrils of smoke winding up from Samantha's cigarette and noted that she'd put some highlights in her long brown hair.

"Did Keisha do your hair?"

"You like it?"

"Takes ten years off."

"I wish it would take ten pounds off!"

"Lord, Samantha!" Desiree laughed, her southern accent drawing out her syllables like taffy. "You need to start coming to the club with me!"

"I don't have time to be sweating on those machines! I sweat enough just taking care of the house!"

"Look: If you want to keep Reggie's eyes where they belong, you got to give him something worth looking at—"

"Reggie better not even *think* about looking someplace else!"

"Come on, girl. They're *always* looking!"

"You can speak for Marlon," Samantha said with a bray of laughter. "I'm not tolerating any of that nonsense from *my* husband."

They both shot sly glances in my direction, but I let their voices fade into the soft clinking of their wineglasses. Traces of B.B. King now pounded up from the study like a sulking heartbeat, and then I heard Carl's laughter leap out in response to a murmured joke.

"That's right, girl," Samantha went on. "If Reggie starts that shit, he'll be sleeping in the street. I'm taking everything—the cars, the house, the bank accounts and his NBA ring, too!"

My thoughts wandered to the wall of windows in the living room of our custom-built home. Carl had chosen the site—nearly an entire acre on a heavily wooded cul-de-sac with the improbable name of Lavender Lane. We'd actually hired a professional decorator to create this showcase. Carl insisted that we'd often be entertaining his clients, and we needed a house that looked like success—tasteful, elegant, low-key.

What I ended up with was a living room full of shell carpets, ivory sofas and taupe walls, with large abstract paintings of wheat-toned swirls. There were glass tables and glass shelves and a wide marble mantel over a looming sandstone fireplace.

What Carl ended up with was an image of perfection.

"The rest of the house is yours," he reminded me as he surveyed the interior designer's work. "You can decorate with a blowtorch, if you want."

I took him at his word. The house, a collection of sun-soaked platforms constructed into a sloping hill, had four large bedroom suites on its top floor. The sunken living room, warmed by enormous windows, faced the front. The formal dining room and Carl's study both looked out over our deep backyard, and had French doors that opened to the slate patio.

The kitchen, breakfast nook and pantry were nestled beneath the bedrooms, along with my office, and the lowest level of the house had an enormous family room—big enough for Carl's widescreen television as well as Marisa's baby grand piano.

I'd papered the master bedroom in a deep, earthy brown, and furnished it with woven raffia rugs and a big mahogany bed. Marisa had a loft, with thick emerald rugs beneath the swaying palms painted on the ceiling. The guest suite was done up in ecru and periwinkle. My office, which was in the fourth bedroom, had graceful Danish bookshelves and a matching desk. And I let Carl have a forest green study, with plenty of space for his golf gear.

My attention was snatched back to the party by Desiree's little-girl voice.

"Look, Reba. You need to let me know if you're going to Chicago with us."

"Chicago? I really don't need to fly halfway across the country to go shopping."

"The flight's less than two hours," Samantha cut in. "And believe me, the stores are fabulous. Heaven knows, if you're going to have meetings with the big guys on the Hill, you need to accessorize your wardrobe!"

"First I got to find some cash to pay for those lovely little trinkets."

"There you go again, whining about money!" Desiree complained. "You need to stop it, Reba! You and Carl are doing just fine.

And a trip to Chicago would actually be good for your savings account."

"Desiree's right, honey," Samantha agreed. "The shopping on the Mile is worth whatever it takes to get there. The money you'd save on shoes alone is worth the trip."

"I'll think about it," I said. "Marisa's orthodontist bills are coming up. And I'm still paying off that hot tub that you all love soaking in every chance you get!"

"But just look at this place," Samantha said. "You had a professional decorator! You've got Carl's clients and those Washington bigwigs over here all the time—"

"And I have to get excited if Marlon can get his boring dermatologist buddies to even come to our parties!" Desiree added. "If I had the chance to entertain like *you*, I'd have the wardrobe to show for it!"

"And you never have any trouble with your weight," Samantha said, her eyes narrowing as she took in my casual pants and sweater.

"Girl, if I had your figure, I'd be power-dressing every day of the week," Desiree added. "You can go into any store and just buy stuff off the rack—"

"But she doesn't even have to," Samantha exclaimed. "Our girl can go designer all the way. I hear Carl's making a bundle with all that government consulting he's been doing—"

"Samantha—" I began.

"Oh, don't bother denying it. Carl's been telling Reggie all about it. He told Reggie that his most recent contract got you that new Volvo. And I hear you're planning to buy a limited edition Beetle Cabriolet for Marisa as soon as she gets her license."

"You two need to slow down," I said flatly. My friends exchanged glances. "Look—Marisa's only fifteen. I don't want her wrapping herself around a tree the day after her sixteenth birthday."

"The point is that you have nothing to complain about," Desiree asserted. "I would say that in the lottery of life, you definitely got the right ticket. Or should I say that you made the right choice the *second* time around!"

Four eyes fastened on me with dry irony. Even now, after twenty long years, they still wondered exactly how I had done it. Although Samantha considered herself far more beautiful than I could ever hope to be, and Desiree had enjoyed the privileges of being both a doctor's daughter and a doctor's wife, I had managed to snare the men they both wanted.

Yes, I meant to say *men.*

It made no sense to me, either. Though Joseph had explained it to me twenty-four years earlier, on our first real date: *"You are a crystal maze, Reba. You are made up of many twists and turns, but still I can see your heart clearly."*

"If you can already see how to get there, then I can't be a maze," I'd replied with youthful honesty.

"On the contrary. The maze is all the more difficult because the paths have no walls. It will require a very special hero to appreciate the complexity of those twists and turns, and to really value the treasure once he finds his way."

Now I stood up and began moving casually around the patio, collecting dishes. Two pairs of eyes measured my full hips, long thighs, good breasts. It's true—although far from slender, I was one of those lucky women whose proportions had remained intact as she grew older. Food bored me and I hated wasting time eating. That was one of the things that Joseph had claimed would make me an excellent teacher in his country.

"There is never enough food. So we learn to do without it. You people in America are surrounded by food all the time. You don't even realize how much you eat."

"Hey, Reba," Samantha called out, interrupting my thoughts. "How about some more of that dip? Did you really make it yourself?"

"Every damn slice of onion and scoop of scour cream," I replied, walking the few steps to the sliding door.

"That's what you get for taking those cooking lessons," Samantha laughed.

Inside the house the hum of the air-conditioning almost hid the noise from the large-screen television below. Marisa and Jimmy were watching some horror movie, screaming and laughing out loud at inappropriate moments. When did kids quit dancing? I remembered the way we'd grooved to the latest Motown singles when we were their age. Well, maybe things had changed since television had taken over Black music and begun dishing it out in white-sized portions.

"Hey, honey." Carl swung around behind me, setting three foamy beer glasses in the sink. He reached into an overhead cabinet—bleached maple, of course—while expertly caressing my rear with his other hand as he took down a trio of rocks glasses. "Mmmm," he grunted softly. "Very nice."

"Could you guys think about keeping it under control?" I replied, swatting at him irritably. "I don't want anything spilled all over that carpet."

"Don't worry," he grinned. "We're not exactly amateurs."

"Somebody's got to drive home tonight."

"I'll be driving, all right. But I won't be in any car."

"What about Reggie and Marlon?"

"That's what *their* wives are for."

"Carl—"

"I know," he said quietly. "You're busy looking out for everybody, as usual." He paused for a moment, considering me with a half smile. "You know, Officer Reba, you should take off your badge and just enjoy the evening."

I bit back an answer and looked carefully at my husband—tanned, trim and still staggeringly handsome at forty-three. It was always hard to stay angry with him. Even when he caused me pain.

"Come here, baby," he murmured, moving close enough to brush my forehead with his lips. "You've still got that look on your face. Now, unless I'm very mistaken, it's Saturday night, our best friends are over, and pretty soon I'm going to be kicking them out so that I can turn all my attention to you." Raising my chin with the tips of his fingers, he looked lovingly into my eyes. "Now let me see a smile," he coaxed me gently.

"Carl," I repeated, trying to look away.

"Come on, Reebee," he whispered, bringing his lips gently to the side of my mouth. "Let me see my baby smile."

He got his smile. Then he kissed me again and vanished into his study.

I began rinsing out the glasses. Once again my eyes wandered toward the living room and the vision of that crabapple tree, now glowing ghostly white in the moonlit darkness. The sliding door opened behind me and I smelled Desiree's perfume.

"You hiding out in here?"

"Just getting a head start on the cleanup."

"Let me give you a hand." She picked up a dishcloth and began wiping the plates that were already stacked on the counter. "You seem kind of quiet tonight."

"Just tired, I guess. Saturdays are always tough."

"You're supposed to take it easy on the weekend, Reba. I know how much you run all week."

"The weekdays aren't so bad, once you get used to the routine.

It's all the extra stuff—you know, the shopping and the laundry and the piano and tennis lessons—"

"Doesn't Carl help out?"

"Sure, when he can. Although the extra hours he's putting into this new venture really swallow up our family time. And then there's Marisa. She's showing this new level of resistance about the piano, and her concert's only a few weeks away. She's never behaved like this before."

"That's called being a teenager. I've been through it three times, remember? Jack wasn't so bad, because he turned out to be a computer freak. But Jerry almost drove me crazy. You know he tore up three cars and got himself arrested two times with open bottles of beer on the front seat. I can't tell you how relieved I was to get him off to college."

We both chuckled a bit as Desiree shook her head. "Now Jimmy's a little sweetheart until he wants something that he can't get. Then hell hath no fury like my youngest son. I used to send him up to his room, till I realized he was sitting there cutting up all of his church clothes with a pair of my scissors. Now when he acts crazy we make him sit in the garage. The last thing he would ever do is put a scratch on the Mercedes."

I shook my head. "Were we as crazy as our kids?"

"*You* weren't," she said, a note of accusation filtering in beneath her words. "In fact, you were always the calm, cool, never-get-caught-with-your-panties-down girl. While everybody else was smoking reefer, you were curled up in the lounge with your sweetheart."

"Oh, come on, Desiree. I was partying right there with you."

"Not really," she said, setting down a plate. "You were always somewhere nearby. But you were never a part of the party." She smiled, her eyes fastening quizzically on my face. "You always have been a mystery, Reba Freeman. Even to those of us who think we know you well."

The sliding door opened again and Samantha came inside with the rest of the plates. "The mosquitoes won that round," she said, brushing off her arms. "You need some citronella candles."

"I've got a couple in the garage," I began, but she raised her hands.

"That's all right, Reba. I think I'd rather sit in your beautiful, air-conditioned living room, anyway." She walked to the kitchen door, then looked back over her shoulder. "You two hurry up. I can't wait to tell you what I heard about Leona Wesley."

I've been told that many women derive their pleasure from seeing how much pleasure their body gives a man. But I can honestly say that Carl's pleasure came from pleasing me. He was an observant lover; he could catch the softest gasp or the twitch of my eyelash. His hands could sculpt or caress, and his lips worked symphonies on my flesh. I loved the heat that filled his eyes when he sensed me cresting. And sometimes, even in the middle of the day, I caught myself dreaming about the sound of his soft rumbling laughter when the storm was over.

But none of that was happening that night. Carl was snoring like a generator by the time I came out of the bath. Our bedroom reeked of booze, and I felt a riff of annoyance at the sight of his clothes strewn haphazardly across the floor.

Turning off the bathroom light, I walked out into the hall and made my way down the stairs to the dark living room. The shades were open and I could see the curving asphalt driveway, illuminated with little Japanese lanterns all the way down to the street. Winters were mild in northern Virginia, and I'd peppered the yard with magnolia trees that exploded into thick cream-colored blooms long before spring really caught up. Even in the darkness, our front lawn seemed to be littered with doves.

I settled into one of the deep-cushioned chairs, the leather cold beneath my legs. I was in kickback mode, wearing an oversized T-shirt from our last trip to the Bahamas and a short monogrammed robe, a Mother's Day gift from Marisa.

I liked living here in Alexandria, just outside of Washington. Sometimes the scarcity of other Black people unnerved me, but Marisa had made it through the schools just fine. Occasionally Desiree reminded me that some of our friends resented the fact that we hadn't settled in Prince George's County, but I patiently reminded her that Carl's family lived there and I wanted to put a healthy distance between my house and my in-laws.

But there was another reason why I'd chosen exile. Living away from our people helped me to remember what my clients were experiencing. For ten years, I'd worked as an advocate for people who'd fled wars in their own countries in search of safety in the United States. Whenever I met a father who had left his children behind in a combat zone, or a woman whose elderly parents were trapped in a refugee camp, I needed to be able to identify—even if just a bit—with some of their frustrations and fears. Our spacious home could hardly be compared to the conditions those people had escaped and were living in now, but being among the white conservatives of northern Virginia always reminded me what it felt like to be an unwelcome outsider.

"Mom?"

Marisa's voice came wafting out of the darkness as if she were far, far away. She came down the stairs into the living room, her long legs hidden beneath her robe and a bandanna holding back her thick, curly hair.

"What are you doing up at this time of night?" I asked.

"What about you?"

"I shouldn't have drunk that coffee after dinner."

"It's not the coffee," she answered, sitting down on the ledge of the sandstone fireplace beside my chair. "You haven't been sleeping for a while."

"How do you know?"

"I hear you walking around all night. Watching the news at three in the morning. Staring out of the windows like you're in a daze."

I didn't know what to answer. She was, after all, absolutely right.

"I've had a lot on my mind lately."

"With your job?"

"Yes. Since the conflict in the Sudan intensified we've been flooded with refugees and our government isn't willing to give them asylum."

"Why not? Wouldn't they be killed in their own country?"

"Our government prefers to view them as economic refugees who are simply looking for work in the United States."

"What do you think, Mom?"

The leather sighed beneath me as I turned to face her. "I think we should take everyone we can. No one should be forced to spend their life suffering because of an accident of birth."

"Accident of birth?"

"I mean that you and I have the advantage of living in a politically stable country, with uncountable opportunities, for no other reason than the fact that we were born here. No one can help it if they were born in China, or Afghanistan, or Rwanda—"

"Or Liberia?" she said, interrupting me.

"Liberia?"

"Weren't you married to some guy from Liberia before you met Dad?"

"Yes. But it wasn't *before* I met your father. And he wasn't a refugee. We were all in college together."

"Really? What was his name?"

"Joseph," I said, my voice softening involuntarily. "Joseph Thomas."

"Why don't you ever talk about him?"

I looked into her face, which was barely visible in the darkness. Marisa had smooth, unblemished skin with softly reddened cheeks. Her intelligent gray eyes missed very little, and her extraordinary smile—like her father's—could be disarming.

"There's no real reason."

"But Dad never mentions him either."

"They weren't especially friendly."

"Why not? Did Dad break the two of you up?"

"No." I looked away from her, even though I realized that she couldn't see my eyes in the shadows. "No, it was over before your Dad and I got together."

Now there was a silence. It was the kind of silence that happens when the inevitable is about to occur, even though everyone wishes it didn't have to. I sat in my leather chair, my toes resting in the thick shell-toned carpet, waiting for my fifteen-year-old daughter to cut straight to the truth.

"Mom," she asked very softly. "Did you love him?"

"Who? My first husband?"

"Yeah. The guy from Liberia."

"Yes, Marisa. I loved him very much."

"So why did you get a divorce?"

"We were too different, I guess."

"But you must have known that when you married him."

"We came from very different worlds."

"But you just said that those differences don't matter—"

"That's not what I said."

"Sure it is. You said that the only difference between us and the refugees at your job is an accident of birth!"

"Sweetheart, I believe that everyone on this planet should have the chance to live a safe and healthy life. But that doesn't mean that everybody should have to live the way we do in America. People have the right to their own customs, their own religion, their own cultural beliefs—"

"But his cultural differences didn't bother you when you married him."

"Well," I replied, settling slowly back in my chair, "I thought I was marrying a man, not a culture. But it turned out I was wrong."

There was another silence. Marisa was watching my profile, etched in the darkness by the light from those Japanese lanterns.

"If you loved him so much, why do you pretend to be happy with Dad?"

"I'm not pretending. I love your father!"

"It doesn't look that way to me."

"This is real life, Marisa, not TV."

"But you're always different when he's around."

"Different?"

"Yeah. When you're with me you laugh and talk a lot. But when Dad's around you get quiet and"— she paused, searching for the appropriate word—"*polite*. Like he's a neighbor, or a clerk in a store, or someone at your job."

"I certainly don't treat your father like one of those idiots in my office!"

I was hoping she'd laugh at the joke, but instead she pulled her legs up beneath her and lowered her voice.

"The thing that really gets me is that he acts like he doesn't notice," she said. "It's like he doesn't care as long as everything appears to be all right."

"Marisa," I said, genuinely surprised, "where in the world did you get that idea?"

"You said it once. You two were in the kitchen, talking about where to go on vacation. You wanted to go to Aruba, but he said that we had to go to Tortola because one of his clients recommended it. You told him that it was our vacation, not his client's. And he said that it's more important to be part of the club than to be different. And you answered by saying that there's more to life than keeping up appearances."

"Where we go on vacation doesn't really matter."

"I know. But our house and our neighborhood and our cars do matter."

"What do you mean?"

"He wants to live in this big house, even though there's just three of us, because it impresses people. And he chose this neighborhood, even though we're one of the only Black families in this entire area, because his golf buddies all live here. And he went out and bought that gigantic Lexus, when he only has to drive about ten minutes to work."

"Your dad and I work hard so we can afford these things."

"But Mom," she argued, "you're not like that. Not really. I know that you work with people who've lost everything. They can't go back to their own countries and don't have homes or jobs or families. You wouldn't live this way if not for Dad."

"Well, I'm not so sure about that, honey."

"I am, Mom. I *know* who you are."

We both fell silent for a time. Then she rose to her feet and I caught a glimpse of her face, vaguely illuminated by the soft light. "I know you love Dad. And it's okay if you're not *in* love with him," she said with disconcerting calm. "I figure that a little less love probably means that he can't hurt you."

"Hurt me?" I stood up too and reached for her, enfolding her in a reassuring hug. "Your father's never hurt me."

"But men hurt women all the time," she murmured, looking out at our perfect lawn.

"What are you saying, young lady?"

"I'm saying that you don't have to keep up the act for me."

"Nobody's acting!" I said with a brusque chuckle. "And you are going to meet *plenty* of nice guys who are going to love you and cherish you and achieve great things with you! How dare you come moping around me, talking about 'a little less love'? Please get your long-legged fifteen-year-old self up those stairs and into bed before you miss your tennis lesson tomorrow morning!"

She held me close, and for an instant I thought that it was Marisa who was reassuring me. But that wasn't possible. She was too young to understand the complications of her parents' marriage. And she'd never met Joseph, the man I'd loved for the past twenty-four years—despite the accidents of our births.

Someone—yes, I'm sure it was Samantha—had given Carl and me the laughing Buddha, carved from a big chunk of jade, as a wedding gift.

"Look at the expression on his face," she said as I unwrapped the bald, portly figurine. "He'll bestow happiness and fertility on your home."

I looked across the mountain of presents and caught a lingering hint of jealousy in her eyes. "He's great," I said, setting the Buddha on the center of a bookshelf. "But I really hope his services won't be needed."

Mr. Buddha stayed on that shelf for nearly sixteen years. And for sixteen years my eyes seemed to be called to him whenever I passed that bookcase, which eventually ended up in Carl's study. For sixteen years I smiled back at him, gently rubbed his glowing pate whenever I dusted him, and even got into the habit of chatting with him. As the years went by, I started thanking him for keeping things afloat as Carl and I passed through our marital ups and downs.

And then, one morning when Marisa was about eleven years old, I happened to be looking for an unpaid bill Carl had left in his study. It wasn't my habit to go through his desk, though I knew my friends ran regular sweeps of their husband's personal belongings. Carl had never given me any reason not to trust him—there were no unexplained phone calls in the middle of the night, no "business meetings" that kept him away from home, and no anonymous letters addressed to me with stories of illegitimate offspring fathered by Carl.

That morning, however, the insurance was past due on Carl's Lexus, and he called me from work and asked me to find the statement. I'd begun in our bedroom, riffling through the receipts I kept in an orderly file box in one of our walk-in closets. Then I'd moved to the kitchen and searched the stack of magazines and newspapers set out for recycling. Finally I ended up in the study, which was unusual because Carl rarely did any real work there.

Sliding open the drawers on the handsome cherrywood desk, I inhaled the odors of the leather chair, mechanical pencil lead, and the bergamot scent of his cologne. The drawer was packed with yellowing documents, some dating back to the late '80s, and I made a mental note to tell him to clean that stuff out on his next day off—though I knew he'd probably spend the entire afternoon with his buddies on some golf course.

There was no sign of the insurance statement, but I did come across an unmarked envelope holding something that felt like photographs. I opened it without a second thought, certain that they were shots of Carl taken at some work-related event, and my breath stopped in my throat.

A long-haired, ginger-skinned beauty who might have been in her late twenties looked up at me, her full lips parted in a welcoming smile. Sitting at a table in a black evening dress that revealed her ample breasts, she was dangling a wineglass from her diamond-studded fingernails.

In the next photo the same woman was sitting on a lawn chair in a brightly flowered bikini. Her long legs were crossed at the knee and her eyes were hidden behind dark glasses, but her flat belly and generous breasts were still invitingly visible. A pack of cigarettes lay on the ground beside her, next to a half-finished bottle of beer.

In the third photograph she was asleep. White sheets were pulled loosely up to her hips, and one of her arms covered most of her nipples. Her face cleared of all emotion, she seemed strangely childlike—especially in light of the fact that she was sleeping with another woman's husband.

I pushed the photographs back into the envelope with trembling hands and stood up quickly, banging into the bookshelf. A huge world atlas I'd given Carl for his birthday some years before tipped over, knocking Mr. Buddha off his perch, and he crashed to the floor by my feet. Strangely enough, I didn't even hear it break. I stood there, the envelope in one hand, and stared down at the fragments of jade, trying to figure out how they had gotten there.

Then, with that envelope still clutched in my hand, I went and got the broom and methodically swept the pieces up and put them in the trash.

I sat at Carl's desk for a long time, staring at a bronze-plated golf ball he'd won in a tournament some months earlier.

Carl was the key to everything I had. My home. My financial stability. My reputation. He was the father of my child. The man I'd planned to grow old with.

How could I face my friends if they learned about his cheating?

What would my parents think about my getting divorced a second time?

How would I find another man, now that I wasn't young anymore?

What would this do to Marisa?

I wiped my eyes, missing the errant tear that splattered like a drum on the dusty Cross pens and unused leather engagement diary I'd bought him for Christmas the year before.

What if he really did leave me for the young woman in those pictures? The rational part of my mind screamed that no, he wouldn't throw everything we'd worked for away. But then my emotions reminded me that it was very possible for a man to walk out on his wife, even when he claimed to love her. And even when he knew she loved him.

After all, it had happened to me. And I knew damned well it could happen again.

So I placed the envelope on Carl's bedside table that night. He found it while I was in the shower, and was waiting, his gray eyes sharp and guarded, when I came into the bedroom.

"I know what you must be thinking, but let me explain."

"You're going to tell me that Marlon or Reggie asked you to keep them, right?"

He looked down, the envelope flap open in his hand. I could see those satisfied eyes peeking out, and my anger returned, bringing back my tears.

"I could lie," Carl said quietly. "I could make up some shit and repeat it until both of us believed it. But I think you deserve the truth."

He brushed by me and went into the bathroom. I stood waiting while he took out a lighter he used when smoking cigars with his friends. Without another word he set the envelope on fire and waited until the photos were smoldering ashes in the toilet.

"Those pictures have been there for a long time," he said, turning to look into my eyes. "I met that woman at one of my frat conventions a few summers ago. It was that time you had to work and I went alone. I drank too much at the pool bar and spent one night with her. I don't even remember where she came from. I think her name was Donna."

I hadn't realized I was trembling until he reached up and grasped my shoulders.

"I don't want to lose you, Reba. Not over something as stupid as this. It was a mistake. It had nothing to do with how I feel about you or our life together. Please," he added in a low voice, "please forgive me."

Although I wanted to scream, I nodded silently and felt him pull me into his arms. He rocked me back and forth and we wept together, although we weren't weeping for the same reason. I will always believe that Carl was crying with relief because he'd just managed to save the perfect theater of our married life. But I was crying because like that Buddha, my trust in Carl was shattered and I didn't think I'd ever be able to put the pieces back together again.

Still, after a few tense weeks, we slowly settled back into our old routine. We continued seeing our friends, went on vacations together, made plans for Marisa's future, and—after a bit of coaxing with his hoarse, hungry voice—we even made love.

No one ever asked what happened to Mr. Buddha. And no one seemed to notice that anything had changed in our marriage.

No one, that is, except Marisa.

After our late-night "heart-to-heart," I'd coaxed her into bed. Then I sat on the edge of her mattress and tucked her in like a little girl. I went back to our room and lay down next to Carl, thinking about the things I'd just told her.

Sure, I'd been married before. And yes, Joseph and I crashed and burned because our cultural differences were too great. After we broke up I married her father. And I did love Carl—or perhaps I should say that I was trying very hard not to fall out of love with him. Carl was a loving, charming, intelligent man. An excellent provider. An attentive spouse. Wonderful in bed. When it came down to it, we'd built too much to let it all be destroyed by three stupid photographs—or by the rumors about other women that continued to swirl around me.

None of that was Marisa's business anyway. She was still a child. And she had already figured out much too much about my life.

But then, what *did* I have to hide? Why hadn't I ever talked to her about Joseph? Why did I still avoid thinking about what had happened so many years before? Why hadn't I made contact with him for twenty whole years? How could I love a man enough to marry him, only to behave as if I didn't care if he was still alive? There was nothing wrong with wondering what had become of my first husband.

The next morning I sat down at the computer and did something I never thought I would do. I began compiling a list of articles dating back over the past five years about the civil war in Liberia. I began with the databases of the major newspapers, trying not to make duplicate copies of the overseas press reports that are often published in almost identical format in newspapers around the globe. Instead, I tried to match up the news stories by different reporters who were reporting on the same events at the same time. I printed up the stories, then continued my search by typing in the names of the Liberian officials mentioned in those articles.

The search took me the better part of that Sunday, but when I finished I had a bulging file of recent news reports that I hoped would get me up to speed on what had happened in Joseph's country—so that I could begin to find out what might have happened in Joseph's life.

I spent much of the day on Monday using my computer at work to print out all the reports by refugee agencies working in Liberia. I copied the United Nations documents pertaining to the Liberian civil war and its effects on families and children living in combat zones.

And then I began a casual search for Joseph. At first it seemed like fun to scan the Web for lists of schools, teachers and even university professors in Liberia. After a few hours, though, my simple curiosity shifted to concern. Although I tried every variation of his name that I could think of—*Joseph Vai Thomas, Joseph V. Thomas, Joseph Vai, Vai Joseph, J. V. Thomas*—there was no sign of my former husband. No birth certificate. No death certificate. No proof that he'd ever existed.

By the end of that week I'd exhausted every database I could think of. I'd called Absalom Jones College, our alma mater, to see if the alumni association had any address for him. No one was in the office to take my call, so I tried the Episcopal Diocese of New York, which had sponsored his studies in America. No records of Joseph

Thomas. I faxed the Church of England's bishopric in Monrovia. No response at all.

No one had any knowledge of the whereabouts of Joseph Vai Thomas. It was as if he had been wiped clean off the face of the earth.

...And *do you* know what she said? She said she didn't even know he *had* a wife and three kids! Thought he was divorced and the kids were only there on the weekends. Can you believe that?"

It was my practice to have lunch with Desiree once every two weeks. Depending on my schedule, we sometimes met in one of the upscale malls in Alexandria, just across the Potomac and not far from my office. Other times I got on the Metro and rode over to Georgetown, where we'd eat at a sidewalk café.

Now, I like clothes and understand their power. I know clothes are a means to an end—like getting the respect of the folks I work with. But clothes for Desiree had an entirely different purpose. She typically arrived at our lunch dates in high heels and a bright, ruffled outfit. She was all about being the southern belle whose husband made so much money that she didn't have a job to get back to. She always took a long time to order, peering at the menu as if this were her last meal. She typically complained about her food and usually sent something back to the kitchen, as if nothing the restaurant prepared would ever be quite up to her standards.

Still, I chalked these annoyances up to our different natures. Desiree was a doctor's daughter; she had managed to marry a doctor. She had never worked and rarely read a book, preferring to spend her life worrying about the newest fashion trends, celebrity perfumes and the latest and most exclusive spas.

I, on the other hand, was a clergyman's daughter. I was raised to believe that every dollar counts, and even though I had married a successful businessman, I was proud of my full-time job. Call it my ingrained middle-class work ethic.

"I should have ordered the shrimp bisque," Desiree fussed, glancing across at my Caesar salad. "This crab doesn't taste fresh."

"Do you want some of this salad? There's more here than I can eat."

"You know I don't like the garlic they put in the dressing. I think I'll just send this back and get something else," she replied, raising her hand to signal the waiter.

The open-air bistro in the center of the Georgetown Mall was bustling with government workers who were ranked high enough to take more than an hour for lunch. Most of them were easily identifiable by their suits and shirtdresses, while Desiree was dressed as if she were on her way to a cocktail party. Her lavender silk was matched with heavy gold earrings and a necklace set with an amethyst the size of a grape—the "find" of her latest Caribbean cruise.

She raised one of her arched brows and slid her perfect pink nails slowly along the white tablecloth. She had a pair of Gucci sunglasses propped up on her forehead, and the empty lenses reflected the sun's rays.

"So what's going on with you?" she asked after her crab disappeared.

"Going on with me?"

"What's on your mind? You weren't listening to a word I was saying!"

"Crazy week at work," I lied, glancing over her shoulder at a deeply tanned housewife with a Boutiques Anya bag.

"Crazier than usual?"

"I'm having a hard time finding placement for a Somali family. They were university professors in their own country, but none of our colleges wants to recognize their degrees."

"What did they teach?"

"Civil engineering. They were trained in Italy and England and taught for thirty years before their government imprisoned them."

"Why would their government do that? They must need educated people in Somalia."

"It's a sad fact that doctors and teachers are often targeted for persecution when their countries experience political unrest."

"That just proves what I've always said about Africans. They just don't share our values."

"This kind of oppression happens all over the world, not just in Africa," I explained patiently.

"Well, with their credentials it shouldn't be that hard to find jobs for them," she replied, rolling her heavily painted eyes. "So let's get real, Reba. Is everything all right at home?"

"Sure."

"Are you getting enough sleep?"

"Of course I am."

"Marisa acting up?"

"No," I answered, my voice sharper than I intended. "Marisa's just fine."

"So what is it, girlfriend?"

When I didn't answer, she eyed me critically, examining my raw-silk suit and suede silk shell. Her eyes drifted downward to my fawn-toned handbag and low-heeled mules. I knew what she was thinking: I was too well dressed to be worried about money, and I was too confident to be having any real problems at work.

"Well, let's see," she said softly. "I'd say your job's fine and *you* say your daughter is a perfect angel. So is it Carl?"

"Is *what* Carl?" I asked, no longer trying to hide my irritation.

"I don't know. You tell *me*."

"There's nothing to tell you," I snapped, shoving my knife and fork into my half-eaten salad.

"You don't have to get so edgy," she complained, pretending that my refusal to discuss my marriage was something new.

"I'm not edgy," I said as I began pushing my cell phone and wallet into my purse. "I've got an important meeting this afternoon and I don't want to be late."

She blinked slowly, her gaze wavering somewhere between irritation and amusement. "All right, darling," she murmured, letting her southern accent stroll over the last word. "You've got something big on your mind, but you're not ready to talk about it. After all these years you'd think that I would know better than to push you too hard."

"That's right. I refuse to be the latest installment in *Days of Other People's Lives*."

"Well, I'd say that you need to spend a little more of your time looking after your *own* life. And maybe if you listened to some of the things I have to say about other people, you'd save yourself the trouble of being the last to know what's going on in your very own home!"

"Meaning?"

She raised her manicured hands. "See no evil, hear no evil, speak no evil!"

"You know," I said to her with a finality that surprised even me, "now I understand why that proverb is always illustrated with monkeys."

I knew I had blown a very serious fuse on our friendship when she reached into her bag and threw down a fifty-dollar bill just as the waiter arrived with her shrimp. Her face was drawn up tight as she stalked away, in her rage almost tripping on the lowest step of the escalator. I would have laughed if I hadn't been stinging over her remark about Carl. What was it that she knew about my husband? What did everybody else see that I hadn't figured out?

Still stinging, I threaded my way through crowds of shoppers and took the subway back to my office on L'Enfant Plaza. Was Carl sniffing around another woman right under my nose? Was it one of his clients? The wife of one of his golf partners? A neighbor?

Normally I enjoyed working a couple of blocks from the Mall, and on days when I managed to take a long lunch break I often went to one of the museums. Today, however, I had no patience for the tourists flowing down the Mall toward the Capitol. More crowds had gathered near my office, which was located in a modern glass and steel building a block from the Potomac River and just across the street from the U.S. Holocaust Memorial Museum.

Sweating and miserable, I dropped down into my chair and gazed around my office, which was usually the place where I felt my most powerful. After getting my first promotion I'd had the room painted a pale blue and installed off-white blinds. I replaced the drab metal furniture with a beechwood desk and matching armchairs. The office was so handsome that representatives from Capitol Hill were usually ushered directly to me. My colleagues loved stopping in for coffee or holding impromptu meetings at the conference table near the windows. When I was poised at my desk I left all the tensions of my marriage behind and felt that I could take on the world.

Today, however, was different. I tried to shunt Desiree aside by working my way through a number of phone messages. Our agency had succeeded in finding homes for five teenage girls who had escaped from the Central African Republic, where they were facing forced circumcision. The Clinton administration had signed into law a clause allowing such women to apply for refugee status if they found their way into the United States, and word had spread quickly to the African continent. We were getting more and more young women who declared themselves refugees because of this practice, but they were generally easy to place because they were young and eager to assimilate to American life.

I returned a call from Senator Jacobs, who wanted to know more about our ability to assist Bosnian refugees. I promised to messenger over a report I'd done on our successes with people from the former Yugoslavia. Then I sat back in my desk chair, peered out at the sun-speckled Potomac and wondered if Desiree's insinuations about Carl were true.

The phone rang. "Office for the Placement of Permanent Refugees," I answered automatically.

"Reba Freeman? Is that you?"

The woman's voice seemed vaguely familiar, but with my enormous range of colleagues and former clients, it was impossible to place.

"Yes, I'm Reba Freeman-Thornton."

"This is Arlene Masters, from Absalom Jones College. Do you remember me?"

I did, although the face I conjured up was little more than a blur from my heady freshman year, more than two decades earlier. Arlene was that quiet girl who always sat near the classroom windows. In fact, she'd spent more time looking outside than I spent gazing spellbound across the room at Joseph. She'd vanished after our first year, and I'd hardly thought of her since.

"Where are you calling from? And how did you get my number?" I asked, genuinely surprised.

"I'm calling from the college. I'm the coordinator of alumni affairs and I received a message saying that you'd called."

Suddenly I was embarrassed. It had never occurred to me that anyone currently working at the school would have the slightest memory of me—or of my relationship with Joseph.

"So how are you, Arlene?"

"I'm very well. I've just become a grandmother, you know. My son and his wife had twin daughters."

"Son?"

"You don't remember, do you? I left after our freshman year and followed my husband to Europe."

"I didn't realize you'd gotten married."

She laughed graciously. "Nobody knew. I married my high school sweetheart during the Christmas break, just before the Army sent him away to Germany. I spent the rest of our freshman year waiting for permission to join him. I was incredibly anxious to get away from Baltimore and see the rest of the world. I figured that after we got back home I'd end up spending the rest of my life in Maryland. And you know what? I was right!"

"Well, I'm glad to hear from you," I said pleasantly. "I called the college the other day on a whim. After all these years, I was wondering if anyone there had the slightest idea what became of Joseph Thomas."

"Joseph? But Reba—*you* should know that better than anyone."

"It's true that we were married," I said quickly. "But Joseph and I broke up a few months after we graduated. He went back to Africa and I later married Carl Thornton."

"Yes, I'd heard that."

"Carl and I moved into a new house a few years ago and I misplaced an address book that had all the names and numbers of our classmates. So I took a chance and gave the college a call."

"I see," she said thoughtfully. "I've already done a search of our records, and I don't have anything on Joseph. The problem is that with a war going on in Liberia, it's possible that none of the records would be accurate anyway."

"That's true."

"I'll tell you what, I'll look through some other files and see what I can come up with. Can you give me a day or two?"

"Of course. I've got all the time in the world."

I prepared to hang up, and then I heard her voice. "You know, Reba, I never had the chance to tell you this, but I always thought you were a pretty nice person."

"Ah—really?"

"Yes. I saw the way those other girls acted—what were their names—Debra and Sabrina or something? They could get pretty nasty if they were in the mood. But you were always so sweet and kind."

"Well—thanks."

"You know, I never really fit in with you folks. I was so much in love with my husband that I spent most every day wishing I was someplace else. But I really appreciated the times when you made your roommates behave themselves. I know you didn't realize it, but other people were watching."

"I—I really don't know what to say."

She laughed. "Don't say anything. Just hang on and let me see what I can come up with. I'll bet we can find Joseph for you some-how."

□□□

I *watched Carl* carefully after dinner that evening. He settled down in the family room, his strong legs sprawled out on the leather couch, the television tuned to the Baltimore Orioles game.

In the kitchen I finished drying the dishes and poured myself a glass of wine, something I never did on a weeknight. Then, leaning against the sink where I had a clear view of his back on the couch, I did some hard thinking.

The years had been extremely kind to my husband. He'd always been a handsome man, and his charming "southern gentleman" routine had proven too much for most women to resist. He took good care of his beautiful smile, and his flashing gray eyes remained bright and engaging. Even more important, Carl practiced a number of sports and selected clothing that suggested education, wealth and leisure. He had parlayed his degree in business administration into a lucrative private consulting company, and an air of self-satisfied confidence moved with him like a seductive cologne.

The phone rang and he scooped up the receiver, chortling his pleasure when he recognized one of his countless friends. Unlike me, Carl had developed hundreds of contacts in the Chesapeake Basin through his work, fraternity events and social activities. After twenty years my college roommates were still my two best friends.

Marisa came in, a pencil tucked behind her ear, and began fishing restlessly in the fridge.

"What are you looking for, sweetheart?"

"The pecan pie," she said, pushing containers of vegetables to the rear.

"That pie's in the compost, where it belongs."

She stood up, outraged. "But it was still good!"

"Not for our bodies, it wasn't."

"You tell me all the time that I shouldn't be obsessed with my weight."

"That's right. But you don't need to eat sweets while you're doing your homework."

"*Uuugh!* You guys really make me sick!"

She spun on her heel and disappeared up the steps to her room. I took another sip of my wine, my eyes again on Carl.

"Yeah—yeah, that's good," he was saying into the phone. "Friday at seven. Lester's Grill. Right. Okay—see you then." He replaced the receiver and stretched out his muscular legs, slipping his deeply tanned arms behind his head. I noticed that he was wearing the heavy gold chain I'd given him the Christmas before. He rarely wore any of my gifts—that is, unless someone complimented him about them. So did he have a lover who appreciated expensive gold chains? Or did it turn her on to be with him while he was wearing jewelry purchased by his wife?

I went down into the family room and sat beside him. The Orioles were losing by five runs at the top of the sixth inning. Carl didn't take his eyes away from the screen.

"Got plans for this Friday?" I asked lightly.

"I'm meeting Paul Donovan to talk about our new project. You can come along. I'll call him back and tell him to bring his wife."

"No. Marisa's got a special rehearsal for the concert."

"That's too bad," he replied, still staring at the television. "I'll try to set the next meeting up so you can come too."

I set my wineglass on the table. "Carl, we need to talk."

"Right now?"

"Right now."

"Can't it wait? I'm just winding down. It was a pretty heavy day."

"My day at work was heavy, too. And then I picked up Marisa, went grocery shopping, made dinner and washed the dishes."

He glanced across at me, then back at the game. "It looks like you need to cool out as much as I do. Why don't you finish your wine? We'll talk later."

"I want to talk now." I could hear the throbbing bass from Marisa's CD player.

"All right," he said with an air of impatience. "What is it, Reba?"

Leaning forward, I lifted my chin and addressed him as if he were one of my colleagues. "I want to know if you're seeing another woman."

An intense roar poured from the television as one of the Orioles slugged the ball and all three players on the bases scurried around the diamond and headed for home.

Carl kept his eyes fixed on the screen. "Why yes, dear," he said, as if I'd asked him the day of the week.

Although my heart began to slam like a shutter left open in a windstorm, I kept my voice steady. "Is it someone I know?"

"Does that matter?" he asked without looking at me.

"Yes, it does."

"Well, then, the answer is yes. Although I wouldn't have thought you'd care, Reba."

"Of course I care. Who is it?"

"You don't have to worry. It's nothing serious."

"You're my husband, Carl."

He snorted, his voice still dangerously calm. "I'm more of a business partner, really. Let's face it: You're satisfied as long as the mortgage is paid and I show up for the occasional nighttime recreation."

"I'll admit that nothing was the same after I discovered those photographs in your desk."

He looked across at me, his expression cool. "You mean after you found the concrete evidence that this little arrangement isn't working out anymore."

"Arrangement?" I nearly choked on the word.

"Sure," he said, looking back at the screen. "You've got your big house and an accomplished daughter and an impressive career. But this pretense of being one big happy family is a load of crap. We both know that you've never been happy with me."

"What do you mean by that? I've spent nearly twenty years—"

"—pretending that you're not still in love with someone else."

"Who?" I sputtered stupidly.

"Come on, Reba," he said, his eyes still fixed on the screen. "You haven't made it through one day of our life together without thinking about Joseph. Sometimes you're so far away that if you weren't Black you'd be invisible!"

I snatched up the remote and turned off the television. He cocked his head, his bright eyes glittering with malice. "I was watching that game, Reba."

"I'm talking to you, Carl."

He sighed, then got to his feet and climbed the stairs. He went into his study, where there was another small television, and shut the door. A few seconds later I again heard the roar of the game.

Nearly blind with anger, I jumped up and followed him to the door of his study. I grasped the door handle, eager for a fight. Then I stopped. Took a deep breath. Tried to clear my head. After twenty years of arguing I knew damn well that there was no point in going after Carl at such a moment. I'd heard everything he was willing to say.

So it surprised me to find him still awake when I entered our room late that night. He was sitting up in bed with an investment magazine, his reading glasses perched on the end of his nose.

"Who told you, Reba?"

I crossed the bedroom and took off my robe, folding it over our enormous footboard. "What difference does it make? Everybody already knows."

"I just wondered whether you'd heard the truth or some blown-up, fabricated bullshit."

"You're going to tell me that you're not sleeping with her?"

"I won't say it hasn't happened." He took off his glasses.

I lay down and turned on my side, keeping my tear-filled eyes hidden from his inquisitive gaze.

"You don't seem to be very upset," he observed coolly.

"Were you hoping I would be?"

"It might have convinced me that you had some feelings for me." He reached up and turned out the light. "I guess I don't need to have any illusions about that."

"So you're trying to make me jealous?" I snarled. I rolled off the bed and stood up. "You make me sick, you bastard!"

"There it is," he said with a low laugh. "The first honest reaction I've gotten out of you in a long, long time."

"You've been chasing other women for years—"

"And you've been in love with another man since the day we got married. Don't you think I know that?"

"I've never cheated on you!"

"How could you? You've never really *been* with me!"

"That's not fair. I've given you everything I could for the past twenty years. We've built our entire lives together—"

"But one night when we were making love I looked into your eyes and saw that you were wishing I was Joseph. I realized that no matter how good a husband I might be, I could never compete with your memories. No matter how much we achieved, or how good life got for us as a couple, he made you believe you just weren't good enough for him."

"That's not true—"

"Of course it is. You've never gotten over the fact that he left you."

Tears pouring down my face, I stumbled blindly into the bathroom. I stood at the sink with the water running, glad that the sound of the water hid my tears. When I finally came out, Carl was still sitting there, staring into the darkness.

"I don't want her, Reba. In fact, I've never wanted any other woman. They just seem to fill some of the emptiness I've felt since I realized how stupid I was to be so in love with you."

"How can you say you love me?"

"I *do* love you. That's the only reason why I didn't pack up and clear out a long time ago. That's the reason why I've settled for so little, when all I've ever needed was to believe that you truly cared about me."

"I do care about you, Carl."

"Can you honestly tell me you're not still in love with him?"

"I haven't seen him in twenty years!"

"Then tell me, Reba: Are you still in love with Joseph Thomas?"

"That's a stupid question—"

"Say it, Reba! *I am not in love with Joseph Thomas.*"

"That wouldn't prove anything!"

"But I need to hear it. I need to know that I haven't spent my life in love with a woman who saw another man's face and dreamed of another man's touch each time she came close to me. Even now"—he finally turned his head and looked in my direction—"all I really want is for you to tell me that I'm wrong. Lie down with me. Make love to me and really mean it. Prove to me that these twenty years have been more than just a joke."

He paused, his gray eyes very sad. "I'm not such a bad man, you know."

He waited for me to say something, but I didn't know the words. Then abruptly he turned over and pulled the sheets up to his shoulders. I stood in the doorway, staring at his silhouette as if he were a stranger.

Then making my way out of our room, moving by instinct as I

had so many times before, I descended the steps to the cathedral of our coldly perfect living room. Sinking down silently on the fine leather grain of the sofa, I closed my eyes and drank in the emptiness provided by silence.

The house was quiet. Lavender Lane was quiet. The whole world of this northern Virginia suburb was bathed in its illusion of safety. Here on Lavender Lane there were no life-threatening diseases passed between husbands and their mistresses to unsuspecting wives. There were no teenagers on the brink of discovering the temptations of unprotected sex, alcohol and date-rape drugs. There were no gloating "frienemies"—enemies who pretended to be friends—in my life.

And there was no other man—no one singular man—whom I'd loved from the day we met, whom I'd lost, and whom I would go on loving until the day I died.

Chapter 2

Baltimore, Maryland

1 9 8 0

"Please be seated."

Three hundred students arranged themselves noisily on the chapel's pews and looked up impatiently, praying that the speeches wouldn't go on too long.

"Absalom Jones College was named after the first African American to become a priest in the Episcopal Church—a man who dedicated his life to the eradication of slavery and the improvement of life for blacks in the United States. Founded by the Episcopal Church in 1867 to educate the newly freed slaves and their sons and daughters, this institution of higher learning has given more than one hundred years of proud service to the African American community. On behalf of our esteemed President Saunders, the board of governors and the entire faculty and staff of this proud institution, I warmly welcome the Class of 1984 to our college!"

The dean of students beamed proudly from the lectern in the college chapel, a graceful, gothic edifice of sweeping beams and colorful stained-glass windows. Sandwiched on the hard pew between the two girls who'd introduced themselves to me as my roommates, I tried to stave off the perspiration that was already running down my forehead.

I had never seen such heat in mid-September! And the humidity had welded my yellow cotton skirt to my legs like a dishrag. I hadn't wanted to bring that skirt with me, but my mother insisted: "You'll be required to go to chapel at least once a week, young lady, so you'd better take some suitable clothes."

I had sucked my teeth—a brave thing to do in my parents' fanatically disciplined house—and stuffed a couple of matching outfits into my suitcase with every intention of throwing them into the bottom of my closet as soon as I arrived in Maryland. How could I possibly show up at college looking like a preacher's brat? I'd lived in the shadow of my father's profession my entire Detroit childhood, and now, for the first time in my life, I was going to a place where no one knew me or my family. I was finally free!

When the plane set down at Baltimore International, I was, however, already starting to feel the first pangs of homesickness. My grandmother wasn't well, so my parents had allowed me to travel to my new school alone. And although I pretended that finding a taxi to drive me the twenty miles or so to Baltimore would be no big thing, as I exited the terminal I was hit by a wave of fear. What if I couldn't find anybody to drive me into the city? What if I got kidnapped along the way? What if I went in the wrong direction and ended up in Delaware or New Jersey?

Fortunately I noticed a young man in a Morehouse T-shirt and stonewashed jeans whose matching leather suitcases were stamped with stickers from Absalom Jones College. Bravely I smoothed back the loose frizzles on my sweating forehead and crossed the sidewalk toward him.

"Excuse me—are you going to Baltimore?"

He turned his head to look down at me—he had smooth russet skin, warm gray eyes and a sprinkling of freckles across his cheeks—and showed me a mouth full of pearly teeth. My heart began to thud at the sight of his seductive grin.

"Who wants to know?" he asked in a gently hoarse voice, his

bright eyes taking in my face and the shoulder-length ponytail that I wore so proudly.

"Reba Freeman," I boldly answered, hoping to hide my shyness.

His smile broadened. There was a pause while he tried to make out something he saw in my eyes. "Carl Thornton. And yes, I'm going to B-town. I'm guessing that you're on your way to my college, too."

He had a slight southern accent that lulled over his words, and a Rhett Butler manner that my mother would have loved. "Where you from?"

"Detroit."

"Motown, U.S.A.!" he exclaimed. "What's a sophisticated lady like you doin' all the way down here?"

"Well—" I looked down at the pavement, not wanting to tell him that Absalom Jones had been my father's and grandfather's school, and that my enrollment was therefore determined before the day of my birth. "Well, my minister thought it was a good school, and—"

"You wanted to get as far away from home as you could," he laughed. "Sounds all right to me!"

He threw up a confident hand and hailed a cab, which instantly pulled up beside us. The driver got out and Carl began packing all of our suitcases into the trunk.

"You'll like AJC—that's what we call Absalom Jones College," he said as we gained the highway leading into the city. "There's folks from all over the country, and some foreign students, too. It's a church school, but they don't come down with the religion thing too much. After all, everybody knows that college is about having a good time."

"Right," I quickly agreed.

"But coming from Detroit, you must be an expert on good times."

"Sure," I said, hoping he wouldn't start asking me about the newest dance step or the most popular musical group in the Motor City. My father had been opposed to the basement parties that my school friends went to, saying that too much "drinking and drugging" went on at those unsupervised events. I had spent my high school years going to church youth meetings that were conducted in well-lit halls with plenty of scrutinizing adults.

Carl didn't waste any time on getting to know me, however. He was much too busy talking about himself. During that half-hour ride into Baltimore I learned that he was a sophomore, majoring in business administration. He came from a well-to-do businessman's family. He had two older brothers who were already pursuing medical degrees. His mother stayed home to take care of their sprawling house in an area near Washington called Prince George's County. They had a center-hall Colonial with two chocolate labs and a blue point Persian cat. He was on his way back to college after spending a week with his grandparents, who were doctors in Atlanta.

"You're staying on campus, of course," he said with a sly smile.

"Yes. I've got two roommates, but I haven't met them yet."

"*Two* roommates?" he whistled, shaking his head. "You've got to get yourself a single!"

"A single?" I repeated, confused.

"You won't get much action with two other people in your room. You'd better hope they get boyfriends or spend their weekends off campus somewhere."

"Why?"

He took a long, leisurely look into my eyes. "You know, you *really* need a big brother."

"A big brother?"

He laughed. "Sometimes it makes things easier if somebody's around to explain things to you. My older brothers went to More-house, but my mama wanted her baby to stay closer to home. So," he said with a wink as the taxi slowed to enter a pair of stone gates and wound its way down a gracious, tree-lined drive, "I've had to fig-ure things out pretty much on my own. But I'd be happy to look after you."

Before I could respond we cleared the trees and found our-selves in the center of a wide, meticulously landscaped park—the Commons—surrounded by tall, red-bricked buildings. Groups of young people were gathered on the stairs of the white-columned entrances, and at the far end of the grassy space I spied the towers of the small gothic chapel. A fountain sent up a gentle spray in front of the many-windowed dining hall, which I recognized from the ad-missions booklets. The library, an ivy-wreathed stone building on the other side of the green, faced the administration hall. Absalom Jones College was, in a word, beautiful.

"Here we are," Carl Thornton said, reaching into his pocket for his sealskin wallet. I began to dig in my purse, but he handed the driver a pair of twenties and reached across the seat to stop me.

"The ride's on me," he said quickly. "Consider it a welcome gift from—"

A rippling cry went up from a perky young woman who was looking in the window of the cab. She was in his arms before he could get out of the door. The driver laughed and shook his head, glancing into the rearview mirror at me.

"Good luck, miss," he said, tilting his head toward Carl. "Who-ever gets involved with that guy is certainly going to need it."

Samantha Johnson, a part-Seminole beauty with tawny eyes and waist-length hair, came from the southeast corner of Washington, D.C. "I don't care what you've heard about our nation's capital," she was saying as I entered my dorm room. "The capital of *Black* America is Anacostia!"

My other roommate was a petite, chatty girl from Roanoke Rapids.

"Desiree Malene Harris," she said in greeting. "Please call me Desiree, not Desi."

"Why?" Samantha asked. "Because it sounds like *dizzy*?"

"Of course not!" She giggled. "Desiree means 'most desired' in French. My parents wanted everybody to know how I came into the world."

"That's sweet," Samantha said, rolling her eyes.

As we stood together in the doorway of our large triple room, I experienced the first round of a friendly competition that would salt and pepper our relationship for decades to come.

"Well, let's see," Samantha began, peering around the bright chamber. She raised her hand and pointed a scarlet nail at the mattress near the window. "That bed has a real nice view of the campus."

"But you'll have the morning sun in your eyes," Desiree replied.

"I'll have the men's dorm in my eyes, too." Samantha strolled forward and dropped her suitcase firmly on the mattress.

Desiree turned to me. "The bed right here lets you see everything that's going on down our hall."

"Who cares about midnight popcorn and pajama parties?" Samantha said over her shoulder. "Nothing important can happen in an all-girls dorm with an eleven-o'clock curfew and dorm monitors that check under our beds!"

Desiree glanced toward the bed in the far corner. "That one will be the quietest and darkest in the mornings," she said, giving me a questioning look.

"That's fine with me," I said with a shrug. She smiled, glad that I was willing to let her have the bed she wanted.

Both girls were impressed that I'd been in Detroit during the '67 riots.

"Your family didn't leave?" Desiree asked as we unpacked our bags, her eyes round with disbelief.

"Leave? Oh no—my father was right in the middle of it," I answered proudly.

"What is he, a policeman?" Samantha asked as she swept her wavy hair back over her shoulders.

"No," I hesitated. "He's—he's involved in community service."

"*My* daddy's a doctor," Desiree announced. "He was the first Black ob-gyn in our county."

"That's no surprise," Samantha said testily. "You come from the boondocks."

"I think North Carolina's pretty cool," I said, coming to Desiree's defense. "We drove down to the Outer Banks on vacation once. I saw the place where they flew the first airplane."

"Oh, *gee*! I'll bet that was fun," Samantha remarked, shaking her head as she walked out of the room. Desiree and I looked at each other and laughed.

"What are you going to wear to chapel?" she asked as if we were already sisters.

"This old yellow skirt, I guess. God—I hope we won't have to go to church every day."

"Church isn't so bad," she replied as she pulled out a lavender ensemble. "I figure it gives you a chance to scope out the guys."

"It never did that for me," I said, ruefully remembering the way the entire congregation scrutinized the minister's daughter during our services.

Now we were sitting in the packed chapel listening to the college president, who had been talking for over twenty suffocating minutes about the role Absalom Jones had played in American religious history.

"In becoming the first African American priest in the Episcopal Church, Absalom Jones became a model for our spiritual and intellectual development," he was saying. "In letting no man tamper with his right to worship, Absalom Jones declared himself a free and distinct individual, possessing the will to rule himself and the ability to form his own judgments.

"To that end," he concluded, "this college is dedicated to continuing the promotion of growth, self-respect and the strengthening of African American youth to meet the challenges of adulthood."

The chaplain walked to the center of the altar as the president resumed his seat in the front pew.

"We will now join together in singing Hymn 598," he announced, and three hundred sweating students rose gratefully to their feet.

I was feeling hugely exasperated—not only because of the hair-frying heat, but because this was turning out to be way too much like home. I should have known when my parents were so anxious to send me that nothing interesting or exciting could possibly happen at this place!

And then my eyes locked on the student standing directly in front of me. There was something in the lift of his shoulders—a kind of quiet dignity—that made him seem years older than the others. The student had deep mahogany skin and short, neatly shaved hair. When he turned to share the hymnal with the guy standing beside him I noticed that his eyes were nearly slanted, his brows forming strong ridges that swept down gracefully toward his neatly sculpted nose. His square jaw and full lips contrasted sharply with the gazelle-like gracefulness of the upper portions of his face. He didn't look like anyone I'd ever seen in Detroit.

I was staring at him so hard that he glanced over his shoulder and our eyes met. He looked at me curiously, but didn't smile. I lowered my eyes, ashamed. When the service was over he vanished into the crowd of students sweeping hungrily across the grassy Commons toward the dining area, and I forgot all about him.

Almost.

Absalom Jones College was large enough to offer students some anonymity as they went about their lives. Yet it was still small enough to feel like a loosely connected family. So it didn't take long for me to hear about the tall guy with the velvet brown skin.

"I heard he's from Africa," Samantha announced as the three of us got ready for bed a few nights later.

"Africa?" Desiree repeated as she rolled a swath of her hair into a pink foam curler. "Where in Africa?"

"What difference does it make? Africans always look the same to me."

"I don't think he looks like anybody else," I began, but Desiree cut me off with a high-pitched squeal.

"Who cares what he *looks* like? You know what they say about Africans."

"No. What do they say?" I asked naively.

"That they're great in bed," Samantha answered, propping her feet on her footboard so that she could polish her toenails.

"They are?"

"Sure. That's because nobody ever taught them to be civilized between the sheets."

"And they're supposed to be built like steeds," Desiree added.

I didn't have a response for this remark, because I really wasn't sure exactly how grown men were built—I didn't really believe the pictures I'd seen in my biology textbooks—or how they were supposed to behave between the sheets. Despite the movies, books and constant urging of the high school boys to go all the way, my parents had succeeded in sending me off to college a virgin.

"Why would an African guy come here?" I asked.

Desiree pulled up her covers and flicked off her light. "Maybe he's going to be a missionary."

"A missionary?"

"He'll learn how things work in America, then he'll go back to make Christians out of the people in whatever country he came from."

"That's something I really don't understand," Samantha remarked. "People from all over the world are trying to come and live in the United States. Why would somebody from Africa want to go back over there after living here?"

"Maybe he's got family there," I said.

"Well, of course he does," Samantha snapped. "All of those Africans have twenty or thirty kids. Sometimes the men have four or five wives."

I got quiet. Samantha shifted to the other foot and grunted. "One wife or twenty, I'd enjoy trying him out. After all, he's pretty nice to look at. And then, there is that *other* thing—"

"Girl, don't talk that way!" Desiree shrilled.

"Why not? I came here to learn new things!" Samantha laughed. "And besides, we'll never be with the same guy four years from now when we graduate. I'd say I've got two solid years of fun before I even think about settling down. I'm certainly not in a rush to clip my own wings!"

"Well, I think you should try to find the right guy before somebody else takes him away," Desiree countered. "All the good men will be gone by the time we're juniors!"

They both looked at me, and I shrugged.

"Oh, come on, Reba!" Samantha laughed. "Don't pretend that you're not getting your own game plan together!"

"Look," I said sheepishly, "I just hope I'll manage to find somebody somewhere someday."

"*Somebody somewhere someday?* Jeeeezus, girl! There's plenty of fish in the sea. You might as well get out there and see what you like."

"I suppose."

"*Dang*, girl! You sound like you never even went for a swim!" Samantha declared.

When I didn't answer she rolled over and sat up, her eyebrows raised. "No," she said, shooting a disbelieving look across the room at Desiree. "Come on, Reba! You've got to be kidding!"

"Well, I—" Glancing miserably toward Desiree, I was dismayed to see that she was as shocked as Samantha.

"*Oooh*, Reba," Desiree murmured, sucking her teeth. "There is simply no excuse in this day and age for you to still be a virgin. Especially coming from Detroit!"

"That's right!" Samantha agreed, rising from the bed to reach over and slap palms with Desiree. "I know they got a *bunch* of fine guys up in Motown!"

"I guess it was my parents," I began to explain, but both of them laughed.

"No excuses," Samantha declared, scooting over to the edge of her mattress so she'd be closer to me. "We're gonna find you a guy. And believe me, once you get a taste, you'll wonder how you lived without it!"

Two days later I was crossing the Commons on my way to the library when someone tapped me on the shoulder. I glanced around, but nobody was there. Then I realized that a man was walking on my other side, his face wrapped up in a grin.

"I tricked you," he announced with evident satisfaction.

It was the African. He was very tall, which made his slightly baggy pair of pants end some two inches above the tops of his shoes. His shirt and tie seemed strangely formal on a college campus filled with Stevie Wonder T-shirts and Converse basketball shoes, but he clearly hadn't noticed. His bright eyes were shining with a pleasure that seemed weirdly incompatible with the fact that he was only talking to me.

"Yes, you did," I agreed, inexplicably shy.

"How are you, my sister?" he replied, bowing his head slightly. His accent fell somewhere between the British people on TV and a milder version of Desiree's.

"I'm doing okay." It seemed strange that he'd addressed me as a "sister," when he obviously came from such a distant world. "How are you?"

"I'm getting used to things." His voice was very gentle and low, with nothing of the urban "cool" I was so used to hearing from guys in Detroit.

"You must feel like you're a long way from home."

"I *am* a long way from home," he said with a laugh. I flushed, certain that he was laughing at me.

"So, where do you come from?"

"Liberia, on the west coast of Africa. Have you heard of it?"

"We learned in school that it was founded by former slaves."

"Yes. But that was a long time ago. We're a republic now, with a democratically elected president and some of the best natural resources in all of sub-Saharan Africa."

"That's great," I answered vaguely. I was aware of the crunching of gravel under my feet as I struggled to find something to say. My companion fell silent, too, as if unsure how to proceed.

"I saw you in chapel on the first day," he remarked suddenly.

"I'm sorry if I was staring—"

"Oh, no. It was good that someone here was paying attention to me. It is sometimes difficult to be a stranger in a land that's so different from my home."

"Have you been away for a long time?"

"Oh, yes," he said as we walked up the library steps.

I waited for him to go on, but he again paused thoughtfully. "It would require an entire evening for me to tell you about my nation and my people."

At that moment a pack of older girls burst out of the library, took one look at the two of us and began to talk fast and furiously to each other behind their hands.

"I guess I'd better get going," I said, hoping that by dinner it wouldn't be out all over campus that I was getting involved with the African. He reached up suddenly and gently touched my arm.

"When can we speak again?"

"I don't know," I whispered in a flush of embarrassment as Carl Thornton and his roommate, Bobby Watkins, went by. Our eyes met and Carl flashed me a quick, secret smile.

"Do you live in a residence hall?" the African continued, ignoring them.

"Yes. I live in Merriman," I murmured, even more ill at ease. Was this how college men flirted with women? Right out in the open, for everybody to see?

"What about tomorrow, after dinner? If the weather is fine we can take a walk in the neighborhood beyond the campus."

I quickly agreed, noticing that Samantha was approaching with two girls from the sorority she planned to pledge.

The following day was warm and bright, with the first sweet traces of fall on the breeze. I finished dinner quickly and started back across the campus with my head down, halfway hoping that the African wouldn't be there. As I approached the entrance to the dormitory I heard his voice.

"Hello, sister. I was afraid I wouldn't find you. You forgot to give me your room number when we were talking yesterday."

I looked up. He was sitting on the steps beside the door, but he stood to greet me.

Once again I was startled by his height. His plain black pants hung loosely on his lean hips. He had on another one of those white shirts that made him look like one of our professors. Today, however, something had subtly changed: His shoulders seemed straighter, and when he walked down the steps toward me he had the air of a suitor. He smiled with a mouth full of perfect teeth and handed me a single, deep red rose.

"Thanks," I whispered, bringing the dusty petals up to my face. I didn't really want to smell it—I just loved the way the velvety flesh of the flower felt when I brushed the petals against the soft skin of my lips.

"Yesterday I didn't have the chance to properly introduce myself," he said as he touched my elbow and began to lead me away from the dormitory. "My name is Joseph Vai Thomas, but my family prefers to call me Yusef."

"Yusef?"

"Yes. It's the Arabic translation of my name."

"Don't they speak English in Liberia?"

"The people in my village speak a dialect, but English is generally practiced in the schools. Some people in my family, however, are Muslims, and they prefer to use the Arabic translations of our names."

"Muslim? But this is a Christian college."

"That's true," he said with a quiet laugh. "I am, you might say, a kind of ambassador, because my life represents all cultures. I believe that no matter how different we are, we are all loved by the same God. What is your name?"

"Reba Freeman, but I don't think that's very interesting."

"We have a saying in Africa," he replied with his soft accent. "When a person is given a name, her spirit accepts it. Reba is a common form of Rebecca, one of the most important women in Christianity."

"I know," I said, remembering my father's insistence that I study my Bible daily. "Rebecca was Isaac's wife."

"She was a queen to her people, and deeply devoted to her husband and to her desire for a family."

"But she tricked her husband into blessing Jacob instead of Esau."

"Isaac was being repaid for the sin of favoritism. Rebecca wanted to make sure that the less-favored son would not end up an outcast, like Ishmael."

Slightly irritated, I hoped that he didn't plan to interpret Bible stories to me all evening. Joseph, however, didn't seem to notice.

"I imagine your surname, Freeman, was probably assumed by your ancestor when he escaped from slavery."

"I guess so. I've never really thought about it."

"Names are important. They preserve one's history and tie us to those who came before. Take my name, for example. The Vai are a people who migrated to Liberia from Sierra Leone many generations ago."

"You sound just like a teacher."

"I'm training to be a teacher," he replied proudly. "One day I hope to open mission schools in remote regions of my country."

"You mean you want to make kids into Christians?"

"Not really," he said, turning his thoughtful eyes on me. "You see, in some parts of my country there is very little money for buildings, books, paper, and almost no possibility of paying a teacher's salary. So the church sometimes undertakes the responsibility of setting up schools."

"You're planning to become a minister?"

"Oh, no!" He laughed, revealing his stunning teeth. "God has given me no calling to the cloth. I want to teach children and adults to read. After I take my degree here, I hope to receive a commission from the Church of England."

"That's a lot of responsibility."

"It is not so difficult to know one's purpose in the world. The difficult thing is not to corrupt it."

A bird fluttered furiously in the branches over our heads and he glanced up, giving me a chance to really look at his face. His brilliant eyes, almost the same shade as his lustrous skin, were filled with a patient desire to know, to share, to understand. I had never seen anyone so young who carried an air of more maturity, and when he glanced down at me I looked away shyly.

"What are you planning to study?"

"I'm not sure," I answered, still unused to the idea that the classes I took in the next few years might determine the course of the rest of my life. "I'm thinking about accounting. I've always been good in math."

"You will seek work in a corporation?"

"I don't know. I'd like to start my own business. But then again, maybe I'll take a job in the government."

"I'm certain that you'll be successful."

"Really?"

"You are not like the others, Reba."

"Yes, I am—"

"Forgive me, but you're not," he replied, looking down at me with gentle calm. "I sense that you are as kind as you are strong. And this combination is, I think, very rare. Once you have found your path you will move forward with a great deal of power."

"I'm not so sure about that," I answered, laughing nervously.

"Remember, Reba: A baby leopard is still a leopard. Even an egg will walk if you give it time."

No one had ever said anything like that to me before. I stole another curious look at his face. He was gazing at the street as we approached the wide gates that marked the entrance to the campus. I saw his shoulders tense almost imperceptibly, as if he was preparing himself to face the larger world.

"Are you a basketball player? You seem pretty tall."

"Basketball? No, we play football—you call it *soccer*—in my country. And I was never very good, really. I'm afraid that I spent most of my time with books."

We passed through the college gates and began walking down the busy street, now surrounded by the sounds of the evening traffic.

"What did you like to read?" I asked, genuinely curious.

"Whatever I could lay my hands on, of course. I love literature and poetry. But I also like to read philosophy and biology. Every book is a treasure, and to read is a great gift."

I looked away, ill at ease. This time he seemed to notice, for he laughed quietly.

"I have observed that many people in this country do not like to read. In Liberia, where the opportunity to study is offered to so few people, it would be considered a crime to be so indifferent to education."

"But we have to learn a lot of stuff that we don't need."

"Such as?"

"Well, I'm going into business. Why should I have to take English?"

Joseph smiled down at me. "Knowledge is the pathway to riches. You will have to know how to speak properly when you're a businesswoman. You will have to write letters to your clients. And reports about your operations—"

"Okay," I said, smiling back. "But how can I get excited about *The Scarlet Letter* when I'm concentrating on passing accounting?"

"Breaking one's back in the fields is hard, but hunger is even harder. Perhaps you will find others who are also serious about their studies and are willing to work with you."

"Most of the other students seem too busy having a good time."

"In my culture we believe that it takes an entire village to raise every child. We understand that you must work together in order to succeed."

"But everything's about competition in America."

"That is one of the things I find disappointing in your culture."

"*One* of the things?"

"Certainly you have achieved a great deal of technological advancement in the United States," he replied, gesturing toward the display window of an electronics store. "But I do not understand why young people would rather drink alcohol and use drugs than attend their classes. And I am sad about the open exploitation of young women—"

"Exploitation? There are more opportunities for women in this country than any other place in the world!"

"Perhaps. But there are also more pornographic films, magazines and music that degrade women," he said quietly. "A great African leader named Nkrumah once said that one may judge the strength of a nation by the political consciousness of its women. I am afraid that the pressures placed on women in your culture will finally have a destructive effect on the family."

"So you believe that we should just stay home and have babies?"

"No. I believe that men and women should find ways of sharing the responsibilities of raising the family, so that the children will not suffer."

This was a novel idea for me. My mother had worked in a government office for many years, while my father took care of church matters. Some of the people in the congregation were opposed to my mother having a job, saying that she should be available to help out with church activities. But my mother had held fast to the notion that she deserved her own career and her own bank account. There had been lots of bickering about it over the years, but she had raised me to believe that a woman's place was *not* necessarily in the home.

Joseph pushed open the door to a sweet shop that served ice cream at a shiny counter. We were met with the odors of confectioner's sugar and succulent pound cake. Sliding his arm around my back, he led me to a booth in the corner.

"I hope I have not angered you with my frankness," he said after we'd settled into our seats. "My people say that a goat is not always welcome to speak in a town of rams."

"No—I'm just surprised that you see our culture this way. Maybe you'll feel differently after you've been here awhile."

"I have already lived in the States for two years. I went to a junior college to study math and science before coming to Absalom Jones."

"Then you've been away from Liberia for a long time."

"Long enough to be absolutely certain that I want to return. Most foreigners are so amazed by the prosperity of American life that they find it hard to go home. And at first I was the same. Over time, however, I have come to see that the spirit of this world is too very different from my own. I don't believe that I could ever be truly happy here."

"What if the rest of your family came to America, too?"

"The rest of my family?" He laughed. "That would be over fifty people."

"*Fifty* people?"

A waitress came up and I ordered a vanilla milkshake. He asked for a glass of water.

"My family is much larger than most American families."

"Is that because your father has more than one wife?"

"No. My people do not practice polygamy. But my father did marry a second time, after my mother died. I have seven siblings and eight stepsiblings, and my mother and father now have two children together."

"That's amazing!" I blurted. Then I ducked my head in embarrassment. "I'm sorry, Joseph—I didn't mean to sound rude or anything."

"Rude?" he asked with another quiet laugh. "No, Reba. I understand that your culture is very different from mine. Where I come from, we place equal value on all members of our family. It would be very difficult for me to choose one or two people to bring to America while leaving all the others behind."

"But that gives you no choice. You'll have to go back to Africa when your studies are finished."

Now his gaze grew sad for the first time. "What the eye has seen the heart never forgets. Most Americans can't understand that I love my country and my people. I deeply miss my family. I hope that one day, God willing, I will be able to bring learning to my community that will improve everyone's life."

"I'm sorry. I assumed that everyone who came to America would want to stay. I never really thought about it any other way."

"I will never ask you to apologize for what your society has taught you," he replied. "I only ask that you keep your mind and heart open to new things."

"I don't know if I'm strong enough," I answered, struggling under the weight of his penetrating eyes. He answered in a clear, calm voice. And his words brought about the first deep stirrings of womanhood in the depths of my childlike self.

"You are a crystal maze, Reba. You are made up of many twists and turns, but still I can see your heart clearly."

"If you can already see how to get there, then I can't be a maze."

"On the contrary. The maze is all the more difficult because the paths have no walls. It will require a very special hero to appreciate the complexity of those twists and turns, and to really value the treasure once he finds his way."

The waitress brought my milkshake and his water. When he opened his wallet to pay her, I realized that he hadn't ordered anything. Flooded with embarrassment, I pushed the tall glass, topped with whipped cream and a cherry, toward him.

"This is way too much for me. Would you please share it with me?"

He looked at me a long moment, then dipped his head graciously. "I would be proud to do so. And I thank you for offering."

When we got back to the campus that night something about the evening had changed. The early autumn air was charged with an electric sweetness, and the sight of the towering oak trees gracing the college gates filled me with a boundless sense of joy. Joseph had fallen silent as he walked beside me, but his height seemed protective and calm. Our fingers brushed accidentally but neither one of us apologized. When we cleared the trees and came in sight of the dorms, we both automatically stopped.

"Perhaps you would be willing to walk with me again sometime," he said very politely.

"Yes," I answered so quickly that I was suddenly flushed with embarrassment. I glanced up to find him looking intently at me, and a quiver began at my scalp that swept downward to my groin.

"You are the first person who has asked me any questions about my home. I thank you for that."

"It—it was nothing. I really had fun."

"Good night, then," he whispered, turning to walk across the campus toward the men's dorms. I went my own way, feeling as if I was floating across the smooth lawn. Just as I reached the door of my own building, I looked up. He was standing in his own doorway, gazing across the Commons, a tall, still figure in the falling night.

Maryland's autumn bloomed like a deep yellow spring, with the trees igniting into shades of fire as the summer slipped away. The mornings were brisk, but by afternoon the sun still heated the world to a shimmering glow, and my Michigan mind—used to dismal rain and gray, darkening days—could hardly take it in.

Absalom Jones College itself seemed suspended outside of time. The nineteenth-century brick buildings, with their lean windows and creaking wooden floors, always reminded me of the lives of our forefathers—the black men and women who were struggling up from slavery to form themselves into the first generation of America's Black citizens. The walls of the corridors were filled with photographs of corseted girls with neatly coiffed hair and young men in dark jackets and ties. In one photo they were standing around a table laden with glass tubes and Bunsen burners. In another they stood at attention in the choir room, their eyes trained on a choral director whose arms were raised. And in some photographs they were socializing together in carefully chaperoned groups on the tree-shaded Commons.

Their hopeful eyes haunted me as I went about my daily routines. Often I found myself looking for my father in those sepia photographs or, indeed, looking for my father's father, who attended Absalom Jones in the 1920s. Joseph often said his people believed in bringing to the present that which was left behind. I sometimes felt that my ancestors were watching me from those images.

If my roommates shared my interest in our predecessors, they never mentioned it. It was obvious that they were much too busy with the daily routines of classes, meals and their budding social lives to care about the past. I quickly discovered that most of the students discounted earlier generations as hopelessly outdated. Samantha, for example, complained that the university's single-sex dorms were ridiculous now that women had the advantages of birth control: "I had to wait almost twenty years to get away from home and I don't need *anybody* interfering with my sex life!" And Desiree firmly believed that the college should have as many social events as possible in order to encourage the formation of relationships. "I didn't come here for calculus," she complained one evening when she had to stay in to study for a test. "I came here to find a husband."

My life, too, had found a rhythm: meals with my roommates, classes with easygoing students and instruction by old-fashioned, dedicated teachers. We washed our clothes on Saturday mornings and washed our hair on Thursday nights, filling the dorm with the smells of sizzling hot combs and bergamot hair oil. Living out the last days of our adolescence as we made the transition to adult life, there were sometimes raucous pillow fights followed by earnest discussions of whether birth control pills were preferable to IUDs.

Having grown up in Motown I had a certain amount of prestige, but it didn't take long for the other girls to realize that I was a novice in the ways of love. They exchanged ironic chuckles whenever I asked a question that exposed my naïveté, but ultimately accepted me as an innocent who needed their guidance in the great quest for sexual wisdom. What they didn't realize was that in spite of my quiet disposition and girlish demeanor I had developed a thrilling secret life of my own.

Joseph and I had been meeting surreptitiously for weeks. We weren't doing anything forbidden; no, it was much more like playing an enticing, unspoken game. Noticing that he was sitting at the table behind mine at dinner, I'd announce in a loud voice that I planned to go to the library that evening. Inevitably he'd arrive, carrying more books than he could read in an entire month. Taking a seat at the other end of my table, he'd smile at me from time to time as we scanned our textbooks, drafted our papers, completed our math assignments.

Other days I'd go for a late afternoon walk, strolling slowly across the Commons in full view of the men's dorms. A few minutes later he'd magically appear at the entrance gates, smiling at me from his great height. We'd wander through downtown Baltimore, arriving near dusk at Fell's Point, where he'd look to the east and speak softly to me about Africa.

Sometimes we'd watch each other in chapel without turning our heads. We knew we needed to be careful. The other students of Absalom Jones College made it their business to always know everything about each other's relationships. And without ever discussing it, Joseph and I instinctively knew that we needed time to carve out the dimensions of our feelings without interference.

One evening he was sitting across the table from me in the library reading room. He glanced around and, certain that no one was watching, he leaned forward. "You are very pretty, Reba."

"I am?"

He leaned a little closer. "I sometimes find it hard to concentrate when you're so close to me. But when you're not here, I find it even harder."

Carefully, and with great discretion, he slid a cassette tape across the table. I reached out and he stroked my wrist very gently. My fingers opened and his large, warm hand found mine. A thrill shot through me and my mouth went dry, while at the same moment my heart began to flutter.

We remained seated, bound together by his touch, until we heard a group of noisy girls coming up the stairs. I slipped the tape into my bag, returned to the dorm and waited until my roommates were out before slipping it into Samantha's stereo.

After a few seconds of uncertain scratches, a sensuous, lilting blend of throbbing rhythm and delicate melody poured slowly out of the speakers. A wandering guitar was stretched taut over the pulsing bass, which echoed like a heartbeat at midnight. The winds were warm, the blackness rich with the alto murmurs of opal birds. Smoke-scented air bore traces of the sun-ripened earth, and I gasped as Joseph's lips found my breasts. His strong hands steadied my hips and after holding back until I thought I'd scream he thrust slow and deep into the liquid heat of my—

I *think the* African guy's looking pretty good," Samantha announced later that evening as she brushed out her hair. "And he's tall. You know what that means, don't you, Reba?"

She shot me a low-slung glance, then shook her head.

Samantha and I were alone in our room, since Desiree was attending a meeting for the sorority she planned to pledge. She'd begged me to come with her, but I had finally decided against pledging, knowing that joining a sorority would be inviting fifty more girls into my private life.

"I sit right next to him in Government," Samantha was saying. "He hasn't asked me out, yet, but I know it's just a matter of time."

I looked over at her and figured that it was true. Samantha's hair fell in soft, sable waves to the small of her back, and she wore it loose and shining. She had the profile of an Egyptian queen and perfect chestnut brown skin. Walking across campus with her made me feel like a tree stump, for she attracted male attention like wool attracts lint.

"You know," she said, gazing indolently across the room, "you'd look much better if you'd do something with those brows."

"My brows?"

She shook her head as if I were in kindergarten. "You could get busy with the tweezers. Or"— she turned her face to the left and right, considering me carefully— "you could use a bit of eyebrow pencil to even them out."

I looked into the mirror that was hanging on the door. I had spent my childhood, and virtually every day of my adolescence, feeling that nature had cheated me out of any chance of real beauty. My father, a handsome man with a dip of West Indian blood from his relatives in Bermuda, had bequeathed me his narrow hips, square shoulders and strongly built jaw. But I'd missed out on his heavy-lidded, thick-lashed eyes and his wonderfully formed lips.

Instead, I found my face disappointingly ordinary. I had a full mouth, a smallish nose and strangely arched brows. My wide forehead crested in a widow's peak that I hid with girlish bangs, and my dark eyes seemed startling against my milk-coffee skin. My parents had been so strict about makeup that the most I'd ever gotten away with was a little mascara.

"Look," Samantha said, following my gaze. "Why don't you let me give you a makeover? I used to do professional makeup when I worked at Harrison's."

She seated me in front of the mirror, put a towel around my shoulders and went to work. For about a half hour she talked quietly as she brushed and painted.

"Your hair's in good shape," she remarked as she smoothed it away from my face. "It's a good thing your mother never let you get a perm. But you need to get rid of these bangs. They make you look like you're six years old!" She shook her head, then continued her analysis.

"You've got pretty good cheekbones. We can bring them out with a bit of plum blusher."

"I've never really worn makeup."

"Believe me, Reba—my boyfriends have never seen me without my makeup. And they never will."

"But you're beautiful," I said.

"I *make* you think I'm beautiful, sister. Just listen: When I was a little girl—I don't know, maybe five or six—my mother took me aside and showed me my face in the mirror. 'Look at yourself,' she said. 'That face can get you anything you want, as long as you know how to use it.' And she was right. I'm pretty good at convincing people that I'm special. And since most people think with their eyes, all I have to do is make sure they're pleased by what they see."

She laughed coolly and I looked up in surprise. "What is it?" I asked.

"I was just thinking about my mother. She didn't have much, but she made sure her girls had good-looking fathers."

I peered at Samantha's reflection and saw bitterness in her eyes. "I mean, my mother never had any luck with the men she married. So she raised us to take care of ourselves. Still, both of my sisters got married right out of high school. But nobody had to spell *college degree* for me. I decided when I was a kid that I'd only marry a man with looks, class and money."

She glanced down at me. "I know you don't understand what I'm talking about. You grew up in a nice house with both of your parents. And even if you didn't like being a preacher's kid, I'm sure a lot of people in the church were looking out for you. Nobody gave a shit about me in my neighborhood. To tell you the truth, everybody was making bets that I'd get pregnant before I even finished high school."

She pushed back her shoulders and looked at her own reflection. "My philosophy is simple: You're a fool if you don't use what you've got to get what you want. But first you've got to know exactly what you want. And that's one of your problems, Reba."

"I want to be with someone who loves me—"

"That's sweet, but it's not enough." She leaned over my shoulder so that our faces were side by side in the mirror. "Men are devious, Miss Freeman. They'll say anything to a woman to get what they want. You have to look behind their smiles and see what's going on in their heads."

"All guys aren't like that."

She laughed and straightened her back. "You're too smart to be so stupid. Open up your eyes, girl! Get yourself together and go get the man you deserve!"

She did some dramatic work with my eyes, then fumbled around in her dresser drawers until she found a burgundy lipstick. "Always put on your liner, and don't be afraid to add color to your lips. And Reba," she added in a mock schoolteacher's voice, "don't ever go out without your perfume," she said, dousing me in a pungent floral scent.

"What's that?" I said, waving my hands around to dispel the sharp odor.

"That, my dear, is Deception, the newest fragrance by Anya. She's a designer in France. I got all of her stuff at a huge discount when I worked at the store."

Finally she stood back and admired her work, her hands on her hips. "You're a new woman, Reba Freeman. Just look at what some eyeliner, blush and a little lipstick have done for you."

I looked in the mirror and discovered a startlingly older version of myself. Samantha was right: I had darkly powerful eyes and inviting lips, framed by a wide forehead and my father's prominent cheekbones. With my hair swept back I had gained an air of elegance and maturity. Even my arched brows seemed dramatically suited to my boldly handsome face.

"I'd better watch out," Samantha concluded, only half teasing, "or soon you'll be stealing *my* guys!"

The following evening I did my best to transform myself according to Samantha's directions before meeting Joseph at the college gates. Brushing my hair back, I clasped it with a new silver barrette, and borrowed one of her lipsticks—a soft pink that matched my blouse.

When he walked up he looked at me in surprise, and I saw something new in his gaze. For the first time he openly took my hand as we gained the main street, and we began our habitual route through the streets of the city.

"You look even more lovely than usual tonight," he said in his dignified voice.

"Do you think so?" I asked, keeping my eyes on the sidewalk.

"Yes, although—" He paused politely. "Beauty is half of a God-given favor. Intelligence is God's *whole* blessing."

I would have blushed if my skin had been any lighter. Instead, I gulped something about being old enough to wear makeup if I wanted to.

"Oh, I think you seem much more womanly tonight," he agreed, clearly sensing my discomfort. "I meant no harm with my earlier statement. It's just that, well, you are already very beautiful without looking like the others."

I hardly knew what to say to that, so we walked along in silence for a time.

"Did you have time to listen to the tape?"

"Oh, yes," I murmured, looking away quickly so he couldn't see the heat that leapt into my eyes.

"Ali Farka Toure is a favorite of mine. He blends traditional songs with influences from your American blues tradition. He takes African music from exile and brings it back to our motherland."

"He does some other things, too," I replied, still keeping my eyes averted.

Joseph squeezed my hand gently. "I hope you liked it. I would like to share some other African musicians with you."

When we reached the ice cream parlor he leaned forward to open the door for me, but I shook my head. "Let's do something different tonight."

We continued walking as evening fell. It was late October and the darkness came early as we made our way through the city's narrow cobblestone streets. Block after block of tightly packed row houses rose up as we strolled aimlessly into the older quarters of the city. There were few people to be seen, and the sky seemed to close in around us.

For once Joseph, too, seemed to be silenced by our surroundings. I sensed that the cool night weighed heavily on his spirit, and I wondered if he was missing his home. Had he been alone since coming to the United States? Did he ever speak to the family and friends he'd left behind?

"Joseph," I said in the gentlest voice that I could muster, "is everything all right?"

He hesitated before answering. "I am sorry. I was thinking about things that are far away. I did not intend to be rude."

"Do you want to talk about them?"

He turned his head, gazing down a sharply descending street. "I'm not certain I know how."

I reached for his hand, feeling a sudden rush of caring for this strong, solitary man.

"Do you ever call your family in Liberia?"

"It is far too expensive. But we often write."

"Have you sent them any pictures of the campus?"

"Yes, and I often send postcards."

"Have they ever seen snow?"

"Only those who have visited England."

"Do you think they'd like it here?"

Joseph paused. I knew that he was deciding whether to risk my feelings by telling the truth. "They would be very impressed by the size of the cars you make in Detroit."

"Have they ever been in a shopping mall?"

"We have large open-air markets, not unlike your malls."

"And fast-food restaurants?"

"We are used to buying snacks from food stands, as well. But we don't eat hamburgers. We prefer pastries filled with vegetables, chicken or fish."

"What about movie theaters?"

"We have both outdoor and indoor theaters, where families often go to see films at night."

"With popcorn?"

"No," he laughed. "But we do drink plenty of soda."

"And hospitals?"

"We have many fine hospitals with doctors both from Liberia and from around the world."

"And universities?"

"Yes, we have several good schools. They conduct research for the rubber industry and train agricultural specialists."

"When you lived at home did you have a pet?"

"I had a dog when I was a boy," he said, his face bright. "A strong black dog with big yellow eyes. He followed me everywhere and took good care of me when my brothers weren't around. I really loved him, and was glad that he lived a very long time."

"Do you have a girlfriend in Liberia?" I asked, squeezing his fingers playfully.

"I had many friends who were girls," he answered with a twinkle in his eye.

"But was there one *special* girl?"

"There was one—" Joseph froze as someone suddenly loomed up out of the shadows in front of us. He instinctively reached out to stop me from moving any farther.

An overweight white man in a soiled shirt was staring menacingly at Joseph. His swollen eyes slid to me, and I saw Joseph step forward, as if to shield me from the man's view.

Keeping his head raised and his back very straight, Joseph looked directly into the man's eyes. There was a long, silent exchange, and during those tense seconds I felt the weight of three centuries of hatred between the oppressor and the survivor, the European and the African, the ignorant and the intellectual.

Suddenly, without a word having been spoken, the man moved off, muttering something under his breath. Joseph watched him stagger up the short flight of steps into a row house. Then he turned to me. I looked into his eyes and saw a hardness I didn't recognize.

"It's getting late. We'd better get back to campus."

A few days before Halloween, Desiree's sorority sponsored a dance in the dining hall. The excitement in the dorm was palpable as we struggled into our tightest, lowest-cut dresses and forced our feet into our highest heels.

"Maybe I should wear my green dress," Desiree moaned as she squinted into the mirror nailed to the back of the door.

"God, no!" Samantha called from her desk, which was now serving as her makeup table. "You've got to wear something bright so you'll stand out in the dark."

"But this is too tight under my arms," Desiree said as she tried to adjust the straps.

"Nobody will be looking under your arms!"

They both glanced at my "best" dress, a flowered, calf-length calico with a rounded neckline. Samantha simply shook her head and rolled her eyes.

"Can you dance in those things?" Desiree asked as Samantha strapped on her six-inch platforms.

"I don't give a shit about dancing," she replied, turning from side to side in the mirror. "Just look at what they do for my butt."

We took turns doing each other's hair and makeup, and sprayed on so much Deception that the three of us were dizzy when we teetered across campus to the already roaring dance.

The sorority sisters had cleared out the tables and pushed the chairs to the walls, hanging streamers of orange and black crepe paper from the light fixtures and installing a rotating disco ball in the center of the ceiling. With the lights dimmed and George Clinton blasting from shoulder-high speakers, we were in our campus version of Studio 54.

"All right, Reba," Samantha announced in a loud voice as we threaded our way through the crowded entrance and stopped just beside the dance floor. "Tonight is *your* night."

"My night?"

"Yes. I've been doing a little bit of research while you've been holed up in the library. I found the perfect guy for you." She now looked over my shoulder and winked at Desiree, who gave her a smile of complicity.

"The perfect guy?" I repeated, raising my voice over the booming of the speakers. "Who?"

"His name is Andre Chenault," she yelled into my ear. "He's a junior from New Jersey and I think you'd make a pretty cute couple."

"But I don't even know him!"

"Don't worry. I've set everything up. All you have to do is relax and let it happen."

"Let *what* happen?" I shouted, looking from Samantha to Desiree.

"What needs to happen," Samantha answered tartly. "I told him that you have a big thing for him and that you want to spend some time alone."

"What?" I yelled, certain I'd misunderstood.

"He lives on the ground floor of Concord Hall. It's real easy to get in and out through the window, and the floor monitors never check the rooms after ten."

"You must be crazy, Samantha! I'm not going off with a guy I don't even know."

"Some people think it's better like that," Desiree said, speaking up for the first time. "Then you don't have to pretend to like it. I mean, if the guy's your boyfriend or something, there's a lot more at stake!"

I looked from one to the other in angry bewilderment, but at that moment someone walked up out of the blinking lights. It was hard to make out the man's face, but he was clearly too short to be Joseph.

"What's happening, ladies?" he said in a husky voice.

Samantha threw back her hair and slid one hand up to her ample hip. "I was wondering when you'd find your way over here, Andre," she simpered into his ear. "This is my roommate, Reba. She's from Detroit and she's been studying so hard that she hasn't had time to meet any guys."

I felt his appraising eyes on my face, which was half hidden in the shadows.

"A Motown lady?" he said, his gaze now sweeping down my dress. "Then you already know how to dance."

The question was rendered in an insinuating tone that, under the scrutiny of my roommates, I chose to ignore. I let him lead me out into the center of the room, although I didn't like his odor of weed washed down with gin.

Although I had been dancing in the privacy of my bedroom since I was old enough to walk, I had danced in public only a few times in my life. The church parties I had gone to were so carefully supervised that no guy had ever managed to put his hands on me. And at my prom—which I'd attended with Ronald, the son of long-time family friends—there'd been so many people that I'd hardly been able to move around the densely crowded dance floor.

So finding myself exposed to the entire college with a junior whom I'd never met before was terrifying. Even worse was the fact that he reached for my hips and pulled me close as soon as we got to the center of the room. As we swayed to the rhythm of "Rapper's Delight," he began pushing his pelvis against mine. I felt a flush of embarrassment, followed by a wash of crushing humiliation when I realized that nearly the entire room was beginning to watch our performance. A howl went up from a group of men on the sidelines and one of the women laughed shrilly. Andre's face, covered by a thickening sheen of sweat, hardened into a sneer of triumph as he danced around me, thrusting his groin against my rear in time with the beat.

I closed my eyes and tried to block out what we must have looked like. He went right on dancing, his gyrations growing more outrageous as the crowd roared. Trembling with embarrassed defeat, I was unprepared when Andre moved up close behind me and panted into my ear—"Not bad, Miss Detroit. Can you work it like that *off* the dance floor?"

Although his breath sickened me, I was relieved when he took my hand and led me through the crowd to a darkened corner of the dining hall. He sat down on a chair and pulled me expertly onto his lap, instantly planting his greasy mouth on mine. I let him kiss me, feeling his tongue pressing insistently against my lips, but I began to struggle when he made a lunge for one of my breasts. Instead of stopping, he kissed me even harder while wrapping his free arm around my waist to hold me steady against his thighs. I jerked my mouth free and he laughed, clamping his lips hard on my neck.

"Hey—I don't want to do this," I said as he managed to unzip my dress. I looked around wildly, but the partygoers were pretending not to watch what was happening in the darkened areas of the room.

"Come on, baby," he growled, his lips licking my chin as his fingers found a nipple. "You got to try it sometime."

Now my sickening humiliation was drowned out by my enraged realization that *Samantha had told this animal that I was a virgin!*

I began to struggle in earnest, hitting at his back and shoulders and trying to regain my balance. The more I fought, however, the more tightly he held me. I slapped him as hard as I could and he tightened his grip on my breast, forcing his tongue against my lips until my mouth opened.

At that moment we were both aware of a tall figure in a jacket and tie standing over us. Thinking it was a teacher, Andre immediately shoved me away. I fell backward into Joseph's arms. He carefully helped me regain my balance and stood behind me as I struggled back into my dress.

Instantly Andre was on his feet, wavering between rage and embarrassment. "What the fuck do you want?"

I looked up into Joseph's face, praying he wouldn't say anything that would lead to a fight. I couldn't bear the thought that he might get hurt—or end up being expelled—because of my stupidity.

But Joseph just looked down at Andre, his eyes filled with disgust. "I think you need to leave the lady alone," he said softly.

"And you need to get the hell out of my face," Andre snarled, mistaking Joseph's politeness for fear. Several other people had come up and were glancing excitedly from one man to the other. I saw Samantha on the fringe as well, watching.

Joseph turned to me. "Are you all right, Reba?"

I nodded, looking down in shame. Without another word he slipped his arm around my waist and led me through the gathering crowd.

"Fuck you, you African ape!" Andre yelled. Several people

laughed loudly, but most of the room had fallen to a hush. Head held high, Joseph guided me out of the dining hall, down the steps and into the brisk, late-autumn night.

Once we were outside I sank down on one of the stone benches, now icy cold to my legs.

"Did he hurt you?" Joseph asked softly.

Humiliated, I shook my head as I wiped my mouth with the back of my hand. Joseph sat down beside me.

"Do you want to go back to the party?"

"No," I whispered, keeping my eyes on the sidewalk.

"Shall I see you to your room?"

"No, please," I whispered, drawing together enough of my battered self-esteem to look up at him for the first time. In the darkness it was difficult to see what was in his eyes, but still, I was surprised to find nothing more than sadness. "Please, Joseph. I just want to be with you."

He looked to the left and right, knowing we couldn't go to his room. We couldn't leave campus, either, for the streets wouldn't be safe at that time of night. "Well," he said with a sigh, "I suppose we could go to the library."

Without another word we began to walk across the Commons. A cold wind was blowing, and he slipped out of his jacket and draped it over my shoulders. My left heel got stuck in a drainage grate and I began to giggle as he bent over and tried to pull my leg free. He started laughing, too, and when he straightened up I threw my arms over his shoulders and kissed him for the first time.

We stood there kissing for a long while. We walked a few steps, then started kissing again. It took us quite a while to make it the rest of the way to the library. And when we got there, we discovered it was already closed. So we sat down on the library steps, his arms around me, and kissed and talked until we were so cold that our lips wouldn't form words anymore.

"Why did you come to the United States?" I asked him, my voice swallowed up by the muted sound of the bass still pounding in the dining hall.

"Long ago my father's brother went to work in Britain. For many years he regularly sent us part of his wages, and my father used the money to help raise his brother's children. But the problem was that my uncle had to remain alone in Bristol, because if he'd taken his family there would have been no money to send back to Liberia."

"He never came home?"

"No. He lives there now." Joseph paused for a moment, his thoughts far away. "My father wanted something different for me. There was a mission school in our village, and those who could afford it sent their sons to learn how to read. The local vicar approached my father about sending me to a school in Monrovia, the capital, and it was there that I was given the chance to study in America."

"You mean the church sent you here?"

"Yes. Kenyatta once said that the vigor of a nation depends on its ability to renew itself with every generation. I've always known that I wanted to be a teacher, and the church was willing to pay for my studies if I agreed to return to Liberia when I obtained my degree."

"So you've already signed your life away," I said very quietly.

"Quite to the contrary. God has given me this opportunity to help others. You see, your American culture is based on the importance of the individual. My world is based on being part of a *group* of individuals."

"But every person is unique. How can you develop to your fullest extent if you're always tied down by others?"

"How can you develop to your fullest extent *without* the help of others?"

I thought about his words for a few moments. "How will it help your family if you return to Africa? You'd make a lot more money here."

"My uncle has spent his life in England, far away from his family. His children lost the benefit of growing up with their father. He has not lived well overseas, because he spared every penny for us. Now my older brother Kali has gone to join him. I hope that together they will manage to have a better life, but it is terribly hard to be alone in a foreign land.

"When I return, Reba, I will share my knowledge with as many people as I can. Teaching is like engraving one's culture on stone. Every individual I help will, in turn, help others. Some may win scholarships to foreign universities. Others may one day participate in the government and help to run our country."

"Then you have no life other than Liberia."

"I want no other life. Every time someone leaves my nation, part of its potential is lost. And if that person never returns, then the possibility of bringing about positive change is never realized. The Yoruba say that however far a stream flows, it never forgets its source. I come from Liberia, Reba. In many ways, Liberia is who I am."

He smiled down at me. "Do you want to talk about what happened tonight?"

I looked away. "It's all my fault, I guess."

"How?"

"My roommates think I'm crazy because I'm a—" I froze, realizing that I was speaking much too frankly, and filled with embarrassment, I swallowed hard. "They think I need to find a boyfriend. So they set that whole thing up."

"Why don't they let you choose someone who pleases you?"

"Well, they probably would, except that Samantha—well, she sort of has her eye on the person I—" Again I stammered to a halt.

"Yes?" he said quietly.

"Well, she's kind of interested in—in *you*."

There was a long silence. Then he cleared his throat. "I'm sorry, Reba. But which one is she?"

I looked up at him in wonder. "You know Samantha! She's got long hair and sort of yellow-brown skin and green eyes and—"

"I've never noticed her."

"But she's in your Government class—"

"Really? She must sit behind me."

"She sits right *next* to you!"

"Are you sure she was talking about me?"

"Of course she was! She's been talking about you since school started and—"

"Strange. I can't seem to remember who she is."

I opened my mouth, but nothing came out. His smiling eyes wandered slowly over my face as my heart swelled and exploded in my first true understanding of the complexities of love.

"I—I guess she's kind of confused," I murmured.

"Like you Americans say—she's barking up the wrong tree."

"And that guy she fixed me up with tonight—"

"Like you Americans say—he really missed the boat."

"That's true. Because I don't give a shit about Andre whatever-his-name-is—"

Joseph burst into laughter. "Many South Africans say that a bad name predicts bad deeds!"

"I guess," I agreed, "that the South Africans are right. But my roommate Samantha—"

"My people say that the lion is beautiful but its heart is evil."

"I don't believe she really wanted to hurt me."

"The heart of a cruel person is never pure. To trust her would be carrying grain in a torn bag. You must guard yourself against her unkindness, Reba. I am afraid that one day she might do you great harm."

I considered his words while he gazed at me, a strange and strong emotion burning in his eyes. "You must try to know whom you love," he whispered, "because you cannot know who really loves you."

I glanced shyly toward him. "Why do you speak with so many proverbs?"

"Proverbs are the daughters of experience." He drew in a deep breath and took my face between his hands, laughing quietly.

"Reba, I did not think that I would find someone like you in this country. I am glad you don't care about Andre whatever-his-name-is. I hope I will never give you any reason to feel the same about me."

We retraced our steps across campus. The dance had reached its climax, and tired, sweaty students were pouring noisily out of the dining hall and making their way toward the dormitories. For the first time Joseph and I didn't try to hide the fact that we were together. We stopped on the steps of my dorm and he kissed me lightly, in full view of the others. "Remember," he said softly. "Filling your life with other people's anger will leave no place for your joy."

Samantha came into our room a few minutes later and stood at the door, watching as I got out of my dress. "I suppose you expect me to apologize."

I glared at her. "You almost got me raped!"

"It's not my fault that Andre got blasted before the party. And anyway—you didn't tell me you already have a thing with Joseph."

"Joseph and I are just friends," I said, hanging up my calico dress.

"You mean you're not screwing him?"

I turned around slowly and fastened my eyes on her. "That's none of your business, Samantha."

"You think you're better than the rest of us?"

"I just don't care what other people think."

"I could've had him if I'd wanted him!" she declared, throwing her hair back over her shoulder. "But I don't want to be bothered with anybody who comes from nothing!"

I felt an anger rise up in me like nothing I'd ever known before. Suddenly I felt that I would do everything in my power to protect Joseph Thomas from anyone who might try to hurt him.

"You have no right to judge him by what he came from. You can only judge him by the man he becomes. And clearly he's come a whole lot farther and had a lot more to deal with than any of us."

"Then go be a missionary in Africa! That's where preacher's daughters belong anyway!"

I turned to stare at her, the full force of my rage clearly evident on my face. She blinked, then shrugged dramatically. "Calm down, Reba! Why are you getting so pissed off? I'm just messing with you. I really don't care who you go out with. And as for Joseph—" She smiled, a teasing warmth invading her eyes. "The truth is that I'm really happy for you, girl. It's time you got yourself somebody."

Samantha's words were still ringing in my ears when I bumped into Carl Thornton after lunch the following day.

"I heard you were the life of the party last night," he said with his cheerfully mocking grin.

"Weren't you watching, too?" I asked in irritation.

"No. My brother was in town, so we drove up to Philly for the 76ers exhibition game."

"Well, you didn't miss anything." I turned away.

"Hang on, Reba! Where are you going in such a hurry? We don't have class on Saturday!"

I looked up at Carl's spray of freckles and perfect teeth. He'd Jheri-curled his hair into a thick, stiff mass of ringlets that looked strangely out of place with his reddish-brown skin.

"I've got to do my laundry."

"Wouldn't you rather be talking to me?"

"Wouldn't you rather be talking to someone else?" I responded, noticing that a trio of girls was watching from the door of the dining hall.

"Not when you're around," he answered, tipping his head to the side. "Although I almost never see you. What's been keeping you so busy since our taxi ride?"

"School."

"Aren't you pledging a sorority?"

"Why should I?"

"So I can be your big brother."

"Sorry. I'm fine as an only child."

"Have you been to any of the parties over at Morgan State?"

"No."

"Howard?"

I shook my head.

"Have you been up to New York for the weekend?"

"No."

"How about Philadelphia? You know, we could take the train up there together sometime."

"For what?"

"Just to get away from campus."

"No thanks, Carl. I'm too busy going to class so I can get a job when I graduate."

"*Dang,* girl! I already told you that college is first and foremost—"

"About having a good time," I said in a singsong voice.

He gave a low whistle. "I can see you're going to be Little Miss Dean's List. But what about having some fun?"

"Don't worry. I'm having lots of fun."

"You could share some of that fun with me," he called after me.

"I wouldn't want you to overdose," I said dryly as I turned away.

For some reason I glanced over my shoulder as I reached the dorm. The three women had approached him and were pulling playfully on his arms. But he was still staring straight over their heads at me.

Chapter 3

Alexandria, Virginia

0▦▦0

2 0 0 4

I had spent most of the morning in hell.

Otherwise known as the CAD, or the Center for Alien Detainees, this version of hell was a nondescript gray building with the
character of a freight terminal. A windowless monstrosity, the CAD
was hidden some seven miles from any major highways in a rough,
deforested field. It housed hundreds of human beings who had entered the United States illegally and were awaiting the government's
decision on whether they would be declared political refugees or be
forcibly deported to their home countries.

Visits to the CAD, as my colleagues jokingly described them,
were always "more painful than root canals." Indeed, the few hours
I spent there each week talking with hapless and hopeless human
beings always left me feeling battered and depressed. But these interviews were important. The reports I filed on the history and
comportment of the refugees often proved to be the determining
factor in their ability to obtain asylum in the United States.

After arriving at the Center I had to park in a special lot surrounded by penitentiary fences. There were three security checkpoints complete with full-body X rays, and I'd learned long ago to
wear simple clothes and carry nothing more than a briefcase in case
the smirking guard decided to subject me to a strip search. Despite
ten years of regular weekly visits, the staff still took perverse plea-

sure in pretending that anyone who advocated on behalf of the detainees couldn't be trusted. So despite my best efforts to appear nonthreatening, I was often screened like an FBI poster child.

After undergoing a half-hour wait in an antechamber the size of a phone booth, I was led into a gray, windowless holding cell with nothing more than a government-issue green metal table and three chairs. Everything smelled of greasy industrial paint, mixed with the pungent odor of sweat and fear. I still experienced a wrenching nausea when I entered that room, though I'd been there countless times before.

The detainee of the day was an Algerian who had escaped the undeclared civil war in his country by traveling to the Canary Islands, where he'd managed to buy a one-way ticket on a chartered tourist flight to Washington. Arriving at Reagan without documentation, he'd immediately been arrested and placed in detention at a federal army base in Virginia. In the aftermath of the 9/11 terrorist attacks, North Africans were considered particularly dangerous.

So this man—who had lost his wife and five children to a massacre while he was helping his brother harvest crops in a village a few miles from his home—had been subjected to military interrogation. When Homeland Security was certain that he was innocent of any terrorist activity, they handed him over to the immigration authorities, who called me in to assess the veracity of his claim for political asylum.

The man I found in the cell—thirty-two years old, but with the face of an ancient being—was dressed in a prisoner's orange jumpsuit. His olive-toned flesh was lined like the fragile sheath over an onion, and his green eyes were listless as he stared at my feet. I noticed that his head had been shaved and his hair was sprouting back in rough, uneven curls. He had an unkempt mustache that grew in tiny spikes against his soft red lips, and his hands lay open and still on his slightly trembling lap.

Sitting close enough for our knees to touch, I refrained from speaking until an official interpreter entered the room. I turned on my tape recorder. Then I began the interview with a simple greeting.

"Good morning, Mr. Kabyle."

He didn't look up.

"I hope you're feeling well and getting enough to eat."

No response.

"I am here to help you in any way I can. If you're willing to speak with me, I would like to know what happened in your country."

I waited through a silence that went on for several minutes. The interpreter, a young man in a nondescript blue suit, blinked back his irritation and glanced at his watch.

"Mr. Kabyle," I continued, keeping my voice very low, "without your cooperation there's a very good chance that the American government will send you back to Algeria. Please let me help you."

After ten more minutes of silence I slowly stood up, turned off my tape recorder and signaled to the interpreter that the interview was over. I had learned in my years of experience that it was wrong to rush a detainee, but then, some people were simply unprepared to talk. Seeing that I was going to leave, the Algerian also rose. Leaning against the wall for support, he lifted his face to mine. It was then that I saw the bruises under his eyes and along his jaw— bruises that shouldn't have been there.

"I should have killed myself with the others," he muttered, using broken French instead of his native Berber. "Being here is worse than death."

Our eyes met as I heard the translator speak the words in

English. He swallowed hard, his words coming with sudden urgency.

"I had only completed my house a few months before," he explained in a rasp. "It was not a big house. Just three rooms. Big enough for my wife and our girls."

The man pressed his head hard against the wall as he spoke. "My father-in-law and all the neighbors came for the celebration, and we danced long into the night. My wife was pregnant again, and we hoped this time it would be a son."

He fell silent and the interpreter, a little man with an academic's face, paused too.

"Then I went to my brother to help with the crops. I was returning the favor of the long hours he gave to help me build my house. It is difficult for a man who has no sons, because he must rely on the assistance of others."

Again there was a long break. Suddenly the man's shoulders began to shake, though his voice remained preternaturally calm. "That night we came in from the fields. We washed ourselves, and when we were sitting down to eat, we heard it over the radio. The militia had gone to my village and destroyed everything. They had raped the women and girls, then burned them alive in the school building. All the men were shot. Someone had a car, and he drove me as fast as possible back to my village, but it was too late. Everything was already gone."

He began weeping in despair, his whole body wracked with sobs. I looked down on his emaciated frame, wondering why he didn't literally fall apart, right there, before my eyes.

"I should have killed myself with the others," he repeated again and again. "Why do I remain in this life?"

"Tell him I will do what I can," I said to the interpreter.

I made it out to the daylight and slid into the front seat of my car, starting the engine and turning the air-conditioning up as high as possible. Then I leaned my head against the steering wheel, letting the icy air blow directly into my face while I tried to force the man's words into my cave.

Over the years I'd learned to put the refugees' pain in a secret place in the back of my mind—a place that was pitch-black and frigid, and packed with the jagged, bloodstained stories I'd heard throughout my career. As the victims spoke, I ushered their grief and despair down a narrow path between my private memories and my daily responsibilities. Once the interview was done I pushed their voices into that cavernous space and rolled an enormous stone in front of the entrance. Then, if I was lucky, I was free to go on with my normal life, while doing everything I could to help them.

I stared blindly at the CD case in my car, then finally pushed Samite into the CD player and settled back into the leather seat, hoping that the gentle throbbing of his kalimba would help me regain my calm. I would return to my office and write my report, telling the authorities that this man deserved the chance for a safe, new life. I refused to think any further about his suffering. I would not allow the image of his wife and daughters being burned alive to disturb my already overburdened thoughts.

Shifting into gear, I took a deep breath and carefully steered the car out of the lockup and back down the long, lonely road. I tried to think about happy things—Marisa's upcoming concert, our diving trip in Grand Cayman, and even the possibility of that long weekend with Desiree and Samantha in Chicago.

My cell phone had rung several times before the piercing bleep brought me back to the car and the hot summer morning. I pulled over to the side of the highway and answered.

"Reba? This is Arlene. I'm calling from the college."

"Arlene?" I focused my thoughts. "How did you get my cell number?"

"Your secretary. I told her it was important."

I glanced into the rearview mirror. Inexplicably, there were tears in my eyes. I quickly reached up and brushed them away.

"Listen—I've just come out of a difficult meeting and I'm on my way back to the office. Can I call you a little later?"

"I've got something to tell you and I don't think it should wait."

"What is it, then?" I asked, struggling to remain polite.

"Look, it might be better if we meet. It's kind of complicated and might not make any sense over the phone."

I glanced at my watch. It was only eleven, and I didn't have anything on my schedule until a meeting with my boss at two. "I'm about twenty miles south of D.C."

"I'm calling from Baltimore. Why don't I drive down and meet you halfway—say, at The Eateries, just off exit thirty-two in Rockville?"

"I've got to be back in my office shortly after one-thirty."

"Reba," she said, her voice growing serious, "I think you'll want to see this. Trust me: You won't regret the trip."

Twenty-three years had added a few pounds to Arlene's short frame, but otherwise I found myself looking at the same woman I remembered from my first semester at college. As she rose from the table on the restaurant's glassed-in terrace to greet me, I was warmed by her open smile and intelligent eyes. Her graying hair was clipped short and twisted into tiny dreadlocks, and her nose twinkled with a tiny diamond stud.

"You're looking good!" I exclaimed, and she laughed.

"So are you, Reba. But then, you always did have the edge on the rest of us. How do you keep yourself in shape?"

"Running after a fifteen-year-old uses up a lot of calories."

"That's true. How's Carl?"

I looked at her defensively, but found nothing but gentle curiosity in her eyes. "He's doing fine. He has a consulting business that handles a lot of government projects. We live just outside of Alexandria, and you already know that I'm working for a nonprofit down on the Mall."

"Didn't you study accounting?"

"Yes. I know I could make more money as a CPA, but to tell you the truth, working with refugees seems more meaningful."

She nodded in agreement. "I know what you mean. I was in Germany for fourteen years. I got my bachelor's and master's degrees over there, then came back here and started teaching languages at Chesapeake Community College. Since most of my classes are at night, I help out with alumni relations at the college during the day. It keeps me busy now that my son has grown up and has a family of his own."

The waitress appeared and we each ordered iced tea and a Caesar salad.

"Is your husband a professor, too?"

"No more husband!" she replied, grinning broadly. "Perry and I divorced a few years ago. We did all right while we were overseas, but he turned into an entirely different man when we got back home. It seems the temptations of civilian life were more than he could handle."

"I'm sorry."

"I'm not! I got to see most of Europe, learned to speak French and German and raised a wonderful son. It was time for both of us to move on to other things. So we wished each other the best and went our separate ways."

She reached across the table and touched my arm. "I really was glad to talk to you the other day. It seemed as if I'd finally found a link between my present and my past. You know, most of the people who were at the college twenty years ago barely remember me. But I remember all of you."

"Then you remember Joseph."

"*Very* well. And I remember how much in love the two of you were. I used to see you going for walks together in the evenings. And I often saw you in the library, but you were too busy staring into each other's eyes to notice."

"Really? We thought we were being discreet."

"You were. Joseph was a very private man. I had to do a project with him for our Government course, and occasionally we talked about his home. I think that he deeply missed his family. But as the semester went on he began to feel torn by a terrible desire to stay. I think that desire had a lot to do with you."

My mouth opened but no words came. How could she know so much about Joseph and me? Had our feelings been so obvious?

She laughed gently. "No one else seemed to notice what was going on. I used to hear some of the girls talking about how handsome he was. They wondered why he didn't flirt with them. They had no idea that he was already so deeply in love with you."

Luckily at that moment our food arrived. It gave me an excuse to go to the ladies' room and dry off the tears that had again flooded my eyes. When I got back to the table she had already started eating.

"My mother sent me the alumni magazine in Germany, so I knew you and Joseph got married. I was happy for you. It seemed to me that if you had the courage to marry a man from such a different world, Perry and I had a chance of making it."

"But it didn't work out for either of us."

"Oh, I just outgrew my husband. And I think that on some

level, you and Joseph simply took on too much too early in your young lives."

"Maybe," I said lightly, not wanting to reopen those wounds.

We chatted for a while about her classes and my work. Then I pushed my plate aside. "Well, you said you had something to tell me."

Arlene bent down and pulled a large envelope from a woven grass tote bag. She laid it on the table and opened it, her expression growing serious.

"I had a hard time putting this together. But I think that when you've looked it over, it will all make sense."

She took out a manila file bearing the seal of the college and turned it toward me. The first document was a copy of Joseph's college admission application, dating back to his arrival in the United States as a community college student in 1978. A picture of the young man in a white shirt, his eyes filled with quiet confidence, met my gaze.

"How in the world did you get this?"

"Well, I'm pretty close to the people in Admissions. They let me borrow this with the promise that its contents would remain confidential."

I nodded and turned the page to find a copy of his college transcript, a hand-typed document bearing the registrar's seal. The document noted that Joseph V. Thomas had graduated summa cum laude on May 26, 1984.

Then there was a copy of a 1985 letter from the office of the Church of England in Liberia, requesting a reference for Joseph Thomas. Scanning the letter quickly, I noted that Joseph was being considered for an appointment to start a school in a village in northern Liberia.

"I never knew exactly when he went back to Africa. This was just a few months after our breakup."

"Then you lost all contact?"

I nodded again and closed the file. Arlene returned it to the envelope and handed me another set of papers.

"I spent some time in the library putting these together. I think they'll answer some of your questions."

An article from a 1990 edition of *The World Church* met my eyes. There was Joseph, now wearing a beard, standing among a throng of children in front of a simple wooden building. The caption beneath the photograph read:

> *Schoolmaster Joseph Thomas conducts courses in reading and agronomy in his Liberian Learning Institute. Mr. Thomas is the recipient of the Church of England's Queen's Medal for his dedication to spreading literacy in his native Liberia.*

I found myself smiling at the lean, dignified man whose arms were stretched wide to embrace as many of the children as possible.

"So he's done well. I always knew he—"

"Reba, you have to read everything."

The following page was a 1994 *New York Chronicle* article on the growing conflict in Liberia. My blood seemed to freeze as I stared at a blurred photograph of a blood-smeared man carrying a child's limp body out of a pile of mud bricks.

"You don't think—" I began, squinting to make out the features.

"Read it," she insisted.

CIVILIANS ATTACKED IN LIBERIAN CONFLICT

MONROVIA, LIBERIA (FPF)—*Joseph Thomas, an American-educated teacher who returned to his native country to open a school almost a decade ago, found himself at the center of the na-*

tion's civil war when fighting spread to northern Liberia. Trapped in his schoolhouse, Thomas was one of the few survivors when troops destroyed his village.

"Our people are peaceful," he explained. "We have nothing to do with the struggle for power in the capital. We merely want to take care of our families and lead quiet lives."

Thomas's sentiments have been echoed by numerous local authorities, who have called upon government forces to halt their raids against unarmed villages. The attacks on unprotected farms are seen as a primary means of providing both food and young men, who are conscripted into the military. Thomas reported that as many as twenty-five children, some as young as seven, were forcibly taken from his region.

Arlene touched my arm. "I'm sorry, Reba, but there's more."

The following page was a 2000 press report taken from a magazine I'd never heard of, *The Global Review*.

REBEL FORCES STORM AREA
NEAR LIBERIAN CAPITAL

MONROVIA, LIBERIA (FPF)—*Authorities state that a rebel group has gained new ground in fierce fighting near the capital. The group, which calls itself the Rimka Liberation Front, is led by a former teacher, Yusef Vai, who lived in the United States before returning to run a school in rural Liberia. Reached in his temporary headquarters in Taylorville, some ten miles from Monrovia, Vai stated that the government's inability to bring its militia under control required the formation of a resistance movement.*

"Over the past decade Liberia has seen violence unlike anything in her entire history," he said. "Such inhumanity necessi-

tates swift and definitive retaliation. My organization will work to restore peace and bring an end to the cruelties that have become a routine part of Liberian life."

Whether the Rimka Liberian Front's actions will lead to a cessation of violence is yet to be seen. At present, the death toll in the current round of fighting has risen to well over one thousand and the aggression shows no sign of abating.

"There's no photograph," I protested without raising my eyes. "Without a picture you can't be sure that this man is Joseph."

"I did everything I could to be sure before calling you, Reba. I looked for other references to the RLF. I ran computer searches for Yusef Vai. And then it occurred to me that I was going about it the wrong way."

"What do you mean?"

"I was looking for traces of Joseph through my American eyes. The only real way to find an African is to ask other Africans."

"You mean that you know someone in Liberia?"

"No. But I know plenty of Liberians living in Washington. I called a friend of mine who teaches African history at Howard. He knew all about the resistance movements and he was familiar with the name of Yusef Vai."

"What did he tell you?"

"He said that Vai, like many of the more sophisticated leaders, had risen up out of nowhere and created a faction of young fighters who were determined to beat back the military."

"I don't understand. Does this group support the president of the country or not?"

"Well, my friend said that although Vai spoke publicly about democratic elections, his men could be just as violent as their opponents."

"Then it can't be Joseph!" I said sharply. Two or three people at nearby tables turned to stare at us, and I lowered my voice. "I'm telling you that he'd never be capable of hurting other people. It's just not possible."

She closed her eyes for a moment, then looked down at the table. "There's one more article, Reba. I think you'd better have a look at this before you say anything more."

My fingers had begun trembling even before I turned the page. The final article, written in French, came from a publication called *Verité d'Afrique*. I glanced up at her and she looked into my eyes. "My friend suggested that I look this newspaper up on the Web. I downloaded the article last night and translated it this morning."

I lifted the page she'd typed out and held it close to my face, hoping she wouldn't see the despair that I knew was in my eyes.

Berne, Switzerland, April 2003

A number of suspected war criminals in detention in Switzerland will stand trial for crimes perpetrated against the citizens of their nations. All of the detainees were engaged in military activities in their respective countries. Many were leaders of resistance groups that engaged in terrorist acts against civilians.

Of the twenty-two prisoners brought to Switzerland, six were citizens of African nations, ten were inhabitants of former states of the Soviet Union, and six were suspected of belonging to underground terrorist organizations in Europe.

Trial dates for the detainees have not been set, but a spokesman for the Court of Human Rights said that the cases will be heard when the Court convenes for its autumn session in September.

"I don't see any reference to anyone who might be Joseph."

"Look at the sidebar of the original article."

I cast my eyes down a list that began with the words "*Détenus politiques.*" I didn't have to look very far, for the third name from the top was "Yusef Vai: Liberia."

Arlene shifted in her seat, suddenly producing a tissue that she wordlessly slid toward me. I hadn't realized that my face was bathed in tears.

"Perhaps you're right. This could all be an ugly coincidence. Joseph might be teaching quietly in a tiny village, oblivious to all the horror that's going on in his country. Or he might be living in another African nation, or even in London or the United States. These articles are not necessarily proof that he created some kind of paramilitary organization and became a—"

She suddenly broke off as if she, herself, was becoming aware of the full implication of what she was saying. "Look, Reba. I know you've got lots of friends in the government who can help you take care of this, but if there's anything I can do, just let me know."

"Help me take care of what? Yusef Vai has been accused of crimes against humanity."

"Even Yusef Vai is innocent until proven guilty, Reba. And if there's even the slightest chance that Vai really is that beautiful young man who once attended Absalom Jones College, then there's still something good inside of him. I'm sure of it."

"This can't be Joseph," I repeated as if the force of my words alone could make what I said true. "I don't care what these articles say. I won't believe it until I see more proof."

I dropped my gaze and my eyes fell on my watch. "Christ, Arlene! I'm going to be late to my meeting!"

"I'll tell you what," she said as we hurriedly gathered up our belongings. "Give all of this some thought and let's talk some more when you're ready. Here—take these articles. I've got my own copies."

I fumbled for my wallet and felt her warm hand on my wrist. "I'll take care of the bill," she said. "You just drive carefully. And remember: Whatever happens, I'll do my best to help you."

"I wish it was that simple," I murmured as I again climbed behind the steering wheel. Arlene had just blown the entrance to my cave wide open—and I wasn't sure that I would ever be able to really close it tight again.

I was sitting in the kitchen in the dark, the International Station silently broadcasting the latest images of human suffering in Ethiopia. Stick children in rags were picking their way through a muddy field, turning over stones in a desperate search for something to eat. The scent of roses eased its way in through a window I'd opened despite the steady purr of the air conditioner, and I was startled when I saw Marisa standing in the doorway like a ghost.

"It's four A.M., Mom."

"Go back to bed, honey."

"Why are you up?"

"I had some work to finish, so I drank some—"

"Not the coffee excuse again!" She shuffled through the kitchen and pulled out a stool, dropping down sleepily at the counter beside me. Her hair, which she'd cut short on a whim the summer before, had nearly grown down to her shoulders, and she'd tied it back with a rhinestone-studded bandanna. Resting her face in her hands, she looked up at me with her father's gray eyes. "Why don't you just put a futon in your office?"

"Why would I do that?"

"Because you obviously don't want to sleep in the same room with Daddy."

"Believe it or not, baby, this has nothing to do with your father."

"Then what is it?" she asked, her face reflecting the flickering black and white of the silent television.

"Nothing, honey. I can handle it."

"That's right," she said sarcastically. "I'm too young to understand. I'm just supposed to stay on the honor roll, play piano with a symphony orchestra, pass my driving test, supervise a bunch of seven-year-old nature scouts, behave properly around guys, refrain from alcohol, tobacco and other drugs and never miss a tennis lesson. But of course I'm much too immature to know what's going on in my mother's life!"

"Okay. I guess that you're more grown up than I like to admit. It's just hard for me to get used to the idea that you're almost a woman."

"Mom—" she said, genuinely annoyed. "I'm not *almost* anything!"

"You're right," I said as I stroked her cheek. "Something from my past has come back to haunt me. Something I really don't know how to deal with."

She lowered her eyes and ran a long finger across the counter. "It's your first husband, isn't it?"

"How'd you know?"

"You've been quieter than usual, and you can't stop watching the International Station."

"That's because of my job, Marisa."

"That's because of the war in Liberia," she countered, her voice exceedingly calm.

"What do you know about Liberia?"

"We're studying it in my world history class. Let's see: Liberia was peaceful for a long time. They produced rubber for our tire companies on plantations all over the country, and had hospitals and universities and a pretty modern way of life. Then—let me see if I can get this straight—the president was overthrown about twenty-five years ago. He was replaced by a guy named Doe, who was murdered ten years ago. And then Charles Taylor, the most recent president, started this war. My teacher said that he tried to start wars in Liberia's neighboring countries, too. I'll bet everybody was glad when he finally stepped down last year."

"Unfortunately things haven't gotten much better for the Liberian people," I said with a glance at the television.

"Look, Mom—there's nothing to be ashamed of, you know. If I'd been married to someone who went back to a war zone, I'd be worried about him, too."

I looked up at her in surprise. She was watching me intently, as if gauging what she dared to say. "But—is there some reason why you and Dad never talk about him?"

"It was a long time ago, honey."

"Maybe Dad was jealous. He told me once that he knew from the first time you met that you were going to be his wife."

I laughed again. "He was just kidding, Marisa."

"No, he wasn't. He said that he kept trying to get your attention, but the only thing you could think about was that other guy!"

"It was a complicated time for all of us."

"So why does everybody act like it never happened?"

"It ended badly, Marisa. After Joseph left we lost touch, so I've never known what was going on in his life."

She sat thoughtfully for a moment, then turned to stare into the television screen. "Maybe you should try to find him. I mean, every day you help people who come from war zones, and you know nothing about their pasts. You said that their fates shouldn't be decided by their place of birth. So it seems to me that you shouldn't treat this man any differently just because you had a relationship with him."

I nodded and she stood up to give me a hug. "You know, if you don't get some sleep, you'll never make it through my performance tomorrow night. And I'll be pretty embarrassed if everybody in the orchestra, and everybody in the audience, can look in the front row and see my mother sleeping through my solos."

"You don't have to worry about that. Your concert tomorrow night is going to be one of the proudest moments of my life."

"Mom," she said very softly, "do you think you can love Daddy and still love your first husband, too?"

"Yes, pumpkin. There's space in my heart for both of them. And I still have plenty of love left over for you."

She smiled. "That's one thing I never worry about."

The Rimka Liberation Front appeared twenty-nine times in the Internet databases I searched at work later that morning. There were many articles describing the activities of the secret organization, which consisted of a growing group of fierce combatants dedicated to the eradication of pro-government militias. The RLF refused, however, to align itself with any political party, preferring to remain neutral while fighting to protect the nation's democratic system. In a number of interviews its articulate leader, Yusef Vai, described the RLF's doctrine as a policy of "using the oppressor's tools to dismantle the oppression."

Strangely, there were no photographs of Vai. Several journalists reported that the leader refused to allow his picture to be taken. Others said that he insisted that he was really nothing more than a spokesman for a number of resistance groups that had sprung up throughout the Liberian provinces.

Leaning back as far as possible, I rested my feet on the top of my briefcase.

Nothing in the twenty-nine articles on the Rimka Liberation Front proved that Joseph Thomas was the same man as Yusef Vai. Joseph had explained to me once that "Vai" was the name of his people, who were spread out across the northern regions of Liberia and southern Sierra Leone. There were hundreds—possibly *thousands*—of men who bore that name. Yusef Vai's aggressive style was totally different from the gentleness of the man I'd known, and the resistance leader's willingness to use violence as a means of bringing about change was the opposite of everything Joseph stood for.

Gently tapping my pencil against my cheek, I wondered where the RLF got its guns. Who was funding their operations? What political ideals did they support? Had they planned to fight their way to Monrovia and install their leader, this mysterious Yusef Vai, as the next president of Liberia?

I pulled a government phone directory from a desk drawer. In it was a list of Washington's embassies and consulates. I took out my cell phone and placed a call, deciding that I'd rather not have this inquiry show up on my office phone records.

A woman answered and identified herself as Marian Kamara, Liberian Embassy attaché.

"My name is Reba Freeman-Thornton," I began, speaking very slowly. "I'm an associate with the Office for the Placement of Permanent Refugees."

"How may I help you?"

"I'd like to talk to someone about the case of Yusef Vai."

There was a pause. Then she said very politely, "Please allow me to put you on hold."

I waited while gentle music swelled over the phone line. It took quite a while for someone to answer, and the voice that greeted me was coldly polite.

"This is Paul Kanneh, assistant to the general consul. What can I do for you?"

"Many years ago I was at school with a young Liberian who returned home to take a post as a teacher—"

"I'm afraid that I cannot assist you with inquiries about missing persons."

"Well, my friend isn't missing. In fact, I thought I recognized him as the man who once led the Rimka Liberation Front."

There was a long silence. "Excuse me, but are you a reporter?"

"No. I explained to your staff person that I work for the Office for the Placement of Permanent Refugees."

"The gentleman you're inquiring about is hardly a refugee."

"I'm very aware of that, Mr. Kanneh. To tell you the truth, I believe that Mr. Vai and I were once good friends, but we haven't spoken for some time. Recently I read a disturbing article saying that a man with the same name had been incarcerated for—"

"I am certainly not at liberty to discuss your friend's legal troubles," the officer snapped. "Now, if there is nothing else I can do for you—"

"There is one thing," I said quickly. "You can tell me if Yusef Vai might once have gone by another name."

"I can assure you that I know nothing about this man's identity."

"But surely the Liberian government knows whether—"

"I'm afraid I am very busy, madame. I wish you luck in your search."

The phone went dead. I spun around in my chair, struggling not to kick the wall in frustration. I glared at the stack of articles on the

RLF that I'd downloaded from the computer. Nothing in those articles seemed to offer answers to my questions—and frankly, I had other, more important things to do. In fact, my desk was buried beneath a whole stack of requests for political asylum posted by refugees from political conflicts occurring the world over. These were innocent people who truly needed our support. People who had lost their homes, their families, their worlds. Not people who were sitting in a Swiss prison, waiting to be put on trial for crimes against humanity!

Reluctantly I lowered my feet. Standing up to stretch, I went to the window and stared across the street at the U.S. Holocaust Memorial Museum. A school bus lumbered to a stop before the door and I watched as a teacher led a group of teens inside. I knew that when those young people came out of that building a few hours later they would be different people from the kids who'd left home that morning. They would no longer be able to look at their world as a place of privilege and safety. They would understand that sometimes entire nations engage in the unthinkable—when led by men and women who no longer believe in the sanctity of human life.

I glanced around my office, an island of peace in a world of suffering. Photographs of Marisa and Carl were gathering dust in the late-morning sun. Keith Jarrett was playing on a little boom box in the corner. Two large ficus plants framed the bright window. My bookshelf was filled with the tools of my profession: atlases, dictionaries, name books and publications on economics, political science and world history.

I paused as something on a bookshelf caught my eye: atlases. Dictionaries. *Name books.*

My palms were suddenly sweaty as I reached for the text I often used to establish the ethnic-group identity of African political refugees. I riffled through the pages, coming to a stop on names that began with the letter *R*.

Rah, Rakaya, Ramota, Remi, Rigat—*Rimka*.

I held the book up to the bright morning light. *"Rimka (RIM-kah). Eritrean version of the biblical name Rebecca, which means 'she who ensnares with tender bonds' (as in marriage). Other forms include Riva, Rebecka, Reba."*

I felt a sudden stirring that roared down into the depths of my past as a long-forgotten memory came leaping back into my mind. Twenty-four years before, the young Liberian student and I were walking down the long, tree-shaded drive toward the college gates for the very first time, and we were talking about our families—

"My name is Joseph Vai Thomas, but my family prefers to call me Yusef. . . . It's the Arabic translation of my name."

"Oh lord," I whispered as I stared blindly at the page, astounded at how stupid I'd been. My forehead was bathed in sweat as the rest of that conversation came rattling back into my mind. Joseph had gone on talking, finally remarking that my family name, Freeman— *"was probably assumed by your ancestor when he escaped from slavery."*

I sat down heavily on my desk and lowered my face into my hands. Suddenly it all made sense: Joseph Thomas, now known as Yusef Vai, was a *free man* who was fighting for his people's liberation. And he had named his military organization, Rebecca—Reba— Rimka—*after me.*

W*atching my child* perform in public is always an out-of-body experience. Over the years I had attended countless piano recitals, choir concerts and Christmas pageants, but the night of Marisa's first major solo performance was easily the most stressful experience I'd had in many years of mothering.

Seated beside Carl in the front row of the Kennedy Center, I watched a stunning young woman in an elegant black gown take charge of a Steinway the size of a school bus. Her long, fine fingers flew over the keyboard, her face focused and intense, and the eighty young musicians of the District of Columbia's Youth Symphony played lustily behind her.

Although Marisa didn't display the slightest nervousness as she negotiated the most difficult passages of the Dvořák Piano Concerto, I really thought that I might implode. Hips glued to the scratchy upholstery of the auditorium seat, I sat with a mannequin's smile plastered on my face, nervously anticipating every note, every difficult passage, every possible trip-up. I couldn't bear the thought that the fragile intensity of the moment might be marred by an errant cough, a blurted laugh or—heaven forbid—a mistake from one of the other musicians.

But Marisa leaned over the keys, lowered her head and made magic with the music. I blinked back tears, holding onto the armrests with wet hands, while before my eyes she transformed herself from my tree-climbing, mud-splattered little girl into a confident and gifted performer.

Carl was sitting coolly beside me, his chin braced casually against his thumb. The essence of unconcern, he radiated the attitude of a man who enjoyed the lovely music, but had no respect for the years of struggle it had taken to prepare the performers. Once, during the slow second movement of the symphony, he actually swallowed back a yawn. I cut him such a chainsaw look that he shifted uncomfortably in his seat.

When the orchestra had played its final note and the conductor indicated with a sweep of his arm that she should rise, the audience rose, too, and offered her a roaring ovation. Marisa nodded graciously to her admirers and then smiled unabashedly toward my front-row eyes.

Only then did my smile really collapse into tears. Looking up at my daughter, I understood what an extraordinary child I had borne.

After the reception, the three of us climbed into Carl's Lexus and drove to a nearby French bistro for dessert. I found myself laughing as Marisa, with the energy of a half-starved lifeboat survivor, tore into a double-chocolate mousse with shredded coconut and almond chips floating on a mountain of whipped cream. "It must have been quite a concert," the waiter said as he handed the bill to Carl.

"I never doubted that my baby would be perfect," my husband said, reaching over to stroke her chin.

"Well, what am I going to do when Juilliard comes calling?" I asked Marisa.

"Actually I've been thinking about the Paris Conservatory," she replied, spooning a gob of whipped cream into my cappuccino.

"Paris? How are we supposed to afford that?" Carl asked in pretended outrage.

"I'll get a scholarship," Marisa answered confidently. "There must be some rich people somewhere who want to get rid of some of their money!"

"But why Paris?" I asked, still surprised that she wanted to study overseas.

"I don't know. Too many Madeleine books, maybe. Or maybe it's because you used to let me play dress-up in your Anya originals."

We laughed. Marisa gave a sudden sigh, as if the tension of the evening was finally catching up with her.

"You know, it wasn't nearly as hard as I thought it would be. I knew the orchestra was there to support me. And I had you guys in the front row, even more scared than I was!"

"Great," Carl said. "Maybe next time your mom won't rip holes in my knees with her nails."

"That's not what I mean," she said with a giggle. "What I'm trying to tell you is that being scared shouldn't stop us from doing what we have to do. I realized before I stepped out on the stage that there were still some passages I wasn't too confident about. But I also knew that I had to do it, even if I wasn't sure I wanted to."

Marisa's eyes found mine, and for an instant she held my gaze. Then she pushed the remnants of the mousse to the center of the table. "That was reeeeally good!"

That night I sat on the edge of her bed, smoothing the covers over her young woman's form, still amazed that my baby had grown up so soon.

"I really am proud of how well you played tonight."

"And I really am glad you forced me to practice for the past nine years," she said sleepily.

"Hold on—I've got to get the tape recorder," I laughed, standing up. "I know I'll never hear those words again."

"Oh, Mom," she whispered, already drifting toward sleep.

I walked to the door and turned off the light.

"Mom?" Her voice seemed very childlike in the darkness.

"Yes, baby?"

"I meant what I said. It won't be so bad once you get started. And you've got to do it, even if you're scared."

I stood rooted to the spot, unable to answer.

"Just remember," she murmured, "I'll be in the front row, watching out for you."

After *two days* of mulling over my options, I visited the office of one of my colleagues, an attorney who had begun working on refugees' rights after spending a number of years with the American Civil Liberties Union.

Don Wiley was a paradox. Tall, lean and exceptionally handsome, he was a man who was growing ever more desirable as he aged. His graying hair and husky voice could silence a room full of chattering women, even though he behaved as if he was unaware of his sex appeal. Even more unusual, he avoided any of the clichés usually embraced by men of his social standing: He didn't play golf, he didn't go sailing on weekends and he had never had an affair.

Don was married to a Chilean woman who had survived internment in one of Pinochet's prisons after the assassination of Salvador Allende. Once he'd confided to me that she had long suffered from symptoms of deep post-traumatic stress—she had terrible nightmares, struggled with bouts of depression and, having been raped repeatedly, was unable to conceive a child.

Still, Don was devoted to her. His quiet outrage at the acts perpetrated against citizens by their own governments led him to our office, where he used his legal skills to help refugees gain permanent residency in the United States. I knew that he was the one person who might understand my conflicting emotions about Joseph.

"How is Olivia?" I asked him as I took a seat, coffee mug in hand, in a comfortable armchair just across from his desk.

"She's doing quite well. She always enjoys the spring, you know. She spends a lot of time working on her flowers."

"I want you two to come over for dinner one evening."

"Anytime, as long as you promise that Carl will grill some of his excellent brochettes." We both laughed.

"Don," I began as casually as possible, "what would you do if one of your former college friends was arrested for a crime you're pretty sure he didn't commit?"

"What's the crime?" he asked, stirring his coffee with a plastic stick.

"Let's say murder, for the sake of discussion."

"This friend has legal representation, right?"

"Yes. But I'm not sure it's adequate."

"Well," he said with his brows raised thoughtfully, "I would talk to my friend and try to ascertain what his real needs were." Don paused, setting down his coffee. "But murder's pretty serious, Reba."

"I just don't believe that he's capable of killing anyone."

"In this country people are considered innocent until proven guilty."

"He's not in this country. He's not American. And I haven't seen him in twenty years."

"Where is he?"

"Berne."

"Switzerland?" he echoed, his face furrowing. "You're talking about the International Court of Human Rights?"

I nodded slowly.

"Oh, Reba. If this guy is guilty, then he's violated every law that our office is working to uphold."

"But if he's innocent, this office is exactly what he'll need."

"This could have a very negative impact on your career. Our clients may be hesitant to work with you if you're associated with someone who was arrested for human rights violations."

I was silenced. Don and I regarded each other for a few moments. I dropped my head and slowly pushed my hands through my hair. I felt as if an elephant had climbed onto my back and was growing heavier by the minute.

"This man and I were pretty close."

"How close?"

"He was my husband. Twenty-two years ago. Before I married Carl."

Don's gaze fell. He settled back into his chair, exhaling slowly. "Give me his name and I'll see what I can find out."

〰️

Girl, I'm not allowing my husband to come to any more parties at your house. Carl lets him drink too much and Reggie's useless for the rest of the weekend!"

"And hello to you, too, Samantha," I said, continuing to patiently chop basil for a pesto sauce as I expertly tucked the receiver under my chin. A pot of hot water was simmering gently on the ceramic stovetop, waiting for me to add the gnocchi.

"You can't be *cooking*!" she exclaimed, recognizing the sound of the knife on the cutting board. "Your office is two minutes from the fish market! Why don't you just bring something home for dinner?"

"I don't like buying fish at lunchtime and letting it sit around until evening. And the lines down there are too long after work."

"The truth is that you don't have any decent ethnic food in northern Virginia. If you lived in Maryland you could carry out—"

"Samantha," I said sharply, "it's been a long day and I don't need to hear your opinion of my house, my husband or my neighborhood."

"Your husband? Now where did that come from?"

"Don't tell me you haven't been talking to Desiree. The two of you are like the twins in *The Shining*. One minute you're my friends and the next time I see you, you're coming after me with an ax."

"That's ridiculous! I haven't heard from Desiree all week. What in the world did she say to you?"

I took a deep breath and laid down the knife. I knew that Samantha was lying. I knew that Desiree had called her after our lunch date and played back everything we said. I also knew that Samantha had called to find out how I was taking the rumors that not only was Carl cheating—but that everyone on the eastern seaboard already knew about it. Now it was my turn to find out exactly what my husband was supposedly doing—and with whom.

"Desiree came at me with some gossip about Carl," I said with deliberate calm. "After all these years you would think she would know better."

"What kind of gossip?"

"The kind I've never allowed in my home."

"I'm sure she wasn't trying to hurt you."

"I'm not hurt."

"Maybe she was trying to help you out."

"How can repeating some nastiness about my husband and another woman help me out?"

"Well," Samantha said carefully, "maybe she just didn't want you to be the last to know."

"First you'd have to assume that I don't know."

"You already knew about Carl and Sandra Glover?"

Bingo, I thought. *Petite, pretty and recently dumped by her own husband!*

Without missing a beat I responded. "Carl and I are very honest with each other, Samantha."

"You're trying to tell me that you two have some kind of 'understanding'?"

"I'm reminding you that I've always preferred the truth—even if it gets me into a hell of a lot of trouble."

There was an uncomfortable silence.

"Well, Desiree just thought you seemed distracted during your party. She thought maybe you suspected something and should hear the truth."

"Look, I'm trying to find homes for hundreds of people, keep up with my terribly precocious daughter and still cook homemade dinners. Don't you think that listening to rumors about Carl might be a bit too much drama?"

"Well, I believe you should make him behave or leave him."

"Believe me," I laughed as I finally put the pasta into the water, "if I decide to leave him, you and Desiree will be the *last* to know."

"Reba," she said hotly, "don't forget that I stood by you when—"

"Don't go there, Samantha—"

Again the phone went silent. Finally she sighed.

"You know I love you like a sister. I've never had anything but your best interests at heart. You call me if you want to talk."

That night I was moving very quietly through the house, turning off lamps and checking to see that the doors were locked, when I heard Carl's voice from the top of the stairs.

"Are you coming to bed, Reba?"

"Yes, of course," I said in a low voice.

"I meant," he replied curtly, "sometime before dawn."

I slowly mounted the steps and followed him into our bedroom. Carl had spent most of the evening in his study with the door closed. Now he was bathed in a perfume of bourbon and cigar, and his voice had gained the husky readiness of a man who was looking forward to some serious verbal warfare.

I sank down on the edge of the mattress, pulling my robe carefully over my legs. Carl was wearing only a pair of silk boxers. He leaned against the door, crossing his arms like a Hollywood genie. "Well, it's nice to see what you look like after dark."

"What difference does it make? I'm only here to run the house. You've got Sandra Glover to take care of the rest."

"Ah. You've been chatting with Desiree—or was it Samantha?" He shook his head. "I'll bet they couldn't wait to tell you some exaggerated shit."

"You're saying it's not true?"

"I'm saying that I had a glass of wine with her and she made up the rest."

"But a few days ago you said—"

"I wanted to see if you'd react to the idea that I might really be interested in someone else. Because that's the thing: You really don't care what I do as long as other people don't talk about it."

"I care about Marisa and my job—"

"If you cared about our daughter you'd try to make this marriage work. And as for your *refugees*"— he literally spat the word— "you'll stay up all night worrying about that uncivilized scum, and the first English word they learn is 'nigger'!"

"Maybe they'll think of me and know those stereotypes aren't true."

"Oh, please! Your obsession with these foreigners is nothing but guilt."

"I don't have anything to be guilty about."

"Of course you do," he said with poisonous calm. "You see, baby, I know all about what really happened with Joseph." My face froze and he laughed bitterly. "Come on, Reba. Samantha talks to me, too."

"What exactly did Samantha tell you?"

"She told me he insisted that you give up your life in America to go live in poverty in Liberia—"

Deep inside a part of me relaxed. "Samantha needs to stay out of our business."

"I need her to tell me what's really going on in your head."

"Is that all you need from her?"

"That's all I happen to want from her."

Stung to the core, I raised my voice. "Did she tell you before or after you started seeing other women?"

"She told me when I asked her why you didn't feel anything for me."

"You mean," I replied, "when I finally stopped faking it with you."

His face hardened dangerously and he crossed the room with several long strides to the bed. I didn't resist as he pushed me down, his hands on my upper arms. He leaned over me, his eyes bright and his boyish face hardened by the shadows.

"Why don't you want me, Reba? Is it because you can't get over the fact that Joseph didn't love you enough—"

"No, Carl."

"He didn't want to stay with you!"

"You don't understand."

"He cared more about Liberia than he ever cared about your marriage!"

"That's not true. Joseph left me because I failed him as a wife."

"That's crap!" With those words he released me, leaning back in disgust. "Why do you refuse to see him for the man he was—or the man he *wasn't*? Joseph Thomas couldn't live up to the challenges of making a life in this country, so he went back to Africa where he could become part of the elite."

"Joseph wasn't looking for power—"

"*Every* man is looking for power, Reba. And he found a way to give himself power in both worlds." He drew in a long breath, watching me as I lay there.

"Joseph left you with a fantasy of what your life might have been if you'd stayed together. And that fantasy has controlled you for more than twenty years. You've never really been my wife."

"I've done everything I could to make our marriage work."

"And I've been a good husband."

"*Good?* I'm supposed to be happy about your other women?"

"None of that started until I realized how little you care about me."

"You knew who I was before you married me. You watched me fall in love with Joseph. You were there when I married him. You saw how devastated I was after he left. And I never, ever gave you any reason to believe that I was over him."

"But you married me anyway. You had a baby with me. You let me hope that one day you would love me, too."

Now there was a very long silence as we considered each other. His gaze moved carefully from my face to my breasts, belly and thighs, and lingered there, on the soft folds of my robe.

"Even if I can't have your love, I'm still your husband."

Something in the way he spoke caused my breath to quicken. "How can you say that, when you've been with those other women?"

"Disposable wipes," he said. Lifting his shoulders, he once again turned his gaze on me. "It's you, Reba. Always was. Always will be. I've never wanted anybody else."

I closed my eyes as I felt his weight shift on the bed. "Do you know when I started wanting you?" he asked, slowly tugging on the sash of my robe. "That first day at the airport. When you looked into my eyes and told me your name."

His fingers were suddenly beneath the fabric, stroking the soft swell of my belly. "You looked straight into my face. You didn't try to flirt with me. You didn't even try to"—he touched my breast—"attract my interest."

He leaned down and kissed me, then pulled my robe open and moved his hand to my thighs. "You must have been the only woman on that campus who didn't know I was alive. You never even saw how much I wanted you. How much I needed you."

Suddenly he became very still and I opened my eyes to find his expression unexpectedly vulnerable. "You still don't see it, do you?" he whispered, his face inches from mine. "You still don't understand that everything I've done has been for you. How can I make you forget him, Reba? How can I make you love me?"

I lay beneath him in silence.

"He's gone," Carl said as he took me in his arms. "He's gone and he's not coming back. Do you hear me, Reba? You're never going to see him again. Joseph Thomas is out of our lives."

⬚⬚⬚

Got *a minute?"* Don Wiley came into my office and shut the door. His expression seemed even graver than I expected.

"You look kind of serious for a Friday," I quipped, but he didn't smile. He sat down in the armchair across from my desk and rested his arms on his knees. Ignoring my offer of coffee, he leaned forward and lowered his voice.

"Reba, I ran some government security checks on Yusef Vai and came up with some information."

"Something I can look at?"

He shook his head. "Most of the material is classified." Pausing, he ran his thumb absently along the edge of the folder. "The Rimka Liberation Front is said to be part of an international terrorist organization."

"Is there any proof?"

"That will probably come out at his trial."

"Did you find out any other details about his arrest?"

"There isn't much. It appears that he was imprisoned for more than three years in the capital, Monrovia, before being handed over to the UN Peacekeepers."

"The charges?"

"Well—" He paused uncomfortably. "The Liberians claim that his group murdered a number of civilians."

"And Yusef?"

"They say that he was personally responsible for over thirty deaths."

The purr of the ventilation system was the only sound in my office as I struggled against a sudden, rising nausea. "When is his arraignment?"

Avoiding my eyes, Don opened the file and scanned its contents. "Late July, apparently."

I clasped my trembling hands together and stared out of the window. Don cleared his throat quietly. "Reba—you and I have been working together for a long time, right?"

I nodded without turning my head.

"Long enough for you to trust me?"

I looked over at him. "Yes."

"I want to explain something to you." He lowered the manila file and reached up to scratch his neck just behind his ear. It was a nervous gesture, one I'd seen him repeat in the midst of stressful meetings with immigration officials who wanted to deport our clients.

"You know, my wife Olivia has never really recovered from what she went through thirty years ago in Chile. She's constantly afraid that when she's in the supermarket, or at the movies, or even on a beach, she's going to come across one of the men who hurt her. You see, most of the people who commit crimes against humanity aren't monsters. They're everyday folks like you and me, who get caught up in a series of circumstances that lead to them doing things they never could have imagined. And often when circumstances change they become everyday citizens again and go right on with their lives."

He lowered his eyes. "I imagine you're struggling with the idea that this man—Yusef Vai—could be the same person you loved twenty years ago. You must be telling yourself that there's been some mistake. That it's just not possible.

"The problem is that your first husband ended up in a place that might have changed him into an entirely different person. No matter how much you loved him, you must understand that he may well have committed these crimes."

I managed to find my voice. "I really don't know what to do, Don."

"I believe you have two options. You can try to find out if Yusef Vai really is your first husband. If he turns out to be another person, then perhaps you'll feel more comfortable about letting the case follow its course."

"And the other option?"

"Just wait and see what happens. Once he's been arraigned, there should be far more information available."

I looked into Don's eyes. "I can't just sit back and wait."

He smiled faintly. "Knowing you, Reba, I didn't think you would." Reaching into his back pocket, he pulled out his wallet. He fished through the folds of leather that were stuffed with scraps of paper and sales receipts, finally pulling out a business card.

"Four years ago my wife and I had a real crisis when she thought that one of our neighbors was a man who—well, a man she had known in Chile. We found someone who looked into the guy's past and came up with enough information to convince Olivia that he probably wasn't the same person."

"Is this a detective?"

"No. She's an attorney. She came to Washington some time ago. Her husband worked with Veterans Affairs, and she started out re-uniting Vietnam vets with the children they'd left behind in Southeast Asia. Over time her work with overseas cases has grown. I think that she could help you to establish whether Yusef Vai really is your former husband."

Don stood up. "This office has four-hundred twenty cases pending at the moment, Reba. You should hand this Liberia business over to a professional so that you can get back to your work. After all, we're supposed to be helping the victims, not the perpetrators."

Arlene's Toyota moved tentatively up our winding drive. She pulled to a stop near the crabapple tree. I saw her emerge from the car and cast a quick glance at the wide picture windows with their professional draperies. Her gaze then fell on the slate walkway, which matched the slate shingles on the roof.

I swung the front door open and ushered her into the wide foyer, which always bore the lemon-pepper scent of the lavender stalks I kept in a large vase near the door.

"My goodness, Reba!" she exclaimed. "Your home is really beautiful!"

"Ah—thanks," I stammered, unprepared for her genuine warmth.

We descended the curved steps into the living room and she looked around, openly admiring the furniture and paintings. "What a gorgeous room! You must do a lot of entertaining."

I glanced at Arlene's open face, her handsome hand-printed dress and small Fulani earrings. We were dressed very similarly, for I was wearing a batiked caftan from Thailand and had my hair wrapped in a scarf.

"Come on," I said, leading her through the house to my office. "I know we'll be more comfortable in here."

We were soon settled in my wide armchairs with tall glasses of iced tea. Her eyes twinkled when I found a yearbook from our college years.

"Do you remember that girl who came all the way from California?" she asked, pointing to a picture of my dorm mates as we posed on the steps of Merriman Hall.

"Carmen Albright," I said, looking at the photo of the buxom young woman with honey-colored hair and hazel eyes. "She took off to New York after our sophomore year and tried to be a model."

"Whatever happened to your roommates?"

"We're still friends, actually. Desiree and Samantha both live in Prince George's County. They both married guys they met after we graduated, and they're both doing pretty well."

"It's hard to believe that the years have passed so quickly. Sometimes it seems as if it was just yesterday—"

"I'm home, Mom!" The door opened and Marisa stuck her head in, her tennis racket slung over her shoulder. "Oh—sorry! I didn't know you had company!"

"Come and meet Arlene Masters, my friend from college," I said, and my daughter ambled into the room and stuck out her hand. Her long colt's legs vanished beneath her baggy shorts and her strong arms were bronzed by the early summer sun.

"Marisa is a musician, sportswoman and a very impressive scholar, and her mother's very proud of her!"

"Oh, Mom!" Her freckled face flushed a deeper cinnamon and her gray eyes twinkled beneath their thick lashes.

"She's a beauty, too," Arlene added. "You know, young lady, it sounds to me like you're the perfect blend of your mother and father."

"Thanks," Marisa said, showing off her radiant smile. Her eyes twinkled and she took a step closer to Arlene.

"Mrs. Masters," she said craftily, "what were Mom and Dad *really* like back in college?"

"They were two of the nicest students on campus."

"But that's so boring! There must be at least *one* juicy secret you could tell me!"

Arlene laughed. "I'm sorry to report that your mother was a dedicated student who spent most of her time in the library. And your father was a handsome and debonair young man who was always friendly to everybody."

"Oh, well," Marisa said with mock disappointment as she backed up toward the doorway. "I'm going to take a shower and go over to Kelsey's, okay?"

Once we were settled again, Arlene turned to me with perceptive eyes. "You have a beautiful family, Reba. Are you worried that helping Joseph might somehow hurt them?"

"Yes, I am."

"I get the impression that things weren't exactly reconciled between you and Joseph when he left for Africa."

"That's true. The breakup was pretty painful. He left before we figured things out, and I never heard from him again."

"If you could speak to him, what would you say?"

"I guess I'd apologize for what happened between us, and I'd wish him well."

"You're not angry about the past?"

"No. It was my fault that our marriage fell apart. If anything, I'd like to ask him to forgive me."

"How does Carl feel about what's happened to Joseph?"

There was a strained silence. Arlene reached out and touched my hand. "Carl knows what's going on, doesn't he?"

Without looking at her, I shook my head.

"You have to tell him, Reba."

"Carl and I are going through a difficult period right now. I don't think he'd be too happy about this."

"You're going to need his support."

"I've helped hundreds of refugees build new lives. This shouldn't be any different."

"But this isn't work, Reba. It's going to affect your personal life."

Arlene looked at me for a moment, then leaned forward and rested her arms on her knees, studying her glass. "Once when I was studying in Germany I received a summons from the Ministry of Education. I knew that as the wife of an American serviceman I wasn't going to have any real problems, but I was still a little bit nervous when I went into this gigantic government building alone. I found the office and discovered that another young man was already waiting in the foyer. He was holding his passport, and I could see that he was Iranian."

She looked up slowly. "Now, this was just a few months after the hostage-taking crisis in Tehran, and American servicemen had been warned to avoid contact with any Iranian nationals. Naturally I was insecure about being alone with him. Just as I decided to leave, he turned to me. He gazed at me for a moment, then asked if I was American. I nodded and waited for his reaction. To my surprise, he held out his hand and whispered, 'You are truly blessed by God.'

"You know, Reba, until that moment I had never really thought about what it means to be born in the richest nation on earth. I mean, our parents lived through Montgomery, Little Rock and Selma. Americans murdered Kennedy, Malcolm and Dr. King during our childhood. When I lived in the United States, I was Black, and that meant that I automatically had less than equal power. So it was an amazing moment when this young man, who was supposed to be my enemy, reminded me of how lucky I was."

She clasped my hand. "There is nothing wrong with what you're doing. You are privileged to be able to help Joseph. I'm sure Carl will understand."

She smiled and I felt a strange connection to this woman I'd barely known in my college days.

"Oh—I almost forgot!" She reached into her bag and rummaged for something. "I was down in Adams Morgan yesterday and I came across this book. Somehow it made me think of you."

She handed me a palm-sized volume entitled *Dawn Songs: Poetry by the Women of Africa.*

My heart turned over as I recognized the cover. Joseph and I had kept a copy of the same little book on our bedside table, and we had often read the poems aloud before falling asleep.

"Thank you," I said, wondering how this woman, who seemed so determined to help me heal the wounds of my past, had suddenly appeared in my life.

Late one morning Don Wiley came into my office. I had been staring out the window, pondering what prison conditions were like in Switzerland, but I quickly returned to the open file on my desk as he pulled up a chair and sat down beside me.

"You haven't called Simone yet, have you?"

"Simone?"

"The lawyer I told you about." He smiled gently. "And don't bother to tell me that you're not worrying about your first husband. It's pretty obvious."

"What do you mean?"

"We had a ten o'clock meeting with the senator's people about those Bosnian refugees. Remember?"

I glanced at my watch and was shocked to see that it was already 10:40. Before I could speak, however, Don held up his hand.

"It's okay. They called to cancel. But Reba, I think you've taken on something that's too big for you to handle without professional help. I know it's not your style to ask anyone to do something you can do for yourself, but this time you need to do it. I gave Simone a call this morning and asked her if she'd be willing to speak with you."

"You did what?"

"She said she'd be happy to help out if she can. She's waiting for your call."

He stood up and took a scrap of paper from his pocket. "Here's her number again, just in case you lost it."

Without another word he walked to my door. "Senator Jacobs is sending his people over after lunch. Let's see if we can find these Bosnians a home."

Simone James-Ashford agreed to meet me in her Washington office at seven o'clock the following Tuesday morning, despite the fact that she was due in court at ten. This meant that I had to be on the road at dawn, but that didn't matter—I hadn't managed to sleep for more than three hours the night before, anyway.

The attorney's office was located in an elegant brownstone in northeast Washington, just a few blocks from Capitol Hill. This quarter of the city had only recently been renovated, driving out the elderly black residents who had lived there for decades.

Finding a space that would accommodate my car, I lifted my now-bulging file, which included Arlene's research and the downloaded copies of the articles I'd found on the Internet, and made my way to the address Don Wiley had given me. The brownstone rose four stories from its half-submerged basement windows to the dormers on the sloping roof. I climbed the steps to the entrance and rang the doorbell beside a steel plaque that read: JAMES-ASHFORD, LLP.

The smell of fresh coffee wafted out of the open first-floor window. Footsteps approached and the doors swung open to reveal an athletic woman in her mid-forties with a short, carefully groomed afro. Her sharp gaze took quick measure of my face and attire.

"Reba Thornton? I'm Simone." Her voice was deep and rusty—the kind of voice that suggested nights of sensuality to most men—but sounded no-nonsense to me. "Come on in." She was wearing running pants and a Pistons T-shirt.

"Thanks for seeing me so early, and without a regular appointment."

She waved my thanks away. "No problem. But you'll have to excuse me. I'm kinda scruffy at this time of morning."

I followed her into a hallway that opened to a modern, skeletal staircase sweeping both up to the higher levels of the house and down into the basement. Following my curious gaze, she smiled. "In case you're wondering, I have my offices in the three lower floors. I use the top floor as my apartment."

"This is really lovely," I remarked, making note of the gleaming hardwood floors and exposed brick walls.

"I bought this house ten years ago because it was close to the Capitol. Then I found myself working so late that it didn't make sense to drive out to the suburbs every night. The only drawback is that if I'm having a bad day I'm very tempted to go upstairs and get right back into bed!"

We both laughed and she ushered me into her office.

The room was simply but elegantly furnished, with tall cabinets and a curved desk set close to the bay window. She led me to a quartet of leather armchairs set around a low table.

"Coffee? I've just made a fresh pot."

"Thank you." I set down my file and watched as she swept across the room, which was painted a soft marble white. The deep gray carpets complemented the pale walls, which bore a pair of dusk-toned watercolors. A fine balance of the personal and professional, her bookshelves were packed with leather-bound legal volumes, but topped with a collection of wonderful blown-glass paperweights.

"How are Don and Olivia doing?" she asked as she returned.

"They're fine. Don said that you were very helpful to them a couple of years ago."

She smiled warmly and sat down across from me, placing two mugs of coffee on the table. "You said on the phone that you're interested in finding out more about a man who's been taken into custody for human rights violations."

"Yes," I answered, appreciating her directness. I briefly described my relationship with Joseph and showed her the articles Arlene had assembled. When I told her what Don Wiley had learned about the Rimka Liberation Front, her expression grew troubled.

"What's Yusef Vai being detained for?"

"Mass murder."

She didn't react. Instead, her gaze went inward as she began to consider the few facts I'd given her. She crossed her legs and took a sip of her coffee, her clear brown eyes fixed on the marble table. For a few minutes the silence was broken only by the melodious ticking of a brass clock on the mantel and the chortling of car engines starting up in the street.

"Reba," she said suddenly, "where are you from?"

"I was raised in Detroit, went to school in Baltimore, and now live in northern Virginia."

"Ever think about going back?"

"To Detroit? No. I guess the Michigan part of my life is over."

"If you discover that this man really is your first husband, what do you want to do?"

I set down my coffee mug. "I'm determined to help him in any way that I can."

The attorney now placed her own mug on the table. "It won't be terribly difficult to ascertain his identity—unless he's done something to deliberately obfuscate the truth, such as altering his fingerprints or appearance. What we really have to think about is what happens once we have the facts."

She reached across the table and gently touched my shoulder. "You need to be prepared for the possibility that even if he's innocent, his experiences in the civil war may have marked him forever. And you need to understand that even if you care about him, the 'Reba' part of *his* life may be over."

"I know. I see people like that every day. People who want nothing more than to forget the things they've seen and find some sense of peace with their grief."

She smiled. "I like the fact that you don't refer to them as 'cases.' "

"No. I could never see them like that. They've already been stripped of everything they love. The last thing they need is to be further dehumanized."

"That's why Don thinks so highly of you," she concluded, standing up. "I've got to get ready for my court appearance, but one of my associates will look into this and I'll get back to you as soon as possible."

"We'll need to move fast. He'll be arraigned in three weeks and his trial is set to begin in September."

"Don't worry. I enjoy working under pressure."

That evening I had just stepped out of the shower when the phone rang and I heard her throaty voice on the other end of the line.

"Reba? My associate did some research this afternoon and I think I have some answers for you."

I sat down on the bed, glad that Carl was off playing golf and Marisa was having dinner at Kelsey's. I moved the receiver to my other hand, finding that the fingers grasping the phone had broken into a sweat. "I'm listening."

"All right. First of all, we were able to check the birth records in Liberia. A child named Yusef Vai Thomas was born on March 9, 1960. Does that sound right to you?"

"Yes," I whispered. "That was Joseph's birthday."

"The American embassy in Monrovia has a field report that suggests that Joseph began referring to himself as Yusef at some point after his village was destroyed by a government paramilitary group. It appears that the group targeted villages that were considered pro-American."

"But Joseph's village was miles from the capital."

"Unfortunately, these villages were often selected because they had mission schools, or government training programs, or teachers who'd been educated—"

"In the United States," I guessed, finishing her sentence. "But even if Joseph was a member of the RLF, it doesn't mean that he's guilty of murder."

"Clearly we don't know that yet. Do you want to take this any further?"

I heard a car in the drive and knew that Carl was home from his golf game. He would certainly shower, order a pizza, then drink cold beer while watching whatever sporting event was on television that night. Soon Marisa would arrive, tanned and exhausted from a day with her friends at the pool. She'd retire to her room and put on her newest CD. Neither one of them would suspect that I had spent my day lost in this labyrinth of split devotions that now went by the name of Yusef Vai.

"Reba? Are you there?"

"Yes, Simone," I said, now certain that I was committing myself to a journey that would change my world. "I'm going through with this. So what's next?"

Chapter 4

Baltimore, Maryland

1 9 8 0

"I just can't get over it—Reba never even dated before and now she's the first one of us to get a boyfriend," Desiree enviously observed as she packed her suitcase the night before the beginning of Thanksgiving break. Her hair was wound tightly into curlers and she'd rubbed a green cream all over her face in the hope that she'd clear up her dorm-food complexion before arriving in North Carolina.

Samantha sucked her teeth from her corner of the room, where she was tweezing her brows while waiting for her mother to arrive to take her back to D.C.

I said nothing. While Desiree felt a grudging admiration for me for actually finding someone, Samantha still hadn't gotten over the sting of defeat.

"Actually," Desiree said a bit guiltily, "I think he's kind of cute."

"He's too thin. Someone really should have invited him over for Thanksgiving dinner. I'll bet he's never seen so much food on a table."

"Reba hasn't told us if he's any good in bed," Desiree remarked.

"That's because they still haven't figured out how to do it!"

Squeezing my lips together, I turned on my bedside lamp and tried to read. My roommates, however, became even more incensed that I was ignoring them.

"You know," Samantha announced, "I've heard that women in Africa have to do all the work while the men sit around drinking. Then, when their heads get square from carrying those big jars of water, their husbands marry younger women."

"You're kidding!" Desiree exclaimed, throwing a quick glance in my direction.

"Of course their titties go all flat from hanging their kids in those slings so they can nurse all day. They've never heard of combs or underwear. And God only knows what they do without tampons!"

Desiree's shrill laughter fell somewhere between curiosity and embarrassment.

"And they won't let girls go to school," Samantha continued. "Women can't wear pants, either. And they have all these crazy rules about sex—"

"I could *never* live there," Desiree said, shaking her head.

"It doesn't matter if you live there," Samantha replied. "African men think that way even when they live here!"

"How does Reba stand it?" Desiree asked, stealing another look in my direction.

"I don't know. But I wish she'd take some advice from the people who really care about her. After all, we're the closest friends she's got."

Without a word I turned off my lamp and gathered up my books, pens and a jacket.

Doing my very best to force them out of my mind, I made my way down the hall, passing other rooms with other girls in cold cream and curlers, and walked out into the night. The cool November evening felt remarkably warm to my Michigan blood, but I realized that Joseph must be terribly uncomfortable. He rarely complained about anything, though I sensed that he often felt very alone. Everyone else on campus seemed to be obsessed with alcohol and sex, with their schoolwork coming in a distant third. The other students kept a careful distance from him, as if they were ashamed of how they appeared in his eyes. If Joseph felt lonely, however, he concealed it by walking tall and always keeping a book by his side.

Now I wound my way slowly across the campus, which was bustling with students who were preparing to depart for the long weekend break. I wouldn't be going home until Christmas, but I didn't mind. My world seemed full enough, now that I had Joseph.

I called Joseph's room from a telephone in the foyer of his dormitory.

"I'm not quite ready, Reba. Please give me just a few minutes."

"That's okay. I'll be waiting outside."

I wandered out to one of the benches that faced the Commons. The grass was still thick and green despite the late November chill. Over the years the classes of graduating seniors and various alumni groups had dedicated trees, planted ceremonial gardens and placed a number of small monuments along the sidewalks, so that the Commons was a pleasant enough place to rest—or watch the college's social life unfold.

I hadn't been sitting long when someone took a place on the bench beside me.

"Want to share a taxi to the airport?" Carl Thornton was bathing me in his radiant smile, his gray eyes dancing suggestively above those boyish freckles.

"I'm not going home for Thanksgiving."

"Neither am I. I'm going back to my grandparents' in Atlanta."

"That should be nice."

"That's right." He leaned closer to me and lowered his voice seductively. "I'm going to tell you something nobody else knows on this campus. I've got a girl down there."

"Why are you telling me?"

"Because I know you'll keep my secret."

"How do you know that?"

"You're the type who hates gossip."

"Why is it a secret?"

"It would mess things up for me here if everybody knew what I had going on down there."

"So what does your girlfriend in Atlanta think you're doing while you're in Baltimore?"

"She thinks I'm planning on getting engaged to her."

"And what do you think she's doing down in Atlanta?"

"Well," he said with a laughing shrug, "she's probably checking out her choices, just in case things don't work out with me."

"If you two can't trust each other, why are you together?"

He looked out at the dorms, where students were getting into cars with their families. "Didn't you ever feel that being with someone would make everybody happy?"

"What do you mean?"

"Her parents went to school with my parents, and they have money and we have money and she looks good and—" He broke off, still staring across the park.

"Do you love her?"

He didn't answer.

"Do you even *like* her?"

He remained silent.

"Well, maybe it doesn't matter since the two of you live so far apart."

"That's right." He pushed his hands resignedly along the top of his thighs and rose slowly to his feet. "I still have two and a half years till graduation. And who knows? Somebody else just might come into the picture before then."

He glanced down at me. "So what about you and Joseph?"

"What about us?"

"I heard you're a couple."

"Maybe," I answered, hoping he'd hear by the tone of my voice that our relationship was not a topic for discussion.

"I'm happy for you. In fact, I'll give Joseph a hand if you want."

"Give him a hand?"

"Sure. I could go shopping with him. Help him get some decent rags and a good haircut—"

He saw the rage that leapt into my eyes, and before I could respond he backpedaled. "Hey—don't get mad. I was only kidding!"

Still, I didn't smile.

He stepped away from the bench and raised his hands in a gesture of surrender. "Arrested, tried and found guilty as charged. All right?"

I shook my head, staring stonily into his face as he moved away. Just as he reached the edge of the grass, he turned and shouted over his shoulder, "Have a happy turkey day, Reba."

A few moments later Joseph strolled down the steps of his dorm and, spotting me, jogged the short distance to the bench.

"Were you talking to Carl Thornton?" he asked after kissing my cheek.

"Carl was talking to me."

"King Carl likes holding court," Joseph said, his tone somewhere between irony and amusement. "He spends a lot of time entertaining his friends with stories about his romantic exploits. His family is, it seems, so powerful that he doesn't have to worry about his classes." Joseph paused. "In Liberia we sometimes say that when a man is rich, he should dance in private."

We stood up and began walking toward the library.

"I've only talked to him once or twice," I answered offhandedly. "And besides, there's nothing about me that would interest him."

Joseph gave me a quizzical look. "You are very wrong about that, Reba."

"No, I'm not. Carl Thornton wants somebody who looks like a model and has lots of money."

"Perhaps that is what his parents want. But I sense that he is unhappy with the role thrust upon him by his background. He thinks there may be something more to a relationship than those superficial things, but he's not sure how to go about finding it."

"That's not my problem."

"No. But I wish that I could help him."

"That's funny. He just said the same thing about you."

"Let me guess—he wants to make me look like an American."

"That's right."

"All of the people on this campus would feel more comfortable if I looked and talked like them. But an elephant never tires of carrying his tusks. I have no wish to leave my culture behind."

"Carl doesn't get it."

"Perhaps he will, in time."

"It sounds as if you like him."

"There are things about him that I admire. He is friendly to everyone and tends to be honest about what he feels. Sometimes I think that he brags because he is very uncomfortable with his privileges. Equality is difficult, but superiority is painful. He actually hopes that someone will tell him how to bring more meaning to his life."

"That has absolutely nothing to do with me."

"I'm not so sure," Joseph said, and I looked up at him in surprise. "I think that beneath all the noise he is very observant. Perhaps he is drawn to the same qualities in you that I find so compelling."

"Compelling?" I asked, slipping my arms around Joseph's waist. "Nobody's ever called me compelling before."

Joseph smiled gently down at me, his intelligent eyes filled with something I didn't recognize. "Flowing waters make standing waters move, Reba. You are stronger than you realize. And a much better woman than you yet understand."

"You're talking to me like you're my grandfather," I complained.

"Some women can only attract a man's eyes. But you will always attract a man's heart. And once you have his heart, you will always have the best part of him, no matter what."

"Does that include you?" I asked, grinning up at him flirtatiously.

"Perhaps," he answered mysteriously. He leaned down and kissed me. My whole body seemed to bloom at his touch. "And by the way, you are indeed as pretty as a model."

When he looked into my eyes I again saw an elusive thought in his eyes. At that moment, however, I was certain that it was love.

⬛

Mid-December—and the end of our first semester in college—found me closer to Joseph than ever. We spent hours in the library, smiling silently at each other over the tops of our textbooks and holding hands as we completed our homework. We ate all of our meals together and figured out how to meet—even if only for a few minutes—between each of our classes. We spent all of our free time walking in the brightly decorated city or, if the weather was bad, sitting together until the dining room closed.

The other students steered a clear path around us, as if we no longer belonged to their world of fraternity parties, intense rivalries and shallow one-week affairs. Left to our own devices, we finally had the time to talk, to laugh, to really get to know each other. Many evenings found me wrapped in his arms, sitting before the wide stone fireplace in the student lounge, listening to his richly detailed descriptions of Africa. He lent me tapes of his favorite music: Ladysmith Black Mambazo's songs of faith, Thomas Mapfumo's calls for Zimbabwean liberation, and Fela Ransome Kuti's mesmerizing indictments of international political oppression.

I put off my departure for Detroit until the day before the dorms officially closed for the Christmas holiday. With exams over, most of the students had already left for home and the campus was more deserted than I'd ever seen it. The college had arranged for Joseph to spend his holiday as the guest of a wealthy couple who had attended the college many years before.

"I hope they'll be cool," I said to him on the evening before my flight home.

"They are very nice. Mr. Farmer once taught in Liberia. He knows something of my culture and I'm sure I'll enjoy spending the holiday with them."

"I wish you could come home with me."

"Perhaps I will have that chance one day."

"You might regret it. My father can be pretty tough to live with."

"It is difficult to be the father of a girl. He must protect her while she is young and be certain of the character of the man who wishes to marry her."

"Women decide who they want to marry in this society."

"Giving women such freedom has not resulted in happier marriages. There are fewer divorces in my world, and men are usually respectful toward their wives."

"You're telling me that nobody ever cheats?"

"Yes, there are still men who cheat. But choosing one's spouse carefully helps to ensure that most children will grow up with both of their parents."

We were alone in the dining hall. The room was very quiet, and most of the Christmas decorations had already been taken down so that the hall could be cleaned before the students returned in January. Joseph was wearing a handsome hand-knitted sweater and a pair of jeans we'd selected together at a nearby Sears. The wife of his minister in Liberia had made the sweater for him when he received his letter of acceptance at Absalom Jones College, and he wore it very proudly.

"What's your father like, Joseph?"

"He worked so hard to support our family that I've never spent much time with him. My older brother Simon was like a second father to me. He is the master metalworker in our village. He builds tools, fences and car parts, and melts down scrap metal for use as pots and plates and other utensils."

"How did he learn to do that?"

"In our village, each craftsman chooses several young men as apprentices and trains them from the time they're very young. This way, the village is almost certain to have at least one person who'll remain in the trade when the older man dies."

"What about girls?"

"Many are trained as nurses or teachers. Some go to the city and return as doctors."

"Does your family live in a house?"

He laughed. "Of course, Reba. You don't really think that African people live in trees?"

"No, but lots of photographs show Africans sleeping in mud huts."

"Life in Africa varies widely, according to the climate and economy of the region," he replied patiently. "Countries that were European colonies have cities that were built according to European styles of architecture. But a wooden house may not be the most appropriate use of our natural resources. Many people believe that it is an affront to nature to destroy trees if buildings can be constructed from mud. And dwellings built with reeds can be quickly constructed and easily moved. Remember, Reba—we don't have to contend with cold weather."

"So what's your house like?"

"It is a brick house within a compound that was once owned by a British company. It has a parlor, a kitchen and four sleeping rooms."

"Did you have your own bedroom when you were growing up?"

"Of course not. Why would I need a room to myself, when I only went there to sleep?"

I thought about that for a moment. My own room had been a great source of pride to me. My parents had given me some freedom to decorate it, and I'd covered the walls with posters of my favorite singers. Although it was small, I'd managed to cram my entire world within its walls.

"Do women wear makeup in Liberia?"

"Some do."

"Do they straighten their hair?"

"Rarely. I found it very strange to see black women with hair like whites when I first came to this country. In Africa we have many beautiful styles of braids with patterns that represent our communities."

"Women can wear pants in Liberia, can't they?"

"Once again, there are wide variations in cultural expectations about women's dress across Africa. Even within a single country, women dress differently depending on whether they live in a city or in a distant rural area. Many women would tell you, however, that it is preferable to wear skirts that are light and comfortable in the heat. Most would find your blue jeans cumbersome and unattractive."

"Do *you* think my jeans are ugly?"

He laughed gently. "I would be happy to see you in a skirt sometimes. But I recognize that your jeans are appropriate to your culture."

"What would your mother think of me?"

"My mother? Well, she would find you to be a very modern, independent woman."

"Do you think she'd like me?"

"Of course," he said, his slanted eyes lost in a memory.

Satisfied, I settled more deeply into his arms. "What do you eat at home?"

He closed his eyes for a moment, as if savoring a distant memory. "My mother is considered an excellent cook. She makes some of the best okra in Liberia!"

"Okra?" I echoed with disgust.

"Yes. In a perfectly spiced sauce. Sometimes she will cook her yams in large quantities and sell them at the market. Most of her vegetables come from her own garden. And the bread she makes with my sisters is also excellent."

"What do you think of American food?"

"It's too heavy, and you eat too much. But I have learned to enjoy macaroni and cheese."

I giggled at the thought that my calmly intellectual boyfriend liked to eat kid's stuff.

"If your life was so good in Liberia, why *did* you come to America?"

"Eyes that have beheld the sea no longer fear the lagoon. We pursue degrees in foreign universities so that we can bring the newest and best learning back to our country."

"But what about the universities in Liberia?"

"You must realize, Reba, that many Americans study in foreign universities, too. That does not prove that you come from an inferior culture."

"I didn't say that Liberia is inferior!"

"No, but I am well aware of what most Americans think of my continent. I have seen your Tarzan movies. I have seen the way that African people are represented in photos and music. Often we are shown as savage, uncivilized people when human civilization, in fact, developed in Africa."

"Black Americans don't think Africans are inferior."

"Many students at this college do. I have often heard negative stereotypes about my home. I have been told that the only reason that Liberia has continued to exist is because former Americans founded it. In the eyes of many, the fact that many African cultures are much older than the nations of Europe counts for nothing."

"You're right," I agreed sheepishly.

"It is certainly not your fault," he answered with a smile. "But in the end I feel that such people should stay away from my home. I don't want Americans thinking that they should come to Africa and 'Americanize' us."

"But won't you be taking American values back to your home?"

"Clearly I am being influenced by my life here. But all rivers have a source. I am trying to retain my cultural values, despite living among American citizens."

"What's the hardest part?"

He looked directly into my eyes. "You."

"Me?"

"Yes. The more we're together, the harder it is for me to think about leaving without you."

I became very still. "Why do you have to leave without me?"

"I have to leave. I have never questioned where I would spend my life."

"But what about me? I don't have to go back to Detroit."

"Reba, I have no right to ask you to leave your family. I cannot promise that you would be happy outside of your community. And I do not know if you would be comfortable with African life."

"You don't think your family would accept me?"

"It would be hard for you, and for my family, to learn to accept each other," he answered truthfully. "But my people are not judgmental. They would be proud that an American thought enough of our culture to live among us."

"But I would be there for you."

"And of course, my people would be happy for me."

"But"— I paused—"would *you* be happy?"

"With you?" He looked into my eyes, but he didn't smile. "Reba, a marriage is only happy when out of two minds comes a single future. A man and a woman may love each other very much. But they must also share a sense of purpose and a similar vision. They must be happy with the way their lives unfold together, and satisfied with the manner in which they live."

"Those things aren't so difficult if they love each other enough."

He smiled. "That is an American idea, based on the relative ease in which so many of your people live. The truth is that even the deepest love is tested by poverty. In places where life is difficult, love matters less than a willingness to work hard together. And in a culture where the lack of medical care leads to the death of many infants, large families are valued."

"We like big families in America, too!"

"But having a large family here is easier in many ways. My mother gave birth to ten children. Several died in infancy. She never had disposable diapers or plastic milk bottles. She didn't have a washer or dryer. And she has to find the means to feed her children every single day."

"Well," I answered meekly, "don't the other kids help out?"

"Yes, of course. We assume responsibilities for our families at a much younger age than most Americans. But motherhood can still pose a tremendous challenge."

"Don't you think I'd make a good mother?"

"Oh, yes," he whispered in return. We were both silent for a few moments. Then he sighed. "I think we are moving too fast."

"No, we're not. Isn't it true that people in Liberia get married when they're much younger than we are?"

"Yes, but—"

"I'm almost nineteen. And I'm not a kid anymore."

"We haven't completed our studies, Reba."

"But I'm in love with you, Joseph. I don't want anybody else."

"We haven't known each other very long."

"How long is long enough? I'm not one of those idiots like my roommates. I didn't come here just to find a man. I know what I want to do with my life, and I can make my own decisions."

"Hasty unions make hasty divorces," he began, his voice trailing off when he saw what was in my eyes.

"I love you, Joseph," I said, my voice full of intensity. "You and nobody else. I don't care what anyone says. I don't care what anybody thinks. I want to be with you, and nobody can stop us from being together."

I reached down with tentative fingers and touched his pants. He moved against my hand, emitting a sound deep in his throat. "Oh, Reba, please stop. It's already so difficult."

"It doesn't have to be. You're the only one I've ever wanted. The only one. Joseph"—my voice acquired a strange hoarseness—"I want to make love with you."

He stared into my eyes, then nodded as if making a decision. Slowly he rose to his feet, still holding my hand. I stood, too. We walked to the door of the dining room and, without a word, went out into the night. Our steps took us directly across the Commons and in the direction of the dorms.

"I am the last person in the building," he said softly. "If you'd like to come to my room, I promise you that we will be alone."

I had never been in Joseph's dormitory before. We tiptoed down the hall and slipped into his room, leaving the lights off so that the dorm monitor would think that he was away. The full moon etched the silhouettes of matching beds, twin desks and chests of drawers, and I could make out a poster of the African singer Fela tacked on one wall.

The world was silent except for the tree branches scratching the windowpanes. Joseph locked the door and helped me out of my coat, laying it neatly on his roommate's bed. Then he turned to face me.

"I cannot pretend to be a teacher tonight," he whispered, taking my hands.

"I don't want to be your student. Let's just be a man and a woman."

Much later that night, as I drifted off to sleep, I heard him whisper something in the darkness: "*Please, Lord—let me live my life in this richness. Let this love bloom into a garden, for there can be no wealth without children.*"

Spring came early to the East Coast that year, and buoyed by the fragrant warmth of ripening earth and the sudden explosions of magnolias, I suggested that we take the train from Baltimore for a day of exploration in the capital.

Washington proved to be as beautiful as I'd always heard, with swaying clouds of cherry blossoms littering our path as we made our way down the pebbly sidewalk from Union Station to the Smithsonian museums on the Mall. To the east the domed Capitol shone in the hot spring sunshine; the obelisk of the Washington Monument beckoned at the other end of the long grassy park.

"I don't think that I can stand being away from you for three whole months this summer," I remarked, thinking about my return to Detroit in the weeks ahead.

Joseph slipped his arm around my waist, pulling me close. "Some say that the greatest obstacle to love is fear. But you don't have to worry. Our time apart will ensure that I will love you even more when we return to Maryland in September." A school bus packed with squealing children roared past with little hands waving at us from the windows.

"I don't see why we should be apart at all. We should both get jobs and look for rooms to rent somewhere in Baltimore."

He kissed my forehead. "I already have a job waiting for me with the government in Monrovia. I must work in Liberia to pay back a portion of my scholarship."

"But I want to be with you!"

"I want to be with you too. For now, however, circumstances dictate that we both must wait." He looked into my restless eyes and continued in a fatherly voice. "You must learn patience, Reba. It is very American to expect that your wishes will instantly be fulfilled."

We entered the Mall at the eastern end, closest to the Capitol. Morning joggers were bouncing along the gravel paths lining the Mall, and an open-sided tram ambled along with a tour guide pointing out the sights to a load of tourists. Several television vans were parked at the bottom of the stairs leading up to the Capitol, and a number of reporters were speaking live into microphones with the dome as their backdrop.

Joseph became very still as we stood at the bottom of the stairs that swept upward to the massive structure. "This is truly very impressive," he remarked quietly. "After seeing it in photographs for so many years, it's hard for me to believe that I'm finally standing here."

"Hey—I was talking about *us*!"

"I *am* talking about us," he retorted sharply. "The men in that building have the power to create order throughout the world. They can provide the military and economic support to either maintain or destabilize governments. They can provide food and books to the poor in nations such as my own. Whether you understand it or not, that building is indeed very important to my nation."

I blinked back my hurt at his reproving tone. He glanced down at me, his expression unexpectedly cold. "You must not take your democracy for granted, Reba. Many people in the world would love to live in a country with elected representatives whose acts are judged by a free press."

"You sound like some kind of politician," I said, pulling away from him.

"No, Reba. I sound like someone who has lived in a nation of political instability. I sound like someone who has been unsure about my own government."

"Then stay here! You can graduate and get a job in the United States!"

He turned and looked down at me. "No matter how heavy, the tortoise does not throw off its shell. I have responsibilities, Reba. My family is sacrificing to send me to the United States. What would it say to them if I never returned?"

I looked away angrily. It made no sense that Joseph was tied to endless numbers of brothers and sisters—some of whom didn't even share his blood. He had the right to his own life. He had the duty to make the most out of his unique gifts—and he'd *have* to stay in the States in order to do that.

We turned and began walking slowly down the Mall.

"Plenty of people come to America and stay—"

"Those people cannot go home for political or economic reasons," he answered calmly.

"There's nothing wrong with starting over and creating a life for yourself here."

"That's true, Reba. But I simply do not want to live in the States. You're going to have to accept that. And besides," he added, his voice growing softer, "not long ago you spoke about coming to Liberia. Have your roommates managed to dissuade you?"

Embarrassed that he somehow knew about Desiree and Samantha's constant carping about everything African, I ducked my head.

"Words can do more damage than weapons," he said as we

walked along slowly. "My roommates are often insensitive, too. Black Americans are not at peace with their ancestry. European culture has provided you with another set of values, and you have come to look at Africa through the eyes of exile."

"But we're Americans, Joseph!"

"Without a past, a people can have no dignity. If Black Americans learned more about Africa, you would have more pride in yourselves and be less vulnerable to the deep racism of this nation."

I stared up at the man I loved. I had known him to be dignified, tender, considerate and deeply passionate. But I had never heard him speak this way—with an edge of razor-sharp bitterness that hardened his handsome features to stone.

"No matter what you say, you could have a good life in America."

"I am not seeking a better life for myself alone, and that is the major difference between us, Reba." He stopped walking and reached over to take my arms.

"You have been raised to think first and foremost about yourself. I have been raised to think of myself as one of many. This is why I do not conceive of a future in which I alone enjoy its benefits. My purpose on earth is to share my advantages with others."

"You keep on repeating that. But you don't love somebody on the basis of how she'll serve other people. You should love a woman because of her own unique qualities."

"I agree," he said, a sadness entering his tone. "And I already know that this will be the challenge of our future. You spent your youth under the scrutiny of your parents' church, and now you want to live your life outside of others' eyes. All that I can offer you is a life within a compound of many people who will, indeed, expect you to conform to their values. This is the way of my world."

We began walking again, moving silently toward the National

Gallery. That day we visited a number of museums, and I watched Joseph as he stared thoughtfully at the art, historical and scientific exhibits, learning everything that he could.

I was also aware that he was watching me, measuring my long silences and trying to understand my inability to think beyond the confines of my own culture.

When we finally got back to campus that night, exhausted from the long day of walking, the train trip back to Baltimore and the bus's slow crawl across the city to our campus, he kissed me gravely.

"I will always love you, even if you come to feel that I'm not right for you," he said cryptically.

"Not *right* for me? What do you mean by that?"

"God's thoughts are as distant as the stars, Reba. I do not know what lies before us, but I will always love the dream of what we might have been if we'd not come from such different worlds."

Welcome Week fell in mid-June, and the entire college was bright with scarlet and silver banners rippling gently from every window, staircase and balustrade. The graduating seniors had already finished their exams, so they were dashing about the campus in their black and gold gowns, taking photographs and playing pranks on the underclassmen. The rest of the students were packing for the trip home, cleaning their dorm rooms for final inspections and preparing for the visits of hundreds of family members and prospective students.

My parents had decided to drive down and participate in my father's thirtieth class reunion before taking me back to Detroit for the summer. I had prepared myself for their arrival by pushing it to the very rear of my mind, behind my exams, my packing and my desolation at being parted from Joseph.

My father was almost swaggering as he emerged from the shining black Continental and walked around the car to assist my mother. Even from my dorm window his broad back was confident and imposing, and I was surprised that the little flecks of gray that were salting his hair made him appear even more distinguished. My mother, on the other hand, had grown portly since I'd last seen her, as if my departure signaled that she should start looking like a woman of middle age.

Despite my nervousness before their arrival, the sight of their car sent me hurtling like a child down the stairs to burst out into the hot afternoon and into my mother's arms.

"My goodness!" she remarked, looking down at me with glowing eyes. "I think you've aged about ten years since we saw you at Christmas!"

My father, too, gave me a measuring look. "My alma mater must be sitting well with you, Reba! You look like a million dollars!"

While I hadn't adopted all of Samantha's makeup suggestions, I had learned how to wear a bit of eyeliner and lipstick to bring out my best features. I'd gotten rid of my bangs, too, and was wearing my hair pulled away from my face—a style that Joseph really liked.

"I want to meet those roommates you've been writing about," my mother was saying. "And I know your father wants to have a look at his old classrooms. What time is dinner?"

I ushered them into Merriman Hall through a rush of students and their families. My mother instantly loved Desiree's air of a gentle southern belle, and my father ogled a simpering Samantha. After a few moments of meaningless conversation, I pushed my parents out the door, thankful that neither one of my roommates had dared to make any stupid comments about Joseph.

I had planned to introduce my parents to Joseph at dinner, after giving them time to get used to how much I'd grown up during my year on campus. I wanted them to see that I was old enough to choose my own friends, make my own decisions and, in fact, to have a serious boyfriend.

But as we strolled across the campus, my newfound maturity was the last thing on my parents' minds. Each building we passed triggered another of my father's stories about his wild and reckless undergraduate years. Caught up in his nostalgic tales of the girls he'd wooed and the capers he'd undertaken with his fraternity brothers, I barely noticed Carl Thornton observing our progress from the library. Carl muttered something to the two girls who were accompanying him and jogged down the steps, strolling directly across the grass toward us.

"Hey, Reba," he said, grinning sunnily. "Are these your parents?"

That afternoon Carl was the picture of collegiate perfection—he'd cut off his permed curls and replaced his T-shirts with a striped button-down shirt and a pair of ironed trousers. He'd attached his little gold fraternity pin to his collar and even scrubbed his pricey basketball shoes.

"Yes," I said hesitantly. Carl introduced himself to my parents, explaining that he was finishing his sophomore year with a major in business administration. Ignoring my quizzical stare, he then told them that he'd helped me find my way from the airport to the college last fall. He was, in his own words, "the first person Reba met at Absalom Jones College!"

"Really?" My mother's voice had gone up an octave. "That certainly was nice of you, Carl. I'm sure that Reba was glad to make a friend even before she got to campus."

"I do my best to look after our new students, Mrs. Freeman. That's one of the advantages of studying at a family-sized school."

"That's one reason my own parents sent me here," my father exclaimed.

"Are you an alumnus of AJC?" Carl asked with dramatically raised eyebrows.

"I certainly am. And no college could have prepared me better for my divinity studies."

"I didn't know that your father's a minister," Carl said, glancing mischievously at me. "That must be why you're always so serious about your books!"

"I hope Reba didn't spend the entire year in the library," my mother replied, her eyes still fixed on Carl's wide smile. "College should be fun, too."

I turned to my mother in shock, just as my father piped in. "Do I see a *Phi* on your lapel, young man?"

"Yes, sir. I crossed during freshman year."

"Congratulations and welcome to the brotherhood. I crossed thirty-two years ago and I feel I've got kinfolk all over this country."

"I'm the sixteenth *Phi* in my family," Carl bragged. "My father would never have let me consider any other fraternity."

"Well, it's always nice to meet a young man who represents the values of our brotherhood so well," my father declared pompously.

"How long will you be in Baltimore, Reverend Freeman? It would be great if you could meet my father."

"Oh, Mrs. Freeman and I can only stay for two days, I'm afraid. I've got to be back in Detroit for my Sunday services."

I looked away to hide my irritation. I couldn't understand why Carl was pretending to be so interested in me when we'd only spoken a few times during the entire school year.

"It was really nice to meet you," he now said with the most pronounced southern accent I'd ever heard. "I really do enjoy going to school with your daughter." He turned to go, then glanced back over his shoulder and threw up his hand. "Have a great summer, Reba!"

"What a nice young man," my mother murmured as we walked away. "Who are his people?"

"I wouldn't know. After all, we've had a grand total of three conversations."

"Well, he certainly seems to like you," my father observed. "And I agree that he appears to be a very decent fellow."

"Appearances can be deceiving. Carl Thornton's dating about twenty women on this campus and he's got a fiancée in Atlanta. He's really not my type."

"Oh, Reba," my mother cooed. "Most boys—and that included your own daddy—need to sow some wild oats before they're ready to settle down."

"I will *never* be interested in settling down with Carl Thornton. And besides—" I stopped speaking for a moment, unsure whether I wanted to tell them so soon. My parents came to a halt and looked at me with curious eyes. I glanced quickly around the park, wishing with all my heart that Joseph would somehow materialize and give me the support that I needed.

"Besides," I said, my voice croaking strangely, "I've already got a boyfriend."

My parents exchanged glances quickly. My mother spoke first. "That's great, honey. But why didn't you tell us?"

"I didn't have a chance," I lied, knowing it was pointless to explain that I really hadn't wanted them to know.

"Is he a student?" my father asked.

"Yes, of course. He's in my class."

"Well," my mother said, determined to appear supportive. "What's his name?"

"Joseph Thomas."

"I wonder if we know his family," my father stated. "There was a Raymond Thomas in my class."

"He's actually an international student from Liberia."

"You mean he's African?"

"Yes," I answered, trying to hold my voice steady. Again they exchanged glances.

"Does he speak English?" my mother asked softly.

"Of course. Liberia was founded by Black Americans."

"I assume that if his name is Thomas and he's attending this college he must be a Christian," my father said.

"What difference would *that* make?"

"It's a question of values," my mother said quickly. "You see, people who come from other countries sometimes think very differently from Americans."

"And particularly when they don't come from the Christian heritage," my father added.

"He's not so different from us," I replied defensively. "He loves his family and his country and he takes his studies very seriously."

"I'm sure he does," my mother interrupted soothingly. "When are we going to meet him?"

"At dinner," I answered firmly.

We continued our tour across campus, and my father went on with his excited boasting about his time at Absalom Jones. But a cool distance seemed to have sprung up between us, and I found myself insistently matching his fanciful stories with some serious tales of my own. When he told us about draping a rival fraternity's campus office with toilet paper, I told him about visiting Washington with Joseph, and how much I'd learned in the museums on the Mall. When he described a chemistry final that he was certain he'd fail, I mentioned that both Joseph and I had achieved the highest grade point averages of all the students in our dorms.

Finally we came to the wall of photographs in the main classroom building. He went from frame to frame, identifying his friends and family members as they'd looked a generation ago. As we moved to the door I showed him the list of students on the dean's list, and pointed out Joseph's name, written just above mine.

"I'm very impressed by everything you've done here at Absalom Jones," my father said. "But coming from our family, I wouldn't have expected anything less."

"Nobody from those photographs helped me with *my* chemistry final," I said. "Joseph was my tutor."

"This Joseph sounds like a very special young man," my mother said.

"That's right. And imagine—he doesn't even belong to Dad's fraternity."

By the time we retraced our steps across the Commons, a sweet summer evening had banished the blazing afternoon sun. Smiling parents were strolling along with their graduates, and mobs of screaming children were running back and forth through the thick grass.

I saw Joseph waiting beside his dorm, his tall figure straight and still in the midst of so much movement. He was dressed in one of his white shirts, and despite the heat he had put on a tie. His neat dark trousers were ironed to a crease, and he'd trimmed his hair the night before.

He recognized me and began walking toward us, and I was struck by the grace of his dignified stride. For the first time I realized how beautifully he moved—head raised, shoulders relaxed, with an air of confidence that made him appear to be years older than the other undergraduates.

I stole a glance at my mother and saw that she was watching

him, too, with an expression bordering on awe. Joseph's square jaw and gentle eyes had fascinated me for months—in fact, I had never grown tired of looking at him. There was something different about the way he carried himself, and at that moment, watching him through my parents' eyes, I suddenly understood what it was.

Joseph had grown up in a Black world, ruled by Black people. He had never been taught to doubt himself or to feel shame for his color. Joseph had a kind of confidence that was too rarely visible in Black men raised in this white man's world.

We met near the center of the Commons. Joseph extended his hand and introduced himself to my father, then greeted my mother. Impulsively I reached out and grasped his fingers, and our eyes met for a brief, intense moment.

My father was watching, and his face stiffened. "Well, Mr. Thomas," he announced, "we've heard a great deal about you this afternoon."

"Reba speaks often of you too, sir. I believe that your achievements on this campus motivate her to be a very fine student."

Joseph's lilting accent and mature manner made it seem as if he was a professor evaluating my academic performance. My father blinked once or twice, unused to a younger man speaking up as if he were his equal.

"Reba says you come from Africa," my mother said, breaking the silence.

"Yes, Mrs. Freeman. I was born and raised in Liberia."

"How nice," my mother said vaguely. "Has it been difficult for you to get used to our country?"

"I was warmly welcomed by the students and faculty of the college," Joseph answered with a smile, "but I confess that the winter seems very cold to me."

"Joseph certainly grew up with some sense of kinship with the

United States," my father said to my mother. "Liberia was founded by American citizens."

"Our founders were former slaves from the United States," Joseph agreed, "but there was a large indigenous population in my country as well. Liberia is a nation of many ethnic and religious groups, and we continue to struggle with the challenges of sharing our resources equally among all of our peoples."

"You can learn a great deal about the struggle for civil rights from your American cousins," my father said with a trace of irritation. "After all, we invented the idea of civil liberties."

"Of course, sir." Joseph turned his head slightly to include my mother. "We Liberians are proud to share the blood of Dr. Du Bois and Dr. King. We look to their selfless acts as models for our own behavior."

"Many lesser-known people have also dedicated their lives to the struggle," my father retorted stubbornly.

"God loves simple folk," Joseph agreed. "That is why there are so many of us."

"I think we need to get some dinner," my mother declared, politely attributing my father's testiness to hunger.

We began walking across the park. Joseph fell into step beside me and glanced down reassuringly.

"Are you going back to Africa for the summer?" my mother asked him.

"Yes, Mrs. Freeman. I will work in a government office in the capital, Monrovia."

"Really? I work in the mayor's office in Detroit. Are you planning to go into government service?"

"No ma'am," Joseph said quietly. "I don't feel that I would make a good administrator. I am drawn to the classroom, so I plan to teach once I've finished my studies."

We entered the dining hall, where many families had already taken seats at the colorfully decorated tables. I expected my father to regale us with further tales from his youth, but he had grown sullen, and led the way through the food line without speaking.

Once we were seated my mother valiantly tried to revive the conversation.

"How did you choose Absalom Jones College, Joseph?"

"I've studied in mission schools all of my life, and I was recommended to Absalom Jones College by my bishop."

"Then you could certainly be a candidate for the ministry," my father cut in, peering hard into Joseph's eyes. I knew my father was challenging Joseph to make a comment on the church, and I shot him a warning glance. Joseph, however, carefully wiped his mouth with his napkin and looked directly into my father's eyes. He addressed him in a calm, clear voice.

"I have been fortunate enough to have enjoyed great support from the men and women of the church. To that end, I understand the importance of their calling, and I would never minimize it by pretending to feel so inspired myself." He paused.

"God's great wisdom guides us toward our proper paths. I am aware of my particular strengths in dealing with children, and I feel confident that I will repay the kindness of the church by returning to my community to serve as a teacher."

"That is a very fine mission," my mother agreed. "Have you ever considered pursuing your graduate studies in the United States and going on to be a university professor in Africa?"

Joseph smiled at her patiently. "I admit that I love studying. I think that I could spend my entire life learning new things. But my hope is to prove myself useful to those who might otherwise have no opportunity to learn basic reading and writing."

"Lots of foreigners change their minds about leaving once they've had a taste of American life," my father said brusquely.

"I think," Joseph replied, "that if I decide to continue my studies, I would like to attend a university in Europe. It would, indeed, balance my understanding of the world, and better prepare me to work in Liberia."

"How can studying in Europe help you in Africa?" my father said. "You need to be here, around Black people."

Joseph cast his eyes on the tablecloth for a moment, as if formulating the most diplomatic answer. "I do not find it so difficult to understand my Black kinsmen in America. But there are still many Europeans living in Africa, and I would appreciate knowing more about their cultures."

"But everyone knows that America is the most important nation on earth," my father bristled. "You can learn everything you need to know right here."

I couldn't count the number of times I'd heard my father criticize the United States for its violence and racism. Yet now he was pretending that the nation that had enslaved millions of African people was the greatest nation in the world! Lowering my eyes in shame, I realized that I had said exactly the same things to Joseph without realizing how stupid and hypocritical they sounded.

Joseph's face remained fixed in a mask of calm, but I saw something pass through his eyes. He was ashamed for my father— ashamed that this educated, respected and successful man should be insecure enough to show the extent of his shallowness. And I was ashamed of my father, too, for making it so obvious that he was jealous of my twenty-one-year-old boyfriend.

"I agree with you, sir," Joseph said politely. "The wise goat eats the grass where it is tied."

We all chuckled at the timely proverb, but I heard the disappointment in my lover's voice. When he glanced at me a few seconds later there was a growing understanding in his gaze, coupled with something else—a new respect for me.

"Will your family be visiting you while you're here?" my mother asked.

Although the question seemed harmless enough, I knew that my mother wanted to find out if his parents were wealthy.

"I would be pleased if my parents came to Baltimore. But I think that it is more likely that my younger siblings will visit first. Two of my brothers are planning to pursue their studies abroad as soon as I finish my degree, and three of my sisters are already undertaking careers in medicine in the capital."

"Oh, my goodness!" my mother exclaimed. "You come from quite a large family!"

"By American standards, yes. But my family is actually quite typical of my culture."

"Well, I'm sure your parents are very proud that you've all chosen to study."

"My parents place a high value on education. As we say at home, wisdom is the finest beauty of a person."

My father's eyes had grown more subtly malicious as he listened. "It must be quite a change for you to live in a modern city."

Joseph's shoulders stiffened slightly, but his face remained open. "I studied in our capital, Monrovia, before coming here. Although our architecture is somewhat different from what I've seen in Maryland, my city is actually quite large."

"Well, perhaps one day you'll visit us in Detroit."

My father's words set a cold challenge to the young man who so obviously cared for his daughter. And it was obvious that Joseph *did* care—otherwise, why should he have accepted my parents' smallness with so much dignity?

"Joseph and I are having a contest," I said without raising my eyes. "We've decided to see which one of us can graduate with the higher grade point average."

"Really?" my mother replied. "Well, I'm glad you're both so success oriented, but I hope you have time to get out and meet other people, too."

"I'm afraid that I'm not a very social person," Joseph apologized.

"I've discovered," I added, "that neither am I. I suppose that all those church groups I went to over the years have paid off. I'd rather spend the evening discussing good books with Joseph than going to the latest dance or trying to pledge a sorority."

"Well," my mother said lamely, "I just hope you're making the most of your time while you're here."

I looked across the table and stared deep into Joseph's eyes. "Don't worry, Mom. I am."

It was at that moment that I was sure that nothing and no one would stop me from loving Joseph Vai Thomas. And I was finally certain, as he smiled back at me, that nothing would ever stop him from loving me.

Chapter 5

Alexandria, Virginia

2004

In our nearly twenty years of married life I never once cheated on Carl.

Not because I didn't have the chance. There were plenty of men in our circle who would have been happy to engage in a little "off-the-record" time with Carl Thornton's wife. Sometimes in the middle of one of our parties, I'd catch my friends' husbands watching me with an invitation in their eyes. And once or twice—particularly after I'd found those photographs—I'd actually given it some thought.

But then, I'd never been attracted to any man in quite the same way that I was attracted to Carl. It was strange: Joseph understood me better than Carl. He challenged my intellect, taught me about empathy and expanded my world merely by telling me stories.

Yet being with Carl was an adventure—he was always finding new friends, developing new projects, making new plans. Joseph made me think; Carl made me laugh. And even after twenty years, Carl still knew how to make love.

So even though it made no sense at all, my plan to try and help Joseph felt like I was cheating. And even though I truly believed I had nothing to feel guilty about, I decided to take Arlene's advice and come clean about what was going on in my life.

I should have known better.

Thornton Consulting was located in a lovely suburban complex just a few blocks from our home. A winding drive led to a group of single-story buildings set off by landscaped flower beds and white-barked aspens. Carl's Lexus was parked near the entrance, and the absence of other cars told me that he was probably finished with his clients for the day.

I parked beside his car and walked into his office. His secretary, a middle-aged widow who looked after him like a mother, glanced up at my arrival.

"Reba! How nice to see you. Let me ring your husband and tell him you're here to see him."

"That's all right, Esther. I'll just go on back."

Carl's personal office was located at the end of a short corridor; other doors opened to a small conference room, a kitchen and a large storage space where he kept his files. I knocked on his door and opened it before he could reply. Carl was sitting at his desk, turned toward his computer with the speaker phone on.

He looked up in surprise, then raised his hand.

"Larry, I've got to go now, but I have your business plan right here on the computer. Why don't I print it out and fax it over before I leave?"

The person on the phone made affirmative noises, and Carl completed the call. He got up to hug me, sliding his hands slowly down my back to my hips.

"The sky must be falling. My wife actually left her job early and came by to spend some time with her old man."

"One of my meetings got postponed so I decided to get a head start on the traffic. Don't you have a golf game tonight?"

"I usually meet Chad and Douglas at the club on Wednesdays, but if there's something else you want to do—"

"No—well, yes. I just thought we could talk."

He motioned for me to take a seat, despite the cautious look that had entered his eyes. He sat down on the edge of his desk and leaned forward, no longer smiling.

"Is this about the other night? If so, I want you to understand that there's really nothing going on between Sandra and me. She's pretty upset about Alan leaving, but that's not my business."

"I didn't come here to talk about other women. But I do want to talk about us."

"All right. I'm listening."

I looked at my hands, searching for a way to bring Joseph up without setting off another argument.

"Things have been pretty rocky between us lately, and I want to take responsibility for my part in our problems."

He grunted softly in surprise, but didn't speak.

"I know that sometimes I've seemed distant," I continued. "I'll admit that there are times when I feel overwhelmed by the bad things that are happening in the world. But the truth is that I love you, Carl. I value the life we've built together. And I think that our marriage is worth fighting for."

"I feel the same way, Reba."

Speaking very slowly, I looked up into his eyes. "I think I've found a way to make things better. But I'll need your help."

"What is it?"

I took a deep breath. "It involves Joseph—"

"Damn! I knew you wouldn't be able to resist bringing him up!" Carl jumped to his feet and began gathering up his papers.

"I think you should hear me out."

"I'm sick of this shit, Reba! I'm not listening to any more non-sense about him. You need to get over whatever it is that keeps you tied to that man. Can't you see that he has his own life? Can't you understand that he has no interest in you?"

"Actually—"

"Has he called or written to you in the past twenty years?"

"No, but—"

"Has he made any effort to find out if you're still alive?"

"Carl, I—"

"Then don't come in here telling me anything about Joseph Thomas. I want him out of our lives. Do you understand, Reba? No more Joseph!"

He shoved his files into his leather briefcase and looked down at me. "If that's all you've got to say, I can still make my golf game."

There was nothing I could do but wait.

Wait to hear from Simone.

Wait by the television in case Joseph's story appeared on the news.

Wait for some understanding of what the hell I was doing with my life.

Those were strangely unreal days—full of summer's richness and sweet with nature's inner peace. The leaves on the trees, fat and full and a deep, Sherwood green, danced lazily in warm breezes that sent perfumes of blossoms wafting through the night. It was hard to believe that Joseph Thomas—now known as Yusef Vai—was sitting in a Swiss prison waiting to go on trial for mass murder.

And then, on the twenty-first of July, Simone called me at my office.

"Reba," she said with her characteristic directness, "someone from the court just returned my call. Yusef Vai will be formally ar-raigned next Monday, on the twenty-sixth. The charges against him will be fully disclosed at that time, and a list of prosecution witnesses will be made public. I expect that if no delays are imposed, the actual trial will begin in early September."

"Have you learned anything about his representation?"

"He has a court-appointed attorney, but I don't know anything more."

"How can we find out?"

"Why don't we try speaking to him? I'm told that we can set up a conference call."

"When—when do you want to do it?"

"There's a six-hour time difference between Washington and Switzerland. Why don't we shoot for one o'clock?"

"*Today?*"

"Will you be free?"

I was waiting at my desk as the hands of the clock swung toward one. I hadn't been able to eat any lunch, but my stomach was still roiling as if I was a ship caught in a perfect storm. I was so nervous that I was no longer thinking clearly about anything. Even the soft Abdullah Ibrahim playing in the background couldn't slow down my ragged breathing. I couldn't even hold a pencil.

I locked the office door, removed my fawn-toned linen suit jacket and even unbuttoned my blouse. Perspiration already darkened the fabric, though my skin felt prickly and cold. My feet were aching, so I took off my shoes and pushed them out of the way.

The phone rang at precisely 1:01 P.M. The sound nearly caused me to jump out of my seat, and I had to steady my racing heart before lifting the receiver. The secretary's voice sounded flat and distant, though she was sitting just on the other side of the wall. "Mrs. Thornton, there's a call for you from Ms. James."

"Yes, I'll take it. And please hold all my other calls."

There was a series of clicks as she transferred me to the external line.

"Hello, Simone?" I said in a strangely creaking voice. "I'm here."

"Good. The international operator is on the other line. Just hold for a moment."

I heard her speaking French with amazing fluency, and a distant voice replied. There was another static pause, followed by a formal greeting by a man.

"*Paul Merceau, Directeur Général.*"

"*Monsieur Merceau? Ici Simone James des États-Unis.*"

"Ah, yes," he said, switching instantly to English. "We received your request for a phone interview with Mr. Vai. He is being escorted to a telephone cabin and will be on the line in a moment. I must first, however, review the protocol of this interview with you."

"Thank you," she said with self-assurance.

"Mr. Vai has not yet been arraigned, and no formal charges have been brought against him. His attorney will not be present, but we reserve the right to audit your conversation. Therefore, it would be wise to proceed accordingly. You may stay on the phone for a maximum of thirty minutes, and all charges for this interview will be billed to you. Do you have any questions?"

"None at present."

"Good. Then I will have your call transferred." The line went silent and I heard Simone breathing lightly. My anticipation was so great that my nervousness vanished, leaving behind a deep, almost unquenchable thirst to hear Joseph's voice again.

Suddenly there was a click. "Hello?" a man said softly.

"Mr. Vai? This is Simone James, calling from the United States."

"Mrs. James? How may I help you?"

I knew in an instant that my search was over. With those calmly uttered words any doubts I had about Yusef Vai's identity were dispelled. No other human being held in an international prison for crimes against humanity would have begun a conversation with an unknown caller by asking not "Who are you?" but rather "How may I help you?"

Simone must have felt it, too, because when she answered, some of the edge had vanished from her voice, and I heard an almost instinctual warmth enter her words.

"Mr. Vai, I am an attorney in Washington, and I have a client who would like to speak to you."

"Hello, Joseph."

Now the silence was so heavy that I thought I had spoken into the void of the past twenty years. My mind was filled with the weight of all the nights I had lain awake, thinking of his face, remembering his voice, longing for his touch. I thought of the times I had played music that seemed to recall his laughter. The times I had spoken aloud to him when trying to resolve some difficult case. The times that I had looked at my daughter and wished that she were his child.

"Reba," he answered, the two syllables as necessary as light in a cavern of darkness. "I am so happy to hear your voice."

Again there was a silence, but this time it was mine. I struggled with what to say when there were so many things to be said.

"Mr. Vai," Simone interjected. "Are you satisfied with the conditions of your detention?"

"I am not being mistreated. The food is more than adequate, and I am allowed an hour each day for exercise. The only thing I miss for the other twenty-three hours is a view of the sky. My room is windowless, you see."

This was the first time that it really came home to me: Joseph was in prison for crimes that were nearly beyond imagining. Except that, in my role as a person who helped the survivors of such crimes, I didn't have to use my imagination.

What should I say to him?

I should have guessed, however, that it was Joseph who would know exactly what to say to me.

"Are you well, Reba?" His voice had exactly the same timbre of calm gentleness that had made me love him so long ago.

"I'm well—in fact, we're *all* well. You probably don't know that I'm married to Carl Thornton. We have a daughter, Marisa."

"I think that you made a very good choice in Carl. And I expect that your daughter is sixteen or so by now."

"How do you—"

"I received the college alumni magazine for some time after I returned to Liberia."

Now we both paused. There was so much to tell him, and yet—

"Mr. Vai," Simone interrupted, "I am going to let you speak with Reba now. Before I go I'd like to know the name of your legal counsel."

"Mr. Matthew Pope. He was assigned to me by the court."

"Are you satisfied with his representation?"

"We have not spent a great deal of time discussing my case, but he seems to be a very bright and earnest young man."

"You realize that you are to be arraigned in one week?"

"No, I was not aware of the exact date. I am very thankful for your interest."

I heard a click and knew that Simone was gone. Now Joseph and I were alone on the line. I glanced up and noted that twelve minutes had magically vanished. Where should I begin?

"We don't have much time," I said slowly and clearly, my interviewing skills kicking in. "I need to know what I can do for you."

"It is enough that you called, Reba."

"That's nonsense. Do you have enough food? Clothing?"

"Those things have been provided for me by the court."

"What about pens and paper? Are you doing any writing?"

"Yes, I have adequate supplies."

"Have you been able to contact your family?"

He didn't answer. There was a strange pause that seemed to explode with my sudden, terrible understanding. "Joseph—where are your parents?"

"They are no longer living. I have also lost many of my siblings in the past twenty years. I have one brother who now makes his home in England. But I have not spoken with him."

"Why? Don't you know where he is?"

Again there was a silence. Then he spoke, the words dark and filled with despair. "I have led him to believe that I am dead."

"Dead?"

"I don't want him to know what I've become. I never intended for anyone to realize that Yusef Vai is, in fact, my father's son."

"You've hidden your identity from your *family?*"

"The man they loved did, indeed, die many years ago. I could not do what had to be done while I still had blood ties."

"What had to be *done?*" I echoed, remembering that the prison director stated that this call would certainly be monitored. "Surely you're not saying that the charges they're bringing against you are true?"

He was quiet for a moment. "No, Reba. I am not admitting to the crimes of which I have been accused. But it makes no difference, really. The life that I've led over the past ten years is not fit to be shared with anyone I love—nor with anyone who loved me."

I began breathing again with those words. "If you're not guilty, you can't accept unjust imprisonment!"

"I cannot go back to being Joseph Thomas, either. I think it is best for me to remain here, far away from everything that's happened."

"What? You're saying that being in prison is better than being a free man?"

"Reba," he murmured, his voice like ash, "whether I remain in this prison or not, I will never be free."

"That's not true! You can't just throw your life away!"

"There is no life for me to return to."

"Then you create a new life!"

"Where? I have no home, no family—"

"But you have *me*, dammit!"

"No, Reba. You have a husband and a daughter. You cannot tie yourself to a man whose hands have been washed in blood."

For a moment I floundered, then I took a deep breath and let my heart choose my words.

"Listen to me, Joseph Vai Thomas. There was a time when I didn't understand what drew you back to Liberia. I didn't understand the sacrifices we have to make for those we love. I didn't have the strength to swallow my fear and fight to see my dreams through. But those days are over, Joseph. I know what I have to do, and I will do it. I will not let you sacrifice yourself. Do you understand?"

There was another long silence, and I realized that I had spoken to him with more assertiveness than I'd ever dared during our time together. When he answered me, he seemed almost amused.

"You have clearly found your power, Reba," he said with some of his old dignity.

"You have no idea how much power," I replied, nearly smiling. "Joseph—you just hold on tight. I'm going to find a way to set you free."

There was another pause. Then suddenly his voice seemed very close. "I will try not to fail you, Reba."

"Joseph Vai Thomas—" I paused, gathering all the courage I had. "I swear that this time I'm not going to fail *you*."

Forty-eight hours after speaking with Joseph, I had made the necessary reservations, secured a short personal leave from work and prepared myself for the argument that had to happen.

Just after seven that evening, Carl came roaring in from the golf course, his voice pitched at the three-beer register, and went straight through the kitchen to the shower. Marisa and I were halfway through our spinach quiche when he passed by us again, another beer in hand, on his way to the family room.

"Do you want some dinner?" I asked lightly.

"Had a sandwich at the club."

"Could I talk with you for a few moments?"

"Can it wait? Preseason football, Reba!"

"It's important, Carl."

Tanner than usual from a charity tournament he'd played the weekend before, he glanced with regret toward the wide-screen television. "Well, what is it? Another bill from the tax man?"

"No, it's something else," I said, avoiding Marisa's inquisitive stare. She'd decided a few weeks before that she was going to lose three pounds, so her plate had only a half slice of quiche.

"I'll leave so you two can talk," she said, standing up. She took her dishes to the sink and proceeded up the stairs. A moment later I heard her CD player.

As he continued to stand in the doorway, Carl's face had grown wary. "All right, General," he joked. He sat down and took a demonstrative swill of his beer. Lowering the bottle, he squared his shoulders. "Where's the war zone?"

"It's in Switzerland," I answered, ignoring his bad joke.

"Switzerland? Why Switzerland?"

"Because Joseph Thomas is being held there for crimes against humanity."

"What are you—" His face shifted as he took in what I was saying. "Reba, I told you—"

"He's been accused of leading a resistance group that might have been responsible for a number of murders in Liberia," I said, keeping my words as clear and simple as possible. "I'm leaving for Switzerland tomorrow night to help him in any way we can."

I watched as Carl's face mirrored his confusion, disbelief and growing understanding. He pushed his beer bottle out of the way, his eyes hard.

"Are you for real?"

"Do I look like I'm joking?"

"Do I have any say in this?"

"No, Carl. The reservations are made."

"You're leaving your family to take care of a man who abandoned you twenty years ago?"

"I'm going to make sure that he gets the same fair treatment that any person deserves."

"And how are you going to do that?"

"I don't know yet, but I have to try."

"And how long are you planning to be gone?"

"Three days. I'll arrive on Saturday, see Joseph over the weekend and be back home on Monday night."

"You can't do anything in three days."

"Maybe not."

"And what if he's guilty?"

"You know damned well Joseph isn't capable of committing any crime."

"I suppose your office likes the idea of your helping a war criminal?"

"As far as I'm concerned, Joseph is innocent until proven guilty."

"Let somebody else help him."

"Clearly there is nobody else."

"Where's his family?"

"I don't know."

"Why don't some of the people in his so-called resistance group come to his aid?"

"I don't know that either."

"What about us?"

"I guess you'll just have to survive for three whole days without me."

"That's not what I mean, Reba."

"Then say what you mean."

"Joseph left you twenty years ago. He has no right to expect you to help him now."

"This is my choice, Carl."

"What if I object to my wife flying halfway around the world for a man she's no longer married to?"

"Then perhaps I'll start objecting to my husband's encounters with women he's *never* been married to."

"Mom!" Marisa wailed, and I looked up to find that she had come back down the stairs and was now standing in the kitchen. I heard her steps as she clattered through the house and threw open the sliding door leading out to the patio. Carl and I were still staring at each other.

"You're a bitch," he said softly.

"You're wrong. I'm the alpha bitch."

"If you leave this house and go to Joseph Thomas, I may not be here when you get back."

"What difference will that make? You're already nothing but noise."

Snatching up the plates with my half-eaten dinner, I walked into the kitchen, set everything on the counter and stared out the window, my chest heaving in anger.

So much for telling the truth, I thought, struggling to calm myself. Gradually my eyes focused on the scene outside. I left the dishes in the sink and went to find my daughter.

It wasn't difficult. For years Marisa's favorite place to daydream about boys, mourn the untimely loss of her pet rabbits or simply celebrate the beauty of her growing womanhood was a tire swing hung from a thick-branched oak tree in the deep green of the backyard. Though they'd never been tended, a copse of rose bushes I'd planted years before had exploded into a forest of speckled blossoms. The roses were now draped like a fragrant web over the fence delineating the borders of our property, sending a stunning perfume over the entire yard.

Marisa was sitting on her swing, her long legs dangling childlike to the petal-strewn ground below. She was holding a pink-white rose, staring into the labyrinth of petals toward its pollen-dusted navel.

"I'm sorry I upset you, baby."

She was quiet for a moment, her eyes still fixed on the flower. "Are you and Daddy getting a divorce?"

I sighed and sat down on the grass beside the swing. Reaching into a thick bank of clover, I silently wondered whether four-leaf clovers really existed.

"I hope not," I said, looking up into her eyes. "But Marisa, part

of being a woman is having the strength to make tough decisions. Your dad and I are having some problems right now, but with luck everything will work out."

She pondered this for a while. Then she looked down again at her flower. "Why didn't you tell me you'd found him?"

"I met with a lawyer a few weeks ago who managed to track him down. I spoke with him by telephone two days ago, and then gave myself some time to decide what I wanted to do."

"But why didn't you tell me? You can trust me, Mom."

"This isn't a question of trust, Marisa. I knew that my choosing to help Joseph might really hurt your father. I knew that my leaving town would be difficult for you. And I'm certainly aware that if Joseph is a war criminal, supporting him might make things really difficult for me at work."

"Then why are you doing it?" she asked, looking directly at me for the first time.

"Because he's lost his family. He's no longer in his country or his culture. He has no support from his government. He has no friends. Certainly, like every human being on this planet, he deserves something better."

"It's also because you still love him," she challenged.

"Yes. I'll always love him."

"Do you love Dad?" she asked in a small voice.

"Yes I do. And I love you, too."

She let my words sink in. Then she straightened her back and sat up slowly. "Can I come to Switzerland with you?"

"Not this time, baby."

"But you're not going by yourself—"

"No, Arlene is going with me."

"Not Daddy?"

"No, I thought it would be better if Daddy stayed home with you." I climbed to my feet and she reached out to grasp my hand.

"Mom, this may sound strange, but—but I'm really proud of you."

I *had visited* Switzerland twice—once on my honeymoon with Carl, and again when I attended the International Conference on Political Asylum, which was held in Geneva. Now, as I stared out the plane window into the darkening stratosphere, I was almost glad I was returning.

Switzerland seemed to be one of the few places where social stability and political neutrality promised fairness—if fairness really exists anywhere on earth. I remembered the impressive cleanliness of the streets, stores and public restrooms. The calm demeanor of the people. The trains that ran on time. The waiters who asked if the meal was satisfactory. The dogs that never barked. The children who never seemed to cry.

When I attended that conference of over five hundred representatives from governments throughout the world, I'd been astounded to find that our room reservations were correct, our name tags properly spelled, and that the security was virtually airtight.

And that was one reason why, if I had to travel to Europe on such a desperate mission, I was glad that my destination was Switzerland. Deep in my heart I believed that the international court would conduct a thorough and impartial investigation into Joseph's case. They would review the evidence, agree to his innocence and set him free.

Or at least, that's what I prayed as I stared out of the plane window into the endless night.

I was also very glad that I wasn't alone. Arlene Masters—who spoke fluent German and had "millions of frequent flyer miles and no chance to use them"—had instantly offered to come. Now she slumbered beside me, her reading glasses hanging on a chain near her breasts and her neat dreadlocks pressed like soft graying twigs against the seat cushions.

As usual, I couldn't have fallen asleep if I'd tried.

An amazingly stupid screwball comedy was playing on the video screen a few rows ahead, but I found myself unable to concentrate on anything other than Joseph. Simone James had helped me prepare for the trip, putting together more files on international criminal cases and formulating a list of procedural questions for me to pose to Joseph's attorney. Arlene had, in the meantime, conducted as much research as she could into the Liberian conflict. I spent most of the flight reading, and as we drew closer to our destination I tried to convince myself that I would know what to do for Joseph. That is, if anything could be done at all.

I tried to imagine what he would look like. Had time put more weight on his once-lanky frame? Had he lost the grace that took my breath away as he strode across the campus? Were his hands still slender, with long, square-tipped fingers? Had his hair begun to turn gray? Were his eyes still filled with the patient kindness that had drawn me to him from that first day in the chapel?

And how would I appear to him? I hadn't gained much weight since our college days. I kept my hair short, which emphasized my slender face. My skin had remained unwrinkled—my mother said it was my father's Caribbean blood. And Carl often joked that time had actually put some much-appreciated "meat" on my breasts and rear.

But those things didn't matter as much as my one burning fear: Would Joseph see me as just another affluent American, wallowing in the privileges of wealth, education and power? What would he think if he could see my luxurious home, my silk-stuffed closets and my shining new Volvo? What would he say if he knew the truth about my marriage to Carl? My so-called friendship with Desiree and Samantha? Had I become the kind of woman he would despise?

Slowly I fingered the papers in the folders, letting my mind wander toward my greatest fear: *What if he asked me to explain the thing that drove us apart so many years ago?*

Fortunately Arlene stirred beside me, stretching her legs in the narrow space between the seats. "I hate flying," she muttered without opening her eyes.

"I thought you were asleep."

"Just resting. I never sleep on planes." She craned her neck and reached up to run her fingers through her locks. "Flights like this give me muscle cramps for weeks, yet I never stop traveling."

She turned to look at me, her eyes immediately falling on the open documents on the tray table before me. "Are you okay?"

"I never dreamed I'd be involved in anything like this. It's one thing to work with perfect strangers. But for this to be Joseph—"

"It's the wages of love," she replied, turning her body in the narrow seat so that she was facing me. "God knows that we're often forced to do unbelievable stuff for the people we care about."

"I'm not sure I'm strong enough to handle it."

She reached over and touched my arm. "When my mother was diagnosed with cancer, I was faced with the same feelings. And I promise you, I found reserves of strength I never would have expected."

"But this is different, Arlene. If he did these things then he *de-*

serves to stay in prison for the rest of his life. Your mother did nothing to deserve her illness."

"God will help you find the strength."

God? I thought. What god? I turned again to the window, thinking about the refugees I'd worked with over the past decade. People from countries as close as Mexico and as far away as the former Soviet Union. Mothers who had witnessed the execution of their children. Fathers who had been forced to watch their wives and daughters being raped. Elderly people whose entire families had been deported, imprisoned, "disappeared." And the orphans: countless children who had no words, even in their own languages, to describe the unspeakable things they'd survived.

Yes, I'd found the strength to help them. I'd used my attitude of calmly detached professionalism to lobby the government on their behalf. I'd found housing and schools and jobs for them. I'd given them the opportunity to share something of my opulent American life.

But *this* was different. Joseph wasn't a stranger stepping out of one of those late-night news reports. Joseph's story would not fall neatly in place beside the others. Joseph had been my life.

We landed in Zurich at 6:43 A.M.—just after midnight, Washington time—which meant that we wouldn't get another chance to sleep for many more hours. Nearly dazed with exhaustion, I followed Arlene through passport control. The agent, a tall man in a dun-colored uniform with matching hazel eyes, peered at her dreadlocks and carefully examined her papers. He typed something into his computer and waited for a moment.

"Are you here for business or pleasure?"

"*Nichts geschaeftliches. Nur zum Vergnügen.*"

"*Sie sprechen Deutsch?*" he asked, raising his eyebrows coolly.

"*Ich bin Professorin der germanistischen Literatur,*" she replied. He nodded without speaking, closed her passport and waved her through the barrier.

"You are also a German professor?" he asked me as he scrutinized my documents.

"No. I'm here to visit an old friend."

"Where are you traveling in Switzerland?"

"I'm going to Berne."

He closed my passport and slid it over the counter without another word.

We rented an Audi station wagon at the airport despite the fact that the train would have taken us to Berne in less than two hours.

"This will be faster and a hell of lot more convenient," Arlene said as she steered the car into the raging traffic. "Just sit back and count the cows."

"Are you sure you can handle these roads?" I asked as a silver BMW streaked past.

"Handle *these* roads? Honey, you're forgetting that I drove on the German Autobahn every day for years—and they don't even *have* a speed limit!"

"Arlene—" I began nervously.

"Reba," she interrupted, her voice growing serious. "I know you're used to taking care of business all by yourself. But you've got enough to deal with right now. Just relax and let me help out where I can."

I closed my eyes for a moment, trying to remember how it felt to relax. But it wasn't possible. My hands lay clenched in my lap and my neck had begun aching from sitting so rigidly during the ten-hour flight. My stomach was also complaining about the half-frozen omelet the airline had served as a pretense of breakfast.

"Tell me something," she said to make conversation. "What made you and Joseph decide to get married halfway through your sophomore year?"

I opened my eyes and stared into the unfolding asphalt. "I'm not sure it was something we decided. It just seemed to happen."

"You mean you went for a walk and ended up at a justice of the peace?"

"Exactly. We went for a walk and when we came back we were husband and wife."

"How in the world did you do that?"

I thought about it for a moment. How *had* we done it? How could I describe it, when I had never told *anyone* about it? For twenty-two years, no one—neither Samantha, nor Desiree, nor even my mother and father—had ever heard about the night I married Joseph Thomas. Carl, of course, had never asked. And after Joseph left me, I had pushed our wedding as far as possible into the deepest, darkest corner of my cave. That's how much it hurt to even think about it.

"Reba? Are you okay?"

I opened my mouth to speak. Then without any warning, all the images of that period came flooding back in a terrific rush, and suddenly I saw Joseph's face and heard his voice with an immediacy that brought tears to my eyes. I began digging in my bag for tissues but it was too late. I began to sob.

"Do you want me to pull over?" Arlene asked gently.

"No, I'll be all right in a minute."

"I'm sorry—I hope I didn't—"

"It's not your fault," I managed to say, raising my head to catch a passing church spire. "It's just that I've never talked about it before."

"Then we'll talk about something else."

"No," I insisted, struggling to bring my emotions back under control. "I want to tell you, Arlene. You're the first person in all these years who—"

I paused, ashamed of what I was about to say. "You're the first person who's ever cared."

Her brows came together in concern, but she remained silent. I leaned back in the car seat and closed my eyes. My words began to flow, blocking out the sound of the trucks racing past us on the highway. I drew my thoughts back to the happiest night of my life—January 29, 1982. And I told Arlene how Joseph and I, without forethought or planning, suddenly took the boldest step that any two people can take: We committed ourselves to spending the rest of our lives together.

She listened patiently, sometimes laughing, other times shaking her head in wonder. "So you just held hands and jumped."

"Yes," I whispered, realizing that my eyes had again filled with tears. Arlene remained focused on the road, skillfully negotiating the Audi between flatbeds loaded with bales of hay and late-model German sports cars.

"You didn't tell anyone?"

I looked out on a pair of auburn horses galloping across a rolling green field. A wooden barn with a steep, sloping roof loomed out of the dawn.

"Not until the end of the school year. And we only admitted it then because we wanted to remain in Baltimore over the summer. We wanted to find jobs and look for a place to live. But to tell you the truth, it probably would have been better if we'd told everyone right away."

"Why?"

"We went through so much crap that winter. My parents were writing and calling, threatening to take me out of school if I con-

tinued to see Joseph. The dorm monitors noticed that I was spending lots of time in his room, and we had to make up all kinds of stories about class projects and math tutoring."

Again my eyes were drawn to the peaceful scenes beyond the highway. Light brown cows were standing together in small groups, their bells ringing plaintively. Carpets of bright pink impatiens blanketed the plots beside wooden farmhouses. A farmer was climbing up on the seat of his tractor.

"Hey, Reba—" Arlene called. "You hungry? I don't know about you, but there's a restaurant up ahead and I'm ready to take a walk and get some grub!"

I glanced across the car at Arlene and realized that for the first time in more years than I could remember, somebody was looking out for me and expecting nothing in return. Maybe—just maybe—this is how it really felt to have a friend.

Berne, the capital of Switzerland, is an old city nestled on a plateau near the Alps. Elegant cobblestone streets bordered by stone buildings lead to the city center, where the huge domed government building looms over a deep green ravine. Living on the border between the German- and French-speaking regions of the country, the people of Berne seem used to the many guests who roam their streets. Arlene and I had no trouble getting directions to the prison where Joseph was being held.

It was just after ten o'clock in the morning when we arrived at the building, a modern brick structure with dark windows and ten-foot-high steel gates. Several police cars were parked in the drive, and an armored vehicle stood grumbling beside the entrance.

We parked in the visitor's lot and made our way to the front doors together. Arlene had changed from her loose-fitting traveling clothes to a gray pantsuit and covered her braids with a scarf when we'd stopped for breakfast. I, too, had put on fresh clothes, choosing a navy skirt and jacket with a comfortable sleeveless blouse. I'd washed my face and put on very light makeup. This was an occasion for absolute professionalism, not forty-two-year-old vanity.

We entered the building and found ourselves in a small antechamber. A guard's station stood to the right, so I squared my shoulders and led the way directly to the officer.

"Good morning," I said confidently. "I have come to request an interview with a prisoner."

The man looked up. He was in his fifties, with a carefully trimmed mustache and cold blue eyes. "Whom do you wish to see?" he asked in heavily accented English.

"Mr. Yusef Vai, of Liberia."

"You are his lawyer?"

"I am an advocate for detainees' rights," I answered, placing one of my business cards on the officer's desk. "This is my assistant," I added, gesturing toward Arlene.

He looked at the card, typed something into his computer and watched the screen for a few moments. Then he picked up the phone. A short conversation ensued in which he responded in monosyllables. Arlene cocked her head, listening intently, and once again I was terribly glad she spoke German.

"You may visit Mr. Vai for one-half hour," the officer finally announced, hanging up the phone. "He has his routine exercise hour at eleven o'clock each day, and we do not normally allow any changes in the scheduling."

I nodded and stole a glance at Arlene. Her brow furrowed as the officer searched our bags, spending some time on my briefcase. He then led us through a doorway and into a corridor marked by offices bearing long German titles.

At last he unlocked the door to a windowless white room furnished with a rectangular metal table. There were four chairs and a video camera mounted on the ceiling. It was not unlike the conference rooms where I met detainees at home.

Arlene and I sat down. I glanced at my watch; it was 10:20 A.M. How much time would we lose while waiting for them to bring Joseph from his cell? Would they explain to him that someone had come from the States to see him? Would he be afraid when they broke with his normal schedule by ordering him to follow them to an unknown location?

"How're you doing?" Arlene asked me gently.

I peered across at her in surprise, having forgotten that she was there. Looking down, I saw that my hands were clasped so tightly that my knuckles were white. Perspiration wreathed my forehead. I didn't trust myself to speak.

"Reba," she murmured, "you've worked with political refugees for years. Stay calm. You can handle this."

Five minutes passed. Then ten.

The door suddenly jerked open and a pair of uniforms stepped inside. They were followed by a very thin, very old man in an orange prison overall. I started at the vision of white hair, skeletal cheeks and haunted, protruding eyes that fastened on mine. He wavered, grasping at the back of a chair for support. His mouth opened and I saw that both of his front teeth were gone.

There had certainly been some mistake! This man wasn't Joseph Thomas! At least, he wasn't *my* Joseph!

"Reba—is it really you?"

My heart nearly leapt out of my chest with those words. I was out of my chair and around the table so fast that the guards couldn't stop me before I was in his arms. Despite the fact that his bones felt like matchsticks, he held me with the force of a vise. He pressed his face desperately into my hair and I felt his heart thumping against mine.

"*Entschuldigen Sie!*" one of the guards snapped. "*Sie duerfen sich nicht umarmen! Jeglicher Kontakt zwischen Gefangenen und Besuchern ist verboten!*"

"Reba," Arlene said calmly. "You've got to stop or they might take him away."

I reluctantly released him and he carefully let go of me. I stepped back and looked into the ghost of the young man I had once known—the wasted phantom of the man I loved.

"*Nehmen Sie auf der anderen Seite des Tisches Platz,*" the guard said coldly.

"He's instructing you to sit down on the other side of the table," Arlene translated. The guard looked at her and continued to speak. She nodded, then turned to me as I sat down.

"He says that we only have thirty minutes. There can be no physical contact between you and the pri—— Joseph—and we are only allowed to exchange materials that have been previewed by prison security."

"I understand," I said, nodding briefly to the guards.

The men withdrew, leaving the three of us alone. I was aware of the video camera poised on the wall directly over the table, and assumed that microphones were on. Joseph had lowered himself painfully into the seat in front of us and had placed his frail hands palms down on the table. His eyes were closed and I thought he might have been praying.

"How are you doing?" I asked, and found to my surprise that my nervousness had been replaced with a low-burning anger, fueled by the sight of his broken figure.

He didn't look up. "I am fairly well, as you can see."

"No, Joseph. I don't see that at all."

Slowly he raised his eyes. His pupils, yellowed by some un-known, and perhaps undiagnosed, illness, were filled with sadness. "I was confined in a Liberian prison for a few years before being turned over to the Swiss. Sometimes it became—difficult."

"What did they do to you?"

He spoke carefully, as if to hide his shattered smile. "It really doesn't matter now."

"Are you getting medical attention?"

"Yes. The Swiss have been most kind." He paused. "I did not think that you would come here."

"I told you I'd help. Didn't you believe me?"

He didn't answer, and for a long moment he stared at the floor as if unwilling to look into my eyes. And then I knew. He had nei-ther forgotten nor forgiven me for our past.

"I am glad to see you," he said, as if guiding the conversation away from the memories that still lay between us. "Thank you for coming."

"Don't talk to me as if I'm a stranger. You should have known that I wouldn't let you down!"

"Reba—" It was Arlene who was speaking, her voice a warning murmur. "Remember—others are listening."

Joseph's eyes flickered to her, and I saw his brows come to-gether thoughtfully. "You are from Baltimore. From Absalom Jones College, I believe."

"I'm Arlene Masters. You knew me during our freshman year. Then I got married and moved away."

"I see," Joseph replied. He looked back at me. "I never meant for you to find me."

"It wasn't easy," I admitted, glancing wearily at Arlene. "Now, Joseph—tell me what we can do for you. Your arraignment is the day after tomorrow."

"There's nothing to be done. The prosecution has offered me a plea bargain that would lead to a reduced sentence. With any luck, I will be able to return to Liberia in some years and live out the rest of my life there."

"A plea bargain?"

"Yes. I would plead guilty to a certain number of the accusations, allowing the court to close the books on the case. It appears that admitting partial responsibility might save the court from having to go through with a trial."

"But on the phone you said they don't have a case—"

"No, Reba," he quietly replied. "I told you that I am not guilty. The prosecution most certainly feels that it does have a case. And since there is no other defendant, I am likely to be found guilty as charged."

"But you can't accept responsibility for crimes you haven't committed!"

"My attorney believes it would be better for me to accept limited responsibility than to be found guilty for everything they are prepared to charge me with."

I stared at him blankly, my head beginning to ache with disbelief. "Your attorney is allowing you to plead guilty to *some* crimes, in order not to be convicted of *other* crimes, when you are innocent of *all* the charges?"

Again he looked down at the table. "Actually it was my idea to do so."

"Joseph," I said very softly, "please tell me the truth: Are you responsible for those killings?"

There was a long pause. Then he looked up slowly. "I would not lie to you, Reba," he said, his voice wavering slightly. "I swear on the love we shared that I have never been responsible for the death of another human being."

"You can't plead guilty to crimes you haven't committed. You must not throw your life away."

One of the guards stepped forward and tapped on his watch. Without another word Joseph began to rise.

"Do you hear me, Joseph? You cannot accept the plea!"

For what seemed like an eternity he didn't speak. Then he nodded slowly, with something of the old dignity returning to his face. "Can you come again?" he asked quietly.

"I'll be here tomorrow."

"Then I will think about it until then."

Arlene and I were staying at a Sheraton just outside the city. Our room was spacious, with a view toward the dome of the capitol.

"There's something mesmerizing about Switzerland," she commented as she sank down on one of the beds. "It's overpriced and overclean, but it certainly is peaceful."

"I don't need peace," I said as I stretched out on the other bed. "What I need right now is some way to keep Joseph from giving up."

"Well," Arlene replied, "I would start by finding out what's left of his old life. I got the distinct impression that he feels he has nothing to live for. Does he have a wife?"

"A wife?" I responded, scrambling to keep any hint of jealousy out of my voice. "I don't know. And there was nothing about his family in any of the articles you found." A vision of the old man in the prison came into my mind. "He must have gone through something terrible. I should have been in Liberia with him, Arlene. Maybe I could have prevented this from happening."

Her head snapped in my direction. "Reba," she said sharply, "don't waste time on talk like that! There's nothing you can do about the past. You should be glad that you're healthy, wealthy and powerful enough to help Joseph now."

"God knows I don't feel very powerful."

"That's because you've left your family, language and culture behind. You haven't seen this man in nearly twenty years. And you're up against a foreign legal system. But Reba—what Joseph needs right now is your moral support. The same clear-headed, down-to-earth openness he came to love all those years ago. He needs your courage and your strength, and I guarantee you those things haven't changed a bit with time. If they had, God wouldn't have guided you here."

I sat up slowly and let my head drop between my shoulders. "I don't know if that's completely true. You see, I'm great at work. I can handle refugees, government officials, even congressional committees. But my home life is a mess. Carl and I are still together, but things are bad between us. He has his own friends, his own social life, his own lovers—and I just pretend not to care."

She moved toward me and took my hands. "Do you love Carl?"

"I've spent my whole life with him."

"But do—you—love—him?" she repeated, emphasizing each word.

"Yes, Arlene, I do. But Carl blames everything that's wrong between us on the one thing I can't defend—the fact that I still care about Joseph."

"I see," she replied quietly. "Your first marriage has become something to be ashamed of."

"Yes. I've never been able to talk about my past, even to my own daughter."

"It's time to break the silence. Carl will never be able to accept your helping Joseph until he understands everything that happened twenty years ago. Maybe if you let go of your secrets, he won't feel the need to have secrets of his own."

She let out a sigh and, clucking like a mother hen, wrapped me up in a big hug. "Things are going to work out, Reba. But we have to get there first. Listen: I have an idea."

Arlene called the prison early the following morning and, using her excellent command of German, talked the official into allowing us to see Joseph for a full hour. When we arrived we were loaded down with bags—and the plan we'd worked out the night before.

Once again a pair of guards brought Joseph into the chamber. He looked even more tired than he had the day before—if that was possible—but there was a slight glimmer of light in his eyes. He sat down across the table and greeted us both politely, but his eyes lingered on me.

"How are you doing this morning, Joseph?" I asked in my calmest, most professional voice.

He smiled faintly, and I noted that his missing teeth had been replaced with a bridge. "I confess that I didn't sleep much last night. I kept thinking that I'd conjured you out of my fantasies and I might wake up to discover it was all a dream."

"Well," I said cheerfully, "it's okay if you'd rather think of us as your fairy godmothers. In fact, just to prove it, we've brought you some presents."

"Presents?" he asked in a cracking voice.

I glanced at Arlene, who was smiling broadly. "Yes. And they've all been examined and approved by Big Brother."

We pushed several plastic bags across the table. He looked puzzled, then reached forward with uncertain hands and opened the first bag.

Out came a snow-white button-down shirt.

"This reminds me of my days at Absalom Jones," he said with a faint smile. He opened the next bag and produced a gold and black striped tie.

"Oh, my," he said softly, picking it up with his twiglike fingers. "I believe these are our school colors."

"Yes," Arlene said. "Everyone back at home expects you to represent our alma mater proudly."

He looked at her quickly, his lips opening in surprise.

"There's a pair of slacks and a matching jacket in the other bags. I want you to try on the clothes," I said in a firm voice. "Arlene and I will wait in the hall, and if they don't fit we'll exchange them."

"But why?"

"Because you are not going into that court tomorrow in a guilty man's clothes."

Arlene and I stood silently in the hall while one of the guards watched Joseph change. We were strangely nervous about whether this makeover would actually serve any purpose at all. It had been Arlene's idea to buy the clothes, and I'd been shocked when she pulled the school tie from her bag. "I intended it to be a gift," she explained. "Now I see that it might serve a more important purpose."

The door opened abruptly and the guard motioned us inside. We found Joseph standing beside the table, an uncertain look on his face. The stooped posture we'd witnessed when he entered the room had vanished. He was standing tall, his hands at his sides. The shirt was a bit too large at the neck, but Arlene had guessed right about the size of the fine wool jacket and pants. They filled out his prisoner's frame and gave him the air of an aging academic. With a little bit more flesh on his face—and a decent haircut—he might even have been mistaken for a diplomat.

He hadn't managed to complete the knot of his tie, and instinctively I stepped forward to correct it.

"*Kein Kontakt, bitte!*" the guard warned, and I stopped just short of touching Joseph. We looked into each other's eyes, and my heart began to pound uncontrollably.

"Well," Arlene said brightly. "I'd say we did a pretty good job. You look like a million dollars, Joseph."

His face melted into a smile. "It has been a long time since I have worn clothes such as these. I fear it will take some getting used to."

"Hang on," I said, "we're not finished with you yet." I reached into my bag and took out a new watch, a silver pen set, and a battery-operated hair trimmer. "Joseph," I said as I pushed the objects across the table, "I want you to ask someone to trim your hair properly before your court appearance tomorrow. You should also ask your lawyer for a decent notebook of some kind. I'll expect you to take notes during your hearing. And you must go to sleep early tonight so you'll be alert. I want everyone in the room to see you at your best."

"My best?"

"You can trust my advice. It's part of my job to help people prepare for court."

"I am ashamed that I have not asked you about your career. I have been very selfish with our limited time together."

"There will be plenty of time to talk about me in the months to come. Today we only have about thirty minutes more to talk about you."

"Please excuse me," Arlene said quietly. "I think I'll find the ladies' room." She stood up and said something to the guards, and one of them opened the door so that she could leave.

I took Arlene's files from my briefcase and laid them on the table. Then I looked directly into Joseph's eyes.

"I know I'm not your attorney, Joseph. But in order to help you I've got to know what's happened over the past two decades."

I opened the file and slid the article from *The World Church* across the table. Joseph looked down at himself as a much younger, bearded man, his arms spread wide around the children who so obviously loved him. His lips moved slowly as he read the caption beneath the photograph:

> *Schoolmaster Joseph Thomas conducts courses in reading and agronomy in his Liberian Learning Institute. Mr. Thomas is the recipient of the Church of England's Queen's Medal for his dedication to spreading literacy in his native Liberia.*

For a long moment, neither of us spoke. Then he sighed.

"In 1985 I received the commission I'd been hoping for from the church. After a year of training in Monrovia I traveled to the northernmost region of my country to open my school. I instructed the children during the day and taught their parents at night. There had been a school there some time before, and some of the older children helped me with the beginners.

"Of course, such things go very slowly. The parents were hesitant to release the older boys from helping out in the fields, and most of the girls were needed at home to care for infants. I had to convince some of the older women to create a nursery so the girls could be excused from their duties for several hours a day. And holding classes in the evenings meant that I was teaching both day and night. There was little time for anything else, but I must say I was very satisfied with my life."

Slowly I pulled out the *New York Chronicle* article and its blurred photograph of a blood-smeared man bearing a child's lifeless body from a scene of flames and rubble.

Joseph looked at the photograph for a long moment. Then, as if forcing himself to face the past, he began reading the article aloud.

> *"Our people are peaceful. . . . We have nothing to do with the struggle for power in the capital. We merely want to take care of our families and lead quiet lives."*

Tears formed in his eyes, and he didn't look up.

"I don't even remember exactly when the fighting started. We watched it on the television as if it was worlds away. We refused to believe that it would ever come close to our village or affect our way of life."

He paused. "And then, one day, the soldiers arrived. In a matter of hours they had burned everything and taken the life of anyone who stood in their way."

"Why your village?"

"Why *any* village? They wanted food, money and young men for their army. They assaulted the women and burned our homes after trapping many of our people inside."

"Where were you when this happened?"

"I led the children into the school, hoping they would be safe. But the soldiers mortared the building. Most of them died when the roof collapsed. The others passed away within hours without medical attention." His head lolled to the side and he traced out an invisible name on the tabletop with one unsteady finger. "It really was for the best. Their parents were already dead."

I pressed my feet into the floor as hard as I could to stop myself from reaching out to touch him. Without speaking I slid the 2000 article from *The Global Review* toward him.

REBEL FORCES STORM AREA
NEAR LIBERIAN CAPITAL

MONROVIA, LIBERIA (FPF)—*Authorities state that a rebel group has gained new ground in fierce fighting near the capital. The group, which calls itself the Rimka Liberation Front, is led by a former teacher, Yusef Vai, who lived in the United States before returning to run a school in rural Liberia. Reached in his temporary headquarters in Taylorville, some ten miles from Monrovia, Vai stated that the government's inability to bring its militia groups under control required the formation of a resistance movement.*

Joseph read the first paragraph and smiled darkly. "Yes," he whispered, peering at the print.

"What happened then, Joseph?"

He looked up at me, and something in his eyes had changed. I saw a stony resolve, distant and cold, in his gaze.

"Those of us who survived decided that we had to do something to defend ourselves. We had to protect the other villages from the slaughter. So we armed ourselves and began to fight back."

"You planned to take power in Liberia?"

"No. We didn't even want to leave our region. Our only goal was to rid the area of those marauders who preyed on civilians."

"Then you *were* involved in the things described in this article?"

"I was involved in describing them."

"I don't understand."

"I am saying that much of this is pure propaganda, intended to give the impression that our movement was much grander, and more powerful, than it ever really was."

"Then it's not true?"

"We were poor and untrained. Although many survivors from other villages joined us, we were never a true militia."

"But you engaged in combat—"

"We managed to defeat our enemies when we encountered them by chance. But we spent much of our time roaming the countryside, trying to defend other villages. After all, we had no home to return to."

He picked up the article and began reading aloud.

"Over the past decade Liberia has seen violence unlike anything in her entire history," he said. "Such inhumanity necessitates swift and definitive retaliation. My organization will work to restore peace and bring an end to the cruelties that have become a routine part of Liberian life."

"Those are my words, Reba. I was the spokesman because I was the only one who had the education and the ready facility with the Queen's English to make an impression on our enemies. The reporters came to me because I could explain the conflict in terms their readers could understand. Because believe me, when you're in the middle of a war, you understand almost nothing."

"But what kind of 'swift and definitive retaliation' did the Rimka Liberation Front undertake?"

Our eyes locked for a long moment and I was frightened by what I saw in his gaze.

"Joseph," I said very softly, "you can trust me."

"It is not a question of trust," he answered coldly. "Every person who is drawn into such a conflict is changed, Reba. I am not the same man you once knew."

"Then tell me who you are. Help me understand."

"Understand?" he repeated, his voice flat. "How can you understand? You have spent the past twenty years in safety and security, untouched by the horrors faced by so many in this world. You can't even imagine the things I have witnessed in my own nation, committed by my own people, against those who were helpless—"

"You don't know anything about my life!" I said sharply, feeling the door to my cave spring open. "I'm not that naive young woman you used to know."

There was a moment of stony silence as we stared into each other's eyes. Then he leaned back in his chair and lowered his gaze.

"After six years of fighting, my men were tired. We could barely remember what it meant to have a normal life. We wanted to do something definitive—something to convince the government to end the fighting.

"When we arrived in that village outside the capital we learned that the government was amassing its soldiers for a full attack. I was opposed to any military action that might lead to the death of civilians, but some of our younger soldiers did not share my views. They believed that with the help of the villagers, we could take Monrovia.

"We argued well into the night. Most of the older men agreed that we should retreat. The younger men wanted to fight, but they saw that they could not face our enemies with only a portion of our soldiers."

He sighed, and the sound rattled as if he had only half a lung.

"At dawn the Rimka Liberation Front split into two factions. I departed with the older soldiers, and we began a march toward the north. Our only desire was to find our surviving relatives and begin building our villages anew. The younger men went east, hoping to gather new recruits and continue the struggle. Word came to us of fighting in other parts of the country, but we paid little heed to the news. After so many years, we only wanted peace.

"And then one morning we woke up to find ourselves surrounded. We were taken in military vehicles to the capital. I did not understand why we weren't summarily executed—that was, after all, the fate of most of the captured who were seen as rebels. Instead, we were imprisoned and repeatedly interrogated. After three years I was handed over to the international court and brought here to stand trial."

"Is it possible that the other faction of the RLF killed those villagers?" I asked, staring into his eyes.

"I do not believe the villagers died at the hands of our soldiers."

"But you can't be sure."

"My men would never wound or kill civilians."

"Then why would you consider pleading guilty to any part of these charges?"

Joseph's gaze softened and he lowered his head to his hands. His shoulders began to shake and his sobs echoed weirdly around the airtight room. One of the guards came forward and touched his back, speaking in a low, polite tone.

"You wish to go to your cell now?"

Shaking his head, Joseph wiped his eyes with the back of his hand. Slowly his face came up, and a very old man stared back at me.

"I have already lived my life, and I will accept this imprisonment so the other members of the RLF may go free."

"But you can't, Joseph."

"Yes, Reba. It is fitting."

"How can you say that?"

There was one final pause as he slowly pushed his chair away from the table and rose to his feet. "I can say it because one of those soldiers was my son."

I didn't realize that I had risen too, until I felt the world vanish from beneath my feet. The dizziness made me lurch forward and I had to grasp the edge of the table to keep from falling forward.

Joseph saw what was happening and took my arm to steady me. Both guards moved quickly to his sides.

"I am sorry," he said as he released me, letting his arms drop. "I did not mean to tell you in this way."

"I didn't know that you have a family."

"I *had* a family. The others are dead."

"Where is your son?"

His unhealthy eyes flickered up to mine. "I cannot say."

"You mean that you don't know?"

"The Liberians tried to make me tell them," he whispered.

"They tortured you?"

His gaze went inward. "Let us say they were not always kind."

"If you can identify your torturers I will do everything in my power to find them."

"It would only cause more suffering, Reba."

"You're saying you won't let me help you?"

"I have already said too much," he answered, his expression closed.

"You can't do this," I said, my voice uncharacteristically faint. "You can't go to prison for the others."

"I will be fine," he replied as he started to walk to the door.

"No—please! Please promise me that you won't plead guilty until you've had the chance for a trial."

"I will make no promises, Reba."

"Then let me speak to your son. He may know who killed those villagers."

Joseph's face closed.

"Where is he?" I cried. "Maybe he can stop this from happening!"

"Reba," he said with a sudden coldness, "I forbid you to involve yourself more deeply in this matter."

"You what?"

"I forbid you to pursue any action that might draw you more deeply into my troubles."

"But why?"

"You have other responsibilities and I assure you that I can take care of myself."

"But you can't allow the murderers to go free. If you sacrifice yourself, the killers will go on killing. Is that the way to help your people? The way to help yourself?"

He stopped at the door and considered me for a moment. "Go back to your world, Reba. That is where you belong."

Chapter 6

Baltimore, Maryland

1981

I thought my heart would batter a hole in my chest as I filed out of the airplane behind the line of sluggish travelers. Though the flight from Detroit to Baltimore International took less than two hours, I couldn't wait to get back to my sophomore year. I had managed to survive the summer months by accepting a job in my mother's office and putting in as much overtime as possible, thus staying out of my father's sight. I kept my room clean, held a book in front of my face and didn't even complain when they suggested I go out on dates with a local minister's son.

Joseph wrote to me from Liberia at least twice a week, and often more than one letter would arrive on the same day. His missives, etched with a fountain pen on cracking-thin onionskin paper, were like a secret map to the plethora of emotions he felt as he put his life in America—and his love for me—into perspective. I wrote him nearly every day, but it was clear that he didn't get many of my letters. He warned me that the mail service in Liberia was much slower and less reliable than that of the United States, and that I shouldn't be troubled if he didn't respond to everything I wrote. He wanted me to know that he could feel how much I loved him, even though we were thousands of miles apart, and he only wished that he could afford to hear my voice.

I collected all four of my bags from the airport carousel and

paid a skycap to wheel them out to the taxis. There was no sign of Carl Thornton this time, nor of any other student from Absalom Jones. Still, I moved with the confidence of a world traveler, my thoughts fixed on the things that Joseph had shared with me over the summer.

Reba, my love, he had written from Monrovia.

I am afraid that I will never make an adequate clerk—I make more mistakes on this typewriter than I can count, and some of my coworkers are finding it hard to believe that I really am a student in the United States.

Typing out invoices in an office all day has given me plenty of time to think about all the things I want to do when I return to AJC this fall. I would like to pursue some courses in math and accounting, so that I will be better prepared to set the budgets for my school once I'm a teacher. I also want to visit Philadelphia and New York, and perhaps even Boston. This will require some economies on my part, for I find that travel is particularly expensive, but I'm trying to put in enough extra hours to allow me more freedom during the upcoming academic year.

Most of all, I want to spend more time with you. It was fine for us to meet after our classes, stealing a few hours in the library after finishing our coursework, and to take those long walks in the city. But I think that the first blush of our feelings should now move on to a greater understanding of each other as individuals. I had not realized until I met your parents how difficult it must have been for you to go against any of their expectations. I hope that our relationship has not caused you a great deal of trouble at home. I fear that despite my best intentions, my presence was troubling to your father.

Finally, I find myself assailed with thoughts of touching

you—despite the fact that I managed a great deal of restraint when we were together this past year! I miss your eyes, your voice, your gentle fingers. I have a deep longing for all the rest, too—but I'd better not go into that, in case this letter falls into the wrong hands!

I visited my family last week, and they were all well. They send their greetings to their "daughter in America," and charged me to express their hope that they will meet you soon. Of course, their words are but an echo of my own deep desire. I hope that you are safe and well, dear Reba.

Please remember that I will always love you.

Your Joseph

The taxi seemed to take another two hours to make the twenty-mile trip into Baltimore, and by the time it entered the college gates I was almost giddy with anticipation. The gracious oak trees still dipped their full leaves low over the driveway, and the Commons was speckled with orange-red splashes of late summer mums. A few students were stretched out in the grass; others tossed a football while Kurtis Blow belted "The Breaks" from a portable tape player.

The taxi came to a stop in front of Merriman Hall and I climbed out, looking eagerly across the Commons. As the driver placed my suitcases on the sidewalk, I still craned my head toward Allen Hall, which was where Joseph would be living. It was only when the car had driven away that I heard a voice behind me, and I wheeled around to find Samantha—her flowing hair bleached a light brown with blond highlights—speaking loudly to a man who was following her.

"You shouldn't have gone home so soon," she said in a chastising tone. "Things really heated up after those folks from Howard arrived. I mean, it got so hot that we stripped down to our—"

She was wearing a loose-fitting halter top that emphasized her melon-shaped breasts. Her white pants pulled tight at the hips and thighs, and a sliver of sun-browned skin was teasingly visible at her belt. She glanced over at me and interrupted herself.

"Well, look who's here—Little Miss Motown herself!"

Carl Thornton's eyes met mine as he glanced over Samantha's round shoulder. He had grown a mustache that curled gently toward his soft lips, and his hair was clipped in tight waves that swept back from his forehead. It seemed to take him a moment to recognize me, but then he broke into his glorious smile.

"Dang, Reba! Detroit must have been *real* good to you this summer!"

I wasn't sure what he meant, but the fact that Samantha's eyes had narrowed to a squint probably meant that I looked better than either one of them expected. Still, she opened her arms and gave me a hug.

"Is that what they're wearing in Michigan?" she asked with a glance at my white blazer and neatly pressed jeans.

Ignoring her, I directed my attention to Carl. "How was your summer?"

"Great. I worked as a sales rep for my father. I got to visit New York, Los Angeles and Chicago."

"Not Detroit?"

"No. And I didn't find any particular reason to make it down to Atlanta," he said with a sly wink.

Samantha put her hands on her hips, determined to regain control of the conversation. "Check this out, Reba: I've just managed to snatch one of the three single rooms in the dorm."

"How'd you do that?" I asked, truly impressed.

"I know someone who knows someone who was willing to do me a favor," she retorted with a laugh. "My room is going to be Party

Central. No more egghead roommates to make me feel guilty about not getting enough sleep."

"It really *would* be a shame if you actually learned something while you're here," I said, turning back to my suitcases.

"The trick," Carl offered as he bent to pick up one of my bags, "is to find a way to do both."

"First you have to have the brains to do the schoolwork."

"News bulletin!" Samantha snapped. "Men don't care what's in your head."

"That depends on the man."

Both Samantha and I turned to Carl, whose grin had frozen. He lifted my suitcase over his chest like a shield. "Don't look at me," he laughed. "I'm just the bellboy."

"Reba?" Joseph's voice seemed to crack through the tension like a laser. I wheeled around to find him standing just behind me, a bouquet of roses in his hands.

He hugged me. Samantha snorted sarcastically, and even then he didn't let me go. Carl stood beside her, still holding one of my suitcases. "I guess you won't need my help getting this to your room," he said, setting it down to shake Joseph's hand.

"We'll be fine, Carl," I answered. "You two can get back to your fascinating conversation."

"Our pleasure," Samantha said.

She swung away with Carl walking reluctantly behind her. I gave my attention to Joseph.

He held me away from him, looking down into my face.

"You *have* changed, Reba," he said in his most private voice, and again I wondered what everyone saw in me. True, I'd had my hair cut short, which seemed to bring out my eyes, and I'd really learned to wear makeup while working with the secretaries in that office all summer. I'd also gained some inches in my bust and hips while sitting at that desk all day. But it was obvious that both Samantha and Joseph saw something different—something more—than even I was aware of.

"When did you get back?" I asked him as we lifted my belongings and began walking into the dorm.

"Just yesterday. And I have a surprise, too. The men's dorm reserves a single room for the student with the highest grade point average in each class. And I am the sophomore with the best GPA."

"You have a single?"

"Yes, so we'll finally be able to—" He paused, gazing down at me with smoldering eyes.

"To what?" I repeated innocently, almost walking headlong into the door of my own room. Desiree was lying on one of the beds, cradling the phone against her cheek. She leapt up, squealing, and threw her arms around my neck as if I was her long-lost sister.

"You're back, Reba! I'm *so* glad to see you! And I've got so much to tell you! Guess what?" She pointed excitedly to the phone, which she'd crushed against her breasts. "I'm going out with Monroe Simmons! He's finer than fine! My mother even likes him!"

Joseph gave me an amused glance and set my suitcases on the floor beside the other bed. Sighing, I glanced around the room, which was smaller than the triple I'd shared the year before, but had a view over the entire Commons. Ignoring Desiree's excited chatter, I turned to look at tall, lean, beautiful Joseph, hardly able to believe that I was back in Maryland and he was there, standing before me. It seemed that all was right in my world, and I couldn't ask for anything more.

The summer faded into autumn, then rolled toward winter with astounding speed. Joseph and I went about our life together, studying hard, enjoying each other's company, barely aware of the other students.

Then one night I found myself in the library, waiting in my usual quiet corner for Joseph to arrive from his dormitory. A shadow fell over my geography assignment, and I looked up to find Carl standing over me, a history textbook clasped in his arms.

"Mind if I sit down?" he asked, indicating Joseph's seat.

"Well, in a minute—"

"I know. I can warm it up for him."

I nodded my approval and he settled into the chair across from mine, glancing down to see what I was studying.

"World geography? You joining the Peace Corps?"

"Just getting ready for whatever comes down the road."

"You don't need to know the latitude of Burkina Faso!"

"You never know, Carl."

"Come on, Reba. Some stuff's just a waste of time."

"I used to feel that way about my studies, then—"

"You met Joseph." Carl cocked his head and observed me casually. "I don't see how you have time to be in a relationship when you're so busy studying. Don't you ever just take it easy?"

"You've got to take some things seriously," I answered, my eyes already straying over his shoulder in the hope of spotting Joseph.

"I take lots of things seriously, even if I don't necessarily show it."

"Looks to me like you're always more interested in having a good time, Carl."

"I'd quit it all in a heartbeat if the right woman came along."

"You're so busy partying that you wouldn't know her if you met her."

"You're wrong, Reba. When I'm with that woman, nothing else will matter. I'll only be focused on one thing—building a life with her."

"The famous Carl Thornton is planning to settle down with one woman?"

"My woman will never have to worry about anything. I'm going to give her everything that she wants and needs."

He must have seen the look of disbelief in my eyes, because he went on without pausing. "Look, Reba. Where I come from, a man isn't a man unless he pledges his father's fraternity, plays golf on the weekends and always owns the newest Cadillac. The men in my world love to look at beautiful women, listen to good jazz and live in great big houses."

He lowered his voice. "But there really is more to me than just that stuff. I mean, I respect my parents and everything, but, Reba— this is *my* life, and I'll decide how I'm going to live it—and who I live it with!"

"So you're not going to marry that girl down in Atlanta?"

He shrugged. "She's just doing what her parents want. She doesn't have the slightest idea who I really am. And what's worse"— he smiled dryly—"she doesn't even care, as long as I show up in decent rags and a fat ride."

"I'm sorry," I said clumsily.

"Why? It's not your fault. In fact, you probably know me better than anybody else on this campus."

"That's not true, Carl."

"Yes, it is. For some reason I always want to start telling you about myself, even though I know you're not even interested. To tell you the truth, you're one of the few people I know who really cares about somebody else. Just watching how much you and Joseph love each other is inspiring."

I felt myself flush with pleasure, but before I could reply Carl continued.

"You know, Reba—if you weren't already going with Joseph, I might just try to put in a good word for myself."

"That's crazy. I'm not your type."

"You're wrong about that. Don't look at me through those other girls' eyes."

"You're trying to tell me that you're really a quiet, serious guy?"

"I'm trying to tell you that I'd be whatever you needed if you gave me the chance."

"But love doesn't work like that, Carl."

"Then show me how it works, Reba."

"I can't."

"You could—"

We were both suddenly aware of Joseph, who was standing a few feet away from the table. Carl almost leapt out of his seat. "Just warming it up for you, brother."

Smiling politely, Joseph walked forward and set his books on the table. Carl paced backward a few steps. "Nice talking to you, Reba," he said pleasantly. Then he smiled broadly and walked away.

Joseph's single room was a miracle in disguise. Facing the front of the Commons, the small chamber was always bathed in the warm sun or the cool moonlight. His single also meant that we were finally able to spend a great deal of time alone. Of course, I couldn't be there with him overnight, but we squeezed out plenty of daylight hours to teach each other the ways of love. His gentle strength in dealing with the outside world translated to the bedroom, and I felt wholly safe and at peace when I was in his arms.

Joseph was exceedingly patient with the bawdy teasing he underwent from the other men, and following his lead, I learned to ig-

nore the snide comments made by the women. Desiree was so involved in her long-distance romance—Monroe Simmons turned out to be an undertaker's son from the next county in North Carolina—that she barely noticed my absences. And if the college administration noticed, no one objected to the time I spent in Joseph's room. After all, Joseph and I were two of the best students at Absalom Jones, and plenty of other students were partying their way straight to dismissal.

At Christmas I took the bold move of inviting Joseph home with me. Our house was large enough to easily welcome a guest, and there was, in my mind, no reason for him to remain in Baltimore alone.

I explained to my mother that I wanted to bring Joseph to Detroit to see how we celebrated the holidays. I told her that he had never been in a clergyman's home in the United States, and that he had never seen the north. I arranged for the two of us to ride up to Cleveland along with a classmate who was driving home for the holidays, then to catch the Greyhound for the rest of the trip to Detroit. Although not convinced that my father would approve, my mother reluctantly agreed.

It was snowing when the bus reached the terminal in downtown Detroit. Colored lights were blinking in the windows of Hudson's, and shoppers and businesspeople alike were bundled up in woolens and fur. Joseph had borrowed a heavy overcoat from a professor who often visited his family in New York, but he had no scarf or hat and I could tell that he was shocked by the biting cold. "How do you live in this?" he exclaimed as we stood in the doorway of the bus station, waiting for my father to arrive.

Soon Joseph was staring from the windows of my father's enormous Continental with a bewildered look on his face. Our journey took us through some of the most destitute parts of the city—large, darkened neighborhoods abandoned since the time of the riots. The remaining rafters of burned-out buildings rose like broken spines in the swirling snow, with rusting automobile carcasses strewn along the streets. Corner stores with neon liquor signs were festooned with beer posters showing sinuous black women in carnival makeup who beckoned to us. A few men in bundled rags were gathered around garbage can fires and starving dogs ran wild up alleys. My father, who had turned the car radio to an all-news station, remained stubbornly silent.

We passed by the hulking hangars of factories hunkered down behind walls of barbed-wire fencing. Rows of small wooden houses, their doors and windows barred with iron grillwork, fanned out in the nearby streets. Most were draped in blinking lights or decorated with life-sized plastic Santas listing weirdly in drifts of snow. Sedans rolled past us with music pounding so hard that we could feel the vibrations in our car. Storefront churches with overflowing parking lots and schools with boarded-up windows met our gaze. I was acutely aware of the poverty of my city as I saw it through Joseph's eyes.

I was relieved when we came to the intersection of Livernois and Seven Mile Road, the invisible boundary between working- and middle-class Detroit. Handsome brick stores and shining car dealerships stood shoulder to shoulder with medical and dental practices. Schools in clean, modern buildings with wings specifically dedicated to music and sports were stretched across wide, landscaped campuses. The houses became grander and the automobiles much sleeker with every block.

We finally arrived in our handsome, tree-lined neighborhood of perfectly groomed brick Tudors. The lawns and shrubbery bordering the brick homes were professionally maintained, even with their carpets of snow, and cheerful decorations adorned the windows of nearly every home. Cadillacs were parked nose to tail along the curbs, and warm light poured from windows with their curtains drawn back to welcome the curious gaze. All of the living rooms sported enormous Christmas trees, and many were warmed by roaring fireplaces.

My mother welcomed us at the kitchen door in her apron while my father vanished without a word into his study. The house smelled of gingerbread and roasting lamb, and warm cider was simmering on the stove. I knew that she was trying hard to welcome Joseph to our home, despite my father's rudeness.

"Did it snow all the way from Maryland?" she asked cheerily as she busied herself with our coats.

"Only after Cleveland," I said, automatically heading for the refrigerator to scrounge something to eat. Joseph stood in the large, brightly lit kitchen, an expression of fatigued politeness on his face.

"You just get out of there!" my mother chided when she caught me with a plate of cookies. "Those are for the choir meeting this evening!"

"Can't we just have a couple?" I pleaded, instantly reverting to my childhood behavior.

"You two should just go into the living room and sit down. I'll bring you something to snack on in a moment."

I led Joseph across the tiled foyer and into the living room— which Mom was very proud of—and settled him into an overstuffed armchair. I saw his eyes wander over the matching sofa and loveseat. All were upholstered in a soft blue chintz that matched her sapphire velvet curtains and the sea blue rug. Photos of our family going back several generations stared down from every table, shelf and cabinet. Even the top of the piano had become a spectator zone.

Through the open beveled glass doors he could see into the formal dining room, which was filled with ceremonial dishes my mother had collected from various events over the years. She'd had oak cabinets with little internal spotlights built into each corner, and her heavy oak table was set with an ornate Advent wreath draped with holly and red ribbons.

"You have a beautiful home," he said.

"It's my mother's masterpiece," I whispered as she busily appeared with mugs of warm cider and slices of homemade gingerbread. She sat daintily on the chair across from him and smiled.

"It's so nice that you could come home with Reba. I understand this is your first time seeing snow."

"Yes, it is," he said, trying to eat the cake and respond politely at the same time.

"And have your studies been going well this year?"

"Yes, ma'am. I hope to begin my education courses when I return in January."

"And you've found some time to enjoy yourself?"

"Yes. I have particularly enjoyed visiting museums in Washington."

"Have you pledged a fraternity? I'm fully expecting Reba to join my sorority this year," she said with twinkling eyes.

"I was, indeed, invited to pledge by one of the men on our campus, but I haven't made a decision about it yet."

"You were?" I asked, turning to him in surprise.

"Yes. Carl Thornton offered to sponsor me for his fraternity."

"I remember Carl!" my mother exclaimed before I could answer. "He was such a charming young man! Is Carl a friend of yours?"

Surprised by my mother's sudden burst of enthusiasm, Joseph paused. "Carl and I have taken several classes together," he said reservedly.

"He seemed like a very special fellow. I'm sure that he'd be a very good person to teach you all about American culture."

"Joseph's doing just fine without Carl," I replied, irritated.

"But your college friends stay with you for life," my mother continued in a rolling, maternal voice. "My college roommate at Tuskegee was the maid of honor at my wedding and later became Reba's godmother."

Joseph smiled politely. "I count several students and faculty members as friends."

"Are you getting along well with your roommate?"

"Yes, we continue to be friendly, although we no longer room together. Due to my high grade point average, I have been given the honor of living by myself."

"You're living alone?" my mother answered, swinging her eyes in my direction. "Reba didn't mention that to me." I pushed myself more deeply into the mushy sofa, feeling the interrogation of her gaze. To my credit, I managed to meet her eyes without looking either at Joseph or the floor.

"The major advantage of living alone is that I can study very late without disturbing anyone," Joseph said, trying to regain my mother's attention. "Last year I had to finish all of my schoolwork before the library closed because it was impossible to work in my dorm room."

"Well, I'm glad that living alone has made it possible for you to"—she paused for emphasis—"get more *things* done. Reba," she said in a strained voice, "could you come and help me set the table?"

She followed me into the dining room and closed the heavy glass doors behind us.

"Just what do you think you're doing, young lady? You're much too young to be getting seriously involved with anybody on that campus."

"I don't know what you're talking about," I said, taking a handful of silver cutlery from the sideboard and dumping it on the table.

"Joseph and I spend all of our time doing schoolwork, which is why you sent me to college."

"Don't get cute with me, Reba Janette! I suspect that you and Joseph are doing much more than calculus, and I don't want you to make any mistakes that might ruin your life."

"I'm not going to ruin my life!" I cried, and she put her hands on her hips.

"Don't speak to me in that tone of voice! I'm only saying what any mother would say to a headstrong nineteen-year-old who knows nothing about the world."

I glared at her without speaking.

"Reba," she continued, her voice softening. "Your father and I always hoped that you'd find somebody and settle down near us. When the time comes we want to be a part of our grandchildren's lives. When your father retires you might even want to move your family into this house. That way you wouldn't have a mortgage and your kids could go to private schools."

"You're moving way too fast for me!" I complained, holding my hands up defensively.

"I'm not too sure about that. I don't want you getting brainwashed by that man from the other side of the world. Your future is right here, with your family and community."

"Mom, you've got to let me decide about that."

"We're perfectly willing to let you make all your own decisions after you've finished school," she said. "But that might not happen if this man takes over your life."

"Joseph's the most dedicated student I know—"

"That may be true," she said, "but you're not ready for anything serious."

Joseph stood up when I got back to the living room. "I'm sorry," he whispered. "Perhaps I should have lied."

"You're the one who always says that a single lie can spoil a thousand truths. They would have found out eventually, anyway. And besides, having a roommate has never stopped anybody from having sex."

Dinner was predictably tense, despite my mother's attempts to welcome me home with my favorite foods. The rich aroma of her specialty, roasted lamb and potatoes, filled the dining room. We passed around a heaping bowl of wild rice with peas, followed by a basket of crisp home-baked biscuits with butter. Nat Cole—my parents' favorite singer—was crooning "The Christmas Song" on the ancient record player, and my mother's turquoise parakeet, Eloise, was chirping in her ornate brass cage in the corner.

Joseph ate his food slowly, with his impeccable manners, while my father talked endlessly about his church activities, patently ignoring our guest. Although I could tell my mother was still angry with me, she was more embarrassed by my father's deliberate rudeness, so she changed the subject.

"How do you celebrate Christmas in Liberia, Joseph?"

He set down his fork, wiped his mouth with his napkin and considered her question. "Well, there are always several celebrations. First, we have services in our parish, carried out in the traditions of the Church of England. Then our family gathers for a feast where we sing praises in our own language."

"Do you have something special to eat? Here we like turkey or honey-baked ham on Christmas."

"My family refrains from eating pork," Joseph said, "but naturally we have very special meat dishes and spiced cakes during the Christmas season."

"Spiced cakes? I'd love to get some of your mother's recipes," she said warmly.

My father, whose face had darkened when my mother began talking to Joseph, shot out a question. "Why don't you eat pork?"

"The people in my village do not keep swine, so it is rare to find pork on any table."

"Are you Christian or Muslim?"

"We are Christian, sir, but we avoid foods that are easily contaminated and therefore dangerous to our health."

"I hope your people don't confuse Christian and Muslim traditions."

"Joseph isn't responsible for the traditions of his people," my mother said quietly.

"No," my father replied testily, "but I would ask him to examine the legitimacy of those traditions."

"There are lots of different ways to be a Christian," I said. "Joseph's village doesn't have to celebrate the holidays the way we do."

My father's eyes went hollow. "You have no business trying to explain the traditions of the church to me, young lady!"

"Raymond," my mother said, "Reba didn't mean it that way!"

"Yes, I did," I replied, staring across the table at my father. "You're sitting there pretending you're superior to all of us. But Jesus wouldn't want you to act this way to a guest in your own home!"

"Both of you should be ashamed of yourselves!" my mother scolded as she put down her napkin and rose from her chair. "I've never seen you behave this way in front of company."

"But Dad is not the only person who understands Jesus," I sputtered. "And Joseph isn't just *company!*" I retorted, turning to look at her. "You both should get used to the fact that he's a part of our family, because as far as I'm concerned, he's the most important thing in my life."

"Reba!" my mother said in shock.

"Mrs. Freeman—" Joseph's clear voice broke through the mounting layers of anger. "Reba is only suggesting that as I have no family in the States, I would be happy if you would think of me as a godson."

This pronouncement was met with a ringing silence. I was still staring at my mother, who was looking at my father. But my father's eyes were trained on Joseph. A few moments passed, and I realized that Nat Cole had stopped singing. Eloise had stopped chirping. We could hear the winter wind blistering the windowpanes.

"Our godson, eh?" my father said sarcastically. Joseph gazed at him, his face a study in honesty.

"Sir, I would never do anything to hurt your daughter or to dishonor your family. And since you are uncomfortable with my presence, I will take a bus back to Maryland tomorrow. I did not come here to cause you any trouble, and I apologize to you both if I have done so."

"No!" I stared open-mouthed at Joseph, who now turned to me.

"It is for the best, Reba."

"No, it's not," I repeated in a voice meant for him alone. My father heard the privacy in my tone and drew up his shoulders authoritatively.

"Just what exactly is going on between the two of you?"

"Isn't it obvious? I love Joseph, and if he'll have me, I intend to be his wife."

"Reba," Joseph whispered, registering his own surprise at my pronouncement.

"You *what?*" my mother sank into her seat.

"Reba," Joseph repeated, shaking his head in caution.

"No," my father said. "Let her talk. I want to hear everything my daughter has to say."

I snapped my head in his direction. "You heard me. I love him, and I'm going to marry him when we finish school."

"When did you two come to this decision?" he asked, his face frozen in a menacing smile.

"We—we haven't really decided—" I stammered, despite my best attempt at bravery.

"You've invited a stranger into our home and announced unexpectedly that this man is the person you plan to spend the rest of your life with—"

"Joseph isn't a stranger—"

"On the contrary," my father spat, "that's *exactly* what he is. I've spent no more than two hours with him. I know nothing about his family or his background, and you have no business bringing him here and asking me to give you permission to become his wife!"

"I'm not asking for your permission!" I shouted, pounding the table. "I spent my childhood trying to please you, but I'm not a little kid anymore. I'm old enough to make my own decisions. I love Joseph and there's nothing you can do about it!"

I knew that despite my claims of maturity, I was edging dangerously close to tears. I looked quickly at Joseph and was surprised to find that he was staring down at the tablecloth.

My father cleared his throat. All the air seemed to vanish from the room as he drew in a deep breath.

"You are absolutely wrong, young lady. There's a *great* deal that I can do about your obvious immaturity, evident disrespect and inexcusable rudeness."

"Raymond," my mother cautioned, "let's just stop for now and get a good night's sleep."

"Be silent, woman! I am speaking to my daughter!"

"But Raymond," she persisted, "we have a guest!"

"I have been led to believe that this young man is soon to be a part of our family," he said sarcastically, "in which case, he might as well get to know me.

"I have dedicated my life to two things: my ministry and my family. It is a life that I can be proud of. I have built a model of decency and humility within my home. Never have I tolerated the kind of disrespectful behavior that other people have come to accept as normal in their children.

"Reba Janette, I have provided you with food, clothing, education and a very fine home. You have wanted for nothing, and nothing was required except that you lead a good, Christian life. Now this evening you have repaid your parents' devotion by bringing a man we hardly know to our table and announcing, in defiance, that you plan to marry him. You have forgotten that there are proper and necessary requirements involved in a courtship. You have ignored the fact that we are still paying for your education, and thus deserve the opportunity to know who you are seeing. And finally, you need to remember that you have an obligation to your parents to study, graduate and obtain employment, because we have made everything possible in your life."

He paused to take a breath and my mother, making one final effort to rein in my father's anger, interrupted. "Raymond, Reba didn't say that she wants to marry Joseph right away. She said that they plan to wait until they've finished school."

"What do you have to say to all of this, young man?"

His eyes still fastened on the tablecloth, Joseph responded quietly. "I am sorry to have brought discord into your home, sir. That was never my intention." He looked up, his face calm and sad. "I intended no disrespect when I came here. But you should know that I do care very deeply for your daughter, and I hope that you will give me the opportunity to prove to you that I am worthy of becoming her life's mate."

"You hardly know my daughter—" my father began.

"I hope that, given time, that will change."

"You have absolutely no prospects in this country!"

"That is true, sir. But I am doing my utmost to prepare myself for the future."

"You cannot support her on a teacher's salary."

"I will be proud if Reba has her own career."

"And I will under no circumstances give you permission to take my daughter off to Africa."

"If you will excuse me," Joseph said very softly, "there are over thirty independent nations in Africa. Liberia is very different from some of the more politically unstable countries."

"That makes no difference to me. In my opinion, African Americans belong in the United States. We built this country and we deserve to reap the benefit of our forefathers' labor."

"Liberia was founded by African Americans," Joseph replied. "My forefathers also worked hard to make it one of the most modern nations on the continent."

"Then why did you come here?" my father snarled.

"I came because Absalom Jones College has educated some of the finest minds in America. I am proud to have this opportunity, and I am trying to learn as much as I can so that I might one day better serve my own community."

My father blinked several times, unable to respond to Joseph's selfless reply.

"Please excuse me," Joseph said as he rose with dignity and left the room. I stood up and quickly followed. He was already halfway up the steps, moving resolutely toward the guest room.

"Don't go!" I pleaded to his firmly set shoulders.

He paused at the top of the banister and turned to look down at me. His face was expressionless, but a universe of emotions passed though his eyes. "Reba, please call the bus station."

"No, Joseph!"

"You know very well that I must leave. This is your father's house and it would only create further tension if I were to stay."

"But this is my home, too!"

"I'm sorry. I must respect your father's wishes. Otherwise, he would be justified in objecting to our union."

"You mean that you're going to break up with me because he doesn't approve of our relationship?"

Joseph looked deep into my eyes. "I think," he said, choosing his words carefully, "that the differences in our cultures already pose many difficulties. If, in addition, we go against our families' wishes, it will make our relationship almost impossible."

"You're giving in to him?" I asked in a shocked whisper.

"No," he said. "The hunter who speaks too much returns home without food. I am merely withdrawing until I can find a better way." He walked to the door of the guest room, then turned back to face me as I stood rooted at the bottom of the staircase.

"By the way, you told your parents that you plan to be my wife. But I don't believe that I've asked you to marry me."

I dropped my eyes. There was a long silence—longer than any silence between us in all the months we'd been together.

"Reba Janette Freeman," he said, "will you one day do me the honor of becoming my bride?"

I looked up to find him gazing down at me with his calm, loving smile. I don't even remember shrieking as I clambered up the stairs, but I know that when my mother came out of the dining room to see what was going on I was still in Joseph's arms.

Although they had strictly forbidden any more talk about a "life-time" with Joseph, my parents had no way of stopping us from continuing our life together at Absalom Jones. Joseph and I spent every free moment together throughout that winter, and when we weren't studying for our classes, we luxuriated in the drowning pleasure of our love. Our feelings were so strong that we never even spoke about my father, whose threatening letters arrived with military punctuality. It seemed that the more my parents protested, the more certain we were of our feelings.

And then a certain kind of breeze, blowing away the winter cold on January 29, 1982, brought it all to a head.

A front of coastal air had blown up from the south, bringing with it a springlike sweetness. The air was prickly and warm and the earth smelled rich and damp, like a field after a rainstorm. After classes Joseph and I decided to get off campus for a couple of hours. The afternoon sun was unexpectedly warm, so I put on a skirt and a wool blazer, and he had on a pair of black trousers and his beloved hand-knitted sweater.

Soon we had passed through the college gates and were waiting at a bus stop. His arm was around my waist and he was describing the hot rains during the monsoon season in Liberia when a young couple came up pushing a baby carriage. The child was wrapped in a furry blue snowsuit with a matching cap, and Joseph told the mother that her baby was very beautiful. She thanked him and turned to me. "You two are going to have gorgeous kids, too!"

I looked up at Joseph, thinking he might be embarrassed, but instead I found his eyes filled with a deep, almost painful anticipation. And for the first time in my life I knew what it meant to be truly desired. The expression in his eyes was so intense that I began to ache somewhere in the depths of my body. I wanted to make a new life with him. I wanted to have his children and love him even more through loving them.

We were just standing there, and we both seemed to look up at the same moment. There, on the inside of the bus stop, was an advertisement for a wedding chapel in Elkton, Maryland, that issued instant marriage licenses. We both stared at the poster. Then we looked at each other.

"Reba?"

"Yes."

"Are you certain?"

"Absolutely."

We asked the young couple if they knew how to get to the chapel. They told us which buses to take, and within an hour we were standing at the chapel door.

As it turned out, the "chapel" was the front room of an old Victorian house. A white-haired man answered the door and ushered us warmly inside. He explained that the fee for the ceremony was $39. We could also spend the night in their house, which was actually a bed and breakfast, for $60, but of course Joseph and I had to get back to school.

We emptied out our pockets and discovered that we had just enough to cover the ceremony and get the bus tickets back to Baltimore. The old man smiled and assured us that his wife would be along to act as our witness as soon as she finished washing the dishes. We stood there looking around the room, which was papered in white brocade and decorated with satin draperies and overflowing pots of ivy. The old man busied himself with lighting rows of white candles and producing a corsage of pink carnations and baby's breath from a little fridge in the rear. He turned on a tape of quiet organ music.

A few moments later we were joined by our witness, a bustling elderly woman in a light blue dress. They introduced themselves— "Mr. Frank Hallworth, fully licensed and registered justice of the peace for Baltimore County, State of Maryland, and his wife, Sally Smith Hallworth, acting witness to the ceremony."

Joseph stood beside me in front of a white wooden podium. The justice took out a Bible and a smaller book, pressing it open to the Rite for the Joining of Couples in Holy Matrimony.

I felt Joseph's fingers entwining mine. He smiled down at me, and we repeated the vows in strong voices, without the slightest hesitation. When the time came he took off his one ring—a simple gold band given to him by his father—and slipped it on my finger. Then we sealed our bond with a kiss of dignity and love.

On the bus back to campus, we talked quietly about what we had just done.

"I don't think we should tell anyone yet," he suggested, his face close to mine. "The news will travel very fast to the administration, and I don't want to risk losing my scholarship."

"Do you think they would send you home?"

"I think your parents would try to make that happen," he answered. "And your father will certainly have some influence over the school."

"Then what do you think we should do?"

"Carry on as usual. We will have to be very mature, my love. Or perhaps I should say, my wife." He looked down at me, his eyes brimming with joy. "I hope that you will not regret this when you wake up tomorrow."

"Of course I won't!"

"We have defied your parents, Reba, and put our studies at stake."

"I've respected my parents' values by marrying the man I love! I'm not acting like a slut, like Desiree and Samantha!"

"Still, they will not easily accept the fact that we chose to marry without informing them."

"If my parents love me, they'll learn to accept the fact that I'm taking responsibility for my life. And you're a wonderful man, Joseph. I know that my father will eventually come to love you too."

He reached down and stroked my cheek. "I am richer by far than the most powerful king. I will never regret this day," he said very softly, "no matter what happens in the future."

We made it through the end of that long winter and into a brilliant spring. The morning that the semester ended, I took a deep breath and slipped my wedding ring onto my finger. I'd worn it on a chain beneath my clothes since that night in January, making sure that the only other person who ever saw it was Joseph. Of course, once I put it on my finger, Desiree instantly noticed the thick gold band, proving that she was watching me even more closely than I'd realized.

"What's that?" she asked, pointing at my hand.

"It's a ring."

"An engagement ring?" she asked, coming closer. "It doesn't have a diamond."

"It's not an engagement ring," I said, borrowing some of Joseph's extraordinary calm.

"But it's from Joseph, isn't it?"

"Yes. It was his father's."

"So you *are* engaged?" she shrilled, her eyebrows rising almost to her hairline.

"No, Desiree. We're married."

An instantaneous chain reaction was set off, and within minutes every student in the dorm had crowded into our tiny room to confirm what Desiree's hysterical shrieks had announced: *Crazy Reba Freeman eloped with her African!* This brought the dorm monitor to the door; she then sent me straight to the dean of students, who convened an emergency meeting in the administration building with Joseph, the chaplain and the president of the college.

A crowd assembled on the sidewalk outside the building while Joseph and I were grilled about our relationship. We could hear their voices as they milled around in the hot May sun, all hoping to be the first to get the news of our expulsion. Never had students defied the Absalom Jones College code of conduct by eloping, then returning to school to continue with their studies. Never had those students also managed, after breaking the rules, to continue to *adhere* to the rules by attending all classes, coming in by curfew and earning the highest grade point averages in the college.

Joseph and I were seated side by side in stiff wooden armchairs in the president's cobalt-carpeted, bay-windowed office. Photographs of the founders—craggy white men with abolitionist scowls and high-collared suit coats—surrounded us. President Saunders, a rotund man with thin brown hair combed over his delicately balding pate, and Dean Crawley, a handsome tennis ace who had been known to date the teachers, began to play interrogation tag with each other as they grilled us about the reasons for our elopement. My turn came first.

President Saunders: "Young lady, were your parents aware that the two of you were seeing each other?"

"Yes, sir."

Dean Crawley: "Then they've already met Joseph?"

"Yes, sir."

The president: "Did you have their permission to marry this young man?"

"No, sir."

The dean: "Are they aware that the two of you absconded from this campus and were secretly wed?"

"No, sir."

The president: "When, if ever, did you intend to tell them?"

"When the semester was over, sir."

"May I ask why you waited five months to share the news of your wedding with your mother and father?" That was President Saunders, speaking out of turn.

"Yes," I replied politely. "We knew that telling them would cause an uproar, and both Joseph and I wanted to focus on keeping our perfect grade point averages."

The president looked down at me in wonder, then cleared his throat in frustrated anger. He wheeled around on Joseph.

"Do you realize that the Bishop of Liberia might be disposed to withdraw your scholarship because of your unorthodox behavior?"

"Yes, sir."

Dean Crawley: "Do you realize that as a foreigner in this country you have no legal right to work, and therefore cannot support your wife?"

"Yes, sir."

President Saunders: "Do you have any other means of paying your tuition should the bishop refuse?"

"No, sir. But I am willing to do whatever you ask of me."

Dean Crawley: "Have you broken the rules of this institution by sleeping outside of your dorm room at night?"

"Of course not, sir."

The two men exchanged glances. Then they looked helplessly toward the chaplain.

He, too, cleared his throat, then finally spoke. "Have you—have you two—ummm—consummated your marital bond?"

There was a momentary silence as Joseph and I stole a glance at each other for the first time. I dropped my gaze modestly to the floor. Joseph nodded without speaking and lowered his eyes too.

At that point the chaplain began to bluster, asking us if we understood that Absalom Jones was a religious institution with a reputation to uphold in the community. The dean sent me straight to the clinic, where the school nurse was waiting to ask me a number of embarrassing questions before making me submit to a pregnancy test. When everyone was satisfied that Joseph and I had married out of love—not necessity—the debate began about whether our marriage was in itself grounds for expulsion.

Joseph and I once again sat with expressionless faces while the dean, who was outraged that this "breach of decorum" had happened on his watch, argued for our dismissal. However, the president, who realized we were two of the college's best students, suggested that they move a bit more slowly in coming to their decision.

The chaplain reminded them that I was a third-generation student, and as the president pointed out, Joseph and I were legally adults. The dean reluctantly agreed that there were no rules in the code of conduct that prevented *married* students from attending Absalom Jones—they were simply not allowed to live together in the dorms. My dorm monitor was then called in to confirm that I had never spent a night out of my bed. So, everyone concluded, there were no real grounds for my dismissal.

Joseph's case, however, was more complex. Because he was a scholarship student whose tuition was paid by the Bishop of Liberia, phone calls had to be made to Africa. Joseph and I sat in silence in an adjoining conference room, exchanging occasional glances of mutual encouragement, while the president held a closed-door telephone conversation with the bishop. After nearly an hour he returned to announce that the bishop was not opposed to our marriage, for it was common for students to marry young in Liberia. He agreed to continue to offer financial support for Joseph, and actually wanted to commend us both for managing to earn such excellent grades after taking on the added responsibilities of married life. The only thing he asked was that we present ourselves to the chapel to allow the chaplain to formally bless our union.

By the end of that sweltering afternoon the president, who deemed it inappropriate for us to live off campus, decided to allow us to move into one of the faculty apartments that were used by the unmarried teachers on campus. We would be permitted to continue our studies without any penalty, but were strictly admonished not to encourage other students to follow in our footsteps. Such behavior simply couldn't be held up as an example for others.

Joseph and I emerged from the administration building holding hands and beaming, and the rest of the students crowded around us, cheering—not because they particularly liked us, but because they believed we'd taken an incredible gamble . . . and won. Desiree gave me a big hug, her eyes full of a newfound, jealous respect, while Samantha stood beside Carl, her arms folded. She seemed oddly calm. Then she turned and walked away.

"You really did have me fooled," Carl murmured in my ear while Joseph was explaining things to his former roommate.

"What do you mean?"

"I honestly didn't think you were that interested in him."

"Not everybody gets engaged to please their parents."

His gray eyes lingered on my face for a moment. Then he leaned forward and kissed my cheek. "My mistake," he murmured. "I hope the two of you are very happy."

Detroit, however, didn't exactly share Carl's sentiments.

My mother screamed for nearly an hour. She cataloged every time I'd disappointed her since I was in diapers, proving that I'd always been a liar, a cheat and an ungrateful tramp. When she began to get hoarse my father got on the line and told me that I'd disgraced the family in the eyes of our church and his alma mater. He then demanded to speak to Joseph. He accused my husband of brainwashing me into forsaking my family and nation, and threatened to have him deported if he did anything at all to hurt me.

When the call to Detroit was over we sat and looked at each other in utter exhaustion, the words of the chaplain, dean, president, our roommates and my parents ringing in our ears. I might have burst into tears if I hadn't been so happy. After all—we'd done it. We had each other. And we had our entire lives before us.

So while the other students were packing to go home, Joseph and I prepared to move our few belongings into a furnished, two-room faculty apartment.

"You're not going to Detroit at all this summer?" Desiree asked for the tenth time as I dropped an armload of books into a cardboard box.

"Not until things cool down with my parents," I explained once again, avoiding her envious eyes. "Anyway, Baltimore is my home now."

"How are you going to pay for that apartment?"

"I've already told you that Joseph is going to work for the dean of students, and I've got a job in the accounting office."

She stood by the empty closet, eyeing me closely. Her envy seemed to harden into an impotent fury.

"I still can't believe you didn't tell us."

"I didn't tell anybody."

"But we're your friends!"

"Joseph's my husband."

"So he comes first?"

I peered across the room to find her staring back at me, enraged. "Of course he does," I answered.

She turned away, pushing the last of her party dresses into the suitcase. "And you're going to leave it just like that?"

"Leave what like *what*?"

"You're going to pretend that you're *really* married, just because you repeated the oath to some fly-by-night guy in a no-tell motel."

"Our marriage is perfectly legal in the eyes of the law."

"But aren't you going to have a *real* wedding?"

"We had our wedding five months ago."

"But you didn't have a dress or a cake or anything!"

"Those things don't matter to me."

"But that's the whole point of getting married!"

"The point of getting married," I said patiently, "was to legally declare my intention to spend my life with Joseph."

"But the ceremony's important, Reba!"

"Not as important as the love."

"What about your reception?"

"We don't need a reception."

"But you'll need gifts to furnish your house!"

"It'll be years before we can afford a house."

"Then your parents can help you with the mortgage."

"I'm not worried about that, either," I said as I began emptying out my closet. "Joseph and I will be moving to Liberia one day."

"Haven't you heard anything we've been saying? You can't possibly be serious about going to live in the Stone Age!"

"You don't know what you're talking about, Desiree."

"Joseph's made you blind. All I'm trying to do is open your eyes!"

"You're starting to sound like my parents!"

"Well, maybe they're right!"

"How can they be right about someone they've barely met?"

"They just wanted someone better for you."

"*Better* for me?"

"Someone from our culture, who understands our way of life."

"You don't judge people by where they happened to be born, Desiree."

"But you didn't *have* to get married, you know."

"What do you mean?"

"Just because you had sex with him—"

"I didn't marry Joseph for sex!"

"But he *is* your first guy. Maybe you should have tried out a few other people."

"It wouldn't matter if he was my fiftieth! We love each other, Desiree! Why can't you understand that?"

By this time we were standing face to face, where I could look directly into her eyes. Suddenly I realized that Desiree and Carl and Samantha and the others actually *did* understand. They just couldn't stand the fact that Joseph and I were brave enough to declare our love, despite the world's disapproval.

Desiree pushed out an exasperated sigh. "Well, you can always come back and bunk with me next semester when the dishes start flying."

I raised my chin. "Nothing and nobody's going to break us up."

A strange expression passed over her face. She shrugged elaborately and zipped her suitcase shut. "We'll see."

Desiree wasn't altogether wrong about one thing: The dishes did fly more than once during that first long summer of our married life. Ensconced in the nearly empty faculty apartment building, we both worked in the college offices all day and tried to get used to married life at night.

The campus was empty of students, except for groups of high schoolers who came in for daily summer camps in reading and math. The dorms were closed for cleaning and repair, and the dining room only served cold sandwiches.

The problem was that I'd never had so much freedom—coupled with so many responsibilities. At first my job in the accounting office entailed some record keeping and the payment of staff salaries, which were fairly challenging duties. My supervisor, a woman who had been at Absalom Jones since my grandfather's time, found it charming that I wanted to be an accountant and decided to teach me as much as she could over the summer. So without warning I was suddenly responsible for balancing books and overseeing a number of internal accounts. She worked me hard from the moment I arrived in the morning until I nearly crawled out of that office at night—all the while congratulating herself that by September she'd make a professional out of me.

Joseph was far happier in his position in the dean's office, where he handled the campus correspondence and took care of inquiries from prospective students. His supervisor loved his accent and calm demeanor and soon allowed him to handle the phones. Between calls Joseph had time to read, write and even study ahead for his fall classes.

Our married life quickly fell into a routine. We went to bed soon after dark and, not having a television, improvised other ways of amusing ourselves. After making love we often read African poetry by candlelight, or listened to the music of Joseph's homeland until we fell asleep, wrapped in each other's arms. Waking at dawn, we left for our offices at eight-thirty in the morning, then met for a picnic lunch every day under the sweeping oak trees. Joseph picked me up at five o'clock and we walked hand in hand across the Commons to our apartment, where we were delighted to be on our own.

Of course, that meant cooking, washing, cleaning. It was one thing to cook a meal on special occasions, and something entirely different to have to cook every single day. Unlike the women of Joseph's culture, I had never really learned to buy food and prepare meals. We had to take the bus to a supermarket and purchase enough provisions with our meager paychecks to last the entire week. And we had to turn our minuscule two-room flat, with its battered furniture and paper-thin walls, into a home.

But Joseph, who had lived away from his family for many years, already knew a lot about those things.

"Let me help you with that," he said in a gentle voice as I tried to prepare my first loaf of bread from scratch. I was determined to do it without a mix, because I knew that his mother and sisters baked that way in Liberia. But everything seemed to go wrong as I stood in our tiny kitchen. I'd poured flour into a mixing bowl, following the instructions in a cookbook I borrowed from the library, but watched everything turn into a thick, gluey paste when I'd added the eggs straight from their shells.

With flour stuck in my hair and my eyes, I was fuming as I raised my sticky hands from the mess. Joseph laughed quietly.

"You look as though you're about to bake bricks, not bread. Here—let's see if we can't thin out this dough."

He stood behind me and slipped his arms around my waist, pouring warm water into the bowl. Then he reached in, pressing my hands into the soft flour. "Just push a bit here and there," he murmured into my ear. "Feel the way that it moves beneath your fingers. You see how the texture changes. You sense it responding to your touch."

He kissed my ear, sending a hot trembling down my back. "There. You see? You're already making it rise."

I caught my breath as his mouth moved slowly to the nape of my neck, his hands still guiding my fingers through the softening dough. "You mustn't forget the salt," he whispered, pressing hard against me as he reached for the shaker. "And maybe," he added as his hips pushed insistently against mine, "we need a little bit of oil. It's better when it's smooth."

His body moved slowly against mine, his hands still pushing, pushing. "Yes," he whispered as the dough began to spring back to our touch. "I'd say it's almost ready."

He helped me form the mound into the shape of a loaf, wetting it with warm water and covering it quickly with a towel. "It needs to sit for a while before it goes into the oven."

"Well," I said, slipping around to face him, "that will give us a chance to go over the lesson."

"As you Americans say," he murmured, his lips brushing my face, "practice makes perfect."

Occasionally we did disagree—usually about money—and particulary when I wanted to go out to a restaurant or a movie. Sometimes we argued about American life. Joseph saw evidence of selfishness and wasted opportunity everywhere.

"I could not think of staying here," he announced when I mentioned that I was looking forward to moving into a real house. "The deceptions played on people of color are far too great to be ignored."

"But plenty of Black people have very good lives in this country."

"Black Americans are expected to participate in the economy, but they have no real social or political power."

"My parents have power in their community."

"But it is a very small community."

"I wouldn't exactly describe Detroit as 'small.'"

"Even the whole of Detroit can do nothing to stop whites from flooding its neighborhoods with drugs. Detroit cannot protect its people from the abuse of racist policemen. Detroit cannot keep its young men out of prisons or protect its own economy or stop this white government from sending Black men to fight in white men's wars."

"My family has a higher standard of living than many whites."

"Yet there are neighborhoods just outside Detroit where your parents cannot purchase a home. There are white colleges that will not admit you as a student. There are regions of this country where you cannot safely travel."

"But the American government is the most stable political system in the world. We live in a true democracy—"

"You live in a nation in which political leaders are chosen by a small percentage of the population, which is mostly white."

"That's because so many people choose not to vote."

"That's because so many Black people feel that they have no real representation in your government."

"You don't know what you're talking about, Joseph! You've only been here four years."

"Yes, but I read everything I can, Reba. I suspect that I know more about America than many people who have lived here all their lives. Which is another very serious problem with your culture."

"Don't bother to pretend that it's so much better in Liberia."

"No," he said, suddenly growing very quiet. "No, my home is far,

far worse. But I can return to Liberia and try to make a difference. I can convince people that they must learn. I can show them how to create opportunities for their children. In America I am powerless, but perhaps I will one day have some small influence on the health and stability of my own nation."

He went to the window of our tiny living room and looked out at the falling night. Once again I clearly saw his profound loneliness. His gaze restlessly followed a bright yellow oriole that flitted across the lavender sky, and the anxious drilling of locusts roared in to replace our angry voices.

"I'm sorry," I said as I came to stand beside him. "I've never lived anywhere but here and Detroit. Sometimes it scares me to think about moving so far away."

He looked down at me and smiled faintly. "It is unfair for me to expect you to see the world through my eyes. Let's go for a walk and talk about other things on this fine summer night."

"Actually," I said as I wrapped my arms around him, "I'd rather stay in and do other things on this fine summer night."

His gaze softened, then deepened with desire. "I think," he said as we moved toward our bedroom, "that you have made a very convincing argument."

When the autumn came, we cut our working hours back in order to fit our classes into our days. We were able to eat in the dining hall with the other students, but we had so much schoolwork to do that we had very little time for socializing. Not that it mattered. The gossip, parties and undergraduate romances seemed far, far away from our lodgings across campus. The other students treated us with the awe of visiting celebrities. Even my former roommates refrained from criticizing me—perhaps because they found it so prestigious to visit me in our flat in the faculty dorm.

Desiree had broken up with her boyfriend at the end of the summer and was starting to seriously worry about whether she would find a husband before we'd graduate. Samantha had dated a law student from Howard University while working in Washington, but she didn't believe it would last now that she was back in Baltimore.

"There's too much willing snatch right there in D.C.," she said with a shrug.

"But you can't just let him go!" Desiree exclaimed. "He's going to be a *lawyer*."

Samantha ran her frosted fingertips through her hair. "There's more where he came from. And besides, I'm not cut out to be a lawyer's wife. Think about what might happen if I decide to break some rules."

"But lawyers make lots of money—"

"So do businessmen," Samantha asserted with a feline smile. "And I've got my eye on somebody right here on campus."

"Here on campus?" I asked. "Is there anybody you haven't dated?"

"I just decided to save the best for last."

"Are you talking about Carl Thornton?" Desiree asked breathlessly.

"He's an unattached senior and ripe for the taking."

"But everybody's trying to get him."

"I'm not everybody," she retorted. "Carl and I have been friends since I was a freshman. He came to a bunch of my parties during the summer. He met my mother and knows exactly where I'm coming from. I've made it very clear that if he doesn't want to play ball, there will be other athletes on my court."

Both Desiree and Samantha treated Joseph with extreme politeness, even if they weren't really comfortable in his presence.

They shot sneaking glances at him when he passed through our dayroom and into our bedroom, politely closing the door on our conversation so that he could get on with his reading. Then Desiree looked back at me with hungry eyes, wondering what it was like to really live with a man. Samantha was more cool, and harder to read. There was an interval of tense silence as they reminded themselves that I never discussed Joseph with anyone. Then the conversation would return to some juicy piece of gossip.

The fall slipped quickly into winter, and Joseph and I found ourselves alone again over Christmas. I got a lukewarm card with a reluctant check for $100 from my parents; we bought a small tree and prepared a grand meal, combining African and American dishes. Although I was still learning how to cook, I managed to bake a very succulent turkey, and it was true that Joseph could brew sauces that made okra taste good.

Our January wedding anniversary came up so fast that neither one of us remembered it. One day we simply woke up, our schoolbooks stacked beside the bed, and realized that we'd been husband and wife for over a year. We didn't even talk about celebrating it; we had midterms the following week.

Spring broke; the school year ended and we returned to our full-time jobs. That summer, however, we were more comfortable with the routine. We even managed to save enough money to take the train to New York for a long weekend, where we marveled at the traffic, crowds and sheer heat of the sidewalks. Standing together at the top of the World Trade Center, we gazed speechlessly at a cityscape that seemed to be a million miles away from our little apartment on our little campus in Baltimore. When our feet again touched the pavement Joseph slipped his arm around me.

"This is indeed a very great nation. We are lucky to be living in it."

"Does that mean you'd consider staying?"

"I consider it all the time. But God is calling me back to my people, Reba. When you have lived in my country for a time you will certainly understand. America is a wonderful place. But it will never be my home."

Our last year at Absalom Jones began with the college's announcement that for the first time, upper-level students would be allowed to live off campus. Most of the seniors, including Samantha and Desiree, began looking for apartments in the neighborhoods surrounding the college. Joseph and I, however, knew that we'd never be able to afford anything but our little flat in the faculty dorm.

Samantha was the first to move into the city, taking an apartment with an older girl who'd returned to college to finish her degree. She began throwing parties that attracted students from as far away as Virginia Beach, providing the opportunity for several undergraduate girls to meet their future husbands.

Desiree rented a row house with five of her sorority sisters, but they spent too much time fighting with each other to get any serious flirting done. "If you're going to act like freshmen," Samantha remarked as Desiree complained about her roommates, "you should have just stayed in the dorm."

Joseph and I occasionally dropped in on the celebrations, but more often we enjoyed spending our evenings alone. The mood at the parties was laced with an arsenic of desperation as the women's anxiety about landing husbands before graduation continued to grow.

Samantha thought she was making headway with Carl Thornton, who had taken a job in his father's company after graduating a few months earlier. He'd asked her out several times since the school year began, even inviting her to accompany him to his older brother's wedding. "He's nearly in the bag," she proclaimed in my apartment one evening. "I know it's just a matter of time before my monogram will be SJT."

"Is he good in bed?" Desiree asked.

"You will never know," Samantha replied, lifting her long hair over her shoulder. "If Reba can keep her secrets, so can I."

Desiree excused herself to use the bathroom and Samantha looked at me.

"You know, I think I may have a real chance with Carl now that you're out of the way."

"Me? I was never interested in Carl."

"That may be true, but I always had the feeling that Carl had a secret torch for you. As crazy as it sounds, I suspect that underneath the playboy lurks a real simple guy. Carl really wants a nice, sincere girl like you."

"First of all, I think you're wrong about Carl. He loves beautiful women, which means you're just his type. And now that I'm happily married"—I placed special emphasis on *happily*—"I'm sure you can convince him to see things your way."

She laughed and smoothed back her hair. "I won't lie to you, Reba: I still think you married the wrong guy. But as we get closer to graduation, I have to confess that I wish I hadn't let some of my old boyfriends get away. It would feel good to be wearing somebody's ring."

"Being married is more than wearing a ring, Samantha. You shouldn't get married until you know it's right."

"Wow—we've really reversed roles, haven't we? I was the one telling you about men just a few months ago and now here you are giving me advice."

"Samantha," I said, surprised at her candor, "you will find somebody. I'm sure of it."

The toilet flushed and Desiree returned, dropped down next to me and leaned in close.

"So tell us, Reba. Does sex get boring just because you've tied the knot?"

Just before the Christmas break I got a call from my mother, who admitted that she missed me. She talked a long time, complaining about the church members, my father's mother and two of my cousins, who were unwed mothers. Finally, when she ran out of things to say, she grudgingly asked about Joseph.

"He's fine. It looks like he'll be the valedictorian at our graduation."

"We read about your academic performance in the alumni newsletter," she said, mentioning my father for the first time. "We're impressed that you and Joseph have been able to earn such high grades while having to support yourselves."

"Thanks, Mom," I said, surprised that she'd managed to compliment us.

"You should have given yourself more time to meet someone, Reba."

"Why? I love Joseph and he loves me."

"Life isn't always that simple. You should have thought about your family and your future."

"Did you call me to start an argument?"

"No. I actually called to invite you home for the holidays."

"I don't think Joseph would feel comfortable around Dad."

There was a flustered silence. "Well, I thought you might come by yourself for a few days. I'm sure you'd enjoy a break from living on campus, and everyone here would be glad to see you."

"I'm not coming without Joseph."

"Why not? Lots of women travel without their husbands these days."

"If he's not welcome in your home then I don't belong there either."

"Oh honestly, Reba! You can't expect your father to agree to let him stay in our house after he convinced you to break the school's rules and your parents' trust!"

"Joseph didn't have to convince me of anything!" I shouted, finally losing my temper. "When are you going to accept the fact that he's not going away?"

"All right!" she shouted back. "You are making a major mistake, young lady. We gave you everything we could to see that you'd have a decent life. If you decide to throw it all away for a man who's never even seen a house before, that's your choice. Just don't come running back to us with five or six children when you get tired of living in a primitive country with no running water or toilets!"

The walls of the apartment were so thin that I couldn't scream after she hung up on me. Instead I threw books and pillows around the apartment for an entire hour. When Joseph came in, I was lying on the floor, wrapped in a blanket. He had a bag of groceries and a small poinsettia plant. Dropping the bag just inside the door, he sat down on the floor and wrapped his arms around me.

"Your parents?" he asked as he scanned the overturned books and cushions.

"My mother."

He gathered me up close. "You know, she only wants what's best for you."

"She wants absolute control over me."

"You knew they'd be very angry and hurt about our marriage—"

"They should be proud that we have the strength to make this commitment."

"They want their only daughter to live somewhere close by."

"This is *my* life, Joseph. As long as I'm behaving with decency, they should accept my adult decisions."

He sighed. "In my culture, a parent's wishes are very important. I realize, now, that I should have shown your family more respect."

"More respect? My father didn't show any respect to you."

"Perhaps, but in Liberia we say that whether a father is right or wrong, he is always right. It is his duty to make sure that you live a safe and protected life."

"You're talking as if I'm some kind of object."

"You were your father's responsibility, and now that responsibility passes to me. As your husband, I am supposed to offer you the best I can."

"You know perfectly well that I can take care of myself. If I wasn't capable of making my own decisions I could never have married you."

He pulled me closer. "A man must be prepared to face some very difficult challenges in life. Your father only wanted to be sure that you married someone who would give you everything you deserve."

"Stop talking like I'm a child!" I shouted, wrestling myself out of his arms. "You don't know what I deserve any more than he does! I don't care what your culture taught you, Joseph—I'm an *American* woman, and I'll do what I think is best as long as we're living in my world."

For the first time a sharp distaste for me passed across his eyes. He moved away and silently got to his feet. "The apartment is a mess," he said evenly. "Why don't you straighten up? Then you can prepare something for dinner."

Chapter 7

Alexandria, Virginia

2004

"What did he look like, Mom?"

I arrived home in the late afternoon, jet-lagged and emotionally drained. Marisa had gone out of her way to cook a dinner of spinach lasagna and Greek salad, so I sat down at the table and gathered my wits to share the events of my whirlwind trip with her. There was no sign of Carl.

"Joseph? Well, he was old and exhausted. If I'd passed him on the street I wouldn't have recognized him."

"Was he glad to see you?"

"I think so."

"You *think* so? After you traveled all that distance to help him?"

"I think my presence complicated things. He'd already made some decisions that I asked him to change."

"What do you mean?"

"He was prepared to go to prison to protect his son."

"That's crazy—"

"No it isn't, Marisa. In fact, I'm sure I would do exactly the same for you."

She glanced thoughtfully out into our flowering yard, now hissing with the jets of revolving sprinklers. "He must be an incredible man."

"Yes, baby, he is."

I wearily ate my dinner while she sat with her arms wrapped around her knees, staring out at the pink and blue hydrangeas, which were fighting with an army of black-eyed Susans for a corner of the flower bed.

Suddenly she turned back to me. "If you'd stayed with him I'd never have been born, would I?"

I looked up sharply. "What do you mean?"

"You were married to him for a couple of years, but you didn't have any kids."

"Joseph and I were still in school, Marisa. It was too soon to start a family."

"But after you graduated?"

"We were trying to decide whether we wanted to move back to Liberia."

"And Grandma and Grandpa were totally opposed to your going with him."

"How do you know that?"

"I called Grandma while you were away. I wanted to know more about your first husband, and since you and Daddy have never said anything—"

"Your grandmother only saw him three times, and each time we only spent a few hours together."

"She said they met Joseph on the same day they first met Daddy. She said that you got very upset when Daddy tried to flirt with you, and that she and Grandpa always knew that you and Daddy would end up together."

Anger clouded my eyes and I stood up abruptly, taking my dishes to the sink. I shoved the rest of my food into the garbage disposal, keeping my back turned so that Marisa couldn't see my sudden rage. Still staring out of the window, she went on talking.

"Grandma said that you brought Joseph home to Detroit one Christmas, but he argued with Grandpa and left the next day."

"Is that what she said?"

"Yep. Then she said that he convinced you to elope with him because he knew that he'd never get permission from Grandpa to marry you."

I raised one hand to my temple and touched the spot that had begun to throb. "Did she say anything else?"

"Well, she said that when they came over for your graduation, your husband had an even bigger fight with Grandpa, right in the middle of campus where everyone could see. She said they had come to enjoy the ceremony and your husband humiliated them in front of all their friends."

"You know, there are two sides to every story."

"She said that you broke up really suddenly, and that she was glad you finally saw the wisdom of marrying Daddy."

"Believe me, sweetheart, it wasn't quite that simple."

"I know," she agreed. Standing up to stretch, she brought the rest of my dishes to the sink. "Mommy, I think Grandma must have been wrong about Joseph. I know how much you really loved him. Why else, after twenty long years, would you take off and fly halfway around the world when he's in trouble?"

I turned around and looked into the eyes that had much too much depth for a child.

"You see, Grandma and Grandpa judge people by their position in society. They probably couldn't understand why you loved Joseph."

"That's right, sweetheart," I answered softly. "They didn't understand." She hugged me hard and my heart began beating so fast that I thought my ribs might break.

"There's just one part of the story I really want to hear more about," she said as we cleared away the rest of the dishes.

"What's that?"

She lowered her voice as if sharing a secret. "Did you *really* elope with him? Right in the middle of the semester? And under the nose of the monitor while you were living in an all-girls dorm?"

Three days after my return from Switzerland my boss, Rob Nelson, walked unannounced into my office. I was in the middle of a telephone conference with an official at CAD about living arrangements for a Croatian detainee, so I motioned for Rob to sit down. As soon as I could end the call, I joined him at the conference table on the other side of my office.

"My, your daughter is growing up," he said with a nod toward my collection of photos. "I read in the paper that she brought the house down with the Youth Symphony a few weeks ago."

"That's right. And as soon as she finishes Juilliard she'll probably run off and become a hip-hop artist."

"Well, that's where the money is," he answered, crossing his legs casually. Rob Nelson had worked his way up the government hierarchy to a level where his only chance for advancement would have required a kind of ambition he didn't possess. So he'd jumped to nonprofit organizations, eventually landing in our office, where he earned his salary primarily by making sure that the government didn't disapprove of our work.

"I understand you were overseas last weekend," he remarked, his voice loose and friendly. His fading light-brown hair and tennis-tanned skin cut a sharp figure in his Lacoste polo shirt and khaki trousers. He seemed younger than his fifty-plus years.

"I went to Switzerland to check on the well-being of a family member."

"Family member?"

"My former husband."

"I see," he said, still smiling. "You flew to Zurich on Friday night and came back on Monday?"

"I used personal leave, and the nature of my trip was private."

"Well, you know how it is, Reba: 'Private' means that the whole office has been yapping about it."

"I didn't discuss my plans with—"

"You didn't have to. Someone from the Liberian Embassy called to say that you've been inquiring about a guy who's in custody for human rights violations—"

"Which he's innocent of committing."

Rob shifted in annoyance, his leather loafer bouncing ever so slightly. "I just want to remind you that our mission is to defend the rights of people who've been victims of oppression in their own countries and—"

"Remind *me* about our mission? I've found placements for thousands of people in my ten years with this organization. Tell me, Rob: When was the last time that *you* visited the detention center?"

"It's your job to work with the detainees. My responsibility is to make sure that this office runs smoothly—"

"When was the last time you actually *spoke* to a detainee?" I asked, leaning forward in my chair.

"I am not trained to work with those people—"

"When was the last time you listened to someone describing how it feels to be raped, or burned with cigarettes, or have their ribs broken or teeth knocked out?"

"Reba, that is not relevant to this—"

"It certainly is."

"How so?" he asked, his eyes becoming very hard.

"My former husband is one of 'those people.' "

"But he is not the responsibility of this office."

"You can't tell me anything about the mission of this office. I've dedicated the better part of my professional life to victims' rights."

He stood up with a hostile sneer. "I agree that you have a very impressive record with this organization, Reba. I just hope you won't do anything to spoil it."

I knew that every bit of my rage was evident in my eyes. "There's something you need to realize, Rob. I haven't worked so hard over the past ten years in order to please you. I don't care if you or anybody else in this office approves of my trip to Switzerland. I'm in this to save my first husband's life, because his life is worth saving."

I stood up too. "None of us can judge this man until we've heard his story. And no one can stop me from trying to find out as much of the truth about him as possible."

"Why hasn't he simply told you the truth?"

"That's part of what I have to discover."

Rob's eyes had blackened to a dense rage. "While it's entirely true that I have nothing to do with your personal life, I will certainly be watching your professional performance over the coming days. This organization depends on the funding of a number of corporate and private donors, and I cannot allow your behavior on behalf of a suspected mass murderer to compromise our integrity."

"I know what's at stake."

"I'm not sure you do, Reba. Because we're not only talking about *your* career. We're talking about the viability of this office and the thirty-five other people who are employed here. Since September 11, organizations such as ours are being carefully monitored. The government is not entirely comfortable with our efforts to help political refugees stay in this country. The last thing we need is some kind of scandal attached to us right now. Do you understand?"

"I won't do anything that compromises this office."

"I hope not. Because if you do—make no mistake, Reba—despite everything you've put into this organization over the past decade, I will terminate your employment without the slightest hesitation."

He turned on his heel and strode to the door. "Please consider this your one official warning."

Strains of an old George Benson album filtered out from Carl's study when I turned off my computer and made my way through the darkened house that night. I had hoped to take a shower and go to bed without any further confrontations. Marisa was spending the night at Kelsey's, and Arlene had called to say that she hadn't found out anything new about Joseph. I hadn't heard from Simone either, so my spirits were low as I climbed the thick carpeting to the top floor of the house.

I stepped out of the shower and stood in front of the mirror, preparing for the routine inspection of my body that usually ended with the thought that I didn't look too bad for my age.

I was still staring at my reflection when Carl suddenly appeared behind me. He was naked to the waist and had a tumbler of Scotch in one hand. He'd had his hair cut earlier that day and I noticed for the first time that there was a gathering of gray along the line of his temples. His sun-browned skin caused his boyish freckles to stand out even more, and his eyes, though filled with a yet unexplained emotion, were unusually bright. So bright, in fact, that if I hadn't known better, I would have suspected that he'd been weeping.

"Are you all right?" I asked, despite my resentment that he'd hardly spoken to me since my return from Switzerland.

"Do you really want to know?" he asked, setting the tumbler down on the edge of the tub. He moved behind me so that he could look over my shoulder and see both of us in the full-length mirror. Instinctively I reached for a towel, but he took my hand and held it.

"No, Reba," he said softly into my ear. "Don't cover anything up. I want to really look at you. I want to know the truth."

"The truth?"

"I want to know"—his voice broke and I stared with shock into his eyes, now brimming with tears—"whether it was still there when you saw him."

"What are you talking about?"

"I need to know whether you're still in love with him," he said, reaching out with his free hand to touch my breasts.

He was staring intently into my eyes, his mouth slightly open. Rooted to the spot, I placed my hand over his and forced myself to speak calmly.

"I still care about him, Carl. But—but it's not the same as before."

"Are you lying to me?" he murmured. He pressed his forehead against my hair, inhaling deeply. "Did you make love with him?"

"Of course not."

"But you wanted to—" His other hand traveled the length of my hips while he stared into my eyes.

"No, I didn't."

He continued to stroke me, his gaze fixed on mine. "Did you tell him about us, Reba? Did you tell him about the nights I held you when you talked about him and cried?"

I closed my eyes on the memories of those early days, so many years before, when I thought I'd never survive without Joseph.

"Did you tell him how patient I was when you said you'd never want to make love again?"

Despite my resentment, a fleeting image of Carl's gentle hands, stroking away my loneliness and pain, flooded my mind.

"Did you tell him that you asked me to give you a child?" he whispered, brushing his lips along my neck as his other hand released mine.

"That's not his business," I muttered, fighting an unexpected flood of desire that accompanied my memories of those distant days. "You know that, Carl."

"I only know," he murmured, raising his head slowly, "that he left you in pieces and I put you back together, woman."

He wrapped his other arm around my waist and pulled me against him. His body was a series of hot muscular ridges, and his breath was sweet as he pressed his lips against my face.

"I love you, Reba. I love you even though I can't have you," he whispered, and again I heard the catch in his voice.

"You *do* have me," I said, knowing that he would never be satisfied with those words. He stared at me for another moment, and then I felt him guiding me out of the bathroom, leading me back through our bedroom and out into the darkened hall. With steps that were far more certain than the alcohol on his breath would have predicted, he guided me down into the sunken living room with its elegant furnishings and the huge picture windows staring out over the manicured lawn.

He turned and gathered me into his arms, staring into my eyes.

"Look at this room," he said in a hoarse voice. "Look at the life we've built together."

He spread an arm toward the marble mantel over the wide fireplace, now cast in shadows. "You know those tiles we bought in Italy? Whenever I look at them I think about the time we made love in that little room over the canal in Venice." His haunted eyes returned to my face. "You remember that night, don't you? It was the night when you said he never loved you the way I do."

My breath caught in my throat at the memory of that lie, told so long ago to alleviate some of the guilt I felt for wishing with all my heart that it was Joseph, instead of Carl, who was lying beside me.

"You lay in my arms and begged me to make love to you again and again," Carl said, reaching up with both hands to grasp my face. "You begged me to make you forget him. And I tried. I did everything I could to force him out of your body—and your heart."

"I know," I admitted softly. "I know."

He turned his head toward one of the glass side tables. "Look at those photographs of our daughter, Reba. *We* made this beautiful, talented child. Do you understand? We made her because we were committed to building this life together!"

His voice was growing more intense, and his hands, beset by a sudden trembling, moved to my shoulders.

"Look at our home, Reba. I carried you across that threshold. We raised Marisa here. And we were happy here until you found those"—he paused for a moment—"until you realized that I'm only human."

"Is that what those pictures meant?"

"I never asked you to give up your family and your country. I never asked you to spend your life serving my dreams. I only asked you to give some of yourself to me."

"But Carl—"

"Can't you see that you would *never* have fit into his world? How could you have survived in the middle of that war?"

"Carl—"

"You need to see the truth, Reba! He loved you as his partner. But with me you've had your own life. He loved you because you were young enough to share his dreams. But I've loved you while your *own* dreams came true. I'm the one who has stood by you over the past twenty years! I don't know what happened between you and Joseph, but I would never leave you. And goddamn it, when I fucked up, no matter how much it hurt, you continued to stand by me too!"

The trembling in his hands seemed to set off a like trembling in my own limbs, and despite my confused mixture of anger and frustration, I met his gaze.

"Don't you understand?" he whispered. "We are bound together, Reba. We'll be bound together for the rest of our lives."

"Oh, Carl," I murmured, feeling the wall of resentment I'd harbored since the day I found the photographs begin to fissure. "I just can't do this. I can't fight you and fight for him too."

"Then stop fighting," he said hoarsely, opening his arms to me. "I don't want you to be a warrior—I just want you to be my woman."

Soon I was caught up in his fierce tenderness, and the images of other women were wiped clean from my mind as he urged me in hoarse whispers to give myself to him completely. He labored hard against my resistance, guiding me with his hands and lips to a point where I felt nothing but him.

And somehow I opened myself to Carl and trusted my mind, my body and my life to him. And the pleasure we shared was even more intense because I had fought against it for so long.

Late in the night my eyes opened on Carl's naked form, sprawled in sobering vulnerability on our bed. His left arm was thrown over my side and one of his legs dangled heavily toward the woven grass mat on the floor. His long-lashed eyes were screwed closed and his heavy breathing signaled that he was deep asleep.

I slipped out from under his weight and went into the shower. The hot water coursed in spikes on my face and shoulders, and suddenly I plunged my entire head under the spray, not caring how I looked when I got to the office the next morning. I worried too god-damned much about being perfect—especially when nothing in my life made sense anymore.

For twenty years I had been haunted by a man who had eloped with me and then abandoned me. A man who told me he loved me, but never made the slightest attempt to learn how my life had developed without him. A man who made me believe he could never hurt another human being, but was accused of committing mass murder. A man who rejected my attempts to help him, even though he was alone in a foreign prison.

Yet how should I feel about Carl's mix of treachery and devotion? His very public infidelity and his claim that he had never loved any woman but me? Or that he could give me such pleasure despite the pain he caused me?

As I washed away the touch of Carl's lips from my breasts, his words came echoing back in the steaming chamber of the shower: *"He loved you because you were young enough to share his dreams. But I've loved you while your own dreams came true. . . ."*

Joseph and I had lived together for only two years. We'd juggled jobs, an apartment and the rigors of our studies. We'd worked through our differences with tenderness, patience and love.

But what were two years in comparison to the twenty I'd spent with Carl? Carl had found me at a moment when I thought I couldn't go on, and he'd given me a new reason to live. He'd talked to me and teased me and very slowly taught me to trust him. And when I was finally ready, he made love to me, holding me gently while I wept into the dawn.

Then he'd asked me to marry him, standing on the deck of his parents' retreat on Chesapeake Bay: *"Reba, I know you're not completely over Joseph. But I'm ready to spend my life helping you to feel happy again."* That warm summer evening, Carl's face promised a chance to overwrite my grief with the hope for a new life. *"We'll move away from Baltimore and start over in a place where no one knows us."*

Now I turned my face from side to side, letting his words, like the hot spray of the shower, drench my thoughts: *"He loved you because you were young enough to share his dreams. But I've loved you while your own dreams came true."*

I turned off the water and stood dripping in the shower, my head against the tiles. Why was I on this wild goose chase in Switzerland for a man who'd left me decades before, when my own marriage was disintegrating? Weren't my home and my family worth fighting for? Wasn't Marisa's well-being more important than my need to atone for that one mistake—yes, the *one* mistake that had determined the course of my life?

Carl and I were united by something more than love: We had built a life together, and it was a life worth saving.

"Reba?" I started up to find Carl standing in the bathroom beside me. His eyes were extraordinarily tired, but his face had a strange, almost unknown expression of concern. "Are you all right?" he asked very gently.

"I don't know," I whispered, feeling tears flood my eyes.

"That's okay," he murmured, holding out his arms. "I'll never understand you," he said very wearily. "But I guess I love you even more for it. Please come back to bed, baby."

⧫

Congress *voted this* morning to raise the tax on oversized motor vehicles. This legislation is expected to force auto dealers to lower prices on trucks, off-road vehicles and luxury sports utility vehicles—"

"It's crazy, isn't it?" Simone said as we passed the newswoman, who was standing on the steps to the Capitol with a camera pointed at her face. "With all the stuff that's going on in the world, Americans are still obsessed with buying cars."

We had lunched at the National Gallery and were now walking pensively beneath the sweeping oak trees along the Mall. Tourists pressed by us, headed into the National Air and Space Museum, but we ignored them.

"Reba, Joseph's hostility might have been his way of hiding his guilt," Simone now said gently.

"No. I refuse to believe that."

"Why else would he insist that you have nothing more to do with his case?"

"I don't know. But I can't give up until I'm sure I've done everything I can to help him."

"Well, what's left?"

"One piece. His missing son."

"I found no birth or death certificates for his family in my research. Many documents have been destroyed in the war, of course. But there are no school records or passport applications for them either." Simone paused as a young woman in shorts jogged by, her ponytail dancing behind her. "Do you know anything about the rest of his family—his parents or siblings?"

"The first time we spoke Joseph mentioned that his brother—I believe his name was Kali—still lives in England. When I visited Joseph he said that Kali believes he died along with his family years ago. Still, maybe Kali could tell me something."

"Do you know where Kali lives?"

"Years ago Joseph told me that Kali went to stay with an uncle in—I believe it was Bristol."

"Well, if Kali believes Joseph is dead, he'd have no particular reason to hide anything from you now."

I shook my head. "It's a long shot, Simone."

"Long shots sometime hit their marks. I'll check with International Information. And you should call anybody you know who might have contacts in the local Liberian community."

"I'll speak with my friend Arlene."

We walked a few more steps, then Simone slipped her arm around my shoulders. "I can tell you're discouraged, Reba. But you know that these things are never easy."

"This is different, Simone. The refugees I work with are glad for my help. Instead, Joseph sent me away. Maybe my husband's right—maybe I need to let go of the past and concentrate on taking care of the present."

Simone stopped walking. "Do you believe that Joseph murdered those villagers?"

I turned to face her. "No, I don't."

"Then this isn't about the past—it's about keeping an innocent man from spending the rest of his life in prison."

"I know." I smiled faintly. "Joseph once said that a lost man punishes the man who finds him. I have to do what I think is right, even if no one else understands. And that includes Joseph."

I think I have something, Reba." I could hear the excitement in Arlene's voice as soon as I answered the phone the following day. "I spoke with one of my Liberian friends who happens to have relatives living in England. She called me last night and said they know a Liberian in Bristol whose family name is Thomas."

My heart fluttered. "Is there a way I can contact them directly?"

I heard her rattling something. "I have a phone number. My friend says it might not be correct, but here—give it a try." She recited the number, then paused. "You know, Reba, it's all going to work out."

"One way or the other," I replied, laughing wryly.

Later that afternoon I closed myself into my study and sat down at my desk. Marisa was practicing Debussy's *Suite Berga-masque*, and I held my breath in anticipation of her fingers striking the first chords of "Clair de Lune." Carl was mowing the lawn, a task that would occupy him for at least an hour.

Nervously I picked up the receiver and pressed the cool plastic against my cheek. The dial tone hummed mockingly near my ear, daring me to try to make contact with that distant world. Staring at my scrap of paper, I slowly pressed the numbers. Nighttime in England. Five hours ahead of us. A different life, another culture. And yet—perhaps the only link I could make to—

"Hullo?" The voice was low and gruff, with a strongly inflected working man's accent.

"Is this the Thomas residence?"

"Who is this?"

"My name is Reba Thornton. I'm calling from the United States. Is Mr. Thomas there?"

"What do you want?"

"I want to talk about Joseph."

The line crackled intensely for a few moments. Just as I thought the connection was dead, he spoke again. "Why?"

"I—I used to be Joseph's wife."

Now the silence deepened. Distrust, uncertainty, curiosity, wonder—all of those emotions seemed to race across the ocean from that telephone in England to me.

He finally spoke. "You was Joseph's wife? When?"

"When he was in college in the United States. We were

married in 1982 and broke up shortly after he left the States for Liberia."

"That's rubbish. He never said nothing about it."

"I can prove it, if you'd like to see the documents, Mr.— excuse me, but could you tell me your name?"

"You can call me Kali."

"Kali, I'm calling because Joseph's in trouble and needs his family's help."

"You're crazy. First you say you're his wife, and I never heard of you. And now you say he's in trouble. But don't you know that Joseph's dead?"

"No, Kali. Joseph is alive. He's being held in a prison in Switzerland."

"He's what?"

"He's been detained for his activities with the Rimka Liberation Front."

The phone line exploded. "Joseph never had anything to do with that madness! He was never a part of the war! What are you— a reporter or something?"

"No, sir. Believe me. I'm trying to track down his family because if someone isn't willing to help me, he may spend the rest of his life in prison."

"You're bloody mad," the man scoffed. "Joseph was killed with his family long ago when the rebels attacked his village. He can't be in any prison in Switzerland!"

"I saw him there only a week ago."

"You said you were calling from the States."

"I traveled to Europe to find him after reading about a man named Yusef Vai who led the Rimka Liberation Front. I had reason to believe that Yusef Vai and Joseph Thomas were the same man, and I was right."

There was a pause. "What's this Vai person in prison for?"

"The murder of thirty-seven people in a village outside of Monrovia."

"Oh, no!" The man now burst into rough laughter. "That's bloody impossible! Joseph was too soft to swat a fly. I raised him from when he was a little boy. He was never capable of doing anything other than carrying books around."

"Then you *are* his brother?"

"I was his elder by seven years. I left for England while he was in boarding school in Monrovia. Later he used to write me from college in the United States. He said he was studying to be a teacher. He wouldn't even fight when he was a boy, and now you're telling me that he murdered all them people?"

"No, Kali. I'm telling you that he's being held in prison for the murders—not that he actually committed them."

The phone line tensed. "Look. I don't know what you want from me."

"I want you to help me free him."

"That man is not my brother."

"I'm sure that he is."

"You can't prove it!"

"I've seen him, spoken with him and—and even held him in my arms."

There was a long silence. When he spoke again, something in his tone had changed. "Why do you think that I can help you?"

"I want to know if you have any idea what became of Joseph's oldest son."

"Joseph's children died with him—"

"*All* of them?"

Again the tense silence. "Look, Joseph married a woman from our village about a year after he came back from America.

They had three children before all of them was killed by the rebels."

"You're certain that they died?"

"What kind of bloody stupid question is that?"

"I'm telling you that Joseph is very much alive. One of his children survived too."

"No, that's not possible. They all died in the school."

"You know this to be a fact?"

Kali hesitated, and in that instant I knew that he was lying. "Look, lady—what did you say your name is?"

"Reba Thornton."

"And you claim you was his wife?"

"We met in college and stayed together all the way through school. After we finished he decided to return to Liberia without me."

He laughed gruffly. "I talked to him after he came back from the States. I remember the conversation like yesterday. He said things was too different there. The people had no respect for family, or human life. He never said nothing about a wife. I told him things wasn't so different here in England. He answered that no matter what, he would never leave Liberia again."

"I see," I whispered, defeated.

There was a long pause. "Mrs. Thornton, I don't know why you want to stir things up like this. Joseph was a good man. He loved his wife and his children. He loved our people. He would never have taken another person's life."

There was a low grumble as he cleared his throat. "I spent many years of grief after Joseph died in that school. I know he would not have wanted to live after he lost his children. He was a good man who deserved better. I often think that if I had convinced him to come here, maybe take some more courses in England, he might not have gone to his death."

Kali's voice again went gruff. "That man you talked to in Switzerland—I don't care what he looked like or what he said—that man is *not* my brother."

"Mr. Thomas—"

"I know it is very expensive to call here from the United States. You should save your money."

The line went dead. I listened to the smothered silence, which suddenly clicked and became a rude bleeping. Exhaling slowly, I hung up.

So Joseph had returned to Liberia and married a woman who had borne him three children. She had been burned alive in the schoolhouse with their offspring. Joseph had not died with them, but he had let the world believe that he was dead. But why?

The answer seemed obvious. Joseph went on to form the Rimka Liberation Front. Under the name of Yusef Vai, he led the RLF in warfare against the men who had killed his family. He fought for some years, until his group finally reached Monrovia, where government forces captured them. It was possible that Kali knew nothing about what had really happened in Liberia. And Kali made it clear that Joseph had never told him anything about me.

"Good lord," I whispered. "I really have been a fool."

Suddenly I realized that Marisa had stopped playing. I couldn't hear the lawn mower, either. There was no sound in the house. Even the clock on my desk had grown strangely silent, as if the entire world was holding its breath.

I glanced toward the window to see my daughter strolling out into the garden, strands of her hair slipping free from her scarf, her soles stained by the cut grass. She was holding a thick paperback and eating an apple. Sitting carefully on the tire swing, she opened her book and began to rock herself gently without looking up.

This was my life. This was what I had worked so hard to create. This is what mattered. This was real. It was time for me to let go of the past and hang on tight to my husband and daughter. I needed to leave the past alone—before I destroyed what was left of the present.

I took Marisa to the mall that night and strolled silently beside her, only half listening as she chattered about her friends, the newest recording artists and the ugly clothes on the store mannequins. I took in the sterile world in which we lived and the bland, mind-numbing Mozart wafting out from unseen speakers.

A couple passed us, the blond woman smiling through whitened teeth while her husband, whose sun-browned wrist sported a heavy Swiss watch, stopped to inspect a set of Italian leather luggage. I looked away, my gaze coming to rest on a pair of teens with navel rings on their bare midriffs, wearing T-shirts emblazoned with the word *maneater*.

Who would Joseph have become if he'd remained in America? One of these empty, materialistic people? Or would he have been consumed by loneliness, spending his life longing for the culture he'd left behind?

What would have become of me if I'd remained his wife? Would I have survived in Africa, or was this the world in which I *truly* belonged?

Marisa and I were sitting in the food court sipping drinks made from blended bananas, kiwis and strawberries when I heard my name and turned to find Desiree and Samantha bearing down on us. Samantha's streaked hair was tied away from her face in a loose

knot, and Desiree had put reddened highlights into the hair around
her forehead. Dressed in pastel linens with matching cork sandals,
they might easily have been mistaken for sisters.

"What are you two doing so far from home?" I asked as we exchanged kisses.

Their arms laden with shopping bags, they dropped down dramatically beside me. Marisa excused herself to go and sit at another
table with some of her school friends.

"I needed something new for the Theta luncheon," Samantha
answered, "and I didn't want to shop anywhere near home. There's
nothing worse than showing up in a dress that half the women in
the room tried on!"

"Didn't you find anything on your trip to Chicago?" I asked.

Desiree looked down at her perfect nails. "The shopping was
great, and we bought so much stuff we had to buy more suitcases.
You really should have come with us."

"Well, it looks like you're both doing pretty well right now," I
said, indicating their bags.

"But I'm worn out," Samantha declared as she tucked loose
strands of her hair back into the knot. "This is it. I won't be doing
any more shopping or traveling for a while."

"And how's your summer been?" Desiree asked. "I haven't seen
you since our little lunch in Georgetown."

"I've been working, spending time with Marisa and taking care
of the house, as usual."

"That's all?" Samantha asked. "Because we heard a rumor that
you'd been overseas. Where was it, now? Sweden? Swaziland?"

"I spent a few days in Switzerland," I answered, not even both-
ering to ask who had told them. "I went there to see Joseph."

"Joseph?" Desiree asked, feigning surprise. "You mean Joseph
Thomas?"

"Not that man who eloped with you, then deserted you?"

"And who's now sitting in a prison for mass murder?" Desiree added in a sweet, mocking voice.

There was a moment of tense silence as I looked across the table and saw two middle-aged women whose fading beauty had been replaced by a raw bitterness, sharpened by an adolescent jealousy that had grown more cruel with time.

"Yes," I said simply.

"Reba, are you sure about this?" Samantha whispered, leaning forward in her creaking plastic chair.

"And do you have *any* idea what everybody's saying?" Desiree added eagerly.

"Or what this is going to do to your already shaky marriage?" Samantha echoed.

"Yes," I answered again.

"And?" Samantha said, the single syllable thrust across the table like a knife.

I stared into her eyes, stunned by the cruelty of that single syllable.

"Reba?" Desiree said uncertainly, her voice betraying her surprise at what she was seeing on my face.

My eyes flickered to Desiree. Suddenly, with blinding, crystal clarity, I finally understood: *I didn't need to have these women in my life.*

"Samantha," I said softly. "Desiree," I added with a calm smile. "Go fuck yourselves."

With the television as my only companion, I was once again sitting in the kitchen late that night, staring vacantly at the screen. The news stories swirled around me like a sick soup: war in the Middle

East, ethnic cleansing in eastern Europe, AIDS in southern Africa, starvation in China.

I had spent years trying to make a difference in the world, yet what hope did I have when there was so much pain and hunger and violence? What difference did it make to find homes for one hundred people when there were millions whose lives were threatened? Why was I aligning myself with Joseph when there were people in my own backyard who deserved my help?

The news droned on: another political assassination in Italy. Another synagogue burned in southern France. Another mass grave in Guatemala. Another village massacre in Sri Lanka.

Sad and exhausted, I opened my wallet and took out the scrap of paper with Kali Thomas's phone number. It was ridiculous that those twelve digits were the only link I had between my world and Joseph's. And it was even more ridiculous that Kali Thomas, the one person with whom I should have been able to share my deepest feelings about Joseph, refused to speak with me.

No, it wasn't just ridiculous. It was stupid and unacceptable.

I dialed the number and stood up, carrying the phone to the window, where I watched the leaves of the crabapple tree stirring faintly in the moonlight.

The line clicked nervously as the connection was established with that faraway city in another corner of the world. I knew that the five-hour difference in time zones would make it just after dawn in England. Perhaps, with any luck at all, someone would still be at home.

"Hullo?"

The voice was calm, low and gently accented—a voice not unlike that of the young man I'd fallen in love with so many years ago. It sounded so much like Joseph that I caught my breath, momentarily unable to speak.

"Hullo?"

"Excuse me—is this Kali?"

"No, it's Daniel. Who's calling?"

"This is—my name is Reba Thornton. I'm a representative of the Office for the Placement of Permanent Refugees, in the United States."

"The what?"

"I'm calling to speak to Kali Thomas."

"What about?"

I caught my breath, deciding to take a chance. "I've called to talk about Joseph Thomas."

The crackling silence on the line roared with such intensity that I braced myself for the dial tone. Then he spoke. "Why are you calling?"

"I want to help free him from prison. Surely you're aware that he's being held by the Court of Human Rights in Switzerland."

"You've made a mistake. Joseph Thomas is dead."

"There's no mistake. I was with him a few days ago. I know why he's being held, and I believe he's innocent."

"Who in the world are you?"

"I'm an advocate for people whose rights are being violated," I said, enunciating every word. "Joseph Thomas is not a murderer. It is wrong for him to be imprisoned for crimes he didn't commit."

"Why are you calling here?"

"I spoke to Kali last night. He claimed that the man who calls himself Yusef Vai is not the same person as Joseph Thomas."

"You cannot produce any evidence that Joseph Thomas and Yusef Vai are the same man."

"I can document everything Joseph did, right up until the time that the Rimka Liberation Front was born."

"Coincidence," he said belligerently.

"Perhaps. And perhaps Yusef would rather let the world believe that Joseph really did die with his wife and children—"

The young man stammered something, but I went on speaking.

"—but I cannot allow him to live out the rest of his life without the love of his family. Those few family members who are living should have the courage to come to his aid when he needs them most."

"He gave all of that up a long time ago."

"He only did it to give others the chance for a decent life."

"How would you know that?"

"I know how much Joseph loved Liberia and her people. I know how much he valued his village and its way of life. And I know how much he loved his family."

"Who *are* you?" he asked again.

"I'm just an old friend."

"You must understand," he said, a note of anger entering his voice, "Yusef is a strong man. He makes his own decisions. He has chosen his path, and there is nothing I can do about it."

"Think very carefully before making that decision," I said quietly, "because it's a decision you'll have to live with for the rest of your life."

I heard someone speaking in the background.

"Joseph is being held by the Court of Human Rights in Berne, Switzerland," I said. "His trial will begin on September seventh."

The young man cleared his throat. "I'll think about it," he said before hanging up.

Chapter 8

Baltimore, Maryland

1984

I never intended to get pregnant so soon. I'd been on the Pill since before Joseph and I got married, and had religiously swallowed the little tablets every morning. Perhaps it was my anxiety over my parents' arrival for our graduation that made me misplace the little plastic compact for almost a week. A week that Joseph and I spent in very sensuous celebration, as he'd been named valedictorian and had been invited for a job interview at the New York offices of the Church of England.

I hadn't spoken to my mother since our argument before Christmas, but I had received a letter informing me that my parents intended to be present to witness the graduation of the third generation of Freemans from Absalom Jones College. She didn't say anything about their hotel arrangements, nor how long they planned to stay in Baltimore. It was clear that their trip was more symbolic than personal—my father wanted to catch up with his former classmates, and he really didn't care how I felt about it.

As graduation day approached I began to sleep badly, and I often snapped at Joseph over meaningless things. He was, as always, patient and forgiving, but there was a strange kind of tension in his eyes.

"If the Church of England should choose me for this position," he explained as we sat at our small table after dinner one evening,

"I will be able to move back to Liberia much sooner than I thought."

"How soon?" I asked, staring into my plate.

"I believe that they want to hire someone to begin in September. I would serve as an educational administrator for about a year, then finally receive a mandate to open a school of my own."

His eyes were gleaming with excitement and I realized, perhaps for the first time, that nothing I could say would stop him from returning to Africa.

"Will they approve of your bringing a wife?"

"Of course. They will be impressed that I achieved such high marks while married. And they will believe that a married man will have more stability."

"Do you—do you think there'll be a job for me?"

He chuckled quietly. "There are uncountable jobs for you in my country. You will be able to work as little, or as much, as you desire."

"Then we'd be living in Monrovia?"

"At first. Then I would be posted to a different region. Of course, I would prefer to go somewhere near my home."

He stood up and held out his arms. "This is exactly what I've always wanted, Reba. If I am selected, then everything I have worked for will come to fruition. And"—he paused, his expression leaping to a memory of something far, far away—"and at last I will see my family again."

I heard the desperate longing that he so rarely showed, and I realized with a jolt that he loved his family as much—and maybe even more—than he loved me. "I know you've missed them," I began hesitantly.

"Oh, yes. Just think, I have younger siblings who could barely walk when I went away. Now they're almost in secondary school. Imagine what my tales of America will mean to them!"

"Do you think they'll like me?"

His face burst into a smile. "They will find you as beautiful as a movie star and as smart as the president. Everyone will envy me my wonderful bride!"

He swept me into his arms and hugged me with enthusiasm. We waltzed around the apartment, while he laughed with unadulterated joy. It was the happiest I'd ever seen him. He was so thrilled, in fact, that he didn't notice the sudden quiet that seemed to root in me.

Samantha, Desiree, Joseph and I were graduated along with seventy other students in a beautiful ceremony under the college's sweeping and venerable oak trees. Dressed in gowns of black and gold, we filed proudly out of the dining hall across the sunlit Commons, heads held high. The families were arranged in rows of chairs facing low wooden stands where the faculty and college administration were seated. Many of the parents were carrying bouquets for their daughters. Some of the mothers were wiping tears away as their sons or daughters took their place on the bleachers.

The honors students filed in last, our silver stoles rippling gently, their scarlet sashes flashing in the sunlight. Joseph's robes were further decorated with ceremonial strips of turquoise. He was the last student in the line, and he proceeded to the podium, where he took a seat beside the president.

Soon the ceremony was under way. After the national anthem and the school song, President Saunders greeted the guests, congratulated the graduates, and introduced the valedictorian, Joseph Vai Thomas.

Slowly, my husband rose to his feet and stepped up to the podium. I knew that I had never succeeded in hiding my pride, but there are no words to describe the love that flooded my heart at that moment. Joseph's robes hung handsomely on his tall frame, and unlike most of the other students, he looked both confident and erudite in his black mortarboard.

"I would like to thank all of you for receiving me so warmly," he said, his voice wafting pleasantly over the Commons. "But then, my entire experience at Absalom Jones has been extremely positive. I must give particular thanks for the support I have received from Frederick Martin, my professor of American history, who helped me to understand so much about this great country. I also found a friend in Professor Lorna Terrence, who is as comfortable with chemistry as with calculus, which I believe is a very rare quality, indeed."

The audience chuckled politely.

"Finally, I want to thank President Saunders and Dean Crawley for their support when I became the husband of a wonderful woman two years ago. My wife, Reba Freeman-Thomas, and I owe our success as students to the kindness of this college. And I must admit that as her grade point average is only a single decimal point lower than mine, she certainly deserves to be standing on this dais beside me. In fact, she *really* deserves to be the valedictorian at our commencement, because on top of excelling at her own work, she has guided me through so many of the difficulties of living in a world that is quite different from my own. We will take Absalom Jones College's message of brotherhood and learning with us when we begin our professional careers in my native country of Liberia. Please indulge me in introducing my wife, Reba."

Flushing with pleasure, I rose to my feet. The lawn exploded into warm applause, but I hardly heard it. All of my attention was focused on that wonderful man. My husband. My life.

Joseph and I were halfway across the Commons after the ceremony when we heard my father's voice. "Reba! I'd like to have a word with you!"

We both looked back to see my father approaching swiftly. His eyes were riveted on us and his mouth was a thin line of rage. My mother, hampered by her sandals on the thick lawn, was struggling to keep up.

My father reached us first. Ignoring Joseph, he directed his assault wholly at me.

"How dare you announce your departure for Africa to the public without first having spoken to your parents!"

"I didn't announce anything to anyone," I answered, my own anger rising like a volcano despite the fact that we were standing in the dead center of campus. Several students standing nearby with their families stopped talking to watch.

"In the midst of my former classmates and friends, you made an open declaration of your shameful relationship and then followed that with the news that you're leaving the country!"

"Excuse me, sir," Joseph said in a low voice. "I am certainly the one to blame for both of those things."

"I refuse to hold you, a stranger from another continent, responsible for my daughter's poor judgment," my father replied dismissively, "though it is clear that you have done everything in your power to brainwash her."

"He's done no such thing!" I shouted, oblivious to the crowd that was starting to gather as our argument progressed. "Joseph and I waited over a year before we decided to get married, and as you can see, it hasn't prevented us from being the best students on this campus. In fact, Joseph and I have made better grades than you did when you studied here—"

"How dare you speak that way to me?" My father was standing

so close to me that I thought he might strike me, but my mother, who finally caught up with him, reached for his arm.

"Raymond, you're making a spectacle of yourself. Let's go now."

"I think this young man needs to understand that he hasn't gotten away with anything," my father said in a menacing voice. "If I die tomorrow, you will never touch a penny of my money."

"What are you talking about?"

"I'm talking about the *real* reasons why he convinced you to sneak away without your parents' knowledge. After he saw our home he thought that by marrying you he might just be in line for—"

"That's ridiculous! We've never asked either one of you for a cent."

"Let's take this discussion somewhere else," my mother insisted, pulling at my father's arm. More than twenty people were milling nearby, openly listening. My father glanced around, his face filled with self-righteous disdain.

"I studied at this fine institution," he declared in his pulpit voice, "as did my father before me. I believe that my daughter owes me some respect, particularly while she is a student at my own alma mater."

"I fail to see how our marriage or our academic achievements at Absalom Jones signify disrespect," Joseph replied softly, openly challenging my father for the first time. "Perhaps it would be more appropriate for you to recognize our accomplishments."

"And perhaps," my father answered as he leveled his bitter gaze on my husband, "you should remember that I will always be Reba's father, even if you tricked her into becoming your wife."

"Why is it so hard for you to believe that she *chose* to be my wife?" Joseph asked with quiet dignity.

"Reba has never gone against my wishes before!"

"It was time for me to make some decisions on my own," I answered.

"Stop this, all of you!" my mother hissed. "You're embarrassing me!"

"Not nearly as much as Reba has embarrassed me," my father argued.

Joseph slipped his arm around my waist. "Once again, I do not wish to be the cause of discord in your family, sir. But I think that your comportment toward us is unfair. We love each other and have committed ourselves to that love by marrying. We have supported ourselves by working, living very frugally and continuing to do very well with our studies. My parents are very proud of me, and will be very proud to welcome your daughter into our family. I hope that in time you will feel this way about me too."

My father lifted his chin. "I have only one child, young man, and I have spent my life protecting her. I will *never* trust a man who encouraged her to abandon her family, face expulsion from her college and openly flaunt her disregard for her parents to the community."

"Then I apologize," Joseph said with grace. "But sir, I want to make it clear that I love your daughter and would never do anything to hurt her."

"Well, I do *not* apologize. And I am formally opposed to your taking her off to live in Africa."

"When the time comes," Joseph replied, "Reba will accompany me of her own accord. I would never make her do anything she does not wish to do."

"Come now, Raymond!" my mother exclaimed. My father threw back his shoulders and straightened his back, but he still had to look up to meet Joseph's eyes.

"Make no mistake. You will *never* be welcome in our family or our home. The only reason I haven't cut all contact with my daughter is that I predict this marriage will not last, and she is most certainly going to need my support once you're gone."

I looked over my father's shoulder and realized that Samantha was standing with her family in the crowd. She quickly glanced at me as Joseph met my father's stare. After I had spent four long years refusing to discuss any aspect of my relationship with Joseph with anyone at the college, my father had publicly humiliated me before the entire campus—and on the day of our graduation.

"Come on, Joseph," I pleaded, lowering my head to hide my burning tears. He broke eye contact with my father and looked down at me, his brows drawing together in concern. Without another word, we turned away to the raging murmurs of the curious spectators.

Dean Crawley offered to let us keep our small apartment over the summer. Joseph was hoping that he'd land the position with the Church of England, in which case we'd be moving by the end of August. Everything depended on his interview with the church in New York, which was scheduled to take place two weeks after commencement.

My former roommates asked me out to lunch a week after the graduation ceremony, claiming that they wanted to spend some time with me before they moved out of their apartments. We met at the harbor and sat on a terrace, eating crab cakes while wealthy Baltimoreans guided their sailboats in and out of the harbor.

"I can't wait to get back to Washington," Samantha began as she sipped a glass of Chablis. "I need to be in a city with a bankable supply of men."

"I thought you were on your way to the altar with Carl," Desiree remarked, smothering her crab cakes with hollandaise sauce.

"He's moving way too slow for me," she replied, her eyes narrowing.

"Did that law student you were dating ever get married?" I asked.

"No. But I'd still prefer Carl. Our kids would be so pretty."

She went on for a while, talking about the advantages of living in a city with so many colleges. "They provide an inexhaustible inventory of fresh prospects." She glanced up at me. "Have you spent any time in Washington?"

"Joseph and I take the train down from time to time."

"But have you hung out and enjoyed the nighttime groove?"

"I'm married, Samantha, remember?"

"Well, you can still have some fun," she said, touching my arm reassuringly.

"You and I have different definitions of fun."

"True. But what are you going to do around here this summer? We've graduated, Reba. You shouldn't be stuck on an empty campus."

"If everything goes well, Joseph's going to get that job and we'll be moving by fall."

"That's all the more reason why you should get out and party. Once you're in Africa—"

"Don't start, Samantha!"

"Okay. I know you don't want to hear it. But you should think about the fact that you're planning to leave everyone and everything you've ever known behind. Women don't have the same freedoms over there. Men are in control. I really think you should just enjoy this last summer of American life. Who knows? You might look back one day and be glad you did."

I glanced uneasily at Desiree, whose eyes issued me a challenge: Was I still free enough to accept Samantha's invitation—or did Joseph already wield complete control over my life?

"I'll think about it," I said evasively.

"Why don't you stay with Samantha while Joseph's in New York for his interview?" Desiree asked.

"I was planning to go with him."

"Are they paying for your hotel?"

"Actually, we're going to stay in the seminary."

"Seminary!" they shouted together. "You're going to be sleeping in a dorm with a bunch of priests?" Desiree shrieked.

"We'll have our own room, and it's only for two nights—"

"*Two* nights? You're thinking about going to New York and staying in a place where you can't even drink!" Desiree said.

"Or laugh out loud," Samantha added.

"And don't even think about sex!" Desiree howled.

"Listen," I said. "Joseph's going for a job interview, not a party. And anyway—hotels cost money. We can't afford anything else."

"Then let him go by himself," Samantha concluded. "You can come and stay with me in D.C."

"I should be with him for moral support."

"What if the priests want to invite him to dinner?" Desiree said. "Won't you be in the way?"

"If you're not there he can concentrate on getting the job without worrying about you," Samantha added. "And you can have some fun before you start packing for your move."

"If you want, I'll come down to Washington too," Desiree said. "I'm not moving home until the end of June. We can spend this last little vacation together as a tribute to Absalom Jones and our lifelong friendship!"

———

I began feeling queasy a few days before Joseph left for New York, but I didn't tell him about it. He needed to focus all of his attention on his interview. He prepared himself by reading for hours, expecting that he'd be given a series of tests to determine the range and depth of his knowledge. Every evening we practiced his interviewing skills by role-playing difficult questions and various answers. As the day drew closer he became increasingly tense, talking endlessly about the decadence of America and the wonders of his own home.

"Monrovia is really quite modern," Joseph said as if to reassure me the night before he was to leave for New York. "And even though we have a new government, our economy remains stable."

"New government?" I asked as I ironed his best white shirt.

"The old president, William Tolbert, was deposed by Samuel Doe four years ago," he said. "My family says that once things settled down, life has gone on in much the same way as before."

"I didn't realize that anything had happened with the government in Liberia."

"We were freshmen."

"Why didn't you tell me?"

"We've rarely talked about politics in Africa."

"We talked about everything else. You just never mentioned the political situation."

"I didn't think you'd care," he said, sitting up and turning away. "After all, most people in this country barely know what's going on in the American government, much less show any interest in the rest of the world."

"But you've let me think that everything was perfect in Liberia."

"That's not true, Reba. I have always been completely honest about the need for great change in my home country. That is one reason why I am so anxious to return."

"You should have said something, Joseph."

"Reba," he said angrily, "we have been together for nearly four years. You have been my wife for two. You have had many opportunities to inform yourself about life in my country. Absalom Jones College has a very fine library full of books and newspapers. There are courses offered in African history and anthropology. If you now profess to be ignorant about your future home, you have no one to blame but yourself."

I stared at his back in wonder. Joseph had never before spoken to me with such contempt. His shoulders, stiff and square, formed an unyielding wall between us, and for the first time in our entire relationship I felt a real sense of uncertainty.

"If it was unsafe, would you tell me?"

"Of course."

"How would you know?"

"My family would inform me."

"But they don't live in the capital."

"Neither will we."

"But we'll be there for at least a year."

"You don't have to worry, Reba," he said, staring stubbornly at the wall before him. "The change in political leadership only affects people at the upper levels of government. We will hardly be important enough to garner any attention."

"But they'll know you've come back."

"Hundreds of Liberians study abroad."

"But the government paid part of your scholarship. Won't they expect something in return?"

"They will expect me to be an effective teacher in the region where I'm assigned."

"Is that all?"

"What do you mean, Reba?"

"Won't you have to pledge allegiance to them or something like that?"

"No. That's the kind of jingoistic nonsense that you Americans ascribe to. No one in my country says prayers to their flag."

"But no one in this country simply _deposes_ the president!"

"No. Presidents are assassinated here."

"Still, most Americans live well."

"Thousands of Americans are murdered every year, Reba. Millions more live in poverty. Despite your nation's wealth, uncountable people are functionally illiterate. It isn't even safe for us to walk in certain neighborhoods of this city."

"Then why don't you stay here and do something for _this_ country? After all, you owe your education to America, not Liberia."

"I have been a model guest while I studied in your nation. But I cannot accept the disinterest Americans feel toward the rest of the world. The waste of food and water that I see every day, even on this campus, sickens me. And I refuse to dedicate my life to people who assume that I am inferior, simply because of the place of my birth."

"All Americans aren't like that."

"You will _not_ make me give up!" he shouted, jumping to his feet. "I will not hesitate to take this position should it be offered to me! Do you understand?"

"Don't I have something to say about it?"

"Not as far as I'm concerned."

"But you're expecting me to go with you—"

"I will be returning to Liberia whether you choose to accompany me or not!"

A ringing silence filled the room. Joseph had never raised his voice to me, much less shown me any sign of rage. Now his eyes were wild and his breath came in gasps. I looked into a face that was shadowed with a kind of anger that left me speechless. We stared at each other as if we were strangers.

"I—I'm not trying to stop you from going home."

"Then what is the point of this discussion?"

"I just wanted to know—" My words failed at the sight of his glowering eyes.

"You *don't* want to know," he retorted, his face tense. "You have no idea what life's really about. You have never been hungry or cold. You have never watched someone you loved grow sick and die because there were no doctors to care for her."

He tore his gaze away and rolled his shoulders nervously. His eyes fell on his small suitcase, which was already packed for the trip to New York.

"I do not know what's facing us in Monrovia," he admitted emotionlessly. "I did not know what was facing me when I came to America. Some people are born into uncertainty, Reba. We have to overcome our fears and move forward, no matter how difficult it may seem."

"I won't be afraid if I'm with you," I said over the hammering of my heart.

"You *still* don't understand. It doesn't matter if we're afraid. The needs of my people are more important than anything we might be feeling."

"I can't stop my emotions."

"No, but you can overcome them. Do you think that I'm made of stone? I have been terribly lonely in your country. I have missed my family more than words can describe. I have not spoken my language or eaten my food in years. I have not smelled the earth of our country or the perfume of our flowers or heard the songs of our birds in the night. Many nights I have lain awake, even while you slept beside me, aching for my home."

He shifted restlessly. "No matter what I was feeling, I have never let these emotions interfere with the things I came here to do. I disciplined myself to work and study and abide by the customs of your world. Now I am ready to go back to Liberia, and I will do whatever it takes to get there."

My stomach began to ache and I reached down instinctively. His gaze followed my fingers.

"If you are going to be my wife and the mother of my children, you will have to accept the role that I have prepared myself for."

"What about *my* life?"

"You can find great happiness in devoting yourself to others, Reba."

"I thought I was devoting myself to you."

He let out a long sigh, as if emptying his heart of many years of sorrow. "I *am* my people. I exist to better their condition. You have known this from the start."

"But I fell in love with *you*."

"Then give yourself the chance to fall in love with Liberia. You may find that it is a far better love than simply dedicating your life to one man."

"But I make love with *you*."

"We make love to create life. And in making life we will add to the life of my people."

"I don't want to give birth to a people. I want to give birth to your child."

"They are one and the same, Reba."

"Not for me."

"That is because you were raised in a culture of selfishness."

"No, Joseph. It's because I pledged myself to you."

He drew his lips together and looked toward the window. "You will understand better when you've lived in my world for a time."

He had dismissed my feelings in a few words, reducing every-thing I'd said to a difference in culture. Turning on his heel, he left me alone in our room, my head ringing and my stomach aching with a deep, wrenching cramp. I felt like throwing up but fought back the nausea, determined not to let him know how upset I was. Then I climbed into bed and turned out the light. Pulling the sheets over my head, I curled up into a ball and wept, feigning sleep when he finally came to bed much later that night.

What's wrong with you?"

Wearing a poppy-red sundress, Samantha leaned out the window of her mother's black Cadillac as I emerged from our apartment, my overnight bag clutched in my arms. A blazing sun had emerged from a bank of morning clouds and the afternoon was already sweltering. Samantha's long hair was wound into a coil above her head and her dangling gold earrings glittered as she rested her chin on her arm.

"I think I've got food poisoning," I complained as I slid in beside her, my blue jeans and cotton T-shirt already clinging damply to my body. "Maybe I should just stay home."

"Food poisoning?" she blurted, laughing out loud. "You're just scared to be on your own for a few days. Was Joseph mad that you decided to come to D.C. instead of going to New York with him?"

"Of course not," I said, avoiding her cat's gaze. I was determined that she wouldn't see my eyes, still reddened from weeping for most of the night. I didn't want her to know that Joseph had barely spoken to me before he left for his interview that morning. I could hardly believe that he climbed into a taxi for the ride to the train station, his small suitcase in hand, without even saying good-bye.

"Well, since this is probably the last time we'll be doing any partying for a long time, I've made some very special plans."

"Nothing like Andre Chenault, I hope."

"Reba, you still haven't forgiven me for that, huh? Look, we're going out on Carl's boat tonight with Desiree and a couple of friends from home. There's a guy in the crowd who just moved up here from Florida to go to med school, and I'm planning on setting the two of them up."

"You're giving a doctor away?" I asked disbelievingly.

"Marlon's way too slow for me," she said as she flicked the air-conditioning on and shut the power windows. "Besides, I dated him when he was up here visiting his cousin last summer. That's why I know he'd be perfect for Desiree."

I grabbed my stomach as another cramp reached deep into my body, bending me almost double on the car seat.

Samantha shot me a concerned glance. "You really aren't kidding, are you?"

"Yes," I said sarcastically, "I'm just making this up."

"Is it your period?"

"It can't be."

"Look, we'll stop by the health center where my cousin works and get you a prescription, all right?"

I don't remember much of what happened during the next couple of hours. Samantha drove us straight into Washington and stopped in front of a women's clinic a few blocks from Howard University. Her cousin, a nurse practitioner, agreed to see me even though it was her lunch break. Thirty minutes later she called me into her office, a stern look on her face.

"Samantha says you used to be roommates," she said as she motioned me into a chair beside her gray metallic desk.

"Yes, freshman year." I caught my breath as another cramp rolled through my body.

"She said you got married two years ago."

"Yes. My husband's in New York for a job interview."

"And you graduated last month?"

"Yes," I muttered. "Why?"

"That's all good news," she said, sitting back in her chair to consider me with a half smile. "Well, Reba, I can give you something very mild to help you with the pain, but I certainly wouldn't want to do anything that might interfere with the health of your baby."

I looked up. Her smile was now a grin. I felt my forehead moisten and my whole body began to shake. "There must be some mistake. I—"

"No mistake, sweetheart. Four weeks, give or take a few days."

"But I'm taking the Pill—"

"Have you ever missed a day?"

"Well, I—" I stammered to a halt, realizing that I had, indeed, lost track of the little pink compact for nearly a week.

"You're young and healthy," she said, leaning forward to touch my arm. "That makes it much easier."

Speechlessly I glanced up at the posters depicting a woman's reproductive cycle. I had looked at those posters in doctor's offices for years, never realizing that those colorful drawings of the Y-shaped fallopian tubes, superhighways for the intrepid sperm, might one day have *real* relevance to me!

"I had no idea. . . ." My voice faded away again, as hundreds of voices roared through my head. I knew how Joseph would react when he learned that he was soon to be a father. I also knew what Samantha and Desiree would say. But I could only imagine my parents' horror when they understood I was due to have a baby just as I was leaving for my new life in Africa.

"Are you feeling okay?" the nurse asked gently.

"I—I guess."

"You've got a place to live?"

"Yes."

"Your husband wants children?"

"Definitely."

"And he's interviewing for jobs?"

I nodded silently.

"Well, then everything's going to be all right."

I reached up to wipe the sweat away from my forehead. She found a tissue and I automatically wiped my eyes. I hadn't even realized I was crying.

"Listen, sweetheart. Lots of young women are surprised to find out they're pregnant. I would say that you're really lucky to have a husband and a degree. This may have happened a little bit earlier than you intended, but if you give yourself a few days I'm sure you'll be very happy about it."

I lowered my eyes and she stroked my arm. "You'll need to see a doctor in the next week or two. You're going to need to take some tests and get a prescription for special vitamins. For the time being, try to get more sleep, cut out the coffee, alcohol and cigarettes, and eat saltines if you don't feel well."

I staggered out into the waiting room, where Samantha was pacing impatiently. She looked over my shoulder at her cousin, who was smiling warmly. "Let's go," I said without further discussion.

Once we were in the car, however, she immediately looked at my hands.

"Didn't she give you anything for your stomach?"

"No. I don't have food poisoning."

I looked away, blinking furiously at the tears that still threatened to fill my eyes. She put the car into gear and swung out into traffic. My stomach lurched and I lowered the window, gasping for air.

"Reba, what's going on?" Samantha asked nervously, glancing across the seat in wonder.

"Nothing. I—I just don't feel well."

"Damn, Reba. If I didn't know better, I'd say you're pregnant!"

I should have reacted more quickly, but at that moment I was struggling to keep myself from throwing up. She smoothly guided the car to the curb and shut off the engine, turning to me.

"Reba Freeman—*are* you pregnant?"

For four years I had managed to keep my vow never to share the details of my private life with anyone. But at that moment, sick and alone and deeply hurt by my husband's dismissal, Samantha's concern felt like a buoy in my sea of confusion. Tears spurted from my eyes and I nodded my head, unable to form any words.

There was a surprised pause. Then she reached across the car seat and pulled me roughly into her arms. "I should have known," she said with an exasperated sigh. "Why the hell didn't you say something?"

She drove very slowly back to her mother's row house in southeast Washington. Amazingly, she didn't speak for the whole trip, which gave me a chance to calm down.

Alone in her room, she sat beside me on her bed.

"You didn't know, did you?" she asked perceptively. When I didn't answer, she grasped my hands. "So Joseph doesn't know either?"

"He'll be very happy."

"And what about you?"

"I'm happy too."

"You don't look very happy."

"I just have to get used to the idea."

"OK," she said. That cool gaze that I knew so well returned. "How are you going to handle being pregnant while you're getting ready to move to Africa?"

"First, Joseph has to get the job."

"Even if he doesn't get this job, it won't be long before he'll be going back. That's all he's ever wanted."

"I know." I avoided her intense eyes, hoping to shield myself from her critical gaze.

"And when you get there, what kind of medical attention will you have?"

"The hospitals are fine in Monrovia."

"But what if he wants to go back to his village?"

"Women have babies every day in Africa."

"Of course they do. But do you really want to give birth like they do, without sterile instruments or painkillers?"

"Liberia is not the Stone Age, no matter what you and Desiree think," I said weakly, but my protest didn't convince either one of us.

"It would be different if you got pregnant after you'd been there awhile," she replied. "Who knows what's going to happen to you in the coming year?"

"Whatever happens, we'll be all right."

"Joseph's not the one having the baby, Reba."

"He'll take care of me."

"Won't he be busy trying to open his school?"

"His family will be there."

"So you're counting on people you've never met?"

"I'm sure I'll be fine."

She stood up and walked over to the phone. "I'm calling the party off. We really don't need to be going out on a boat tonight."

"No—no, I want to go out," I said. "What's the point of me sitting here worrying?"

"Are you sure you don't want me to take you back to Baltimore?"

"I'm sure," I said, uttering the two words that would seal my destiny.

I hadn't seen Carl Thornton since his graduation the year before, but he hugged me warmly when he hoisted me onto the deck of his parents' boat, the *Seven and Seven*. His bright eyes took in my loose-fitting African dress, which Joseph had bought for me in an import store. Then his eyes darkened as Samantha, wearing a red satin halter with matching short-shorts, climbed into his arms.

"Welcome aboard," he said cheerfully after she released him. "Everybody else is already here. There's plenty to eat and drink down below. Make yourselves at home while I get us under way."

The forty-five-foot sailboat, which had cabin space to sleep four, also offered enough deck space to allow the seven of us to move around easily as we sailed out into Chesapeake Bay.

Desiree was too busy grinning at the medical student to notice my piqued face, and Samantha's friends, Paula and Michael, had already drunk half a bottle of gin before we arrived. Samantha led me to some padded benches on the main deck, while Carl climbed fleetly to the top deck and took the wheel.

"Feeling better?" she asked, handing me a cold ginger ale from an ice chest.

"Yes. The fresh air helps a lot."

She looked out at the city lights, which were fading as Carl skillfully guided the boat out of the marina. "Reba, I've been thinking—" She paused as if forming her words carefully. "You know, you really don't have to keep this baby."

"What?" Outraged, I glared up into her face.

"*Shhhhh.* Keep your voice down. Look—I'm not trying to make you do anything you don't want to do, but you should think about it."

"I could never do that!"

"Yes, you could."

I turned away from her and felt the pain in my stomach return. The lights of the dock had receded and the water was still and dark around us. Up on the top deck Carl had put a tape in the cassette player, and a soprano sax was now wailing into the night.

"Listen," she began again, sitting down beside me. "You can take care of it at my cousin's clinic. It only takes a few minutes."

"How would you know?"

"I—well, let's just say I've been there, Reba."

"When?"

"That doesn't matter. What matters is that I couldn't let one mistake keep me from doing the things I have to do with my life. I could never have finished school with a baby. I'd never have had the chance for a career. And I certainly wouldn't be dating anybody like Carl."

"Just because you made that choice doesn't mean it's right for me."

"Reba—do you really want to move to Africa while you're pregnant?" she asked, peering deep into my eyes.

"I—I don't know."

"Will you have a job when you get there?"

"No."

"Do you have any insurance?"

"No."

"Do you have any money saved up?"

"Of course not."

"Do you want to be living in the bush with a newborn child?"

"I don't know."

"Can you handle the birth without any friends or family to help you out?"

I looked away, into the vast darkness of the water.

"Listen, sister," she said with cool formality. "You need to face it: You are just not ready to be a mother."

I closed my eyes, the pain in my gut growing with her words. Deep inside, I knew that she was right. But how could I even think about ending the life of my baby? How could I make such a decision without Joseph's approval? How could I let Samantha, of all people, influence me on such an important decision?

"I can't do it," I whispered, almost forgetting that she was sitting by my side. "I just can't."

"Why not?" she asked. I looked up; it was difficult to see her face in the night.

"Samantha, you're asking me to betray Joseph's trust."

"Does he own your body?"

"Of course not."

"So what if he insists that you keep it against your will?"

I hadn't thought of that. I wrapped my arms around my knees and leaned forward, dropping my forehead to my thighs.

Suddenly, the pain in my stomach seemed unbearable, and my shoulders started to shake uncontrollably. "I need to talk to Joseph!"

"Well, yes"—she stroked my back—"but once he finds out, you won't have any choice, will you?"

"I don't know," I sobbed.

Samantha put her arms around me. "Reba," she said softly, "have you ever really thought about what Joseph's dreams are going to mean for you? You have the right to some dreams of your own. You need to understand that this isn't about Joseph. It's about you, your life and your future. I've never made a secret of the fact that I thought you chose the wrong guy, but now you've got to understand that I'm only looking out for you!"

"Oh, God," I murmured.

"Hey," she said in a low voice. "Hey—are you about to get sick?"

"I don't know," I whispered, my tears pouring between my fingers and running down my arms.

"Hold on," she whispered. "I'll get you a towel."

She vanished with the sound of her bare feet slapping the deck. Almost immediately I sensed the warmth of another body at my side.

"Hey, Reba. Are you okay?" It was Carl. His voice was low and more gentle than I'd ever heard it.

Ashamed, I straightened up and wiped my eyes. My hand came away black. I had forgotten that Samantha had insisted on "helping" me with my makeup before we went out that night.

"Oh, shit," I muttered, looking at the black smears on my palms. Carl laughed softly.

"Here." He produced a roll of paper towels from a compartment beneath the bench. My eyes were burning as the makeup mixed with my tears.

"Let me help," he said, dipping the paper towel into a water glass, then carefully wiping my face. "There, there," he said in a soothing voice. "Does Daddy's little precious feel better?"

An hour earlier I would have slapped his hand away, certain that he was making fun of me. But my misery was so deep that his teasing seemed like a cleansing ray of light in the darkness. I felt a smile tug at the corners of my mouth and, seeing it, he smiled too.

"Oooh, Reba," he said, leaning back to survey his work. "Now you look exactly like a raccoon!"

Gasping, I raised my hands to my face. He burst into laughter.

"That's not funny," I whimpered.

"It's just about as funny as you pretending that my steering is making you seasick," he said.

"That's not what I'm doing."

"Sure it is! None of my lady friends has ever thrown up on the *Seven and Seven*! And I guarantee you, I've had enough guests on this boat to have tested the waters."

"Including your friend from Atlanta?"

"Actually," he said with a shrug, "she never made it this far north." He paused, his face settling into a serious expression. He reached up and placed his hand on my shoulder, looking into my face. "What's going on?"

"I'm just not feeling well."

"Where's Joseph?"

"At a job interview in New York."

"So you're going to stay in the States?"

"No. The job's in Liberia."

He gazed at me a moment without speaking. Then he looked down quickly, examining his hands. "You know, I've been working for my father's company since I graduated. We have a client who sets up nonprofit organizations. He may be hiring right now."

"What kind of nonprofits?" I asked.

"Companies that work with government agencies, mostly."

"Are they looking for teachers?"

"No," Carl said, glancing into my eyes. "They're looking for people with business degrees."

"Then Joseph couldn't get a job—"

"No. But *you* could."

"But I'm not looking for a job!"

"Are you sure?"

"I—we're moving to Liberia."

"But you don't have to move this year, you know. Nothing will change that fast in Africa. And if you worked here for a few months you could save up some cash. Might make things easier when you—"

At that moment Samantha appeared with a wet towel. She glanced from Carl to me, her eyes falling to the blackened paper towel in his hand. Then she cleared her throat. "I didn't realize you were such a boy scout, Carl."

"Reba's been my little sister since her first day of college," he said, chuckling lightly.

"Well, I'll take over the babysitting from here," she coolly replied. He stood up, shrugged and climbed the short flight of steps to the top deck. Samantha sat down beside me.

"Did you think it over?"

"Samantha, I just can't."

"Okay," she said with a sigh. "But I will say this: You are only twenty-one years old. You've only dated one man. You've never had a real job. You've never lived off campus. You've never even had a daydream of your own. As far as I can see, you've let Joseph take over your body, your mind and your life."

She stood up. "If you're sure that you want to spend the rest of your life living with Joseph in Liberia, then you should keep this baby. But if you have even the slightest doubt, you should give yourself the option of freedom. Because once you have this child," she said in a low voice, "it will be very, very hard for you to ever be free."

She disappeared into the lower cabin, where barbs of inebriated laughter tore at the night. Carl came down from the top deck a few moments later. "You need anything, Reba?"

"No, thanks. I just want to sit here for a while."

"Okay. Call me if you don't feel well." He joined the others.

I sat there alone, staring out into the clear summer night. There were uncountable stars in the velvety sky, and I remembered my childhood belief that the stars were angels' eyes, watching over every boy and girl in the world. I wondered if the constellations were the same in Africa. I wondered how the sky would look when I was living in Joseph's village. I wondered if he would sit with me on our porch after a long day of teaching, while our children slept beneath mosquito nets in the room behind us. I wondered if his hand would rest on my belly, where another child would be growing.

And then I wondered if I'd ever have the chance to use the skills I'd learned in college. I wondered if the countless hours of math and statistics would go to waste. Would I ever run an office? Manage a business? Supervise other employees?

I wished with all my heart that I could talk to Joseph. I wished that I could tell him how much I wanted to slow things down. To find a job and live in a real apartment and earn some money. To go to restaurants and movies, and shop in malls and spend time with friends. To live with a sense of security and comfort, even if only for a few months.

Samantha was right. From that first walk with Joseph in our second week of college, my entire world had been built on his dreams. I had taken his hope into my heart, his loneliness into my soul and his determination into my womb. We had never even discussed what I really wanted.

A boat passed us some distance away, its red taillights shining in the night. Another spurt of laughter erupted from below. There

were so many lives in this world—lives that offered possibility.
Growth. Change. How would I change if I left for Liberia with
Joseph? What chance would there be for me to grow? Were there
any possibilities for me to become the woman I *really* wanted to be
if I abandoned my country now?

My eyes fell to my wedding ring, which gleamed softly in the
darkness. This ring bound me to Joseph and to the father who came
before him. But I was bound to other people too. Joseph wanted me
to give birth to the next generation of his people. But what about
my people? What about *my* culture? What about the parts of me
that were distinctively American? Distinctly Freeman?

My heart quavered—even *thinking* this way felt like a complete
betrayal of the promises I'd made to my husband. After four years
of accepting the fact that his quest was so meaningful and real, I
hardly knew how to think for myself.

But as I sat alone on the deck of Carl's boat, looking out over
the still, black water, I knew that I would have to start thinking for
myself. I glanced out into the horizon of endless possibility and uncertain truth. There were no certain truths. We were each responsible for the choices we made, and we could leave those choices to
no one else.

The sky was already bright when we returned to the harbor.
Samantha's friends had fallen asleep after emptying the gin bottle,
and she had a hard time shaking them awake. Desiree and Marlon
had disappeared into the inner cabin, and Carl gallantly decided to
leave them alone. He hoisted Samantha up to the dock, then
reached down for me. As he lifted me gently to land, he looked
questioningly into my eyes.

"Let's go, Reba," Samantha said coldly.

We settled into her mother's Cadillac. She looked across at me.
"Why didn't you come down with the rest of us?"

"I had some thinking to do."

"Really?"

"Yes," I said very quietly. "What time does your cousin's clinic open?"

It was supposed to be painless. But it wasn't. It was supposed to take a few minutes. But it didn't. And I was supposed to walk away with all of it behind me. But I couldn't.

The cramping was so intense that I lay in the clinic in a fetal position for several hours, my body bathed in sweat. When it was time for the clinic to close, Samantha's cousin came into the small room, a worried expression on her face.

"Listen, Reba. I'm going to take you over to the hospital."

"No!" I pleaded. "I can't go to the hospital. I don't have any insurance and I can't afford it."

"But you shouldn't be feeling this bad," she said, once again shaking out the thermometer to take my temperature. "Let me check on the bleeding."

I managed to roll over despite the pain, and watched as she shook her head.

"You're not hemorrhaging, but I still think you should stay off your feet. Did you plan on going back to Baltimore tonight?"

I dropped my head on the examination table, unable to tell her how afraid I was to be alone in our apartment on campus. I didn't expect Joseph to return until late the following day, and there'd be no one to help me if I didn't get better.

She saw my expression. "I'll tell Sam you need to stay with her for a couple of days."

"I have to be back at work tomorrow."

"I'll write you a medical excuse for your job," she said. "But you've got to stay off your feet. And I'd like to see you again tomorrow afternoon. You call me if the bleeding gets any heavier, okay?"

I managed to get off the table and back into my clothes. Samantha helped me to her mother's Cadillac and I lay down on the rear seat, drawing my legs nearly up to my chin to quell the pains. She was unusually quiet as we drove through southeast Washington, and when she helped me out of the car I saw fear in her eyes.

"If my mother says something, tell her you drank too much last night and felt sick all day," she instructed me.

Samantha helped me up the narrow stairs to her room in the rear of the small row house. I lay down on an inflatable mattress beside her bed, and she covered me with a sheet. I instantly fell into a deep, exhausted sleep. I don't know how long I was out, but I was awakened by loud voices in the hall below.

I opened my eyes to blackness. At first I didn't recognize the whitewashed, girlish vanity and bed in the small room. Bathed in sweat, I looked toward the window and found a view of naked telephone poles, not the branches of exploding leaves outside our bedroom in Baltimore. My groin hurt less, but the pain had crawled around to the small of my back. I reached between my legs and the hand that I held up to the streetlight came up black.

The noise outside the bedroom was moving up the stairs. Two people were arguing about something, but I couldn't make out their words. I sat up groggily, trying to decide whether it was more important to mop up the blood or see what was going on outside the door. I thought about Samantha's ruined sheets, a needle of shame piercing my consciousness, then realized that the blood might mean I was in trouble. I had almost forgotten why I was there, on that air mattress. Yes, I'd been pregnant. And yes, I'd had an abortion.

My arms and legs were glued to the soiled sheets, but I managed to roll heavily toward the edge of the mattress. Using a handful of tissues to wipe off my fingers, I tried to staunch the steady flow of blood. A wash of dizziness foamed over me as I sat up, and I felt my heart roaring furiously in my sweat-washed chest. My stomach muscles lurched upward, but I hadn't eaten in almost two days and there was nothing in my belly to vomit. Someone seemed to have forced a bag of sand between my swollen lips.

The voices were coming closer. I heard a man and a woman. They were arguing. They were both very angry. I knew that I should care. But I couldn't. My lids were so heavy that I could barely open my eyes, much less go to the door to see who was making all that noise.

Rolling off the mattress, I went down on all fours. The voices were just outside the door now. I grasped the post of Samantha's bed with my reddened fingers and slowly pulled myself to my feet, feeling the blood pour like syrup down my thighs to splatter at my feet. I swept up the sheet and pushed it between my legs, stanching the flow as I stumbled vaguely toward the door.

Just as I steadied myself to reach for the knob the door jerked open. Light from the hallway spilled into the room to find me frozen in the pose of a black and scarlet Venus, the rose-stained sheet coiled around my body, my hair matted, my lids swollen nearly shut.

Samantha was standing with her back to the door, as if desperately trying to keep the truth from escaping. But it was much too late for that. Joseph's face was frozen in horror, his mouth open as if petrified in midsentence.

No one spoke for what seemed like an eternity. I was trembling so hard that I had to clench my jaw to keep my teeth from rattling.

Beneath the sheet I felt another clot disengage and glide warmly down my glistening thigh.

"I—I need to go—need water," I stammered, and Samantha stepped aside, unable to look at me. Joseph's eyes never blinked as I shuffled by him and staggered into the cold, bright bathroom. As soon as I closed the door I heard his voice, the rage that had fought its way up the stairs now replaced by an icy fear.

"What happened?"

"I already told you that she felt sick yesterday and I took her to see a doctor," Samantha answered with unrestrained hostility.

"What do you mean, 'sick'?"

"I explained to you that she had a lot of abdominal cramping, and—"

"When did this begin?"

"Sometime yesterday."

"Why didn't you call me?"

"You'd gone to New York, Joseph. I didn't know how to reach you."

"Reba knew where I was."

"Reba didn't feel well enough to call."

"What's wrong with her?"

"That's between Reba and the doctor."

"I am her husband."

"That doesn't mean you own her."

"Her health is my concern."

"Not when you're in another state."

"You had no right to intervene."

"She needed someone to take care of her!"

"I have always taken care of my wife."

"You were too busy taking care of yourself!"

"I was making plans for our future—"

"You were making plans for *your* future!" Samantha shouted, her anger again rising.

"You have nothing to say about my relationship with Reba," he answered. I heard his voice move closer to the bathroom door. He tried the knob, but I was leaning desperately against the wood, holding the bloodied sheet between my legs as the blood continued to flow.

"Let me in, Reba," he commanded in a voice that was not unlike my father's.

"Give her some privacy!" Samantha said, obviously standing just behind him.

"Open the door," he said, pronouncing each syllable very clearly.

"Why don't you leave her alone? Can't you see she's in no condition to talk to you right now?"

"My wife has no right to refuse to speak to me!"

"Reba has the right to do whatever she wants!" Samantha retorted. "This is America, not Liberia!" Her voice was so close that she must have moved between Joseph and the door.

"You have nothing to say about what happens in our marriage!"

"And you have nothing to say about what Reba does with her body!"

"You stay out of this, Samantha!"

"You don't tell *me* what to do either—"

"I am asking you to move so that I can speak to my wife!"

"And I'm telling you that when she got into trouble she didn't come to you, Joseph. She came to *me!*"

Behind the door my heart nearly exploded as Joseph uttered the next phrase: "What *kind* of trouble, Samantha?"

"The kind that only another woman understands!" she shouted. I moved away from the door, steadying myself to open it before—

"What has she done—" His words were a statement, not a question, and I realized that he had actually put his hands on her.

"Let go of me, you ape! I'll call the police and get your ass deported!"

I placed my hand on the knob, letting the sheet slip away from my hips.

"What did you make her do?" he shouted, his fury terrifying.

"I didn't have to make her do anything. Reba's smart enough to decide when she wants to be a mother!"

It was as if time stopped. The silence in the hall swallowed everything up, and I opened the door to find Samantha, her eyes snarling, and Joseph Vai Thomas standing before me with a face of stone.

We looked at each other. His eyes wandered down, over my stained breasts, to my heaving belly, and then to the red-brown sheet below. He looked back up into my face, as if studying my features so that he would always remember them. A sheen appeared in his eyes. And then, without another word, he brushed past Samantha and was gone.

The next few hours were a horror-movie comedy. Samantha was frightened, but I refused to go to the hospital. Fortunately her mother was at work that night; fortunately most of the blood had collected in the wells of the plastic air mattress. As she frantically scrubbed the wooden floors and the bathroom tiles, I took a shower and tried to regain some control over my body. Neither of us spoke a word more than was necessary. By the time her mother arrived home after midnight, the sheet was washed and bleached, the bedroom and bath were clean, and my bleeding had slowed. We were lying side by side in her room, not speaking.

Because there was nothing more to be said.

The following morning, at my insistence, she drove me back to Baltimore when no one answered the phone in our apartment. "It's stupid to go all the way back there," Samantha complained as she wound her way through the traffic. "He's just mad. He's not answering the phone because he knows it's you. Why don't you give him some time to cool off? I'm supposed to take you back to my cousin this afternoon—"

I was unable to answer. I could think of only one thing throughout the hour-long ride back to Baltimore: Joseph Vai Thomas's face as he stared at me in the bathroom door.

"I can't believe he just showed up like that. Didn't he even have enough respect for you to call? What if you hadn't been there? I mean, what if we'd gone out on Carl's boat again? He wouldn't even have known how to find us. Did he think he could just sit on my front steps until someone got home?"

The bleeding had slowed to the flow of a normal menstrual period, and the cramping had lessened considerably. The nightmare of the previous day might never have happened, but for my memory of Joseph's face as he stared at me in the bathroom door.

"He came in talking about how he got the offer and couldn't wait to tell you. He said he was hoping you'd be in Baltimore when he got back. When you weren't there he said he caught the next train. He must have found a cab at Union Station, because I don't see how he got all the way to my house on his own."

The highway was a blur, yet it seemed the Cadillac couldn't go fast enough. Samantha's long hair was waving like a banner behind her dark glasses, but I barely noticed the men who brought their automobiles alongside ours to ogle her. I kept seeing my husband's face as he came to understand that I had just aborted our child.

The gates of Absalom Jones College were standing wide open. The gracious oak trees swept downward, as always. And the staid brick buildings stood in silent dignity, the windows open to air out the empty classrooms and dorms.

She pulled up in front of the faculty apartments and turned off the ignition. "It might make things worse if I come in."

I opened the car door and carefully swung my legs to the pavement.

"Reba," she said, "can you handle things by yourself?"

I rose slowly to my feet and leaned down to retrieve my overnight bag.

"Do you want me to come up with you? He won't hit you or anything, will he?"

It felt like ten years—not two days—since I'd been in my own building. The stairs to the top floor seemed endless. I left my bag on the last landing and pulled myself up by grasping the banister. Heart racing, my head began to swim and for a few seconds everything in the hot stairwell buzzed to black. I staggered and sat down heavily on the top stair.

"Reba—are you okay?" Samantha had followed me inside and was now standing on the flight of stairs below. I nodded faintly and pulled myself painfully to my feet. She swept up my bag and ran up the last stairs to take my arm.

"Christ, girl! It wasn't nearly so bad for me. How far along did my cousin say you were?"

I turned my head and the look in my eyes silenced her for a moment. "Hey," she said more softly. "You've graduated, Reba. The college can't do anything to you now."

We reached my door and I fumbled in my pants pocket for the key. There was no sound in the apartment, but I knew that it was very likely that Joseph was at work. Taking a deep breath, I turned the key and pushed the door open.

What met my eyes was the most devastating scene of deliberately ordered chaos I could imagine.

The two-room apartment where I'd spent the past two years of my life was perfectly and impeccably clean. Every dish was washed and shelved; every inch of the floor was dusted. The curtains were open and the pillows were arranged neatly on the sofa. The small refrigerator was filled with the carefully preserved remnants of our last dinner together. The phone answering machine was blinking with three unplayed messages.

But there was no trace of Joseph.

My breath froze in my throat as I realized that the photographs of his mother and sisters that had graced the coffee tables were missing. Two more steps into the apartment revealed that his collection of books—all purchased from used bookstores and loved very dearly—was also gone. I wheeled around to the coat closet and saw that his light jacket, wool blazer and winter coat no longer hung beside my clothing.

Staggering like a blind woman, I made my way around the rooms with increasing desperation as I realized that every one of Joseph's belongings had vanished. It was as if he had existed only in my imagination. Or as if the man who had stared at me in the bathroom door the night before really *had* been a stranger.

Samantha was right behind me, her curiosity dwarfed by her fear. "What the hell—" she exclaimed as she watched my desperate search. "What's that idiot done now?"

When I finally collapsed on the bed, drawing my body up into a ball, she stood angrily in the doorway, berating Joseph for his "stupid, childish game. He has no right to try and scare the shit out of you like this. Where do you think he's gone? Does he even have a friend that he could go and stay with?"

I covered my face with my hands. My eyes fastened on the gold ring shining dully in the morning light.

"Did he say anything before he left last night?"

I didn't answer.

"Do you think he just took off? I mean—do you think he's headed all the way back to Africa?"

I'd hardly spoken a word to Samantha since the morning before, when I'd agreed to go to her cousin's clinic. Now I rolled over very slowly to look into her eyes.

"You can go home now," I said very quietly. "The show's over and there's nothing more to see."

"Reba Freeman! How dare you imply that—" She fell silent at the sight of my face.

I turned back to stare at the impeccable, empty room. I didn't hear her leave.

In fact, I don't remember anything else about that day except the white petals that were drifting from the tangled crabapple branches to the deep green, carefully tended lawns below. Petals that floated on the spring breeze like angels' wings. Petals that touched the earth like tears. Petals that died noiselessly, namelessly, tenderly.

Reba?"

I recognized the voice, but it took me a few seconds to realize that it belonged to Carl Thornton. I looked up to find him striding toward my desk in the accounting office. His sun-browned skin glowed brightly against his white polo shirt, which revealed rolling triceps and a lean, rippling chest. He came to a stop and crossed his arms, grinning down at me like a genie.

"I wondered where you'd disappeared to. One minute you're on my boat in D.C., and then it's seven long weeks before I see you again. I should have known you were holed up here at Absalom Jones."

For a fleeting second I wondered what Samantha had told him. Then I realized that I didn't really care. Nothing mattered anymore. My life had ceased the moment I understood that Joseph was gone.

"I take it you don't remember me," he teased when I didn't reply. "So let me introduce myself. Carl Robert Thornton. Graduate of Absalom Jones College. Recently the founder of Thornton Consulting, my very own company."

He held out his hand, but my nails were chewed raw and I slipped my hands beneath the desk. Shrugging, he returned his arms to his chest and continued to speak playfully.

"And I suppose your name is Reba? Yes, yes, it's great to meet you too. Oh, you attended Absalom Jones College as well? And you just graduated? Now you're working full-time in their accounting office? That's very impressive!"

He beamed down at me as if his banter might crack the thick shell I'd climbed into that morning seven weeks before. Deliberately ignoring my silence, he lowered his voice as if sharing a secret.

"You know, I'm told that Absalom Jones College turns out some of toughest ladies in the United States. They're reputed to be bold and beautiful, stubborn but smart and almost impossible to forget once you've got them under your skin. Could that perhaps describe you?"

He gazed seductively into my eyes. I don't know what he saw in my face, but very slowly the jester vanished. He continued to peer at me, an expression of unusual seriousness entering his gaze.

"You know," he said very quietly, "I never thought the day would come when Reba Freeman wouldn't have anything at *all* to say to me."

"My name is Reba *Thomas*."

"Does it really matter?"

"Don't you care which woman you're talking to?"

"I know who you are. And I know why I'm here. In fact, I have a very good reason to talk to you." He cocked his head to the side as if issuing me a challenge. "I stopped by to invite my smart and spunky little sister to lunch."

I glanced up dully. "Why?"

"Because I haven't had a single meaningful conversation since the last time we met. I really need someone to be brutally honest with me every once in a while."

Tears leapt up into my eyes and he pretended not to notice.

"It's quarter to twelve, Reba. I have to run upstairs and get some copies of my transcripts. Will you have time for a bite when I get back?"

Soon we were driving beyond the college gates in the apple-red convertible Mustang his father had given him when he graduated the year before. He kept the conversation flowing, ignoring my un-styled hair, plain T-shirt and ugly denim skirt. In fact, he ignored the fact that my face was empty of emotion and that tears were never far from my eyes. He chatted excitedly about his new office in a suburb just outside Washington and his first clients, who came from contacts he'd made while playing in an amateur golf championship a few months before.

"It's all about learning the game and then playing it well," he said, looking cheerfully in my direction. "It's amazing how much you can get out of making contact with the right people."

I didn't answer. The streets of Baltimore were filled with jump-roping children and old men digging tomatoes into patches of garden. The sun glinted furiously off the tops of cars and loud rap music argued with heavy metal from teenagers' boom boxes. I hadn't left the campus for weeks, and the sight of so much life was almost more than my dulled senses could bear.

"What have you been doing this summer?" he asked while we waited for a stoplight to change. I lowered my eyes. How could I describe the more than forty days and nights I'd spent doing little more than staggering into work and lying sleeplessly on my bed, staring at the telephone?

Of course, it almost never rang. Desiree had called once to tell me that things were going well with Marlon Cole, her medical student. Samantha called a few times—first to make sure I'd stopped bleeding, and then to remind me that I was better off without Joseph.

"After all," she said, "now that he's gone we'll go to work and find you the man you deserve. And don't worry—I'll never tell anybody what happened the night he left. I consider you to be one of my best friends."

The rest of my life was a long tunnel of darkness. No one on the campus seemed to have a valid address for my husband. The Diocese of Liberia didn't respond to my letters. Nor did their office in New York. Despite repeated searches, I couldn't find even a scrap of paper with his address in Africa, and all the letters and photographs he'd received from home were gone.

Trapped in the present but obsessed with the past, I had retreated into my smothering guilt, reliving my last forty-eight hours with Joseph over and over again. How could I have messed up so badly? Had I lost my mind? Hadn't my love for Joseph meant anything? What had moved me to destroy the thing he would have cared for most in life—our child?

Lying in the darkness, the reedy shrill of locusts nearly exploding in my head, over and over I saw his face and heard his voice. I felt the thick flow of blood on my thighs. I relived my terror when I realized he was gone. Some nights the memories had been so intense that I'd held a bottle of sleeping pills in my sweating fingers, wondering why I shouldn't simply take the tablets and free myself from my pain.

"Reba?" Carl's voice pulled me back to the bright, hot streets, where I caught a glimpse of the ice-cream parlor Joseph and I first visited so very long ago. "You okay?"

I nodded without speaking. Of course I was okay. I had no other choice. Joseph Vai Thomas had made it clear that he was no longer a part of my life.

To my surprise, Carl pulled into the parking lot of a city recreation area that was teeming with mothers and toddlers. He reached into the backseat and lifted up a paper bag and a thermos. "If you'll take these," he said, "I'll get the rest of the stuff."

Soon we were sitting on a blanket spread beneath a sheltering poplar tree. My legs folded beneath me, I could hardly believe that Carl Thornton was relaxing beside me, eating potato chips and urging me to try some of his mother's famous potato salad, which he'd brought along in a plastic container. He'd also packed ham and cheese sandwiches and fresh fruit. The thermos was full of root beer, his favorite kind of soda.

"So my father lent me the start-up money and helped me find an affordable office," he was explaining. "But now I've got these big white rooms with no furniture and I don't have a clue how to decorate them. My wallet is arguing for a visit to the Salvation Army, but my mother wants me to buy new furniture on credit. Of course, if I let my mother in there she'll have the place looking like her bedroom, with pastel wallpaper and antiques everywhere. I've got to do something, but I can't afford a decorator."

His gray eyes questioned mine, but I didn't know how to answer. I was barely taking in what he was saying.

"I'm still living at home to save money," he went on. "But I've been thinking about leasing a condo as soon as I get on my feet. Have you ever seen those places down on the bay near Annapolis? They've got private docks and huge balconies overlooking the water. I could afford one if I could find a decent roommate. I went down and put my name on the waiting list just in case one of the bay-front units comes open. I'd like to get a little boat. Maybe just a cat to start off with. Have you ever lived near the water?"

Carl's words formed vague images in the vast emptiness of my spirit. He was talking about starting a business. Setting up an office. Moving into his own place. Creating his own life.

"By the way—would you have time to take a look at some of my bookkeeping? I'm not very good at that stuff and I don't want the IRS coming after me. But your degree is in accounting, isn't it?"

The flickering sunlight sent dapples of gold across his cinnamon skin, and his gray eyes seemed much brighter in the restless shadows. "I know you have a lot to do," he said, not waiting for my reply. "I know they keep you busy at the college. But if you had some time—maybe on the weekend—I really could use your help."

He stretched out on the blanket and stared up into the swaying branches. I caught the glint of a gold chain beneath the white polo, gleaming against his sun-browned skin.

"I've always loved these trees," he remarked, folding his arms indolently beneath his head. "The leaves are shaped like the spades in a deck of cards. Speaking of which, do you play Whist? I don't remember ever seeing you in the student lounge."

The mention of our days at the college again clouded my eyes and I looked away quickly.

He rolled over on his side, reached down and lifted a black

sticky plum from a bag. "You know, Reba—you really should try one of these plums," he urged, holding it out to me. "The skin's bitter, but the juice is almost too sweet to believe."

Mechanically I reached out and took the plum. Our fingers touched. I lifted the fruit to my lips and, still looking at him, took a bite.

The thick skin of the plum sent a stabbing, lime-sharp sourness into my mouth, but it was instantly replaced by a roaring honey-wine succulence. Juice seemed to explode inside and outside of me, bursting down my chin and onto my T-shirt, finally splattering on my bare knees.

I gasped at the intensity of the flavor. It was the first sensation to vault the mile-thick barriers of numbness that had fortressed my heart since the morning weeks before when I had stood in my little flat and realized that Joseph was gone.

I heard gentle laughter and felt something soft on my cheeks. Opening my eyes, I discovered Carl's fingers stroking my face. He slowly and deliberately wiped the sugary syrup away. Then, one by one, he placed the tips of his fingers in his mouth and sucked off the juice.

I really looked at him then. This man whom every woman on campus desired. This handsome, intelligent and privileged male who had never known rejection or defeat. Whose family doted on him and celebrated his ideas. Whose dreams never seemed far from coming true. Whose eyes were now fixed on mine.

For the very first time in that entire afternoon, I spoke.

"What do you want, Carl?"

Strangely, the seductive grin did not appear. Instead he leaned up on his arm so that he could look directly into my face. "Reba," he said very slowly, "I want *you*."

Without blinking, I replied. "Fuck you, Carl."

"No," he said quietly. "Fuck Joseph."

A blind rage boiled up in me with such force that I was suddenly on my feet. "You have no right to say anything about Joseph!"

Carl was instantly on his feet too. "I know," he said very calmly. "But I'm going to say it anyway: *Fuck Joseph.*"

"Shut up, Carl."

"No, Reba. I won't shut up. I've needed to say this to you for a long time."

"What?"

"For four years you walked Joseph and talked Joseph and didn't let anyone else into your life."

"Joseph is my husband—"

"He *was* your husband. But he's gone, Reba. I don't know what happened between you, and I don't know how he could have been so stupid, but when he left you he abandoned the best and most important part of his life."

"What are you trying to say?"

"What I've been trying to say for the past four years! I want you. Do you hear me? I've wanted you all this time and you haven't so much as even looked at me—"

"That's because you're used to getting whatever you want, and always want what you can't get!"

"No, Reba! It's because you're strong. You're smart. You're beautiful and your heart is good. You're different from any woman I've ever known."

He was standing just inches away, his expression deeply sincere. But the intensity of his emotion only added to my enraged frustration, and I moved away, raising my hands as if to protect myself from his declaration.

"You're just trying to take advantage of me!"

"I don't even *know* what happened to you, Reba. Samantha only told me that Joseph left and that you're here alone."

"I don't need you or anybody else!"

"Maybe," he said very quietly, "I need *you*."

"I'm not interested, Carl."

"But maybe, if you'd give yourself a chance, you could be."

We stood there, facing each other, our eyes locked. He blew out a long breath and, lifting his right hand, reached out to take my fingers. "I promise that I won't hurt you."

"Joseph promised that too."

"I'm not Joseph."

"And I'm not stupid enough to make the same mistake twice."

He folded his fingers into mine. My instincts told me to pull my hand away, but something in his voice made me hesitate.

"No man could ever think you're stupid, Reba. Everyone at Absalom Jones knew that you were smarter and more independent than the rest of us. Whether you believe it or not, I'd be proud to win your trust."

Now I didn't try to hide the tears that formed in my eyes. He reached up and gently wiped my face.

"If it's all right, I'd like you to come and see my new office this weekend. Then maybe we could have a little dinner." He moved a step closer and spoke very softly. "I don't want to rush you. And believe me, if I've waited this long, I can wait till you're ready. But Reba—please give me the chance to make you happy."

"What about Samantha?" I asked in a low voice.

"How did you put it? She always wants what she can't get." He looked straight into my eyes. "She'll live without me, I guarantee you. And maybe, with time, I can help you to go on living without him too."

Carl and I were married twelve months later, in the waterfront clubhouse of our condominium outside of Annapolis. My delighted parents both attended the wedding and gave us their blessing, largely because the chaplain at Absalom Jones had managed to wrangle an annulment of my marriage when Joseph failed to respond to repeated requests for contact through the Diocese of Liberia.

Carl's mother and father were less supportive of our marriage, because I was, in their eyes, a minister's daughter who brought no particular wealth or prestige to the union.

But Carl didn't seem to care. He'd dedicated much of the money from his first big contract to hiring a good caterer and an excellent dance band for our reception, and we'd decorated the spacious clubhouse with yellow roses and white satin ribbons. I wore an ivory beaded gown with a high neckline and narrow skirt. The ceremony was performed by the chaplain and attended by President Saunders and Dean Crawley, who seemed to forget the panic I'd caused them less than three years before, when they found out about my marriage to Joseph.

Carl's older brothers attended with their wives, and his fraternity entertained the reception with a spontaneous step dance that ended with them forming a bridge of their outstretched canes for Carl and me to walk through.

Desiree was my maid of honor, and attended the ceremony with her own fiancé, Dr. Marlon Cole. Samantha came to the wedding too. She was dating a gigantic professional basketball player named Reginald Dixon, and flashed me frequent smiles through narrowed eyes.

No one but Carl and I knew how difficult it had been for me to find a reason to live during those months before our wedding. I would never tell Desiree and Samantha how Carl rented that bayside condo and insisted that I move into the second bedroom. They'd never know how he got me up in the mornings before he left for work and came home at lunch to see that I was all right. I didn't tell anyone about the evenings he put music on the stereo and made me dance with him, then held me tight as we watched movies, sometimes nearly until dawn. And then there were the weekends spent at his parents' vacation house on Chesapeake Bay, where I finally agreed to marry him.

It took me a long time to laugh again, and even longer to look forward to the sound of his car. When I began to wait for his frequent phone calls throughout the day, I knew that maybe, just maybe, I might be ready to explore the possibility of making love. And then, after we'd been together for nearly six months, he arrived home one evening and I went into his arms, hungry to become his lover.

And so after our honeymoon in Europe we came home to our sparkling new life. Carl's business had taken off so well that he could barely keep up with the work. I accepted a position as a bookkeeper with an accounting firm until we were financially stable. Carl and I had already set ourselves the goal of starting a family within three years. He was looking forward to having a daughter to spoil. But I only prayed that I would conceive and give birth to a healthy child. That, in itself, seemed blessing enough to me.

Did I love Carl? Well, I was deeply in love with him. Or maybe I was in love with the promise he offered of a safe, successful life. And perhaps I loved the idea that he had waited so long for me, when I had never shown him even the slightest interest. Charming, attentive, and ready to give me the world, it was almost impossible not to love him.

Carl never asked what drove Joseph and me apart. He seemed

content with the fact that Joseph was really gone. He wasn't a man to dwell on the past, nor to waste time worrying about how my earlier life could affect our future. In Carl's eyes the world was a banquet waiting to be tasted, and he was confident that he was invited to the feast. He never thought about the gift of his fortune, his health or his beauty. He accepted without question the privileges he'd earned merely by accident of birth.

Chapter 9

Alexandria, Virginia

2004

I found Carl in the driveway hauling heavy landscaping stones toward the curb. Shirtless, his strong back gleaming in the waning sun, the muscles of his upper arms seemed to buckle as he lifted each stone and set it carefully in place beside the asphalt.

It was late in the day. The evening shadows were rising earlier as summer prepared her descent into autumn, and a coolness had descended on the yard. Wiping his forehead with a dripping suede glove, he leaned on his shovel and surveyed his work.

Carl was angry. It was clear by the lift of his shoulders, the set of his jaw, and the way he'd forced the shovel into the loose earth.

I walked down our sloping driveway with a bottle of cold water. I knew that he'd have preferred a beer, but I wanted him stone-cold sober for what I needed to say.

"Carl?"

He looked up, his exhausted face creased from his labor. No matter how much he was hurting, he was determined not to let it show.

"I need to tell you something—something I should have told you a long time ago."

"Not another deep dark secret about Joseph," he snapped, pulling off his gloves.

"No. This time it's about me."

"You?"

"Let's just go in the back and sit down."

Exhaling heavily, he picked up his shirt and followed me slowly around the house and into the backyard. Grunting, he lowered himself into one of the patio chairs and I sat down beside him. Marisa's swing swayed gently in the late summer breeze. I watched it while he finished drinking the water.

"So what's going on, Reba?"

"This isn't going to be easy. So just let me get it out, please." I took a steadying breath. "After all these years I have to tell you the real reason why Joseph left me."

"The real reason? I thought it was because you refused to go to Liberia with him."

"I wish it had been that simple."

He set the empty bottle on the ground near his feet and lifted his head to look at me with defiant, vulnerable eyes. "Okay, I'm listening."

"It all began the night that Samantha, Desiree and I went out on your boat just after we graduated. You remember, don't you?"

"Of course. You stayed by yourself on the deck all night. You were crying and Samantha got upset because I wiped your eyes."

"That's right. Joseph had left for an interview in New York that morning. He was sullen and angry because I'd questioned his desire to go back to Liberia so soon. I'd been feeling sick for a couple of days, but that morning it was much worse than before. Samantha took me to a clinic and I found out I was pregnant."

"Pregnant?" He leaned back in his chair with a frown.

I shook my head. "The news came as a complete shock. I was so upset that I told Samantha, and she—"

"Persuaded you to have an abortion."

"No," I said, lowering my gaze. "Samantha talked to me about how hard it would be to be pregnant in the middle of our move to Africa. She talked about the lack of modern medical facilities once I got there. About the fact that my family and friends would be so far away. The fact that Joseph and I had no money. That I might never have the chance for a career, or a life of my own."

"And you agreed with her?"

"No. I believed that Joseph would do everything in his power to be a good husband and father."

"So what happened?"

"Samantha asked me the one question I couldn't answer: She asked what I would do if Joseph insisted that I keep the baby."

"And?"

"There was no question about that. Joseph couldn't wait to have kids of his own." I paused, my mind suddenly full of the star-lit darkness and the sense of solitude that had blanketed me so long ago.

"But that night I realized for the first time that I had something to say about my life, too. I wanted to have Joseph's children, but I also needed to decide when and where. And even though I loved him, I wasn't ready to become a mother.

"It was hard, but that night I faced the truth about some other things, too. I admitted to myself that I had replaced my father's authority with Joseph's. That I had never taken the time to explore my own dreams. I had never made my own decisions. Lived my own life. In other words"—I looked directly into Carl's eyes—"I made my first adult decision on your boat that night.

"I had the abortion the following day. Something went wrong and I ended up staying at Samantha's. Joseph showed up unexpectedly and found me there. He left as soon as he understood what I'd done. I never saw him again."

There was a long silence. I looked steadily into Carl's eyes, which had darkened with his growing understanding. I went on talking.

"For seven weeks I was alone in that apartment, overcome by grief. There were times when I truly wanted to die. I considered taking a bottle of pills and just never having to wake up. I honestly don't know what would have happened if you hadn't come to find me. Without your patience and your kindness I might not have survived. You gave me hope, Carl. You made me want to live—and to love—again."

He made a soft noise but continued to stare at me in silence.

"Still, I've thought about that baby every day of my life. I've wondered what that child would have looked like. What kind of person he or she might have become. And I've never forgiven myself for betraying Joseph."

"You weren't betraying Joseph," Carl said quietly. "You were trying to save yourself."

"But the price was too high. I destroyed more than one life that day. I can't help feeling that everything might have gone better for him if I had made a different choice."

"But he made choices, too. He chose to put his dreams first in your relationship. He chose to ignore your needs. And don't forget, Reba—Joseph chose to leave." Carl pushed his chair back and leaned closer to me.

"You have no control over what happened in Liberia. If you'd gone with him you might have died. Instead, you've used every day of your life in this country to help others." Shaking his head, he reached up to touch my face. "Now I finally understand what's driven you to work so hard to help strangers—and why you're so desperate to help him. You're still trying to redeem yourself."

"I guess that's true," I said.

There was another silence while Carl studied my face. I had

never seen him look at me that way, with an expression of profound, loving consideration. His were the eyes of a man who was seeing his woman for the first time as a singular, independent being—not just a part of his own life. It was as if Carl was finally recognizing that I had struggles of my own—deep, private struggles that I had to overcome in my own way.

He climbed slowly to his feet and pulled me gently into his arms. "I guess you're not going to be at peace unless you see this Joseph thing through. Just remember, Reba, no matter what happens with Joseph, you've got a man to come home to. I wanted you from the day we met and that hasn't changed. We've both done things we're not proud of. But if we forgive each other—and if we work on forgiving ourselves—I think we just might make it. God knows, I'm willing to try."

The flight to Zurich seemed to take much longer this time. I again read through my files, trying to uncover an overlooked detail that might make a difference in Joseph's defense. But there was nothing. I tried to sleep, hoping that the lulling engines would drive the troubled thoughts from my mind. The only thing I had to hold on to was Carl's words as I'd left for the airport that morning: "Just do your best, baby. And don't forget that I love you."

On the train from Zurich to Berne I found myself riding in a spotless, quiet compartment with a young black woman. When I noticed that she was reading *Their Eyes Were Watching God*, I asked if she was American.

"Oh, no," she said with a pleasant smile. "I'm from South Africa."

"Are you vacationing here in Switzerland?"

"No. I am a student at the University of Lausanne," she explained in a lovely, lilting accent. "I just went up to Zurich to see a few friends."

"Do you like living in Switzerland?" I asked, prolonging our conversation to avoid returning to my thoughts.

"Yes. I particularly like the fact that you can learn so many languages by traveling only short distances. That will be very useful to me when I return home."

"Are you going to be a teacher?"

"No, I hope to be a translator for the United Nations. I was lucky enough to learn Portuguese from some Angolan neighbors in my youth. Now I'm spending two years at Swiss universities for German and French."

"I see," I said, deeply impressed. She eyed my small suitcase and asked me if I was in Switzerland on business. "Yes," I said, fighting a sudden urge to share the purpose of my mission with this stranger. "Although I'm also here to spend time with a very old friend. He happens to come from Liberia."

Her face clouded. "The war has taken a terrible toll on that nation. We've had peace in South Africa since I was a little girl, but nothing seems to heal Liberia. Such conflict makes it impossible to lead any kind of normal life. I hope that your friend will find some safety and happiness here in Switzerland."

She went back to her book and I looked out at the lush, rolling countryside. Ironically, my hopes were the same.

My *room in* a small hotel near the center of Berne looked out on the bustling train station. Tourists, shoppers and government officials were going about their lives, oblivious to the terrible dramas taking place in a courtroom only a few blocks away. Throwing my small bag on the bed, I immediately put in a call to Joseph's lawyer.

A secretary answered in German, switched to English, and politely asked me to wait. A moment later a crisp British accent came on the line.

"Matthew Pope."

"Mr. Pope," I began, "I'm here in Berne on behalf of Yusef Vai."

"Ah—you must be his school friend from the United States."

"Yes. I'm his—his school friend. I tried to reach you when I was in Switzerland in July, but—"

"That was a very busy time for me. You must understand that Mr. Vai's arraignment was simply a matter of record. The important facts in his case will come out during the trial tomorrow."

"Is it true that you encouraged him to accept a plea bargain with the prosecution?"

"It is not appropriate for me to discuss the details of this case with you, Mrs. Thornton."

"But I don't understand why he would consider pleading guilty to crimes he didn't commit."

"I have never advised Mr. Vai to plead in any particular fashion, and you can rest assured that he has been an active participant in the evolution of his defense."

"Mr. Pope—"

"I'm sorry, but Mr. Vai specifically asked me not to talk with you."

"He *what?*"

"Please be patient, Mrs. Thornton. The trial begins tomorrow, and I will do my utmost on his behalf."

"Do you think that I could visit him tonight? I'm staying at the Bahnhof Hotel."

"I'm afraid that Mr. Vai will only be permitted to meet with me this evening."

"But I've come all the way from—"

"The trial will be held in a small courtroom, with only a few, select journalists present. If you wish, I will ask Mr. Vai's permission for you to sit in one of the seats reserved for his family."

"Thank you," I said in a small voice.

"Mrs. Thornton," he politely continued, "I understand your concern for Mr. Vai. I have worked with defendants in human rights cases for many years, and I have never known anyone quite like this man. I promise you that I will do everything in my power to see that he has a fair and impartial trial. I realize that you have traveled a long distance to be of service. But I am limited to what he allows me to say—or do."

So, I thought, am I.

Breakfasting alone in the hotel's small restaurant, I picked up the *European International News* and was startled to find Joseph's photograph on the front page.

WAR CRIMINAL TRIAL BEGINS IN BERNE

BERNE (RG)—Yusef Vai was once the speaker of a Liberian paramilitary unit widely known as the "Rimka Liberation Front." Described by his soldiers as a quiet man who rarely discussed his background, Vai is believed to have been educated in the United States. A former teacher, Vai became active with the RLF in the early 1990s and directed its operations until his arrest by Liberian officials in 2000.

Mr. Vai is believed to have participated in a massacre in a village just outside the capital city of Monrovia. He has been of-ficially charged with the murder of thirty-seven people. The trial will begin in Berne's Court of Human Rights this morning. The penalty, if he is convicted, could range from twenty years to life in prison. Mr. Vai has pleaded not guilty.

The words of the article still swirling through my mind, I had just approached the taxi stand when someone called my name. A thin, middle-aged woman in a dark trench coat approached me and held out her hand.

"Excuse me, but the desk clerk told me you are Mrs. Thornton. I am Kristine Schmidt, the assistant of Matthew Pope. I have come to offer you a ride to the court."

"Thank you," I said, following her down the busy Zentral-Strasse to a waiting late-model Mercedes. "This is quite an impres-sive car," I remarked as I settled myself into the leather passenger's seat.

"It is an official vehicle of the court," she explained, signaling before she pulled out into traffic. "We are permitted to use them for court business."

I took a deep breath and looked through the darkened glass at the people moving steadily along the streets. Most of the men were sporting plain, conservative suits, and the women were dressed in somber banking attire.

"Is this your first trip to Switzerland, Mrs. Thornton?"

"No, I've been here several times before."

"I hope that you will have the chance to come back for happier reasons at some time in the future. We have a very beautiful coun-try, with many special places that most tourists never see."

"I'll keep that in mind," I replied, wondering if she really expected me to make meaningless conversation while traveling to watch someone I cared about being tried for mass murder.

The court was housed in a surprisingly modern building with wide, stained-glass windows and a handsomely sculpted sandstone facade. Outside stood a modern sculpture that recalled giant, outstretched hands lifted heavenward. I wondered if the hands were intended to represent a supplication to God for moral guidance. Or perhaps a prisoner's plea for mercy. Or—my heart fluttered—the victim's desperate hope that justice would be served. The car glided into an underground parking area before I had the chance to decide.

Then things began happening very quickly. Kristine Schmidt locked the car and led me swiftly to an elevator. We were scarcely inside the steel cage before it slid upward, spilling us out into a corridor filled with people.

If I hadn't known I was in a courthouse I might have mistaken the scene for an international congress. Men and women of various cultures stood in tight groups, conversing avidly in their native languages while armed military police looked on. Officials in black robes moved purposefully through the crowd, their arms laden with cardboard boxes and fat manila files. Occasionally I spied a person sitting alone on a bench, head lowered, or another person being comforted by someone standing nearby. The din of voices was both soothing and disorienting. Despite the noise, I felt reassured that I wasn't alone.

The attorney's assistant led me through a pair of double doors and into a narrow antechamber. Suddenly everything around me was quiet and she reached up to touch my arm.

"You will be seated in the area reserved for family members," she said. "You will be able to watch the proceedings very closely, but you are not permitted to speak. You will be required to pass through a security screening before you enter the courtroom. Is there anything you wish to surrender to me before we pass through the metal detectors?"

"Why, no," I said in surprise.

"In that case, please follow me."

Joseph's trial was to take place in a compact, octagonal auditorium with a semicircular raised dais behind which the justices and their assistants would be seated. Just below them was a witness stand, placed at an angle so that the speaker's face was easily seen by the justices, attorneys and journalists alike. The prosecution and defense tables were in the center of the room, with places for numerous attorneys and an impressive array of high-tech equipment for presenting evidence. Kristine and I had entered through a side door after passing through a series of searches, and I found myself standing alone in a gallery that faced the defendant's table. It was clear that the gallery was designed to allow prisoners to see and be seen by their family members. I wondered whether that was to offer emotional support or to elicit honesty.

The opposite wall offered an identical gallery that was equipped for journalists. A glass sound booth ran along the highest row of seats, and other seats sported headsets and desks wide enough to hold laptop computers.

Finally, there were several rows of chairs in the rear for witnesses or observers. I noticed that armed security officers were standing along the walls and beside the doorways, and video cameras facing in all directions were mounted on the low ceiling. The entire room—walls, galleries, tables and chairs—was made of bleached hardwood, giving the room a cold austerity. As Kristine pointed to my seat, which bore a name plate matching a security pass I'd been given at the door, I realized that this courtroom was designed to suggest that justice was unambiguous and indisputable, like the clear hard edges of that chamber.

The rear of the courtroom was practically empty. Seven or eight people sitting in the observers' seats were conversing quietly in German. Two young women in dark suits had taken seats at the prosecutor's table, where they were arranging a series of papers in neat, ordered rows. Kristine left me and proceeded to her own table, where she opened her briefcase and began removing manila files. One by one, men and women took their places in the journalists' gallery, putting on their headsets and plugging in their computers. Three court reporters entered and seated themselves at computer stations facing the defendant. The room buzzed with quiet tension as we waited for the proceedings to begin.

Then the bailiff rang a small bell and the entire court rose to its feet. The wall behind the dais slid open, and the justices—three men and two women in black robes—entered, striding swiftly to their places. The oldest, a white-haired man wearing a black velvet cap, placed himself at the center of the dais. Obviously the Chief Justice, he lifted a gavel and tapped it lightly on the bench to signal that the proceedings should begin. As we took our seats I looked around to see a slender, brown-skinned man in a gray suit standing solemnly beside the defense table. Two officers appeared, escorting the prisoner.

The tall, gracious love of my youth now walked uncertainly, his shoulders and hips swallowed by the conservative wool suit I'd purchased for him six weeks before. His head was nearly shaved, but I could see that his hair had gone completely white, and his expression was less focused than it had been even during my earlier visit.

One of the officers pulled out his chair, and Joseph grimaced as he took his seat. He exhaled very slowly, as if trying to ease an unseen pain, then stared blankly forward, avoiding the measuring eyes of the justices. His hands lay lifeless on top of the table.

Someone began speaking and I realized that the proceedings

were in French. I reached forward, put on my headset and fumbled with the buttons in the console until I could hear the voice of the English interpreter, who was sitting opposite me in the glass booth above the press gallery.

The opening of the trial proceeded swiftly. The attorneys and justices were formally identified for the record, and the defendant's name and birth date were followed by the charges against him. Looking down at Joseph, the bailiff repeated the charges in English.

"The accused, Yusef Vai, has been brought before this court on this date of September 7, 2004, to stand trial for the murder of thirty-seven civilians in the village of Taylorville, Liberia. He has also been charged with conspiracy to commit murder and conspiracy to engage in acts of terrorism against the government of Liberia."

Although I'd discussed the charges many times with Simone, hearing the bailiff read them in his emotionless voice made it all horribly real. Joseph kept his gaze fixed on the floor, his long fingers unnaturally still. Though he was seated no more than fifteen feet away, he made no effort to look up at the woman sitting alone in the family gallery. It was as if I didn't exist.

The prosecuting attorney, Michel Declerc, was a heavyset Frenchman with curling dark hair. Speaking in heavily accented English, he faced the justices and began his opening statement.

"If it pleases the court, the prosecution will show that Yusef Vai, self-styled leader of the terrorist organization known as the Rimka Liberation Front, is responsible for acts resulting in the deaths of thirty-seven civilians in the village of Taylorville, ten miles outside Liberia's capital of Monrovia. These men, women and children were guilty of no crime other than refusing to aid the RLF in its effort to gain military control over their nation's capital. We shall produce witnesses who can attest to the purpose and activities of the Rimka Liberation Front, and to Mr. Vai's responsibility for its operations. We will prove that Yusef Vai is guilty of these crimes and deserves the maximum sentence of life in prison."

Now Matthew Pope got to his feet. Delicately slender and nearly bald, Pope looked like a crane in comparison to the bovine prosecutor.

"Your Excellencies," he began in a thoughtful voice, "the defendant, Yusef Vai, is being tried on several charges, the most serious of which is murder. Mr. Vai, however, sees no purpose in attempting to refute the fact that he was a member of the Rimka Liberation Front. In fact, Yusef Vai readily admits to being its founder. The defendant is eager for it to be known, however, that the real mission of the RLF was quite different from that stated in the charges. We shall argue that the purpose of this organization had nothing to do with terrorism, and to that end, it has never participated in the abuse or murder of civilians. Finally, we shall make it clear that Yusef Vai was not responsible for the killings in Taylorville. The defense shall show that the Rimka Liberation Front was not present in the village of Taylorville at the time of the killings. We shall ask the court for the dismissal of all the charges so that this innocent man, Yusef Vai, may go free."

The prosecution called to the stand its first witness, Theo Danqua, a general of the Liberian military. Swollen with self-importance, the barrel-chested officer in a starched khaki suit swaggered to the front of the court, swore to tell the truth and was soon describing the acts of terrorism allegedly perpetrated by the Rimka Liberation Front. Pressing his shoulders into his seat so that his colorful metals glinted in the recessed lights, the general asserted proudly that through the excellent work of his soldiers, the RLF had been dismantled and its leader, Yusef Vai, would now be brought to justice.

As the general made his long-winded speech I took a long, slow look at the justices. I had read that the Court of Human Rights was composed of representatives from throughout the world; each of Joseph's justices seemed to come from a different continent. The men were elderly, stone-faced, and clearly in their late fifties or early sixties. One of them was Asian; another was Black. The two female justices were considerably younger and seemed far less impassive than their male counterparts. Their faces showed both a keen interest and a willingness to react openly to what they were hearing. When the general claimed that his government had brought positive change to his nation, one of the female justices pursed her lips and narrowed her eyes skeptically. The other tipped her head to the side, suggesting her impatience with the arrogance of the witness.

When the prosecution finished, Matthew Pope rose from his seat at the defense table. He paused thoughtfully, slipping on a pair of wire-framed glasses, and arranged his papers with care. Although he was dressed in a suit that seemed drab in comparison to the medals glinting on the witness's chest, when he spoke, his voice was unexpectedly composed and strong.

"General Danqua, have you ever had the occasion to meet the defendant in person?"

"No, I have not. But his reputation as a terrorist leader is well known in Liberia."

"Did you personally witness any of the antigovernment acts that Mr. Vai has been accused of committing?"

"It is well known that—"

"Excuse me, General," the attorney said firmly. "A simple yes or no will suffice."

"No."

Matthew Pope walked a few steps closer to the witness stand.

"What evidence can you present to show that the Rimka Liberation Front was tied to any terrorist organizations?"

"I don't have to present evidence. It is clear that groups such as this can only operate with external funding."

"Did the RLF work from a fixed base of operations?"

"No. They were constantly on the move in order to evade capture."

"Can you produce any written or telephonic records linking them to known terrorist groups?"

"No, but such records are often lost in times of war."

"Did they possess modern communications devices, such as computers and cellular phones?"

"The men we captured refused to divulge where they kept the equipment, but we will certainly find it."

"Did the RLF possess sophisticated arms?"

"Perhaps. We are still investigating."

"Did they ever explode timed devices or set up land mines?"

"We have not discovered such ordnance, but—"

"Did the RLF ever engage in political assassinations?"

"We strongly suspect that they are behind several killings in the capital."

"Can you produce any evidence to prove it?"

"We are still investigating."

"Have you ever arrested a member of the RLF for such crimes?"

"Well," the general responded angrily, "they don't wear uniforms so it is difficult to identify them."

"General Danqua," the attorney said, speaking with slow, carefully nuanced irony, "you have stated for the record that you have no evidence linking the RLF to any known terrorist organization. They had no fixed base of operations. They possessed no sophisticated arms or communication technology. They planted no bombs or land mines. There is no proof that they engaged in political assassinations. So, if you would be so good, please answer this question: Can you present *any* proof that the Rimka Liberation Front ever committed or intended to commit acts of terrorism against the Liberian nation?"

Danqua stared at Matthew Pope with raw hostility. A hateful silence invaded the courtroom. The justices watched the witness as his chest rose up and down. Joseph, who seemed to be staring off into space, did not move.

"The evidence we have collected is highly sensitive and cannot be discussed at this time," the general replied.

After a long, deliberately extended pause, Matthew Pope nodded deferentially toward the justices. "I have no further questions."

The general was followed by a subordinate officer, Isaiah Mulbah, who testified that he had been present at the time of Yusef Vai's arrest. Although less confident than his superior, he too spoke with smirking self-assurance, often glancing up to nod at the bench. When the prosecution completed its questioning, Matthew Pope rose and addressed the officer.

"Mr. Mulbah, on what date did the Taylorville killings occur?"

"March 29, 2000."

"And on what date did your soldiers detain Yusef Vai?"

"April 1, 2000."

"Where did the arrest take place?"

"In a village near the Guinean border."

"Over two hundred miles from the site of the killings?"

"Yes."

"Were the RLF soldiers traveling by car when you detained them?"

"No, they were on foot."

"On foot?" Pope repeated. "Yusef Vai and his men had walked nearly two hundred miles in three days?"

"Evidently."

"Doesn't it seem more likely, Mr. Mulbah, that one of your dates is wrong?"

"My dates are correct. Those villagers were killed on March twenty-ninth and we arrested Vai on April first. Perhaps Vai's men were aided in their escape by another terrorist organization."

"Didn't the killings occur at the height of the monsoon season?"

"Yes. The roads were nearly impassable, and that is one reason it was so difficult to capture them."

"If your soldiers found it difficult to make the two-hundred-mile trip in vehicles, then how did Vai's men accomplish it on foot in three days?"

"I have already said that I do not know."

"Isn't it possible, Mr. Mulbah, that those villagers were actually killed by a group other than Mr. Vai and his men? Perhaps one of the other terrorist organizations that you just mentioned?"

"No. The massacre was committed by the Rimka Liberation Front."

"Can you present any evidence to support this statement?"

"I was not a part of that investigation."

"Then you have no proof."

The soldier paused. "No," he said aggressively, "I was only responsible for his arrest."

Pope moved closer to the witness stand. "Mr. Mulbah, where were the members of the RLF taken after their arrest?"

"They were removed to a detention center just outside the capital."

"How long were they held there?"

"Most were released within several months."

"And Mr. Vai?"

"He was in prison for nearly three years."

"Were the detainees interrogated while they were in custody?"

"Yes, of course."

"Did any members of the RLF confess to participating in the Taylorville killings?"

Mulbah hesitated. His gaze flicked up to the general, who was seated in the rear of the courtroom. "No."

"Even under interrogation?"

"No."

"Was Mr. Vai interrogated as well?"

"Yes."

"More than once?"

"Yes."

"Repeatedly?"

"Yes."

"Over a period of months?"

"Yes."

"For the entire three years?"

Mulbah paused. "Yes."

"Is it true that Mr. Vai's femur was broken during one of those interrogations?"

"Absolutely not."

"Is it true that three of his ribs were broken?"

"Well—"

"Is it true that Mr. Vai was cut with unclean razors and forced to submit to electric shock—"

"Any injuries suffered by Vai during his imprisonment were accidental," Mulbah stated nervously.

"Our records indicate that when Yusef Vai was handed over to

Swiss authorities he was close to death. Are you aware of that, Mr. Mulbah?"

"I am aware that he was ill."

"Is it the policy of the Liberian government to use torture as a means of extracting confessions from political detainees?"

"You have no right to question our methods of handling those who have perpetrated acts of terror against the Liberian state!"

There was a murmur throughout the courtroom, and the Chief Justice pounded his gavel, saying, "*Silence, si'l vous plait!*" into his microphone. The room grew quiet and the attorney continued, modulating his voice so that his questions echoed throughout the chamber.

"During the three years that Mr. Vai was detained and regularly 'interrogated' by your soldiers, did he ever confess to committing the murders at Taylorville?"

The officer leaned back in the witness stand, his face settling into a stony mask. "Vai is a seasoned killer. It was unlikely that he would admit to—"

"Did Mr. Vai confess to the killings?" Matthew Pope repeated.

"No."

"I have no more questions for this witness."

The prosecutor conferred with his assistant for a moment, then rose.

"The prosecution would like to call Yusef Vai."

Joseph got slowly to his feet and moved with some difficulty toward the stand. His head was raised, but I could see that his eyes were distant, as if his thoughts were far away. He took the oath with a trembling hand and sat down, staring straight ahead.

"Mr. Vai," the prosecutor began, "we have heard testimony suggesting you were the head of the Rimka Liberation Front. Was this indeed the case?"

"Yes, sir."

"And the intention of your organization was to destabilize the current government so that a new regime could be brought to power in Liberia?"

"No, sir. Our intention was—"

"You were a military organization, were you not?"

"Yes, sir."

"You obtained arms and used them against the government's forces."

"On occasion."

"You fought your way across Liberia over a period of years, arriving outside Monrovia in March 2000?"

"Yes, sir."

"Is it true that your soldiers were camped in the village of Taylorville for some time?"

"For approximately one week."

"And you interacted with the villagers?"

"Yes. They were quite willing to—"

"But you became aware that government forces were preparing a massive assault against your organization?"

"Yes."

"And you realized that the RLF alone wasn't strong enough to defeat the government soldiers?"

"Yes."

"Would it have proved beneficial to your organization if the men from the village had joined your ranks?"

"Perhaps, but—"

"Did you try to convince the villagers to fight with your men?"

"No."

"But it must have been infuriating for you to be so close to the capital without having enough soldiers to fight."

"It was difficult for some of my men, but—"

"Difficult enough for you to try and force the villagers to join your ranks?"

"No."

"Difficult enough for you to make 'examples' of those who refused to join?"

"No."

"Perhaps so difficult that some of your soldiers lost control and began opening fire on those civilians?"

"No," Joseph insisted. "We did not kill those people."

The prosecutor turned to the justices. "I have no more questions at this time, but I reserve the right to reexamine."

Matthew Pope immediately rose and faced Joseph. "Mr. Vai, when did your men leave Taylorville?"

"March twenty-fourth."

"How can you be so sure of the date?"

"It was my late wife's birthday."

"And where did you go when you retreated from the village?"

"We moved north, toward our home."

"Were you still actively involved in combat at that time?"

"No, sir."

"What were you planning to do?"

"We planned to rebuild our villages and start our lives over again."

"Why did you retreat when you could so easily have marched on the capital?"

"It was never our desire to overthrow the government. The Rimka Liberation Front was founded only to protect our people from attack. Although I was the leader of the RLF, I am a teacher—not a soldier—and have never wanted anything more than a life of peace."

"But you admit that you had fought for the previous six years?"

"Yes, when it could not be avoided. But we had no ambition except to make our nation safe for the people who are defenseless in their villages."

"Mr. Vai, did your soldiers attack the residents of Taylorville?"

"No. We left the village in the hope that they would not suffer reprisals for helping us. We did not want any civilian blood on our hands."

The attorney paused. "I have no further questions at this time."

There was a flurry of activity in the rear of the courtroom and an officer walked forward to confer with the prosecution. Declerc stood up and addressed the justices.

"Your Excellencies, an unexpected witness has arrived, and with your permission, we would like to introduce his testimony."

"I object," Pope responded. "The prosecution has provided the defense with no prior knowledge of this witness."

The Chief Justice signaled that both attorneys should approach the bench. A heated exchange took place, and when they returned to their seats a few moments later, Pope's expression was grave.

The Chief Justice addressed the room. "The court is going to allow this witness to present his testimony. If necessary, we are willing to grant the defense a recess in order to prepare for cross-examination. You may proceed, Mr. Declerc."

"The prosecution would now like to call Abraham Malinko to the stand."

A door at the rear of the court opened and a uniformed youth walked in, his gait nervous and his expression guarded. Tall and perilously slim, Malinko's shirt was too large for his spindly frame and his frayed trousers barely brushed the tops of his worn boots. Malinko's shaved head made his eyes seemed much too large for his gaunt face, and a thick scar stretched across his forehead like a dark seam.

He was sworn in, and taking his place on the witness stand, he set his gaze directly on Joseph. For the first time I saw Joseph stir; his eyes cleared and he looked at the soldier with puzzlement.

"Mr. Malinko," the prosecutor began, "please tell us how you came to be here today."

"I am a soldier in the Liberian army."

"Why were you so late in making yourself available to the court?"

"I learned the date of this trial only two days ago. My commanding officer had to give me permission to travel to Switzerland, and I arrived only several hours ago."

"What is it that you have to share with the court, Mr. Malinko?"

"I was in Taylorville on March 29, 2000, and I witnessed the killing of the villagers by Yusef Vai and his men."

The courtroom exploded into pandemonium. The journalists began drumming their keyboards and the justices spoke quickly to one another. The Chief Justice had to bang his gavel repeatedly to restore order.

Matthew Pope once again stood up. "Your Excellencies, I strenuously object to the court's hearing this witness without the defense having had time to prepare a rebuttal."

The Chief Justice conferred briefly with his colleagues, then looked down at the attorney. "Mr. Pope, we will hear the witness's statement before determining how long a recess the defense will be granted to prepare its reply."

Declerc turned back to Malinko. "Please continue, sir."

The young man squared his shoulders. "I was stationed with my unit outside Monrovia. We heard rumors that the Rimka Liberation

Front was in Taylorville, so my captain sent some of us out into the village to see if we could identify them. We dressed like the villagers so that we wouldn't be recognized as soldiers."

"What did you witness in the village on March twenty-ninth?"

"I was there when the RLF arrived. Vai was their leader. He told his men to round up the villagers and bring them to the market. He announced that his group was planning an assault on the capital and that they needed soldiers. They tried to force the men to fight, and when they refused, the RLF began shooting the women and children. The men then tried to attack Vai's group, so they were also shot."

"And where were you when this was taking place?"

"I managed to hide in one of the empty food stalls. If they had found me, I would surely be dead."

"Thank you," Declerc said. "I have no further questions at this time."

The courtroom went deadly silent. I looked down at Joseph, whose gaze had never left the young soldier, and saw something frightening in his eyes: an expression that I knew well, for I had seen it in my own reflected image for the past twenty years—I saw guilt. And I knew that if the justices were observant, they would see it in Joseph's face, too.

The Chief Justice now addressed the court. "I think, in light of the gravity of the testimony, I will call for a thirty-minute recess. The bench would like to speak to both attorneys in chambers."

The black-robed figures filed out. I wished that I could descend from the gallery and speak to Joseph, but a cadre of security police had surrounded him, so I stood up slowly. Making my way out into the crowded corridor, I was surprised when someone touched my shoulder.

I turned, expecting to find Kristine Schmidt. Instead I came face-to-face with Joseph, looking exactly as I'd known him twenty years before. His tall, slender frame was settled on a pair of long legs, and his short hair revealed a wide, intelligent forehead and somber brown eyes. He stepped forward, holding out his long-fingered hand.

"Mrs. Thornton, I am Daniel. Daniel Vai Thomas. If you have a moment," he said in his father's voice, "I would like to speak to you."

Shocked into silence, I followed him across the noisy hall and to a wide bay window a few paces removed from the rush of people. He was clothed in a simple white shirt and pressed, dark trousers, and I realized in an instant that like his father so many years before, he preferred seeing rather than being seen. Now he looked down at me, his gaze appraising, and then politely averted his eyes.

"I have only just arrived from England," he said, "but I take it from the look on your face that things are not going well for my father."

"No," I answered honestly.

"Is there anything to be done?"

"I really don't know."

He drew in his breath and looked into my eyes. "When you called I didn't realize that—well, my uncle Kali told me that you were once my father's wife."

"Yes."

The young man hesitated, then looked into my eyes. "You loved him very much, didn't you?"

I nodded.

"You must think that I am very weak to have let him go through this alone."

"No, Daniel. I would never judge you for doing what you believed was right."

"But I *didn't* think it was right!" he blurted in frustration. "It was what my father wanted." He stared at me with an ardent expression I knew very well. "When we left Monrovia the RLF split up. The older men no longer had any desire to fight, so he led them north, knowing that the government troops would come in that direction to find him. He sent the rest of us east, hoping we could cross into the Ivory Coast to safety. He said that I should make my way into Guinea, then contact my uncle Kali in England."

Daniel exhaled slowly, looking carefully over his shoulder. He came a step closer to me and lowered his voice. "My father told me that if he was arrested, he was prepared to take the blame for anything that happened."

"But why?"

"He wanted to protect us. He believed that if he could hold the soldiers off long enough, the younger members of the RLF might have a chance to escape to a better life." Daniel paused, lowering his gaze. "You know my father, Mrs. Thornton. He has always done everything in his power for his people."

"Does he even know that you're alive?"

"I don't think so. My uncle refused to let me contact him. He thought it would be better for all of us to pretend that Joseph Thomas died many years ago, and to let the world think that we had nothing to do with the prisoner called Yusef Vai."

Daniel was quiet for a moment. Then he turned his piercing gaze on me.

"My father has always believed that it was his fault that I lost my mother and my siblings. He blamed himself for giving me a childhood filled with war, instead of a life of peace."

"But he wasn't responsible for the things that happened."

"I know," Daniel replied in a voice not much louder than a whisper. "I know."

He gazed out the window, his intelligent face filled with sadness. "Once, long ago, he told me about you. He said that he had known a wonderful woman when he lived in the United States. He said that he wished he could see you just one more time." Daniel paused. "My father said that if he didn't live, he wanted me to tell you—" He broke off. "I cannot say the things he wanted you to know."

"Why not?"

"Because," Daniel answered, "my father is still alive. Joseph Thomas is still alive. And it is up to him to say these things to you now."

We looked at each other for a long moment.

"You know, my uncle Kali was deeply opposed to my coming. He was afraid that the Liberians would try to have me arrested. But no matter what happens, I am glad to be so close to my father."

"Would you like to sit in the family gallery with me?"

"Yes," he said. "I would like to do that, if the court will permit it."

We heard a noise and both looked up to see Kristine Schmidt approaching. "You must come, now," she said urgently. "The justices are returning."

We rushed to the door and she led both of us through the security checkpoints again. Strangely, no one questioned Daniel's identity. He followed me into the empty gallery and took a seat beside me. The journalists were filing into their seats across the small courtroom, and the interpreters were already in place. I noticed that the security officers had already escorted Joseph to his seat, and his attorney was there beside him.

The gavel again called the court to order. The Chief Justice spoke.

"Mr. Pope, are you prepared to question the witness?"

"Yes, your Excellency."

Once again the young soldier took his seat on the witness stand and stared down at Joseph.

"Mr. Malinko," Pope began, "where do you come from?"

"I live in Monrovia—"

"But where were you born, sir?"

The young man shifted imperceptibly in his seat. "In the north, near the Guinean border," he answered with some hostility.

"And how old are you?"

"Seventeen."

"How did you come to be a soldier?"

"I—I joined the army some years ago."

"Exactly how old were you when you became a soldier?"

"I'm not sure."

Matthew Pope paused. He lowered his voice, speaking very calmly. "Do you know how to read, Mr. Malinko?"

"Yes."

"Where did you learn?"

The prosecutor was suddenly on his feet. "Objection, your Excellencies. I refuse to see the purpose of this line of questioning."

"I hope to shed some light on the witness's motives in testifying," Matthew Pope replied.

The Chief Justice nodded. "You may continue, Mr. Pope."

"Where did you learn how to read?"

"At school."

"Where was your school?"

"In my village."

"And who was your teacher?" Matthew Pope asked. Beside me I heard Daniel give a stifled cry, and both Joseph and the young soldier looked in our direction. Joseph's face shifted at the sight of

Daniel, but Malinko's reaction was far more extreme. He visibly jumped, then stared at Daniel as if he was seeing a ghost.

"Mr. Malinko?" the attorney prompted.

"I—I don't remember the teacher," Malinko replied, his gaze falling to his hands.

"Perhaps you can remember whether your teacher worked with both the children and their parents?"

"Maybe."

"And perhaps you remember that your teacher once lived in the United States?"

A whisper went through the courtroom, but Malinko remained stubbornly silent.

Matthew Pope approached the witness stand and stood for a few moments, looking at the soldier.

"Mr. Malinko, was your teacher the man who is sitting before you now?"

Again a rush of whispers moved through the court. The Chief Justice pounded his gavel. Daniel's hands tightened on the bench in front of us.

"Sir," the attorney said, "was Yusef Vai once your teacher?"

Still the soldier did not respond. His forehead began to glisten as his haunted eyes roamed over the court, moving from the general, to Mulbah, and back once again to Joseph. "Yes," he whispered.

"Mr. Malinko, when did you become a soldier?"

"I already told you I don't know," he muttered.

"Is it possible that you were taken from your village ten years ago, when you were still a young boy?"

Malinko stared forward as if resisting interrogation.

Turning to the Chief Justice, Pope raised his voice. "Your

Excellency, I would request that the witness be instructed to answer my questions."

"I must remind you," the Chief Justice said to Malinko, "that you have taken an oath to tell the truth on penalty of perjury. If you do not provide honest answers, you face imprisonment."

Malinko's eyes seemed to flicker. Once again he stole a glance at Daniel.

"Sir," Pope repeated, "I asked how long you have been a soldier."

"Ten years."

"Then you became a soldier in 1994 after your village was destroyed by government troops?"

"Yes."

"Mr. Malinko, please tell the court what happened in your village."

The young man wavered, then began to speak in a tense voice. "The soldiers came. They raped my mother and burned her alive with the other women. They shot all the men, including my father. Then they took me from my village."

"The village where Mr. Vai was your teacher?"

"Yes."

"What did Yusef Vai do when the soldiers came?"

"He told all of the children to run into the school. We hid there, in a closet, listening. We could hear our mothers screaming as they were raped. They screamed our names as the soldiers forced them into the church and set the building on fire. They screamed for our fathers, but our fathers could not come. Hidden in the school, we could also hear the gunshots. One shot after another, while the women were screaming. And then suddenly it was very quiet."

Malinko's eyes filled with tears. "The teacher told us not to move. He said we should wait until we were sure that the soldiers were gone. But I couldn't wait. I couldn't stay there in that closet with my mother's screams echoing in my head. So I ran out the door. And they blew up the school.

"The children were crying out as the roof collapsed. I was alone, there on the street—standing next to the body of my father. The soldiers came out of our houses carrying our food and our belongings. They laughed when they saw me standing there. They took me with them."

"How did the soldiers treat you?" Pope asked him softly.

"They taught me to be a man."

"How did they do that?"

"They taught me how to use a gun. How to defend myself. How to find food and how to fight."

"Did they beat you?"

"Only once," he said, a hand stealing involuntarily to his forehead.

"Did they teach you how to kill?"

"We are at war, and killing is a part of war."

"Have you had the occasion to kill, sir?"

"Only when it was necessary."

"How old were you the first time you killed someone?"

Malinko paused, staring vacantly ahead. "Eight. Or maybe nine years old."

More whispers spread across the courtroom. Matthew Pope waited for silence, then spoke very clearly.

"So you lived with the men who came into your village? The same men who killed your parents?"

"It was his fault they came into our village." Malinko pointed at Joseph. "They came because he was teaching us things he had learned in America. Things that would lead to the brainwashing of the Liberian people. Things that would make us hate our own government."

"Then you believe that Yusef Vai is responsible for the death of your family?"

"The soldiers came because of the teacher!"

"But the soldiers killed your parents—"

"They are good men! They are fighting for the preservation of our nation. They want to keep African people free from American interests."

The court was absolutely silent. Malinko was breathing heavily, sweat darkening his uniform. Matthew Pope now moved very close to the witness stand and looked directly into the young man's eyes.

"Mr. Malinko, have you seen your teacher since that day in the village?"

For a long moment the soldier was silent—so long that the Chief Justice opened his mouth to intervene. And then Malinko shook his head. "No."

"Were you in Taylorville on the day of the killings?"

Malinko looked again at Daniel. Tears formed in his eyes.

"Yes," the soldier said woodenly.

"Were any members of the RLF still present in the village?"

There was another long pause. Malinko closed his eyes. "No."

"Did you see the villagers being killed in Taylorville, sir?"

"Yes."

"Then you know who was responsible for the killings?"

"Yes."

"Were the members of the RLF involved in the killings?"

"No."

"Was Yusef Vai a participant in the killings?"

"No."

"Were you a participant in the killings?"

"Yes," he whispered as his tears began to flow down his sunken cheeks.

"And why were the villagers killed?"

Malinko looked at the floor. "They were killed to send a message to all the people in the area. We did not want them giving aid to the RLF. We did not want them to do anything to help Yusef Vai achieve his goal of selling our nation to the Americans."

Matthew Pope stood very still beside the witness stand. "Mr. Malinko, earlier today you told the court that you saw Yusef Vai kill thirty-seven men, women and children in Taylorville. Why did you lie?"

"I hate Vai," the soldier said. "I hate him for causing the death of our people."

"Then how is the court to know that you are telling the truth now?"

"I have looked into the past," the young man mumbled, "and seen the face of my brother."

"Please explain yourself."

"I had only sisters in my childhood, so I spent all my days with the son of Yusef Vai. We learned to walk and hunt and read together. He was beside me in the school on the day my parents died." The soldier's tear-stained face melted into despair. "I do not care what happens to Vai. But I cannot lie, here, before Daniel, my brother."

Matthew Pope regarded the soldier for a long moment. Then he looked up at the justices.

"I have no further questions."

The bailiff escorted Malinko from the stand. As he passed Joseph the soldier averted his eyes, but just before walking through the door at the rear of the court I saw him turn and look once again at Daniel. Daniel's tear-filled eyes, however, were now fixed on his father.

"If there are no other witnesses," the Chief Justice announced, "the court will begin its deliberations."

The justices withdrew, and Daniel and I rose slowly to exit the courtroom. The guards surrounded the defendant's table and Joseph got to his feet with difficulty. His gaze was fixed on our gallery as he looked from his son's face to mine. I thought, though it was difficult to tell from across the chamber, that his eyes were also filled with tears.

Less than an hour later the justices returned, regained their places and looked out into the tense crowd. I felt Daniel slip his hand into mine. The Chief Justice banged his gavel, and when the room quieted, he spoke in a slow, official voice.

"World citizens, we gathered in this courtroom today to consider numerous charges of murder brought against Mr. Yusef Vai of Liberia. Testimony was offered by officers of the Liberian Army to suggest that Mr. Vai was the leader of a paramilitary organization, the Rimka Liberation Front, which was responsible for thirty-seven civilian deaths. It was claimed that either in his presence, or due to his influence, these men, women and children were put to death in the village of Taylorville, just outside the capital of Monrovia."

The judge looked down at Joseph. "You may rise, sir."

Joseph climbed slowly to his feet.

"The court has listened to the statements given by members of the Liberian military in response to the charges. The court finds it questionable that the Liberian Army has been unable to produce any concrete evidence proving that members of the RLF have been responsible for any acts of terrorism. The prosecution has also failed to show that the RLF was present at the time of the attacks. It also remains to be explained how Mr. Vai could have been arrested so far from the scene of the crimes, when he was traveling on foot in adverse weather conditions. We also find that the testimony of Abraham Malinko that the killings were carried out by government troops clearly supports Mr. Vai's claim of innocence.

"For these reasons the court feels it appropriate to find Yusef

Vai innocent of all charges. We ask Mr. Vai's forgiveness for the months that this case has taken from his life. He is now free to go. This hearing is adjourned."

I would have been happy if someone had cheered, but this was not the United States, where people feel free to share their feelings. Instead, I watched as Joseph's attorney merely shook his hand and patted him gently on the back.

Daniel was waiting to lead me down to his father. Together we left the gallery and approached the table in the center of the room. Joseph was still speaking to Matthew Pope, but he turned his head as we drew near. His face bloomed into an exhausted smile, but he could not hold back his tears when Daniel went into his arms.

I congratulated the attorney for his excellent work. He thanked me graciously.

"Mr. Vai has been released to the English authorities," he said quietly. "He may stay in Switzerland until he is issued temporary residency papers. Then I believe he's planning to go to his brother's home in Bristol." The attorney smiled. "But it's I who must thank *you*, Mrs. Thornton. After all, it's you who ultimately gave Yusef what he needed to obtain his freedom."

"But I didn't give him anything."

"Yes, you did," Matthew said quietly. "Yusef believed that if anyone could find Daniel, it would be you. He knew you wouldn't give up until you had spoken with his brother. And perhaps, if God was willing, Kali would let you know whether Daniel was all right."

"But you could have made contact with Kali."

"No," the attorney said. "Yusef felt that doing so might put the family at risk. In fact, he insisted that you would do what was right. He said that you have always been a woman of honesty and strength, and that we should simply have faith."

I glanced over at the frail man whose arms were still wrapped around his son.

"You see?" Pope concluded. "You have given Yusef both his son and his freedom."

The evening sun filled the air with the cool scents of a Swiss autumn. The crowds of businesspeople had thinned, and Joseph and I moved slowly along Berne's cobblestone streets, seeing everything and nothing.

"I think I will have to buy some more clothing," he said, smiling down at the shirt and the black and gold tie that Arlene and I had provided him for the trial. "Fortunately I now have Daniel to guide me in my selections."

"He's a fine young man, and he loves you very much."

"He is a credit to his mother. I only wish that she could be here to see him."

"She's watching over you both."

"Yes, I believe that's true."

"I have something for you," I said, and digging into my bag, I produced the ring I had worn when I was his wife—the ring that had once belonged to his father. "You'll want Daniel to have this."

Wordlessly he closed his thin fingers around it. He took my hand.

"Joseph, when we first spoke on the phone two months ago, you said that I had made a good choice in marrying Carl. What did you mean?"

"It was clear to me, even back in college, that Carl was almost as much in love with you as I was, Reba. He had never met a woman like you, and he had no idea how to tell you what he was feeling. I was just the lucky one who caught your attention and managed to hold it."

"It wasn't luck," I said, squeezing his hand more tightly.

"But it was. You were destined to do great things with your life, Reba. Both Carl and I knew it. And, of course, you have more than fulfilled your potential."

"What do you mean?"

"After my arraignment the court allowed me to make use of the prison library. I was supposed to be preparing my defense, but I must confess that I found it much more interesting to spend my time learning to use the Internet." He smiled. "Your organization has a very interesting Web site. I have read a great deal about your interests and accomplishments. And Reba"—he let out a long, exhausted breath—"I am deeply honored to have been loved by you."

He stopped walking and turned to look into my eyes.

"I know, now, that twenty years ago I gave you no chance for your own life. I was afraid that if we stayed in America, even for another year, I might never have the strength to go home."

"I would have gone to Liberia with you, Joseph. But I needed time. Time to find my strength and purpose. Time to get to know myself."

"Please forgive me for leaving you alone. I knew when I found you at Samantha's that night that I was also responsible for what happened. And perhaps that is why I couldn't face you the next morning. I began running that day and I never stopped. I ran and ran, burying another family and nearly sending my last son to his death—and all because I could not accept the fact that there were other ways of living than the life I'd chosen."

His eyes grew sad. "I learned many things while living in your country, but there was one lesson that no one in your world bothered to teach me: Education is political, Reba. I thought that reading and writing would give my people the chance for a better life. But instead, the learning I tried to share with them hastened their deaths. My government knew it, you see: If the poor are given knowledge, they will no longer accept their poverty."

Joseph turned his head so that his face fell into shadow. "I will never be at peace with the fact that my learning made me a part of so much death and destruction."

I stood beside him in silence, listening to his words as I had listened to the suffering of so many others over the years. But this was different. This was Joseph, my first husband, my first love.

He turned back to me with tears in his eyes. "Thank you for giving me back my son, Reba. Thank you for giving me the chance for a new life."

"Will you be safe in England?"

"I think so. I am hoping to go back to school. There are so many things I want to know. And one day I will certainly return to Africa. There are many other great nations where I might serve some purpose. Will you be happy, Reba?"

I paused thoughtfully. "I've found some new friends. And although things have been difficult between us, I have a husband who loves me and a wonderful child. It won't be easy, but yes, Joseph, I'm going to be happy."

We both looked out, beyond the dome of the Swiss capitol, to the twilit valley below.

"What will happen to Yusef Vai?" I asked.

"Yusef Vai no longer has a place in my world," he answered. "The storm has passed; the stars remain."

Reading Group Companion

Accident of Birth looks at one woman's journey to reconnect with her first love while also examining the often-ignored cultural tensions between Africans and African Americans. The questions that follow are meant to enhance your discussion and spark conversations about this timely, thoughtful novel that's inspired by real-world political conflicts.

1) How would you interpret the title of the book?

2) Joseph tells Reba on their first date that women are not treated well in the United States. Reba disagrees, saying that there are more opportunities for women in the United States than in any other country in the world. What evidence do Joseph and Reba give to support their statements? Whom do you agree with?

3) What are some of the differences between Joseph's family and Reba's? How do those differences influence their relationship?

4) How does Reba change during her courtship with Joseph? What does she learn from him about her own culture?

5) Why does Joseph say that he is a "cultural ambassador"?

6) Is Reba the "perfect" wife for Joseph? For Carl? Why or why not?

7) Joseph says that "proverbs are the daughters of experience." Discuss the significance of the following West African expressions:

"Even when a father is wrong, he is right."
"The lion is beautiful, but its heart is evil."
"The tree must have a stem before it can grow."
"Work is hard, but hunger is harder."
"A river never forgets its source."

8) How do Reba's feelings for Joseph change over the course of the novel?

9) How does Reba's work as an advocate for political refugees influence her feelings about her community and family life?

10) Carl tells Reba that Joseph "loved her because she was young enough to share his dreams." But Carl insists that he "loved her while her *own* dreams came true." Keeping these words in mind, compare Carl's and Joseph's love for Reba. Which man has had a greater influence on her life?

11) How does Reba feel about her college roommates? How does their relationship change over the years?

12) What does Reba discover about herself through her relationships with Arlene and Simone?

13) When does Reba begin to discover her "power"? Which experiences are most important in her adult life?

14) Reba's parents are deeply opposed to her relationship with Joseph. Are their concerns justified?

15) What is the significance of "white petals" in the novel?

16) What lessons has Joseph learned from his experiences during the civil war in Liberia? How has he changed at the end of the novel?

17) During the trial in Switzerland, a soldier named Abraham Malinko testifies against Joseph. What are Malinko's motives? How would you describe his psychological and emotional state? What would you imagine he's been through?

18) Reba's colleague Don Wiley warns her that "most of the people who commit crimes against humanity aren't monsters. They're everyday folks like you and me who get caught up in a series of circumstances that lead to them doing things they never could have imagined." Do you agree?

19) Heather Neff states in the acknowledgments that this novel was written to examine "the moral complexities of living in one of the world's most politically stable nations during a time of great international unrest." How does this novel explore this issue?

20) At the end of the novel Joseph says, "Education is political . . . I thought that reading and writing would give my people the chance for a better life. But instead, the learning I tried to share with them hastened their deaths. My government knew it, you see: If the poor are given knowledge, they will no longer accept their poverty." What does Joseph mean by that statement? Are there any ways in which this statement can be applied to life in the United States?

For other recommended books for you and your reading group, and more Reading Group Companions, visit www.harlemmoon.com.

About the Author

Heather Neff is a professor of African American Literature at Eastern Michigan University and holds a doctorate from the University of Zurich. She is the author of two previous novels, *Blackgammon* and *Wisdom*, which was named an Honor Book by the Black Caucus of the American Library Association. Her fourth novel, *Haarlem*, will be published by Harlem Moon in 2005. A native of Ohio, Neff has traveled and lived widely in Europe and the Caribbean. Neff currently resides in southeast Michigan, near Detroit.